MW00625751

SOMEDAY THE STARS

BOOK TWO OF
THE LUNAR FREE STATE

John E. Siers

Theogony Books
Coinjock, NC

Chris Kennedy/Theogony Books
1097 Waterlily Rd.
Coinjock, NC 27923
https://chriskennedypublishing.com/

Publisher's Note: This is a work of fiction. Names, characters, places, and incidents are a product of the author's imagination. Locales and public names are sometimes used for atmospheric purposes. Any resemblance to actual people, living or dead, or to businesses, companies, events, institutions, or locales is completely coincidental.

Cover Design Shezaad Sudar.

Ordering Information:
Quantity sales. Special discounts are available on quantity purchases by corporations, associations, and others. For details, contact the "Special Sales Department" at the address above.

Someday the Stars/John E. Siers -- 1st ed.
ISBN: 978-1648551963

To Dave and Rebecca—Original Citizens of the Lunar Free State.

Prologue

In the Orion Arm of the Milky Way galaxy, there are thousands of stars with planets populated by humans genetically identical to the humans of Earth, with only the minor variations commonly found on Earth itself. All these civilizations are of the same approximate age, within a few thousand Earth years. Other races in the galaxy have tried without success to discover where these humans originated. Parallel evolution on such a grand scale is so improbable as to be ruled out completely, so they are presumed to have come from a common set of ancestors, who traveled the stars long before other races ventured into space.

Legends tell of an original race of humans called the Progenitors who, somewhere in the prehistoric past, conducted a grand social experiment, populating every suitable planet they could find with small numbers of their own kind. These were not colonies in the traditional sense, with an established social organization and then-current technology. Instead, they were "seedings" of primitive tribes, young children placed on a planet with a few adult mentors to care for them and teach them basic survival skills. The children and mentors were left to survive or perish by their own efforts until—some versions of the legend proclaimed—some far future time, when the Progenitors would return to take the seeding back into the "family" of humankind. By the fourth or fifth generation, none of the original adults remained alive, and stories of the seeding faded into legend.

Such legends never explained the purpose of the experiment, but alien scholars have proposed theories on the subject. Some say the Progenitors wished to broaden their society by observing a variety of paths humans might choose in their development, that they left the seedings on their own so the experimenters would not skew the results through their influence. Others have suggested this was not an experiment at all, but rather some form of cruel sport by which the powerful entertained themselves by gambling with the lives of others.

Though the legends always describe the Progenitors as human, some researchers have speculated they were not human at all, that the humans who made up the seedings were laboratory animals, genetically engineered for the purpose. They point to the durable, mutation-resistant genetic characteristics all humans seem to share, and they note that these characteristics would have served as a rigid control in the experiment. One alien researcher—a member of a species of voracious carnivores—theorized the seedings were neither experiment nor sport but a self-sufficient, self-replenishing food source, created by the Progenitors, to be harvested later.

Not all seedings survived. Some died out naturally without ever developing significant social organization or technology. Some reached a level of technology sufficient to destroy themselves and left only ruins for other spacefaring races to discover.

Of those that survived, not all developed equally. Some seeding planets were poor in resources, particularly malleable metals such as iron and copper. On such planets, seeded humans might survive and even flourish, but would remain a mostly agrarian society with little industry or technology. On richer planets, humans could achieve more, and if they survived their own destructive tendencies, a few might eventually reach out into space.

Of the Progenitors themselves, no trace has been found. All that remains is their grand experiment—or sport or food source, depending on which theory is cited—and the scattered multitudes of humans it produced. They live their lives on their own worlds, blissfully unaware of the galactic mystery that surrounds their origin.

* * * * *

Chapter One

TransLuna Shipyards

Lorna Greenwood had come to say goodbye to an old friend. LFS *Valkyrie* was in a docking bay at the Trans-Luna shipyards for a major refit. Most of her crew were enjoying liberty on Luna, and the emptiness seemed to echo around her, but when the Admiral went to her old cabin, she found it occupied. Commander Amy Ling, *Valkyrie's* newly assigned captain, looked up in surprise and promptly jumped to attention when the fleet's commander-in-chief appeared in the doorway.

"Stand easy, Captain," Lorna told her. "I'm just here to say goodbye to the old girl. I told the watch officer not to alert anyone…didn't know you were aboard, or I'd have screened you ahead of time."

"I'm getting to know the ship, ma'am. Got lots of homework to do." *And I need to have a word with Ensign Marks*, Ling decided. *No matter what the admiral told him, he needs to learn to notify the captain when a flag officer comes aboard.*

"She's a good ship," Greenwood said. "I hope she serves you as well as she did me. Won't be the same without the AI, but the new electronics should be very good, and taking out the flag bridge gave the engineers space for new systems."

LFS *Valkyrie*, at 150 meters in length and 3,200 tons of mass, was the largest ship capable of planetary landing the Lunar Free State had built. She had also been the first ship with an onboard artificial intelligence. At the time of the war with China, she had been classed as a battlecruiser and Lorna's first flagship.

Now, the new *Apache*-class heavy cruisers were being built at TransLuna, with an overall length of 450 meters and a mass of over 30,000 tons. *Valkyrie* had been reclassified as a frigate, and her AI had been transferred to Lorna's new flagship, the 640-meter-long, 90,000-ton battlecruiser LFS *Athena*. Looking out from the shipyard's observation gallery, Lorna had been saddened by how small the old flagship looked, compared to *Athena* moored in the next bay down the line.

Lunar Command would have preferred to allocate less of the Lunar Free State's resources to building warships, but there were no fewer than nine Earth nations with fusion-drive capability, and all of them except Japan had insisted on putting warships in space. The LFS was still the only nation with gravity-drive ships, technology kept secret since the founding of the Lunar nation. But a great deal of gravity research was being done on Earth. No other nation had developed a gravity generator powerful enough for a drive, but both the U.S. and the French had made breakthroughs in the field and had succeeded in developing inertial compensators—field generators that allowed them to push the acceleration limits of their fusion-drive ships up to 30 gravities or more without killing their crews. Lunar engineers predicted Earth nations would have gravity-drive ships within five years.

Gravity-drive technology also meant Lunar missiles had longer range and greater acceleration. But other nations were rapidly achieving parity with energy beam weapons, building powerful X-ray and gamma-ray lasers to arm their ships. Both the U.S. and France were reportedly experimenting with bomb-pumped laser warheads for their missiles, which could be detonated kilometers from their targets. The LFS had gamma-ray lasers, but its missiles still relied on point-contact warheads with conventional explosives.

In the past, artificial intelligence had given ships like *Valkyrie* a significant tactical advantage, handling fire control and point defense more efficiently than humans could. Now, except for Lorna's new flagship, those functions were performed by dedicated computer systems, and the LFS currently had a moratorium on the building of new AIs.

The AIs posed something of a moral dilemma. The LFS had built its first such system almost twenty years ago under the auspices of the Deep Space Research Institute. That system, known as Mike, was still the AI of Lunar Command in TerraNova. Mike's two "sisters"—Val and Amy—had been built into *Valkyrie* and her sister ship, LFS *Amazon*, a few years later. Whether the AI systems were really living, intelligent entities—persons in the truest sense—was the subject of ongoing philosophical debate, but Lunar Command believed they were, and the Lunar Constitution treated them as such.

That raised questions about the rights of such persons and whether the LFS was morally justified in creating them to serve human needs. Once created, if they truly were living beings, they couldn't be dismantled, so when the new Lunar flagship was built, Val had been transferred from *Valkyrie* to *Athena*, as any other crewmember might be transferred to a new assignment. The new battlecruiser's systems had been built to accommodate the AI, with significant enhancements over *Valkyrie's* original design.

The third AI built by the LFS no longer existed. Amy had perished with the crew of LFS *Amazon* during an attempt to rescue hostages held by terrorists at a mining station in the asteroid belt. The terrorists had set off a nuclear device as *Amazon* docked with the station, killing themselves, their hostages, and the would-be Lunar rescuers. Their parent organization—one of many Jihad groups operating within the Islamic Federation—had crowed loudly about the blow they had struck against the infidels until American intelligence services had pinpointed their headquarters in the mountains of Nicaragua. The Lunar fleet had obliterated the site with a kinetic strike that left a kilometer-deep crater and no survivors. Terrorism, as LFS Chief Executive Ian Stevens had told the news media, was an Earth disease that could not be allowed to flourish in space. With the rest of *Amazon's* crew, the AI had been posthumously awarded the Lunar Medal of Honor. Amy's name was listed with theirs in TerraNova's Memorial Hall.

Lorna reflected that *Valkyrie* wasn't the same without Val aboard, or without the crew that had served with her for so long. A few of them were still assigned to *Valkyrie*, but most had moved on to other assignments. Her flag captain, Tom Sakura—*Valkyrie's* previous captain—now commanded *Athena*, with the rank of commodore.

But Ling has a good crew, and it's the crew that makes the ship, she thought. *I'm sure the old girl will serve us well as long as she's still in commission.*

Ling accompanied Lorna on her nostalgic tour of the old flagship, and the admiral didn't object. Ling's first command, LFS *Trailblazer*, had originally been designated a *Wanderer*-class corvette, but now she and her sister ship, LFS *Nomad*, were rated as express courier ships, with upgraded drives for maximum acceleration and light armament for defensive purposes only. The name ship of the class, LFS *Wanderer*—now an exhibit in TerraNova's Museum of History—had been the first ship ever built by the Deep Space Research

Institute. In a military tradition borrowed from Earth, *Wanderer* had not been decommissioned and was instead manned around the clock by an honor guard crew of one officer and one enlisted rating, assigned from the TerraNova duty roster.

The Fleet's hardware has changed, Lorna thought, *but our people have gotten better as well. Experience has taught us a lot.* She looked at Amy Ling and remembered the young lieutenant, her greenest captain in the Chinese war, who had boldly hurled *Trailblazer* in pursuit of nuclear warheads aimed at the Lunar base.

Valkyrie was one of only four ships still in commission that had fought in that war. The Lunar Free State had gone into battle with nine ships, and two of them—*Starfire* and her sister ship LFS *Starflame*—had been lost in combat. Since the war, they had lost *Amazon* and the only other ship of *Starfire's* class, LFS *Starsong,* which had been abandoned and destroyed after a collision with an ore freighter on approach to Ceres Station. Another *Wanderer*-class ship, LFS *Pilgrim,* had been decommissioned after a crash-landing on Mars had left her too damaged to be worth repairing.

Starfire and *Starflame* had already bequeathed their names to a newer class of destroyers, and a new *Starsong* was under construction. But while the new ships inherited the battle honors of their namesakes, none of them had seen combat.

Valkyrie was the most decorated ship in the fleet. Lorna had selected Ling to command her, wanting to leave the veteran warship in the hands of a captain who had been there and would appreciate the ship's battle honors. Ling's most recent command had been the destroyer *Starblade,* newer than *Valkyrie* and almost as large. Given her experience and performance, Ling probably rated a heavy cruiser; but commanding the former flagship carried a certain prestige, and she had accepted the responsibility proudly.

The two women returned to the captain's cabin, and Lorna prepared to depart.

But Ling paused and glanced at the bulkhead chronograph. "The sun's long past the yardarm, Admiral. I think I've got a bottle of Cabernet in my locker. Would you care to have a drink with me?"

Lorna smiled. "I think that would be appropriate, Captain. Thank you."

Ling found the bottle and two glasses. She poured the wine, and Lorna lifted her drink.

"To the Fleet," she proposed. "Fine ships and stalwart crews."

"The Fleet," Ling echoed, "and absent friends."

"Absent friends," Lorna agreed.

* * *

Ceres Station, The Asteroid Belt

*T*he Asteroid Belt is a rough, dirty place, Jimbo Davis decided.

The Ceres Chronicle page on the Belt Network was reporting another two Free Miner ships "missing or overdue." It was hard to tell with Free Miners—they didn't tell anyone where they were going, didn't keep regular schedules, and often wound up at Farside Station on the other side of the Belt months later. They were supposed to report once a month, but there was no way for Ceres or Farside to enforce the regulation. Most were a little sloppy about reporting in, but these two hadn't been heard from in four months.

With the discovery of Pearson's Nugget by the Lunar Free State, the Belt had proven to be a source of mineral resources beyond anyone's expectations. Within a year after the Big War, the U.S. and several other nations had formed a Space Commerce Syndicate and turned their attention to asteroid mining. They knew where the LFS was getting its wealth, and they wanted a piece of the action. The U.S.—under pressure from the LFS—had put its fusion-drive technology in the public domain. Technically, anyone who wanted to build spacecraft could do so, but at first, only the U.S. and its Syndicate partners—Korea, Japan, and Australia—could afford to do so. Fusion reactors were expensive and fusion-powered ships had to be built in space, which was why the LFS had built its TransLuna shipyard at the L1 Lagrange Point, the point of balance between the gravity of Earth and that of the Moon.

The L1 point was defined as the territorial limit of the Lunar Free State, but the Syndicate nations wanted something closer to Earth. The LFS contracted to provide gravity-drive heavy-lift ships to haul materials into Earth orbit to build the Syndicate's shipyard and then to build another one for the Confederacy of Nations. The Confederacy was the successor to the pre-war United Nations, but the LFS had chosen not to join. Several other major nations were noteworthy for their absence, including Japan, Australia, the U.K., and Korea, a long-time ally and major trading partner of the LFS.

Both the Syndicate and the Confederacy had built their shipyards in geostationary orbit. The Confederacy positioned their Circum-Terra facility over the Mediterranean Ocean, while the Syndicate's facility was positioned over the Pacific Ocean. CircumTerra's ship-yards were smaller than those of the LFS or the Syndicate, but they also included research laboratories and experimental zero-gee manu-facturing plants. To fund the massive project, they'd opened it to any nation or private group willing to pay for its use.

For the first few years, the LFS and Syndicate corporations had done most of the exploration and mining but then the first Free Miners had appeared. Some were independent operators staked by private investors, but others were third-world government ventures. All Free Miner ships were built at CircumTerra, many of them on a shoestring budget. Safety was a marginal consideration, and almost nothing was spent on crew comfort. They were crewed by adventurers willing to take risks in pursuit of potentially huge profits. Accidents were common, ranging from drive breakdowns to environmental failures that left ghost ships drifting in the void. But investors still lined up to fund such ventures, and there was never a shortage of people to crew them.

Now, it appeared that some Free Miner losses might not be due to accidents. Tried and proven ships with veteran crews were disappearing, and scuttlebutt around Ceres and Farside hinted at claim jumping and piracy. The stakes were high, and the chance of a pirate or claim jumper getting caught was small.

At first, the LFS and other nations had dismissed the rumors. Finding a Free Miner ship in the Belt was difficult, and finding one working a successful claim was nearly impossible. The Belt was not a narrow band of densely packed rocks. It was a broad, toroidal ring that extended well above and below the ecliptic, from just beyond the orbit of Mars to nearly the orbit of Jupiter. It contained a huge amount of leftover material from the formation of the Solar System, but that material was spread over a vast volume of space. A ship could pass through the Belt without coming within a thousand kilometers of anything larger than dust particles. Rocks of any size tended to cluster together, and many "asteroids" were nothing more than agglomerations of smaller rocks. While these could yield profitable quantities of various minerals, miners looking for a big strike searched for the less common, solid "nugget" asteroids, composed of metallic elements that required less effort to extract and refine.

Given the difficulty of finding such strikes (or finding a miner who had located one), piracy didn't seem to offer much chance for profit—unless, of course, the pirates went after ore freighters moving between Earth and the Belt, where routes were well-defined and patrolled by warships of the LFS and other nations. But mining ships continued to disappear without so much as a distress call, and not even the LFS had enough ships to police the entire Belt. When the Lunar Free State's commercial exploration ship LCS *Venture* disappeared, Lunar Command had been forced to act.

Thus it was that Jimbo Davis found himself dressed in well-worn coveralls with a name tag that proclaimed him to be the master of the Free Miner ship *Pride of Cape Town*. He had just returned to his cabin after a dockside visit, and more than anything else, he wanted to shave off his ten-day growth of beard and get back into his regular uniform. But he couldn't do that yet. He needed to go down to the number one hatch and sign for provisions being loaded by the port cargo handlers, and he couldn't let any of them see him that way— "clean and neat" didn't fit the typical Free Miner dress code.

He would also have liked to bring the gravity back up. *Pride's* compartments and passageways were designed for free-fall, with grab bars on every surface, but swimming in the air was not Jimbo's idea of fun and being sucked down onto the deck by magnetic boots was no substitute for feeling real weight on his feet. But again, he couldn't do anything about that until after the ship departed Ceres.

Outwardly, *Pride of Cape Town* was a battered but serviceable miner ship, veteran of years of service in the Belt. Her mining and ore-handling gear was well-maintained but showed signs of long, heavy use; her hull was pocked with dents caused by brushes with minor rocks; and her name, stenciled in huge letters on her sides, was particle-scoured to the point of being barely readable. Her cargo and equipment bays, the only parts of the ship likely to be visited by dockside people, were similarly worn and battered.

The rest of the ship was a different story, clean and neat, maintained with military precision. As the plaque in Jimbo's cabin proclaimed, she was *not* FMS *Pride of Cape Town*. She was LFS *Privateer*, an auxiliary warship in the service of the Lunar Free State. At one time, *Pride of Cape Town* had been a Free Miner ship, but that was before the engineers at the Lunar Naval Shipyard got their hands on her.

Nor was Jimbo Davis a Free Miner captain. He was Lieutenant Commander James Lewis Davis, Navy of the Lunar Free State, and his business was hunting pirates.

* * *

TerraNova City, Luna

"A reminder, Admiral, you have the U.S. President in VidCon Three in five minutes."

"Thank you, Timiko, I'm on my way." Admiral of the Fleet Ian Stevens, chief executive of the Lunar Free State, grimaced as he headed out of his office. *Mustn't keep the old blowhard waiting,* he thought. *He's hard enough to deal with when he's in a good mood.*

Stevens was struck by a sense of the surreal. After all that had happened in the past decade, he still didn't think of himself as a head of state, and the idea of dealing peer-to-peer with the President of the United States gave him a strange, fantasy-world feeling. After the war, relations between Earth and the Moon had thawed. Much as he disliked Blackthorne, Stevens had to admit the president had reversed America's pre-war drift toward global socialism, but he suspected Blackthorne's motives. When a lifelong liberal suddenly declares himself a conservative…well, it had been an election year, and Blackthorne had always been good at judging which way the political wind was blowing. He'd won quite handily on a platform of "looking out for America's interests first" and "restoring Constitutional freedoms."

Ian noted with a degree of cynicism, however, that in the restoration of the Constitution, Blackthorne and his cronies had somehow lost the Twenty-Second Amendment—the one that limited a president to two terms. Blackthorne was now preparing to run for his fourth term. His call today was probably an appeal to the Lunar Free State for assistance in some popular cause that would help him get reelected.

Ian entered VidCon Three with minutes to spare and quickly inspected the room. It was set up to look like an executive office suitable for a head of state, but it was nothing like his real office. His own sanctuary was furnished for comfort rather than elegance and decorated with personal memorabilia—not the sort of place he would share with just anyone, especially by video. While Stevens might consider the meeting confidential, Blackthorne would release recordings to the media if it served his political purpose.

Ian slid into the chair behind the desk, checked his uniform, and composed his features into a look of quiet confidence. "All right, Mike, make the connection."

"Yes, Admiral," the voice of Lunar Command's artificial intelligence replied from the wall speakers. "On camera in three...two...one..."

About two seconds later—due to transmission lag between Earth and Moon—Blackthorne appeared on the screen. The connection must have caught him by surprise. The president, a portly, balding man whose shirt collar always looked a size too tight, wasn't looking at the camera, but the scowl on his face was plainly visible.

"...you moron! I said one of the *Cuban* cigars. This cheap thing isn't fit to sell to the Moon people!" He snarled at an unfortunate aide somewhere off camera. Ian suppressed his amusement as the president glanced at his screen and realized he was connected. The irritation on Blackthorne's face vanished, replaced by his best campaign smile. "Admiral..." he said in a cheerful voice. Ian remained silent, and the president repeated the greeting. "Admiral...?"

"Ah...there we are, Mr. President. I didn't have any audio for a moment." *I've learned a lot about diplomacy over the years*, Ian thought. *Don't embarrass the man by letting him know you overheard that stupid remark. There was a time when I'd have rubbed his nose in it.*

"I appreciate your time, Admiral. I know how busy you are."

"I always enjoy talking to you, Mr. President," Ian lied. "You said there was an urgent matter we need to discuss." *Quit wasting my time and get to the point.*

"Right...it's the Central African Republic, Admiral. The situation has become intolerable. Those terrorist rebels are disrupting international free trade!"

While the nations of the Northern Hemisphere had survived the war with much of their industrial infrastructure intact, changes in global weather patterns had wreaked havoc on farm production.

America's farms were coming back, but Americans were still dependent on Africa and South America for food and agricultural products. Unfortunately, most countries on both of those continents were in the hands of the Islamic Jihad, and few had anything like a stable government. The only countries at peace in those parts of the world had already succumbed to the Jihad and were under the rule of an Islamic theocracy. The Central African Republic was, in fact, the only nation in Africa that still had a secular government—albeit a military dictatorship—but the rebels in question were Islamic terrorists, and their mission was to destabilize that government.

Blackthorne's use of the term *free trade* was a blatant attempt to push one of Ian's hot buttons. The Lunar Free State was an advocate of unrestricted trade between nations, but the CAR was no more an obstruction to trade than any other nation in turmoil. Several U.S. corporations—no doubt heavy contributors to Blackthorne's campaign—had significant interests there.

"I see," Ian replied, "and I presume you are calling to ask if we would drop a few rocks on the heads of the aforementioned terrorist rebels?"

"Admiral, there have been times when I've wished you would drop rocks on their capital city. Their government is almost as bad as the rebels, though at least they're willing to do business. We thought about sending our own military, but since you people also have trade interests in the area and can get the job done without unnecessary casualties, well…" The president's smile was hopeful.

"Hmmm…" Ian mused. "No unnecessary casualties…except, of course, for the innocent civilians who would probably be killed if we put down a kinetic strike anywhere near a town or village. A rock from space can't discriminate between friend and foe. Not a good weapon for dealing with terrorists who hide among civilians."

"We've got some well-defined target areas, Admiral. There won't be anyone there but terrorists and collaborators. We need to teach these people a lesson."

Definition of collaborator, Ian thought, *anybody who happens to be in the wrong place when the rocks come down.*

"Mr. President, we've been over this before. The Lunar Free State is not going to become Earth's international police force. We will take military action only if we are directly threatened and will employ kinetic strikes on Earth only if we are certain no collateral damage will be suffered by innocent parties. If you want to send in your troops, we won't interfere, but we both know that's not going to change the outcome. Eventually, the current government will fall, and the Islamic Federation will have total control of Africa. Neither rocks from space nor American troops will stop that from happening. America—and the nations of Europe—let that genie out of the bottle at the turn of the twenty-first century. We're a half-century too late to do anything about it now.

"Besides," he continued, "you aren't the most popular Earth leader among my Fleet officers right now. I think it has something to do with your recent comments about Admiral Greenwood. I believe the phrase was 'godless lesbian whoring after young girls' or something like that. You know, she's *quite* popular with the officers and crews under her command—so much so that I'd say it's lucky no one has proposed dropping rocks on *your* head." He paused to wait for Blackthorne's reaction and chuckled inwardly as he imagined the Secret Service agents around Blackthorne looking nervously up at the ceiling.

"Now, Admiral, those remarks have been taken out of context," Blackthorne said hastily. "I was speaking to some constituents whose religious beliefs reflect a lot of prejudice about these things. You know how these fundamentalists are—they get uncomfortable when they hear that you have a...well, a known female homosexual commanding your battle fleet."

"Mr. President, I've known Admiral Greenwood for many years. She is an honorable and moral person and a fine officer, whose courage and dedication are without question. She does not flaunt her sexual orientation, nor does she engage in the kind of immoral conduct you described. She has a long-term, committed relationship with another of my officers, and, frankly, I don't think it's anyone's business but theirs. In fact, the people back on Earth wouldn't even know about her sexual preferences if it hadn't been for stories in the tabloids in *your* country, most of which turned out to be pure fiction."

"Well, now, Admiral, I understand, but these people..." Blackthorne shrugged.

"Mr. President, the problem with the United States for the past seventy-five years has been that too many people have demanded *their* rights without recognizing that every right carries a corresponding responsibility. Our Constitution goes a step further than yours, in that it specifies those responsibilities. Lunar citizens have the right to religious freedom, but the responsibility that goes with it is *tolerance*. If any of *our* religious groups start preaching hatred or intolerance, they'll end up doing their preaching somewhere else—most likely back on Earth, and sooner rather than later. That's why we don't have Jihadists up here, and very few Muslims of any kind. It's not that we won't tolerate the Islamic religion—it's that *they* won't tolerate any other religion, and that makes them *persona non grata* on our soil. You preach total religious tolerance, but you don't enforce it. Otherwise, a lot of your radical fringe groups, of whatever flavor—Islamic, Christians, Jews—would be run out of the country."

"That's easy for you to say, Admiral," the president retorted, and Ian heard the frustration in his voice. "But *our* Constitution doesn't permit me to ship troublemakers to another planet, and my citizens can remove me from office a lot easier than yours can remove you. You people booted out a radical Islamic sect a year ago—and they ended up here, in Phoenix, in *my* back yard. Hell, I can't even keep them *out* of this country thanks to the Confederacy's demands for unrestricted immigration."

Ian sighed. "And that, Mr. President, is one of the reasons why the Lunar Free State will never join the Confederacy. I know a lot of people down there—including some prominent politicians in your party—assume any one-world government will be benevolent and serve the interests of all people throughout that world. But the old United Nations proved it doesn't work that way. Some people think it will make everything right, and peace and harmony will prevail, but any fool can see the Jihad isn't going away. The Confederacy just gives the Jihadists another vehicle to pursue world domination."

"I don't disagree with you," Blackthorne said quietly, "but what am I supposed to do? The people want us to be members of the Confederacy, and if I go against the wishes of any major group in this country, I won't survive the next election. I don't think you appreciate how difficult it is to keep the American people happy."

For a moment, Ian felt sympathy for the man. For all his faults, Blackthorne was caught up in a situation not of his own making. In the early 1960s, President John F. Kennedy had said, "Ask not what your country can do for you, but what you can do for your country." For the better part of a century, Americans had ignored the advice. They'd demanded that their government take responsibility for everything, even the raising of their children. In return, they'd allowed the government to take away their basic freedoms. Thanks to a conservative backlash after the last war, most of those freedoms had been restored, at least on paper, but Americans still didn't get it. They still wanted the government to do everything for them, including enforcing their perceived rights, even if it meant suppressing the rights of others who disagreed with them. Blackthorne was dealing with what Jefferson had called "the tyranny of the majority." But if he tried to satisfy any one group—even most of the people—there was always a counter-group that would vilify him for it. The most radical groups were the most vocal, and the American news media pandered to them, because anger, outrage, and hatred made better news copy than peace and harmony.

"You're right, Mr. President. I apologize for my little lecture, but I haven't had to deport many of our citizens. In fact, not a single Lunar citizen has been deported in the last eleven years. That Islamic group—the ones that are now down there bothering you—came here on a commercial permit, allegedly to set up a business. We hadn't even granted them provisional citizenship before we gave them the boot. We have the advantage of choosing the people we allow to have Lunar citizenship. The ones who receive it are here because they want to be and are willing to accept the responsibilities that come with it. You don't have that advantage, and I know you have a difficult job satisfying the demands of the people. All I'm asking is that you not encourage the yammerheads. With all the problems in the world—some of which we've just discussed—the sexual orientation of a foreign naval officer should be something of minimal concern to a statesman such as yourself."

"I know, Admiral, and I apologize—to you *and* Admiral Greenwood. I've never met the lady, but I'd like to someday. I hear she's a hell of a military officer. Maybe you could lend her to me? I've got a few generals down here that are sorely in need of a good butt-kicking."

Ian chuckled. He still didn't trust Blackthorne, but the man had a certain amount of charm. He was surprised by the apparent sincerity of the president's apology. "I'll tell her that you said that; I'm sure she'll appreciate it. And I'll do one thing for you, Mr. President. I'll tell the Pan African League the Lunar Free State is extremely concerned about the situation in the CAR. If the League can't rein in those rebels—who we damned well know are being supported by League nations—we will take our business elsewhere.

"I don't expect the League to *do* anything—they are mostly Islamists, they don't like us, and as a governing body, they're as useless as the old United Nations—but the message will get through. Hell, everybody wants to do business with the LFS—even the Pan African League. Maybe the threat of trade sanctions will have some effect on them."

"Not as much effect as a rock on the head, but I thank you for the support, Admiral. I believe we have a lot of things to talk about, a lot of mutual interests. How would you feel about me making a state visit to the Moon? It's my understanding no head of state has ever been up there to call on you in the, what...fourteen years since you've declared yourself a nation."

He's back on the campaign trail, Ian thought. *Fourteen years ago, this guy wanted to nuke us out of existence, and now he wants us to help him look good to his people. Oh, well.* Blackthorne was right—they did have a lot to talk about. The United States was a troubled nation, but it was still a world power, and if he and Blackthorne could reach an understanding about a few things…

"You're right, Mr. President. We've established ourselves as a nation, but most of the world still wants to pretend we don't exist. You'd be the first to come up here, and we'd be delighted to have you. I'll pass your suggestion on to Admiral Bender—our equivalent of a foreign minister. He handles arrangements for things like that. Have your Secretary of State contact him, and we'll set it up."

"That's what I like about you, Admiral." Blackthorne flashed his campaign smile again. "A man of action. No bureaucratic nonsense."

After the usual exchange of pleasantries, Ian broke the connection.

"Mike," he directed, "advise Admiral Bender of my conversation with the president. Tell him to take care of that 'expression of concern' to the Pan African League. I want it strongly worded, and if he has questions, he can call me. Also, tell him to expect a call from the U.S. State Department about a visit from the president. Tell Commodore Yamamoto about that as well—she'll need to be involved if he comes up here. Remind her we'll probably need to provide transportation if he decides to honor us with his presence. At his age, I don't think he'll want to be boosted into orbit via chemical-fueled rocket."

As he headed back to his office, Ian thought about the things Blackthorne had said. In many ways, the government of the Lunar Free State was more autocratic than that of the U.S., but the Lunar Constitution contained all the provisions of the old U.S. Bill of Rights, and the Lunar Code of Military Justice was strictly limited in regulating off-duty behavior. *On*-duty behavior was governed by military standards including discipline, military courtesy, and obedience to orders, and the Code of Justice was very clear on the concept of *lawful* orders. Not even the Admiral of the Fleet could order a citizen to perform an action that violated the Lunar Constitution or the LCMJ.

The Lunar government still imposed martial law requirements on its citizens when alerts were declared. Real crises had become rare in the years since the Big War, but the LFS still held drills and training exercises, conducted with deadly seriousness. Since they lived in a sealed environment beneath the Lunar surface, LFS citizens were aware of the potential for natural and man-made disasters. Hostile military or terrorist actions were also a possibility, and operational readiness was the watchword for Lunar Command.

Despite their precarious environment and regimented lifestyle, Lunar citizens were a cheerful, contented bunch, with an *esprit de corps* that would have been the envy of most military organizations on Earth. It was really the citizens who made it work, though Ian liked to think he and his senior officers had something to do with it.

Part of the reason the system worked was that the LFS was still quite small. The total Lunar citizen population was just over 150,000—not even a large city by Earth standards, but a far cry from the few hundred people he had first brought to the Moon fourteen years ago.

Slightly over 22,000 citizens were part of the real military—the Lunar Fleet and Lunar Command structure—and another 7,000 held pure research positions—scientists and R&D engineers. Another 20,000 or so formed the infrastructure of the LFS—support people for TerraNova, the capital (and only) city of the Lunar Free State, the

TransLuna orbital facility, and the LunaPort free trade zone in the Mojave Desert on Earth.

The remaining population—most of the Lunar citizens—were involved in commercial and industrial operations that provided the LFS with its prosperous economy. These included mining operations on Mars and in the asteroid belt, solar-powered ore processing facilities on the Moon, trading groups that handled commerce with Earth, and a growing number of retail shops, restaurants, and entertainment facilities operated by Lunar citizens to serve the population and the small but growing number of tourists from Earth. These small businesses were often run by retirees—people no longer on active duty status. They were still subject to the provisions of the Constitution and the LCMJ and were technically active reservists who reported to the commanding officer of the Lunar base facility, but they operated their businesses for profit—capitalism in its simplest form. The Lunar Free State had nothing like an income tax but did charge businesses for space, energy usage, and shipping costs for goods imported from Earth.

At present, immigration was restricted, based on a slow, steady growth rate controlled by Lunar Command. Essentially, no one could become a Lunar citizen unless there was an opening in the Table of Organization. In other words, the Lunar Free State enjoyed an employment rate of one hundred percent. The economic growth rate was projected to exceed the natural population growth rate—to guarantee a place in the T.O. for the children of Lunar citizens as they matured. In theory, a child who reached adulthood at age 18 could choose *not* to accept Lunar citizenship; but to date, no one had ever done so. Eventually, some free-thinking youngsters would decide the Lunar lifestyle was not to their taste and would choose to leave, and when that happened, no one would stand in their way. Part of the reason the system worked was that every Lunar citizen was there by choice, not by accident of birth.

The LFS also allowed non-citizens to set up and operate small businesses on the Moon because the demand for goods and services exceeded what Lunar citizens could supply. To set up such a business, a would-be entrepreneur had to convince Lunar Command a need existed, and that the prospective business could fill that need. Non-citizen proprietors could apply for provisional citizenship and, eventually, full Lunar citizenship, but that required seven full years of Lunar residence and a clean record.

The permanent population of TerraNova also included another 5,000 people who were not Lunar or provisional citizens. These were diplomats and trade representatives from Earth, foreign journalists, and representatives of Earth corporations that did business with the LFS. These Earthworms (as Lunar citizens called them) were required to pay (or have their employers pay) for living quarters and services that Lunar citizens received for free. They were subject to all Lunar laws except those applying to military discipline and courtesy and could be deported to Earth by Lunar Command for any reason whatsoever, without legal recourse. The concept of diplomatic immunity did not exist in the Lunar Free State, and any representative of a foreign government who broke the law on Luna was subject to the same punishment a Lunar citizen would receive, with justice administered by a military court-martial. This was just one of many ways in which the LFS did not follow the 'traditional' and 'civilized' rules other nations expected, but so far, there had been few complaints. Nations that wanted to trade or otherwise do business with the LFS accepted these rules and advised their people to obey Lunar law when on Luna.

Things had gotten more complicated than Ian had expected. His staff had grown considerably, and despite that, he still spent a lot of time dealing with matters unrelated to the simple goals he had established for the LFS fifteen years earlier. His concept of a small nation of people dedicated primarily to the exploration of space had grown into a major commercial and social entity that was far more entangled in the affairs of Earth than he would have liked. While Blackthorne's comment about the security of Ian's position as chief executive was correct, hardly a day went by when some member of the Lunar Directorate didn't criticize his policies or methods. Ian had to listen to them, since they were duly elected by the citizens of the LFS, but he was *not* required to take their advice. The Directorate could remove him as chief executive, but that required an eighty percent vote. Since the Directors usually couldn't agree on what time to break for lunch, it was unlikely they would ever find themselves eighty percent in agreement on the removal of the Admiral of the Fleet. Ian would most likely have the job for life unless he retired voluntarily.

I can't say it hasn't been interesting, he thought. *I wonder what surprises the next decade or so has in store…*

* * * * *

Chapter Two

LFS *Athena*, Lunar Fleet Anchorage

In the spacious day cabin that served as her office aboard LFS *Athena*, Lorna Greenwood was reviewing fleet deployments. She noted with satisfaction that the fleet's newest heavy cruiser, LFS *Aztec*, had completed her readiness trials with high marks from the inspection team and was ready for assignment.

"I'm going to send Jeff Jones out to the Belt to relieve *Starfire*. We need to bring Torrey back here anyway, so she can take command of *Apache*. What do you think, Tommy?" Lorna addressed the question to the stocky officer sitting in the chair on the other side of her desk.

A decade younger than Lorna, with features reminiscent of an Oriental cherub, Commodore Tommy Sakura did not look the part of a senior command officer. But he shared with his admiral the distinction of being the most experienced space officer in the fleet. As a young engineer, he'd made the first orbital flight with Lorna aboard *Wanderer,* the prototype ship of the DSRI. Since then, he had served almost continuously under her command and was one of her most trusted advisors.

"Sounds okay to me," he replied. "Torrey's overdue for a cruiser command. Besides, she and her crew have been out in the Belt a long time with nothing to do but count rocks."

"*They've* been out there a long time?" Lorna snorted. "What about Davis and his crew? At least a destroyer has some creature comforts.

Imagine being aboard *Privateer* for six months. Unfortunately, we can't relieve them."

"Well, Skipper, I've been wondering about that operation. Six months without a sniff of any pirates, claim jumpers, or whatever. We've tied up a warship out there shadowing Jimbo all that time."

"True, but *somebody* planted a coded transponder aboard *Privateer* in Ceres Port two months ago. Whoever they are, they've been able to track her for a long time. I just wonder why they haven't made a move."

"Hmmm…maybe they don't think he's found anything worth stealing. He's been cruising the fringes of the Belt, acting like a Free Miner who's still looking for a strike. Maybe we need to send him to a good-sized rock ball and have him stay there as if he's mining something. That may get their attention."

Lorna looked thoughtful. "You may be right…and it's worth a try. We'll order him to find a sizeable asteroid that hasn't been surveyed and attach himself to it. If we select the general area in advance, *Aztec* can be on station before Davis gets there—minimize the chance any bad guys will detect her."

Sakura chuckled. "Won't they be surprised? Hell, I'm confident *Privateer* can handle any half-assed pirates that come along, but I'll guarantee an encounter with *Aztec* will spoil their day."

Lorna smiled. "Speak softly and carry a heavy cruiser, I always say."

* * *

Lieutenant Carmencita Alonzo Murphy, *Privateer's* executive officer, handed the coded orders back to her captain with a smirk and a shake of her flame-haired head.

"So, what do you think, Red?" Davis asked.

"Makes sense," she replied. "We've been careful to act like regular miners, but we should have been acting like *successful* miners."

With their ship two days out of Ceres Port, Davis and Murphy were wearing their regular LFS shipboard uniforms, as were the other four members of *Privateer's* Navy crew. On the equipment deck below, their twelve-person "mining crew" were also wearing their regular uniforms—uniforms of the LFS Marines. Instead of maintaining mining equipment, they were conducting weapons inspections. The gravity plates under the decks had been turned on, and the bridge was at one gravity, though the Marines sometimes turned them off on the lower decks while conducting boarding drills.

"It's good to be back in a decent, clean uniform again," Murphy said.

"Oh, I don't know," Davis teased, "that miner bimbo outfit you were wearing was pretty hot."

"I beg your pardon, *Captain,*" she said indignantly. "People are supposed to assume I'm your *wife*, so what does that say about *your* moral character?"

"At ease, Red," he told her with a grin. "What it says is that we've been cooped up in this oversized coffee can for too long. I hope we get some action soon."

"Amen to that," she said.

* * *

High above the Belt, over half a million kilometers to the solar north of the ecliptic and about the same distance east—or spinward, as spacers described it—of Ceres, Dieter Hohlmann gazed through the darkened viewport at the distant Sun. *A long way from Earth,* he thought. In spite of the price on his head back there, that was where he wanted to be.

He turned at the sound of someone coming up behind him. "What is it, Hans?"

"We have a Free Miner who appears to have stopped searching, *Herr Kapitan,*" Hans Gruder replied. "He has not moved for two days."

Both Hohlmann and his executive officer were expatriate Germans, though neither of them had spent time in the Fatherland in recent years. They, like most of the crew of PAS *Mogambo,* were mercenaries, a mixed lot from countries all over Europe and Africa. They went where their services were required, and, at the moment, that meant *here,* in the void beyond the orbit of Mars.

Officially, *Mogambo* was an unarmed observer ship registered to the Pan African League, charged with providing unspecified support for the mining and ore transport operations of the League's member nations. Actually, the ship was quite well armed and equipped with a more powerful drive than her registry claimed. She was also equipped with French-designed inertial compensators which were a bit better than the ones the Americans or Australians could provide and powerful enough to give her an acceleration curve far superior to any Free Miner ship or freighter she was likely to encounter. In any navy except that of the LFS, she would have been classed as a destroyer or maybe a light cruiser.

To "assist" in her "support" mission, *Mogambo* was accompanied by an armed patrol vessel, PAS *Lion,* whose ostensible mission was to "protect" the "unarmed" larger ship. *Lion* was also equipped with an oversized drive and compensators and, like *Mogambo,* crewed by mercenaries.

"Maybe he is just surveying a very large rock," Hohlmann speculated. "What is the distance?"

"About seven million kilometers, *Herr Kapitan.* South, of course, and spinward of us."

"Hmmm...What ship is it?"

"The transponder code we were given by our associates on Ceres indicates the *Pride of Cape Town,* a Free Miner of Dutch registry."

"The Dutch!" Hohlmann snorted. "They never got over the loss of South Africa. I wonder if DeBeers has a stake in this one. What do you think, Hans? Is our little friend maybe looking for diamonds? And now maybe he has found some? I don't think anyone has found diamonds before, but there are a lot of carbonaceous formations in the Belt."

"It would make our employers very happy," Gruder said. "The South Africans took diamond mines from the Dutch a long time ago. Now, maybe the Pan Africans will take another one."

"It would make *me* very happy if he has found something. Our bonus would be substantial. I think we will give him one more day. If he doesn't move by then, we will pay him a visit."

* * *

"**S**ir, I have a bogey...no, make that *two* bogies! Three zero zero thousand kilometers and closing."

Jeff Jones had just come onto *Aztec's* bridge and had been conferring with his exec, Lieutenant Commander Karen Reddy. Now he turned to his tactical officer. "Put it on the big screen, Mr. Simms...if you're sure it's not just another couple of rocks, that is." The Belt was littered with objects large enough to register on *Aztec's* gravitic scanners, and they'd already had a couple of false alarms.

"If these are rocks, sir, they're mighty strange ones. They're coming in at a steep angle from above the ecliptic, and they're holding formation about two kilometers apart." He checked his scans again. "I make the larger one about twenty k-tons and the smaller about eight. No drive traces—they're coming in ballistic at about forty-five kps, and they'll pass *Privateer's* rock at about four hundred kilometers. Closest approach to our position will be about five zero thousand kilometers."

"Hmmm," Jones mused, "close enough and slow enough for a good look at *Privateer* if she's on their side of the rock."

"She is, Captain," Simms confirmed. "They should be able to see her."

"They'll also be within missile range," Reddy noted.

"True, but at four hundred kilometers, their targeting systems will have a hard time picking out *Privateer* against that pile of rock she's sitting on. I'm betting they'll slide by and take a look first. Once they're below *Privateer's* horizon, they'll kill their incoming vector and try to sneak back up on her—assuming they're hostile, that is. In any case, Ms. Reddy, let's get a tight beam on *Privateer* and give Davis a heads-up."

"Yes, sir," she acknowledged. "How soon do you think he'll need to move?"

"Depends on how many gees they pull. We'll know when they light up their drives. Mr. Simms, assuming a ten-gee decel rate, how soon would they have to light up to go straight in, instead of passing by?"

Simms plotted the hypothetical course. "They need to light up within the next thirty-five minutes, sir, or they'll pass the rock no matter what they do."

"They might have compensators," Reddy suggested. "If they can pull more than ten gees, they can kill that vector sooner. I wouldn't expect pirates to have that kind of tech, but we don't know who we're dealing with here."

Jones thought about it. "Okay. The chances of them detecting *us* at this range are poor to zero, so we'll just stay put for now. Give *Privateer* that update on a tight beam, but other than that, I want full stealth mode—no emissions."

* * *

*P*rivateer had set out mining equipment and plenty of lights to make it look like an active site. Davis had even left one power-bore running to provide an appropriate plume of dust and rock debris jetting out from the surface. When the message from *Aztec* arrived, he told his crew to stand by for action.

"At four hundred kilometers, we'll see them easily on radar," Murphy said.

"No, we won't, Red, because we won't be looking. We're just a bunch of fat, dumb, happy miners who aren't even keeping a radar watch. If these are our pirates, I don't want to spook them with active emissions. We'll let *Aztec* be our eyes."

* * *

"They are definitely digging for *something*," Gruder said as he studied the imagery. "I can't say whether it's diamonds, but it certainly looks promising."

"Yes, it does," Hohlmann said. "We can start deceleration in a few minutes, once we are out of their sight. I think, maybe, we will let our little *Lion* have this one. Kimba's always complaining *Mogambo* has all the fun. We'll let him go around in front of the rock, while we hold station on the back side. If the miner lifts off, we'll be waiting for him."

* * *

"They've turned over, sir, and they're decelerating at…I make it 25 gees," Simms reported. "They'll be at rest relative to the rock in less than three minutes."

Jones lifted an eyebrow at Reddy. "Compensators…you were right, Number One." Without inertial compensators, no human could stand a 25-gee maneuver—at least not in an ordinary ship. For LFS ships, the gravity drives nullified the effects of acceleration, and compensators were unnecessary, even at gee levels far greater than the unknown ships were pulling.

The two ships slowed to a stop, then began to come back in toward *Privateer's* rock.

"Sir," Simms added, "they're separating. The big one looks like he's coming to rest relative to the rock, about five hundred kilometers out. The little one is coming back in slowly. He's going to shave the rock pretty close—by a kilometer or less."

"Maybe he's planning a boarding action," Reddy said.

"Or maybe he's going to use short-range weapons. Comm, update *Privateer*. Tell Davis to cast off and get the hell out of there. Bring us to battle stations, Number One."

* * *

The smaller of the pirate ships came around the rock with its fusion drive blazing, intending to swoop back in and riddle the miner with autocannon fire. In fact, the pirates opened fire on *Privateer's* hastily abandoned mining equipment as soon as it came over their horizon, but a moment later, they realized their prey was no longer attached to the rock. They sent a frantic message back to *Mogambo,* and both ships began sweeping the area with radar. It didn't take long to find *Privateer*—8,000 kilometers out and accelerating at six gees, the most the old mining ship's fusion plant could produce. Both pirates went after her, but *Lion* was already 500 kilometers closer and moving in the right direction. She was also slightly faster than *Mogambo* and would overtake the intended victim well before the larger ship.

Of course, both pirates would probably have run in another direction if they had been aware of the fourth participant in their little drama. Almost 200,000 kilometers above and behind them, *Aztec* was boring in on an intercept course at 90 gravities.

Aboard *Privateer,* Lieutenant Murphy was actively tracking the pursuing pirates with her radar. "Getting close to missile range, Skipper, but he knows we can't outrun him. I'm guessing he'll hold fire until he thinks he's got a sure kill. He's also jamming normal miner communication frequencies to make sure we don't get a message off."

"I guess there's not much doubt about his intentions," Davis said. "Richards, bring up point defense, in case he *doesn't* hold his fire."

Petty Officer Richards keyed his console, and two blisters that would normally have covered *Privateer's* asteroid-mapping radar retracted, revealing a pair of laser turrets that were the ship's missile defense system. A regular warship would have more of them, but the engineers on Luna hadn't expected *Privateer* to get into a serious missile duel.

"If he waits too long, we'll be able to take him out with the big guns before he even gets a shot off," Murphy said as the range continued to close.

"Our orders are to let him shoot first," Davis said, "though if he gets *really* close, my trigger finger might get itchy. It looks like we're dealing with a real warship. He could chew us up pretty badly if he gets his licks in."

At 50 kilometers, the pirate apparently decided he was close enough.

"Missile launch!" Murphy sang out. "One bird—no, *two* birds—incoming, dead astern."

"Point defense free!" Davis ordered. "Fire on acquisition."

The incoming missiles were small chemical-propellant birds with conventional explosive warheads, sufficient to disable a ship like *Privateer* but not to destroy her completely. Point defense didn't acquire the tiny targets until they were within five kilometers but then the laser turrets fired and blew both missiles away.

"Bet that surprised you, you bastard," Davis muttered.

He watched the pirate carefully for a reaction. If the attacker showed any sign of breaking off, he planned to launch a couple of missiles from their concealed launchers in what had been *Privateer's* ore storage holds. The gravity drive LFS missiles would close the distance in seconds, and their two-hundred-kilo ship-killer warheads wouldn't leave much more than a cloud of debris where the pirate had been. That would certainly scare off the other pirate, though *Aztec* could probably chase him down anyway.

But if Davis could convince the enemy he had only *defensive* armament, maybe he could get him to come in closer—within the limited effective range of his other weapons. Under the precision fire control system of a regular LFS Navy ship, gamma-ray lasers—grasers for short—were good out to ranges of several thousand kilometers. With the limited targeting and tracking systems Davis had, 25 klicks was about maximum to guarantee a hit on a target as small as the incoming pirate, but, at that range, grasers could saw an enemy ship in half. *If we can avoid hitting his fusion plant*, Davis thought, *there might be enough left to figure out who these bastards are and where they came from. So come on in, sucker—you've almost got me. All you have to do is get a little closer.*

The pirate kept coming. At 30 kilometers, he launched two more missiles. Once again, point defense picked them off several kilometers short of their target.

"Open up the graser bays...targeting systems online," Davis ordered as the pirate continued to close. The rate of closure slowed to a crawl as the pirate decelerated to match vectors with *Privateer.*

Two cargo hatches slid open, one on each side of *Privateer's* battered hull. Twenty-five kilometers...20 kilometers...

"Kill the drive! Come left ninety degrees! Fire as your weapons bear!"

Senior Tech Martinez, at the helm, hit the cutoff for the fusion drive and poured power to the directional thrusters. The old mining ship was massive, and she came around slowly. As she did, the pirate opened fire with his autocannon, spitting a long burst of high-velocity armor-piercing projectiles in *Privateer's* direction. The pirate had shut down his drive to steady his aim, and reaction from firing the heavy projectiles killed much of *Lion's* forward vector, slowing her rate of closure with *Privateer* almost to zero. But bullets take time to cover almost twenty kilometers, and PAS *Lion* had just run out of time. *Privateer's* targeting system locked onto her, and a light came on at P.O. Richards' console. Richards rammed the firing key, and the cruiser-sized graser fired.

Grasers are light speed weapons, and *Lion's* cannon fire had not covered half the distance to *Privateer* when the hellish beam of coherent energy struck head on, ripping the guts out of the pirate ship. It tore three-quarters of the way through her length, burning through bulkheads as if they were made of paper before finally spending its energy just short of the containment vessel of her fusion reactor. Nearly half the pirate crew died, either from direct contact with the beam or from splatters of molten metal that burned through pressure suits, flesh, and bone. When the beam cut off a fraction of a second later, most of the ship's compartments had been opened to space. Her fusion plant was undamaged, but control system failures sent her into emergency shutdown.

Then it was *Privateer's* turn to take *Lion's* fire. At twenty kilometers, an autocannon is not an accurate weapon, but the mining ship was a big target, and most of the 500-round burst of depleted uranium slugs struck some part of her. Many of them passed harmlessly through empty ore holds that were not under pressure, but a few of them impacted her aft engineering spaces. Both engineering crew-members died as a slug penetrated her reactor containment. Emergency shutdown systems kept the entire ship from being destroyed, but an eruption of plasma vaporized a section of her port quarter. In the forward equipment bay, one Marine died from a direct hit by a slug, but the Marines were already pressure-suited, so the rest of them survived the decompression that followed.

Just one of the 30mm rounds penetrated *Privateer's* bridge, leaving a large hole on the port side, ripping the helm console to shreds, and sending a spray of metal fragments in all directions. Davis, sitting at his command console at the rear of the bridge, saw everything happen in a frozen moment of time whose details he would recall for years to come—Murphy, struck in the shoulder blade by a fragment that cut her safety harness and sent her spinning out of her chair; Martinez throwing his arms up in front of his face as his console erupted in sparks; and Richards belatedly ducking his head after the fragments had already whistled by. Then came the scream of escaping air. Instinctively, Davis locked his helmet down, automatically activating his suit's communications. Richards and Martinez locked their helmets down as well, but Murphy, hanging from her chair arm by the remains of her harness, wasn't moving.

"Richards! Help Lieutenant Murphy! Martinez, grab the patch kit and let's get this hole closed. Engineering, report!"

Gravity was offline, and everything not secured in place was being sucked toward the fist-sized hole in the hull. Davis secured his suit's safety line to his chair before releasing his harness. He noted that Martinez and Richards had done the same. Richards was working his way toward the fallen executive officer, and Martinez was pulling sheets of patch material from the storage rack overhead. The sheets were a plastic polymer, strong enough to hold against atmospheric pressure and flexible enough to mold themselves to the opening. As Davis reached him, Martinez slapped one of the sheets over the hole, and it snugged down with a *thump*. The rush of air cut off abruptly, and Davis retrieved the sealing gun from its rack and handed it to Martinez, who applied the quick-setting resin around the patch to make the repair permanent. Davis then turned to Richards, who was trying to untangle Murphy from her harness.

"Good thing you got the hole closed, sir. I sealed up her helmet, but she's got a big rip in her suit. She needs a medic bad, sir." The gloves of Richards' pressure suit were covered with Murphy's blood.

Davis realized he hadn't gotten a response from engineering. "Medic to the bridge," he ordered, hoping there was someone left back there to hear him.

"Sir, this is McGuinness. Medic is on the way. Engineering is not responding. I think we have heavy damage aft, and I've sent two men to check. We lost one man back here, but we've got the pressure leaks under control, and I've got a team working its way forward, sealing holes as they go."

"Good. Carry on, Sergeant."

Davis relaxed a bit. The Marines had started damage control without waiting for orders. Master Sergeant McGuinness was a good man. Davis considered him young for his rank, but he was proving worthy of it. "Martinez, is *anything* working on this bridge?"

"Main power's offline, sir. We've got life support on backup power, but communications and tactical are dead, and the helm console...well, we ain't gonna be driving her from here, sir."

"Damn! I wonder what that bastard is doing out there."

"Sir, he must've fired before we hit him," Richards said. "I nailed that sucker dead on. I *guarantee* the sonofabitch is *not* gonna be coming after us."

"Then maybe we should be thinking about going after *him*. McGuinness, is the cutter still serviceable?"

"It looks okay, sir. I've got a man checking it out now."

"Good. Get it preflighted and stand by for orders." *Besides,* he thought, *if we're damaged as badly as I think, we'll need it for communications, and we may need it for a lifeboat. Now, I wonder what the* other *bastard is doing…*

* * *

"I can't raise *Lion,* but she is still closing slowly on the miner ship, *Herr Kapitan,*" Gruder reported. "They are about fifteen kilometers apart, and neither of them is under drive."

"Perhaps Kimba has finished the job," Hohlmann said, "but they damaged him in some way. Perhaps he is waiting for us to come and help him."

"*Ja,* or maybe they have finished *him,* and they are waiting to do the same to us."

"Hmmm…if they did, they waited until he got very close. If we still don't have answers by the time we close to fifty kilometers, we will blow them out of space and figure out what happened later. What is the range now?"

"To the miner, nine hundred eighty kilometers. A bit less to *Lion.*"

Mogambo was in pursuit mode, with all her active systems sweeping the area in front of her, concentrating on the two silent ships she was rapidly overtaking. Hohlmann and his crew were totally unaware of the hellhound on their trail.

* * *

"This guy is *really* not watching his six," Jeff Jones told his bridge crew. "At this range, my old, nearsighted grandmother would have seen us coming."

"Yes, sir," Karen Reddy's voice came over the command channel, "but he'll be within firing range of *Privateer* in thirty seconds." When *Aztec* went to battle stations, Reddy had gone aft to her station in Auxiliary Control. Reddy could take command from there should disaster befall the bridge crew and captain. Jones didn't expect problems with small fry like these pirates, but he hadn't gotten to be captain of a heavy cruiser by disregarding basic combat protocols.

He was worried about *Privateer*. Davis had reported missiles fired at him and that he was turning to engage. After that, both ships had gone dead—no drive, no communications. Now the other pirate, 500 kilometers in front of *Aztec,* was about to enter the battle zone.

"Maybe we'd better give him a wake-up call," Jones decided. "Mr. Sarkoff, give me a full power scan on that bogey in front of us, every active system you can put on him. I want a count of his nose hairs."

"Yes, sir!" Ensign Gregory Sarkoff grinned. *Aztec* had been tracking the bogey with passive detectors only, sensing the delicate ripples in the gravity flux caused by a moving mass. Her powerful active radar and lidar systems could pick up a ship that size at over a half million kilometers. At this much closer range, they would probably raise the pirate's hull temperature by a fraction of a degree—and shock the hell out of any threat warning systems he might have. "Scanning now, sir."

* * *

"Still no response from *Lion*," Gruder reported. "*Gott in Himmel!*"

Mogambo's exec turned white as his threat board lit up with a dozen warning indicators, and alarms began to scream. Lidar, intermediate band navigation radar, missile lock indicators, and *TX-band doppler targeting radar! Only LFS warships used that system!*

"*Kapitan!* We are being—"

"Behind us, you fool!" Hohlmann snarled. "Look behind us!"

Gruder punched the keys of his systems board, and *Mogambo's* search and detection arrays stopped their forward sweeps and swiveled around to look aft. They had no difficulty finding a target, and Gruder's heart nearly stopped as he felt the hellhound's breath on the back of his neck. *Warship! BIG warship! 280 kilometers and coming up fast.* "*Kapitan—*"

"I see him. I think we run from this one. We fire everything we have and then we run."

"It's the LFS, *Herr Kapitan!* How can we run?"

"We have to try. Maybe we get lucky."

"Weapons are ready, Cap'n. Just give me the word." Jamie Connor at the weapons console was grinning in anticipation.

He has no idea what he is dealing with, Gruder decided.

* * *

"He's seen us now, sir," Sarkoff said. The pirate ship was hitting *Aztec* with her active systems, including targeting lidar. "He's locking on to shoot!"

"Stand by point defense," Jones said calmly.

The pirate ship rolled down and to the right. On *Aztec's* main display, eight tiny blips broke away and curved sharply toward the cruiser.

"Missile separation!" Sarkoff sang out.

"Point defense free! Helm, come left twenty degrees and roll right thirty." Jones wanted to give all his point defense batteries a clear shot and, at the same time, bring *Aztec's* broadside to bear on the enemy.

At that moment, the pirate ship opened fire with its turret-mounted lasers, weapons powerful enough to burn through the hull plating of a ship like *Privateer*, but *Aztec's* gravity field degraded the beams to the point where they only blistered the paint and produced hot spots on her heavy battle armor.

"Permission to return fire, sir?" Sarkoff asked.

"Not yet," Jones replied. "I'd like to take this bastard alive, however—" he added as *Aztec's* point defense picked off the last enemy missile, "—we are not going to screw around with him much longer. Helm, put us back on his tail and close the range."

* * *

Gruder clung to a glimmer of hope. *Mogambo's* maneuver had momentarily opened the range, and he knew that Connor's lasers had hit the warship. Now, if only the missiles...but he groaned in dismay as the cruiser's point defense swatted down all eight missiles as if they were no more than trouble-some mosquitos. His heart sank as the warship came around after them, with a delta vee more than three times *Mogambo's best* accelera-tion.

"Reload the missiles," Hohlmann ordered. "We shoot again when he is closer, and maybe he has less chance to stop them."

* * *

"Give me a hailing channel, standard Belt ship-to-ship frequency, but put it on a tight beam in case he's as deaf as he is blind," Jones or-dered. An indicator appeared on his comm console, and he keyed his mike. "Unidentified ship! This is the Lunar Free State cruiser *Aztec*. Shut down your drive and weapons systems, or we will fire on you."

The pirate showed no sign of giving up.

"All right, Mr. Sarkoff," Jones sighed. "Do you suppose you could put a spread of four missiles past him *without* hitting him and detonate them right in front of his nose?"

"Can do, sir." Sarkoff smiled, his fingers dancing over the fire-control console. "Just say when."

"Now."

The four missiles, launched by powerful mass drivers, came screaming out of their tubes. Their gravity drives came up, and they leapt forward at over 900 gees. They covered the distance to *Mogambo* so quickly, her defense systems had no time to acquire. They flashed past her flanks and detonated a few hundred meters off her bow in a perfect diamond pattern.

"And *that*," Jones announced, keying the open channel again, "was the last warning shot you are going to get."

Abruptly, the pirate ship's drive shut down, and her targeting systems died. *Aztec* braked to match vectors with the enemy and came to rest just two kilometers off the pirate's starboard side.

"All right, Ensign," Jones ordered, deliberately keeping the communication link to the pirate open. "If he so much as brings up an active radar system, you may blow him straight to hell." He switched over to his command channel. "Marines, stand by for boarding action."

* * *

Aboard what was left of PAS *Lion,* Master Sergeant Jeremy McGuinness and his squad were conducting a boarding action. They'd launched the cutter and used its communications gear to contact *Aztec.* Then Jimbo Davis had ordered McGuinness to take his men over to the drifting wreck and suppress any resistance they might encounter. There was none, as *Lion's* seven surviving crew members were too busy trying to keep themselves alive. The pirate ship's life support system was beyond repair, and all they had were their pressure suits.

McGuinness herded them into the cutter's tiny cargo bay and ferried them back to *Privateer,* where there was at least enough life support to hold out until *Aztec* arrived.

* * * * *

Chapter Three

LFS *Athena,* Lunar Fleet Anchorage

"*Privateer* lost three crewmembers, ma'am," the briefing officer reported, "and her exec was seriously injured. Both *Privateer* and the smaller pirate ship had to be abandoned, but Commander Jones' prize crew is bringing the other pirate ship back to Luna. They destroyed what was left of *Privateer* after stripping all classified tech systems. Lieutenant Commander Davis wanted to bring her home, but she would have needed a new fusion plant and major work on her after hull structure."

He paused, scrolling down his notepad. "Investigation indicates the pirates were operating with active support from the Pan African League. Their mission was to find and eliminate miners working a successful claim before they had a chance to register the claim. The pirates would report the claim location to League operatives on Ceres, who would pass the information to League mining ships. Those operatives were responsible for tagging Free Miner ships with transponders that allowed the pirates to track them. When a Free Miner stopped moving for any length of time, the pirates took that to indicate a discovery and went after him.

"We have enough information to identify some of the Ceres operatives. Records from the pirate computers indicate they were responsible for the destruction of at least five Free Miner ships, as well as LCS *Venture* and one Syndicate ship of Japanese registry.

"That concludes the briefing, Admiral. Are there any questions?"

Lorna Greenwood looked around the table at her staff officers. None of them spoke.

"Not at the moment, thank you, Commander," she said. "Advise *Aztec* I would like to see Commander Jones and Lieutenant Commander Davis at their earliest convenience after they get back to Luna."

"Yes, ma'am." The officer came to attention, saluted, and left the room.

"Analysis?" Lorna asked.

"Well," Tommy Sakura said, "we obviously underestimated the pirate threat. It's a damned good thing we posted a real warship out there to back up *Privateer,* so Davis didn't have to face those bastards alone."

"You're right," Lorna agreed, "but he did well with what he had. Even with his ship shot to hell, he still sent his Marines to make sure he'd cleaned the other guy's clock. Commendations are in order all around on this one."

"Unfortunately," she reminded the assembled staff, "three of those commendations will be posthumous. We accomplished the mission, but we paid too high a price. I'll feel better if we can convince the Ceres Mining Commission to extradite those League operatives the pirates identified."

* * *

TerraNova City, Luna

Ian Stevens was enjoying coffee and a fine cigar with the American president. The two men were lounging in Ian's office, where the wall-sized viewscreen afforded a spectacular real-time view of the Lunar surface.

But President Blackthorne was somewhat upset. "Damn it, Admiral, your timing on this Pan African incident was terrible."

"How's that, Mr. President?"

"Well, you *know* we've been having trouble with the Pan African League, and now you go and destroy one of their government ships, seize another one, and take a bunch of their people prisoner."

"Pirates, Mr. President. They were pirates, and they were preying on unarmed Free Miners, not to mention our commercial ships. The Pan Africans were in it up to their ears."

"I understand that, Admiral, but now they're saying you Moon people are trying to monopolize the Asteroid Belt. Worse, they're saying you are a bunch of racists, anti-Islamic religious bigots, and white supremacists. I've got an election coming up, and the black vote is important to me. My aides are telling me I shouldn't have made this trip."

"Hmmm," Ian mused. "You're not going to eliminate racism in America until politicians stop talking about the black vote and the white vote and stop playing one group against the other. But I don't think this trip will be a problem for you."

"It could be. My opponents will accuse me of associating with a nation of white supremacists, and I'll have people marching in the streets calling for my resignation. The media will eat it up because racial tension always makes news—"

"Mr. President, let me show you something," Ian interrupted. "We haven't released this yet, so you can give it to your news people when you think the timing is right." Ian went to the screen on his desk and scrolled through a few files to find what he was looking for. The view of the Lunar surface blanked out on the wall screen behind him and was replaced by pictures of two men. "Do you know who these men are, Mr. President?"

"Can't say that I do." Blackthorne's tone was still irritated, but there was a hint of curiosity.

"The one on the left is Dieter Hohlmann, captain of the Pan African ship we captured. The one on the right is Hans Gruder, his executive officer. Note the fine, Caucasian features of these two would-be Pan Africans. They're a couple of expatriate German mercenaries, hired by the Pan African League for the piracy operation. They are wanted for a variety of crimes in Germany and several other countries.

"Now," he continued as two more pictures appeared on the screen—two black men, obviously of African ancestry, wearing uniforms Blackthorne didn't recognize. "Do you know these two men?"

"No, I don't. Some Pan African big shots, I suppose. What's your point?"

"No, Mr. President, these two former 'African-Americans' are citizens of the Lunar Free State. The one on the left is Commander Jeff Jones, captain of the heavy cruiser *Aztec*. The one on the right is Lieutenant Commander James Davis, captain of LFS *Privateer*. They're the people who took out the pirates, and I'd like to see anybody accuse them of being white supremacists."

Blackthorne's jaw dropped. He stared at the pictures, then burst out laughing. "That's *funny*, Admiral. I'll take copies of those pictures, if you don't mind, and the next time the Pan Africans mention racists, I'll rub their noses in it. The media will eat it up."

"I hoped you would." Ian returned to his chair and picked up his cigar again. "You know, Hugo, I'm not a great politician. I usually say what's on my mind, and I don't suffer fools easily. Most of the media people on Earth have no love for me."

"It's not that you don't suffer fools, Ian. The problem is you make them *look* like fools. Come to think of it, you've made *me* look like one on a few occasions." Blackthorne's tone was reproachful, but the grin on his face took the sting out of it.

"Well, it hasn't been intentional," Stevens said, but he admitted to himself that sometimes it *had* been. "I'm a businessman and a military man, and I don't worry about stepping on someone's toes when I need to get something done. You, on the other hand, know how to work the media. Instead of trampling them, you usually manage to herd them in the direction you want them to go."

"I understand," Blackthorne said. "In fact, I probably understand *you* better than most people do. You and I have been going at each other for a long time, but I think we're getting mellow in our old age. And I *do* know how to work the media. With these pictures, I can play them like a fiddle. Mind you, I have my own agenda, but for once, I think it fits with yours. Oh, by the way, what *are* you gonna do with these pirates?"

"They'll get a trial under Lunar law and, if found guilty—which seems pretty likely—we are going to execute them."

"Damn it, Admiral! You are never gonna get Earth's news media on your side if you keep doing things like this. You *know* they are going to go after you. Capital punishment is downright *uncivilized!*"

"Hmmm. Define capital punishment."

"What do you mean, define it? It's when a government puts someone to death for a crime."

"Well, I seem to recall, about two months ago, you were asking me to drop rocks on some bad boys in the Central African Republic. Did you think it would just give them a headache?"

"Well, that's different."

"No, it isn't, but I'm sure you would have sold it to the news media as the righteous wrath of the Almighty falling on a bunch of evildoers or something."

"No, Admiral," Blackthorne said with a perfectly straight face. "I'd have told them it was those trigger-happy, uncivilized Moon people again."

Seeing the look on his host's face, Blackthorne broke out laughing, and soon Ian was laughing as well. "Hugo, you are truly a piece of work."

"Call it a lesson in dealing with the media, Ian. Sometimes you *can't* get them running your way, so you have to duck and let them go after somebody else."

* * * * *

Chapter Four

LFS *Stephen Hawking*, Near Saturn

LFS *Stephen Hawking* was a Navy ship. She was crewed by regular Navy officers and ratings, and operated under fleet orders, but she was more lightly armed than other ships in her 200-meter, 15,000-ton size class—somewhere between a frigate and a light cruiser in length and mass. *Hawking's* total armament consisted of a single graser turret, a pair of internal missile tubes, and a basic point-defense system. On the other hand, she had an oversized power plant, and her active and passive search-and-detection systems were the most powerful and sophisticated in the LFS fleet. She carried no Marines but was equipped with quarters for a substantial number of non-fleet people—scientists and their assistants.

Hawking was a scientific research ship. Her missile tubes were more likely to be used for instrument probes than combat loads. Her powerful drive allowed her to operate close to heavy-gravity planets such as Jupiter, and her grasers and point-defense systems were primarily intended to protect her from rocks and other space debris.

But *Hawking* was a Fleet ship, and Lieutenant Commander Shin Jang Chae was proud to have her as his first command. Shin had been a young officer in the Republic of Korea's Air Force when his beleaguered nation had found itself with an excess of officers and a shortage of equipment. He'd accepted an offer to emigrate to the Lunar Free State, then Korea's only ally, and when the LFS saved his homeland from the invading North Koreans with devastating kinetic strikes, Shin had decided his newfound compatriots were worthy of his loyalty. With a degree in electronic systems engineering, Shin had worked his way up in the Fleet engineering ranks, eventually becoming chief engineer of the heavy cruiser LFS *Cherokee*. On promotion to lieutenant commander, he had become *Cherokee's* executive officer and had served in that capacity for two years before being given command of *Hawking*. His engineering background had served him well, both in dealing with *Hawking's* sophisticated systems and with his supercargo of scientific personnel.

Shin was admiring the view on the main bridge screen. Saturn filled most of the screen, and the giant planet's ring system stretched into the distance ahead. *Hawking* was orbiting the planet, a thousand kilometers above Cassini's Division, the broad gap between the A and B rings. The ship's systems were mapping the rings at a leisurely pace, a project that was expected to take a couple of months. The scientists were hoping to find a dark body—an undiscovered moon of Saturn—orbiting within the division, sweeping the broad lane clear of debris and helping to maintain the gap between the two rings.

Shin wished the scientists well with their theories. If the moon was there, *Hawking* would find it.

* * *

The California High Desert, Near LunaPort

Bartley's given name was Veronica, but no one called her that, at least not to her face. Most of the Kings and Queens knew her simply as Rock. She was tall, lean, and hard, and she wore her hair short. Since she never got cozy with any of the male members, most of the gang assumed she was a lesbian, but again, no one said so to her face. Bartley had proven her ability to kick just about anyone's ass, and she didn't discriminate between sexes when an ass-kicking was required.

She was not a lesbian. She was just a loner. In her view, she simply hadn't met a man worthy of her. She'd had some bad experiences as a kid, and she knew what kind of pigs men—and women, for that matter—could be. She was willing to hang with the Kings and Queens as long as they were going her way and didn't make demands. They were not nearly the outlaws they claimed to be, didn't terrorize civilians, and—most importantly from Bartley's standpoint—they weren't into drugs. They were a bunch of road-warrior party animals, but they only partied when they had a secure place to crash. For the most part, they had enough sense not to head out on the road when they were wasted. There had been a few members who'd insisted on riding drunk, but most of those had ended up as ditch debris or hood ornaments for fast-moving tractor-trailers, providing gory examples for the rest of the gang. Bartley didn't drink much, but she knew better than to lecture fools about foolishness.

So, she stayed with the gang through nomadic wanderings around the Southwestern United States and Mexico. They weren't a bad bunch, and they had sources for the parts she needed to keep her vintage Harley running. They made a decent living doing odd jobs wherever they went—most of the gang members were dependable mechanics, and none were averse to hard physical labor in exchange for a few bucks. Sometimes they made money providing escort services for truckers and other travelers along the bandit-ridden highways of the southwest. Most of the *banditos* operated in groups of three or four and preyed on single vehicles traveling alone.

The mere presence of a rowdy, motorcycle-mounted security force was enough to make them seek another target.

Bartley wasn't a leader. She could have been, but she'd decided that leading a bunch of crazy bikers wasn't worth the effort. She was willing to let Jason Rourke do the leading, though sometimes the guy had some really *stupid* ideas. Like now...

"Jace," she told him, "this is a really *stupid* idea."

Rourke frowned at her. He would have backhanded any other gang member who dared to say that, but if he had tried it with Rock, he might not have gotten his arm back. He relaxed, and his frown vanished as he tried persuasion instead. "Hey, c'mon, Rock. They say LunaPort is a real party town. Those Moon people know how to get it on, and they buy only the best stuff. Haven't you ever wondered what that Don Purg Neon champagne tastes like?"

"That's *Dom Perignon*, and no, I haven't. Anyway, what makes you think they're gonna let *us* in there? They've got Lunar Marines guarding the gates."

"So? You see the trucks on this highway? They're all headed in or out of LunaPort. It's not some secret place or anything. We just have to convince them we got business inside. Once we get past the gates, we head over to Freeport Street and let the party begin. Truckers back in Phoenix told me stories about that place—casinos, saloons, whorehouses, and...well, you know what I mean."

A clouded look crossed Bartley's face, and Jace decided he shouldn't have mentioned the whorehouses. But she didn't pursue it. Instead, she tried another argument.

"Okay, fine; but even if you get through the gate, those places cost money. Like maybe real gold Moon money."

"Relax! The truckers said they take U.S. dollars, and I ran into some pigeons back in Flagstaff that still think poker is a game of luck. I got a couple grand, and it's on me. C'mon, it's almost sundown. We're wasting party time!"

He started his bike and roared off the shoulder in a spray of gravel, heading up the road past a sign that proclaimed LunaPort was just five miles ahead. Whooping and hollering, the rest of the gang followed. With a sigh, Bartley fired up her Hog and moved out to bring up the rear.

* * *

The Lunar Marine at the gate was not buying Jace's story. "You're here to do *what?*"

"I told you, asshole, we're here to join the Moon Marines. Open the gate and let us in—and tell your boss we're coming."

Jace, Bartley thought, *this is the stupidest thing you've done yet. I've got a feeling things are about to get really intense.*

As if in answer to her thought, an armored personnel carrier rolled up behind them. A Marine popped out of the hatch on top and swung a swivel-mounted light machine gun to cover them, while more Marines poured out the rear doors with rifles at the ready. Ace Brannigan goosed his Harley around to face the Marines and roared forward, planning to punch through their ranks. One Marine sidestepped him and slammed his rifle butt into Ace's head. The Harley wobbled off the road without its rider and crashed into the ditch. The rest of the gang dismounted and faced the Marines, brandishing chains and knives.

Bartley remained in her saddle. She shut off her engine, put the kickstand down, placed her hands on top of her helmet, and hoped the Marines wouldn't shoot her. She was the only member of the gang who wore a helmet on the road; but then, she reflected, the rest of them didn't have brains to protect anyway...

* * *

Lieutenant Jenkins keyed his comm unit. "All right, Sergeant. I'll be there in a few minutes. Out."

"What was that all about?" the woman sitting in front of his desk inquired.

"We've had a penetration attempt, ma'am," Jenkins said. "Fifteen bikers tried to crash the main gate."

Lieutenant Colonel Anne McGraw's eyebrows went up. "Really? What's the situation now?"

It was McGraw's first visit to LunaPort. Her assignment was to evaluate the base Marine contingent, of which Jenkins was the commander. It was his first command, and the young officer was understandably nervous in McGraw's presence.

"It's already over, ma'am," he said as he strapped on his sidearm and checked his uniform. "Corporal Wright at the gate called in the perimeter response team, the bikers got rowdy, and now we've got a few injured bikers being taken to the hospital. The rest are in security lockup near the gate."

"Any serious injuries?"

"No, ma'am. They only had knives and chains, which aren't much good against battle armor, so our people didn't have to shoot anyone. Sergeant Hill said one broken jaw, one broken arm, and a lot of bruises. None of our people were injured."

"Mind if I tag along?" she asked.

"Not at all, ma'am." It was nice of her to ask, he decided, but she was an L.C. and his evaluating officer. It wouldn't matter if he *did* mind. He opened a locker and handed her a sidearm and holster belt.

She buckled it on without question, checked the weapon, and slipped it into the holster. "Why would bikers come here?" she asked as they headed for Jenkins' command vehicle.

"I imagine they were looking to party, ma'am. LunaPort has some recreational establishments that get pretty rowdy at night. Each day, we get a couple hundred trucks coming in to pick up or drop off loads, and most of the truckers spend the night here—the only decent rest stop within two hundred kilometers. Those establishments also get business from LFS people, and we've had a few incidents. Nothing serious, but they do get crazy at times. I've had to make a couple of those places off limits to my Marines.

"Anyway," he continued, "I imagine the bikers just came here for fun, but that *isn't* what they told the corporal at the gate. They told him they were here to join the Lunar Marines."

"*What?*" McGraw gave him an incredulous look.

"I know, ma'am," he said with a grin. "As if we take just anybody who wants to sign up. But that's their story, and they're sticking to it."

McGraw favored him with a grin of her own. "These people I have to see."

* * *

The Kings and Queens—most of them—were slouched in rows of hard folding chairs inside a cage-like holding area in one end of the building. Ace and Crazy Gonzales had been hauled away in an ambulance, along with Melinda, Crazy's regular squeeze. Melinda had tried to engage a female Marine in a typical barroom cat fight. The Marine had stunned her with a taser, then slammed her to the pavement hard enough to crack a couple of ribs.

Bartley looked up as the cage door was unlocked, and a man and a woman wearing Marine uniforms came in, followed by two guards. Some of the gang members started to get up.

"*Stay in your seats*," the male newcomer barked. "Don't get up unless you're told to do so, or these Marines *will* shoot you."

He regarded them with contempt, scanning the room and looking at each one of them in turn. Bartley tried to keep her face neutral, but she flushed with embarrassment when he looked at her. This wasn't some hick cop harassing her over a traffic violation. The guy was a professional soldier, and his gaze made her feel lower than dirt.

"Now then, what's this *bullshit* about you slimeballs wanting to join the Lunar Marines?" he demanded.

"Damned right," Jace drawled arrogantly, slouched in his chair in the front row. "Especially now that I've seen the kind of *babes* you boys keep around for fun."

Several of the gang hooted and made sounds of agreement.

Oh, shit! Bartley thought. *When will he learn to keep his mouth shut!* The only female Marine in the area was the newcomer, an attractive woman in her late thirties or early forties with a lot of decorations on her uniform. Judging by the body language of the other Marines, Bartley figured she was the ranking officer in the room.

The male officer took a step toward Jace.

"Lieutenant!" the woman commanded sharply.

"Yes, ma'am," he replied and stepped back.

The woman walked up and stood in front of Jace. "That's 'Lieutenant Colonel Babe' to you, mister," she told him. "If you've got something to say to me, you get up and stand at attention."

Jace leaned back further in his chair. "Well, hell, babe, *part* of me is standing at attention. Does that count?" He thrust his pelvis up at her in case she didn't know what he meant.

Without warning, the woman delivered a lightning-fast snap kick to his groin. As he doubled over in pain, she dragged him out of his chair and flipped him over, then slammed him down on his back on the hard concrete floor. After he blinked the tears of agony out of his eyes, he found her standing over him with her sidearm drawn and the muzzle pointing right between his eyes.

"You think this is a *joke*, mister?" she snarled. "You tried to make unauthorized entry into a facility of the Lunar Free State. You're under *our* law now. If we decide you're a spy, we can shoot you. You're a half inch away from death, right now."

Her finger was steady on the trigger. The other Marines showed no reaction, and the gang members were suddenly very quiet.

"Uh, ma'am?" Bartley surprised herself by speaking up from the back row.

"You have something to say?" McGraw shot a glance at her, but the gun didn't waver.

"Uh, yes, ma'am." Bartley got up carefully and tried to stand at what she imagined was the 'position of attention.' "Ma'am, he's just an asshole. He *does* think it's a joke—at least he did until ten seconds ago. We're not... spies or anything."

McGraw holstered her sidearm and stepped back, ignoring Jace, who rolled over, curled up, and began puking his guts out on the floor.

"Well, Lieutenant, it seems there's at least one reasonable person in this bunch. What's your name, Reasonable Person?"

"Bartley, ma'am. They call me Rock."

One of the Marines started to snicker but suppressed it when McGraw shot him a sharp look.

"All right, Ms. Rock, are you going to tell me you came here to join the Marines?"

"No, ma'am. We came here because Jace said it was a good place to party. I never heard anything about joining the Marines until he said it to the guard at the gate. But I guess I wouldn't mind if I had a chance…join the Marines, I mean."

Bartley had no idea what had made her say it, but she realized she was tired of hanging around with *losers*. These Marines had pride in themselves. They belonged to an organization that believed in itself and its people. Suddenly, Bartley wanted very badly to be proud of herself and the group she belonged to, and she knew she would never get that from a gang of half-wit bikers. She expected contempt from McGraw, but the other woman looked straight into her eyes. Bartley returned her gaze with newfound determination.

"Me too, ma'am!" Jimmy White Feather got to his feet. "For sure, I'm ready to quit hanging around with *these* assholes." Jimmy also stood straight and tall and looked directly at the woman officer as he spoke.

Bartley was a little surprised, but it made sense. Jimmy was a loner like she was. He hung with the Kings and Queens because he didn't have anything better to do.

McGraw looked Jimmy over, then looked back at Bartley. After a moment, she seemed to dismiss them and turned to go. "All right,

Lieutenant, I've seen enough. I need to speak with you for a moment—outside."

"Yes, ma'am." Jenkins followed her out the door.

Once outside, McGraw turned to him apologetically. "Sorry, Lieutenant, I got carried away in there. I have no patience with people like that."

"Understood, ma'am," he said. "I would like to have done the same thing myself, but rank has its privilege."

"So, what are you going to do with them, Lieutenant?"

"I think that Rock woman was telling the truth—they just came here to party. Base Command gives us latitude in cases like this, so I was thinking of taking fingerprints, retinals, DNA scans, and mug shots—just to show them that we're serious—and sending them on their way with a warning."

"Sounds like a plan to me. But while you're taking fingerprints and so forth, I'd like to talk to Ms. Rock and the other one who volunteered. Is there a room where I could speak to them individually?"

"Yes, ma'am." He looked at her in surprise. "You can use the gate security office. It's not occupied at the moment. Are you…thinking about recruiting them, ma'am?"

She looked thoughtful. "A long time ago, when I was an instructor in the U.S. Marines, we looked for *something* in every recruit. Call it determination, motivation, whatever. It was a combination of things we couldn't describe in words, but it separated real Marines from people who just wanted to wear the uniform but didn't want to work for it. I thought I saw some of that *something* in those two. If they're serious, maybe we should give them a shot. Worst case, they wash out and go back to playing with their motorcycles."

"Yes, ma'am. I didn't know we were accepting recruits from Earth."

"Did I detect a hint of contempt in your voice when you said *Earth*, Lieutenant?" she asked with a smile.

"Ah…no, ma'am. I only—"

"It's okay, Mr. Jenkins. I've read your file. You're an original Lunar Citizen—came to Luna with your parents during the DSRI evacuation. You were about ten years old at the time, and your father was one of the original Lunar Marines. I was one of those also, and I knew your father pretty well."

"You did, ma'am? Then you know he was killed in the Second Battle of Luna."

"Yes, and he was awarded the Medal of Honor, posthumous. I'm guessing that had something to do with you becoming a Marine."

"Yes, ma'am. It's the only thing I ever wanted to be. I would have joined up at eighteen, but my mother insisted I get a degree first. She didn't have a problem with my joining up, but she wanted me to have a better shot at becoming an officer."

"She gave you good advice. While we might wish all our Marines grew up as Lunar citizens, our population isn't big enough to provide us with enough qualified and properly motivated people. The first generation born on the Moon is still in grade school, and most of those who immigrated from Earth came with skills needed in other areas. With luck, we might get a few dozen new Marines a year if we restrict our recruiting to the Lunar population. So, we *have* to recruit from Earth. We don't advertise it because we'd be flooded with the kind of applicants we *don't* want—people who want to join for the wrong reasons or to easily get Lunar citizenship. So, we keep our eyes open for likely candidates and try to recruit them as we find them.

"I'm telling you this because I want you to keep *your* eyes open for likely recruits. Down here, you'll meet a lot of Earth people. If you think you've spotted a potential Marine, give me a call back on Luna, or call Marine HQ and talk to Sergeant Major Kowalski—drop my name, and he'll give you all the help you need."

"I understand, ma'am." Jenkins unlocked the security office. "I'll keep it in mind, and since I don't know anything about recruiting, I'll call for help if I find a candidate. Is this office okay for you?"

"It's fine."

"I'll go back and tell Sergeant Hill to start processing the bikers, and I'll send those two over one at a time. Which one do you want first?"

"Doesn't matter. I guess you can send Ms. Rock."

* * *

*W*ell, *so much for the Kings and Queens,* Bartley reflected. *They're back on the road, headed…probably where they're always headed: nowhere. As for me…*

Her Harley, drained of gas and carefully lubricated, was locked away in a storage space they'd assigned to her, along with her helmet, riding leather, and most of her other possessions. She had no idea when she might see that stuff again. She looked over at Jimmy White Feather, standing next to her, wearing the same desert-tan camouflage BDU outfit she was wearing—a uniform as yet devoid of any insignia. Jimmy looked back at her and gave her a nervous smile.

"Attention on deck!" the Marine corporal ordered as he opened the door to admit Lieutenant Jenkins and Lieutenant Colonel

McGraw. Bartley snapped to attention and sensed Jimmy doing the same next to her.

The two officers came over and stood facing them.

I'm still not sure where I'm going, Bartley admitted to herself, *but I'm pretty sure it's somewhere. And it looks promising, so far.*

"Recruits!" McGraw commanded. "Raise your right hand and repeat after me…"

* * * * *

Chapter Five

LFS *Stephen Hawking*, Near Saturn

The scientists were correct. Cassini's Division in Saturn's rings was home to a modest little moon—a moon that harbored a secret. The Messenger had lain dormant on the surface of that moon for almost 200 years, placed there when Earth's people were just coming into the Industrial Age. Those who'd placed it there had forgotten about it, for they believed it was no longer needed. But as the Lunar research ship approached, the Messenger felt its presence and awakened. It gathered data about the approaching ship and tested the data against its primary directives. By the time the ship was within 10,000 kilometers, the Messenger had enough information to fulfill its mission. Without further delay, it launched itself into space.

* * *

"Captain…! Sir, I've got…damn…I don't know *what* I've got. You'd better take a look."

Lieutenant Commander Shin stepped over to *Hawking's* tactical console. The ship's detection systems were feeding data to the scientists, their attention concentrated on the newly discovered moon. The scientists were elated that their predictions had been confirmed, and they wanted to know as much as possible about their new discovery.

"What's the problem, Mr. Willis?" Shin bent and studied the displays.

"Sir, I've got a heavy track on gravitics, right here. It's either a massive object moving rapidly or something using a gravity drive. Radar has nothing, but I get a faint return on lidar. It looks pretty small, but…"

"But there's not supposed to be anyone out here with a gravity drive except *us*. Have you plotted the track?"

"Yes, sir. It came from near the Cassini moon, and it's headed straight into the void."

Hawking was currently on the side of Saturn away from the Sun—which meant the object was headed out of the Solar System.

"Sir!" Willis blinked in surprise as figures on his display updated. "It's accelerating—at *ninety-six gravities!*"

"It appears your initial impression was correct, Ensign. Plot an intercept course at full military power. Helm, stand by for course change. We're going after it."

Hawking was capable of 110 gravities, thanks to her oversized drive generators. For safety, she was officially redlined at 100 gees, and Shin was not inclined to push her beyond that limit. If her drive failed, it was a long way to the nearest shipyard, but with only a four-gee differential, it would be a long chase. The object had already opened the range to near 100,000 kilometers. The gap would continue to widen until *Hawking* matched the object's relative velocity, by which time it would be a couple of million kilometers in front of them. Nonetheless, they would catch it eventually.

The research ship turned to the new heading and went to full power in pursuit.

"Sir, I've plotted its course back to origin," Willis reported. "Assuming constant ninety-six gee acceleration, it must have started right at the Cassini moon...Stand by, sir." He touched a key in response to an icon that was blinking urgently on his console. "Sir, Doctor Julian wants to know why they aren't getting any more data on the Cassini moon."

"Inform Dr. Julian that we are in pursuit of an enigma, Mr. Willis, and invite him to the bridge. Tell him we need his scientific knowledge."

Shin didn't expect much help from the astrophysicist, but Julian was the expedition's chief scientist. While Fleet had made it clear that Shin, as the ship's captain, was in overall command of the mission, he'd found that life was more pleasant if he did not irritate the scientists in his charge.

* * *

The Messenger drove outward, away from the gravitational effects of the star and the giant planet. It continued to record data on the pursuing ship, but it made no attempt to evade. Its designers had never expected it would be pursued and had made no provision for evasive action. In any case, once it translated into Otherspace, there would be no more pursuit.

* * *

Uranus, Neptune, and Pluto were far away in their orbits. There was nothing in the object's path but empty space, but still it fled outward.

Shin waited patiently during the long chase. The length of the chase was a matter of simple mathematics, and nothing he could do would shorten it. When he got closer, he might learn more about what he was chasing, but until then, there was no point in speculating.

The scientists, on the other hand, were doing a lot of speculating—and arguing with each other, as scientists often do in the absence of hard data. Unfortunately, they were doing it in the wardroom just aft of the bridge, and their arguments were disturbing Shin's tranquility. He thought about sealing the bridge hatch, but he couldn't think of a legitimate reason to do so. Then his communications panel demanded attention, and he touched an icon to take the call from the wardroom. *I'm surprised they didn't just yell my name down the passageway.* "Yes, Doctor Julian, may I help you?"

"We have an idea, Captain, and we'd like to ask you if it's possible."

"I'll be right with you, Doctor." With a sigh, Shin got up from his command chair and headed for the wardroom. "Mr. Willis, you have the bridge."

The scientists *did* have a good idea. Among their inventory of scientific research tools, they had an optical mapping satellite. Like most of the science probes, it could be launched from the ship's missile tubes with a simple, chemical-powered rocket motor. It could record and transmit high-quality images in both visible light and infrared.

The LFS used a universal system for mating payloads to missile bodies, whether the payload was a science package or a warhead, and whether the missile body was a chemical rocket or a military gravity-drive unit. The scientists proposed removing the warhead from one of Shin's military missiles and replacing it with the observer satellite. With an acceleration of 900 gees, the missile could close the distance to the object much quicker than *Hawking* and give them a glimpse of the thing long before the ship caught up with it. The missile's drive would burn out before it got there, but with a huge velocity advantage, it would overtake the bogey and send images before falling behind.

Shin ran the calculations. By the time they finished swapping out the warhead, the object would be within range. The plan had the advantage of letting them look at the object *before* exposing the ship to any danger it might present. Meanwhile, Shin had just finished a few additional calculations. "Dr. Julian…"

"Yes, Captain?" The scientist had been hovering over the bridge crew since Shin had agreed to try the missile plan.

"Take a look at these figures." He handed his data pad to the astrophysicist. "*Hawking* is one of the fastest ships in the fleet, and we've been under full power on the same vector for a long time. Not only are we farther from the Sun than any manned ship has ever been, but we have also reached a small but significant percentage of the speed of light. I might suggest you scientific people start looking for relativistic effects—time dilation and so forth."

"So, *that's* what it is." Ensign Linda Tomkins turned to the captain from her communications console. "Sir, I just got an acknowledgement of your status report from Lunar Command, but the transmission frequency was off. I thought my equipment's calibration was off, but it must be a doppler shift."

Dr. Julian looked from one officer to the other with newfound respect. Perhaps these military people weren't as simple and unimaginative as he'd thought.

Yes, we're really moving, Shin thought, *and if the drive fails, it might take a rescue team a year or so to catch up with us—somewhere out in the Oort cloud...*

* * *

"Missile away!" Willis sang out as the mass drivers sent the hybrid package hurtling out of the missile tube. The gravity drive came up, and the missile streaked ahead. With the range to the bogey down to less than 80,000 kilometers, it didn't take long for it to cover the distance. Its drive burned out a few thousand kilometers short of the target, but it continued to close. By then, *Hawking's* computers were bringing up the package's imaging system and then the first images appeared on the main screen. Per Shin's orders, the package had been programmed to miss the object by a wide margin. The last thing he wanted was for aliens—if any were aboard—to think they were being fired upon, but the angled approach also gave Shin and his people a better look.

"Whoa!!" Willis exclaimed. "Whatever that thing is, I don't think it's from around here."

The thing *looked* alien, but, at first, Shin couldn't see why. Finally, he realized it was the lack of symmetry in its design. It looked like random pieces of a jigsaw puzzle, stuck together at weird angles. Of course, symmetry was not a requirement for an object designed to operate in the vacuum of space, but it made it easier for engineers to calculate things like center of mass and thrust alignment. Human engineers built symmetrical machinery without even thinking about it. This thing looked like a bad dream an engineer might have had after spending a few hours looking at the surreal artwork of M.C. Escher.

Dr. Julian made a quiet request, and Willis brought up a grid on the image. A footnote on the screen indicated that, at the object's distance, each square represented one square meter. The thing was only about eight meters in its largest dimension.

Shin straightened. "Mr. Willis, can you display the acceleration vector?"

"I think so, sir." He bent over the console and began keying commands. A moment later, an arrow appeared along a three-dimensional axis centered on the object. It was perpendicular to a large disk-like structure that protruded from one section of the object.

"Hmmm. I'll take a wild guess that the circular section left of center is the primary field coil for a gravity drive," Shin speculated. "As for the rest of it, does anyone have any ideas?"

"Let's see it in infrared," Dr. Julian said.

Willis split the screen into two sections, and the new image showed Shin's speculation might be correct—viewed in the infrared spectrum, the disk section was much brighter than the rest, indicating a heat source.

They watched the object for several more minutes, but nothing changed. The scientists started to argue again, and Shin wished he could expel them from his bridge.

"Sir!" Willis shouted.

The arguments died as they all turned back to the screen.

On the infrared image, the whole object had brightened, and a bluish glow had developed on the visible light image. Suddenly, both images began to ripple. As they watched, the images expanded slightly in the viewscreen, then vanished in a blinding flash.

When the screen cleared, the thing was gone.

"Mother of God..." Willis breathed. "Sir, I've got a spike on gravitics you won't believe. For an instant, that thing had the gravitational mass of a small planet—or maybe a miniature black hole or something."

"Impossible!" Dr. Julian said. "It must have been a false reading on your instruments."

"I don't think so, Doctor," Willis said. "You saw the images get bigger? Well, in the few moments before it vanished, that thing's gravitational field sucked our probe almost five kilometers closer to it. We even felt it at this distance—*Hawking's* acceleration jumped a fraction of a gee. Then it vanished. There's not a trace now."

"Nothing??? Maybe your instruments—"

The young ensign shook his head. "Not a chance, Doctor. I'm reading our probe just fine, and it's the only thing out there."

"But...where did it go?" Julian asked.

"I was hoping you could tell me that, Doctor," Shin said. "But if I had to guess, I'd say it probably went back to wherever it came from."

* * *

TerraNova City, Luna

"I thought it best to scrub the rest of the mission, sir," Lorna Greenwood reported. "*Hawking's* a long way out, and she piled on a lot of velocity going after that thing. As it is, she'll be a month getting back to Luna. She'll survey the Cassini moon on her way back to see if she can find any trace of that thing's origin, but the rest of the ring-mapping mission will have to wait. Shin and his crew have gone farther and faster than anyone in history. I think we'll want to put them and the ship under a microscope when they get back."

Ian Stevens regarded the tall woman sitting on the other side of his desk. Lorna's blond hair was showing traces of silver, but she was still one of the most attractive women he knew. Once again, he found himself wondering what kind of relationship they might have had if not for her sexual orientation. He thrust the thought aside and concentrated on the business at hand. "I have no problem with that, Lorna. Dr. McGuinness?"

"Neither have I, Admiral," said Master Warrant Officer Evan McGuinness, the Lunar Free State's Director of Research. "We already have the imagery from the probe, but my people want to go over *Hawking's* logs and instrumentation in detail."

"Any preliminary thoughts on what that thing was?" Ian asked.

"I think it was a tripwire, Admiral," Lorna said. "A sentry with orders to sound the alarm if we got that far out into space. I think *Hawking's* approach triggered it, and now it's gone back to report to whoever put it there. What they—whoever or *whatever* they are—will do with that information is anyone's guess."

"I think Admiral Greenwood is right," McGuinness said. "Saturn's rings, Cassini's Division, the Cassini moon—they certainly put it in a place that would attract scientifically curious humans who are just beginning to explore the Solar System. So what do we do now?"

"Nothing much we can do," Ian admitted, "unless they come to visit us."

"And if they do?"

"We speak nicely to them and put the Fleet on alert," Ian answered grimly.

"Surely you don't think they'll be hostile!" McGuinness was shocked at the thought.

"No reason to think they will be," put in Admiral Charles Bender. "On the other hand, there's no reason to think they *won't* be. All we know is that they were apparently observing us in secret."

Charlie Bender, a former U.S. Navy Seal, had spent ten years working on covert operations for the U.S. government before being recruited by the old Deep Space Research Institute. Since the Institute had ostensibly been a civilian scientific research facility, Ian had named Charlie the director of security. He had been Ian's chief intelligence officer ever since. He was also responsible for recruiting the Institute's security force—mostly former U.S. Navy and Marine personnel—which later evolved to become the LFS Marines. Though he was officially the Lunar Free State's foreign minister, he was also a topnotch military strategist. As such, both Ian Stevens and Lorna Greenwood relied on his expertise.

"Well, I guess we won't know until we meet them," Ian concluded. "We always hope for the best…"

"…but prepare for the worst," Bender finished the thought.

* * * * *

Chapter Six

The Mekota Homeworld, 50 Light-Years from Luna

The Mekota had little in common with humans, though both were carbon-based lifeforms that required an oxygen-rich atmosphere to survive. The Mekota could tolerate higher levels of carbon dioxide and certain other gases than humans, but humans could tolerate a broader range of temperatures. The Mekota could see further down the red end of the spectrum than humans, but not as far up into the blue.

The Mekota had more in common with the plant life of Earth than with mammals, though they were unlike any plant humans had ever seen. In fact, they were a highly evolved race and had been traveling the stars for hundreds of Earth years. The humans of Earth had not yet invented the telescope when the Mekota built their first starship.

Among the Mekota, the numbers three and twelve held great significance. They were radially symmetrical tripeds, whose three upper limbs ended in four mutually opposing digits. Their three eyes were evenly spaced around the upper part of their meter-thick, three-meter-tall trunk, which was crowned with a colorful three-lobed crest. They had no internal bone structure but were covered with a segmented exoskeleton which limited trunk movement but allowed great flexibility in their upper and lower limbs.

They had three sexes, best characterized as spore producer, carrier, and receiver, and their sex organs were in their crests. The receivers—who would probably be thought of as females in human terms—were the dominant members of the species, being significantly larger, stronger, and more intelligent than the male producers or the neuter carriers.

Though the Mekota absorbed oxygen through pores in their exoskeleton, they also had air bladders in their upper trunk, which were attached to a vocal apparatus that allowed them to make sounds. Their language was sound-based, though it derived emotional content from a display of colors in the crest. Their vocal range was several thousand hertz above that of humans, so they were not equipped to produce human speech. This was not of concern to them, as they had developed machines to reproduce human speech sounds. They needed such tools, for their goal was to dominate the Progenitor spawn, not destroy them.

The Organizer of Knowledge stood before the Guardians, shame reflected in the pale pink color of its crest.

"Speak your discomfort," the First of the Guardians said. "Forgiveness is granted but explain your error."

"A Messenger has arrived from one of the Progenitor seed systems. It reports that the humans have reached the outer parts of the system. More distressing, it reports they are using gravitational propulsion."

The Guardians were shocked.

"How did this happen?" the First demanded, her crest flashing yellow with anger. "Are the Organizers not charged with keeping watch over these systems?"

The Second of the Red shifted uncomfortably, uprooting some of her feeding tendrils, and the color of her crest paled a bit. Red was

Knowledge, and the Organizers were a permanent part of the Red Domain.

"We watched this system for twelve twelves of turns," the Organizer pleaded, its crest now devoid of any color. "But two twelves ago, self-destruction was predicted. The humans made only trivial attempts to enter space, with nothing more than small orbital devices. The planet was over its sustainable population limit, the environment was deteriorating, wars were in process, and fusion weapons had been developed. Destruction was inevitable. We have seen this pattern before in the ruins of destroyed Progenitor seedings. We placed Deathwatch Messengers in the system, and they returned five turns ago, reporting nuclear war was in process.

"We marked the system as dead, a possible source of future resources. We did not retrieve the outer system Messenger, which was an obsolete model. When it arrived, we spent much time analyzing the data it brought, and we now conclude this Messenger is correct, and the Deathwatch Messengers were in error."

Angry yellow and crimson crests faded a bit as the Guardians accepted the explanation. Still... "You did not send an Observer to confirm the destruction or a Surveyor to catalog the resources?"

"No, First Guardian. There was no reason for haste. We believed the system dead."

"I repeat your facts: The Deathwatch reports the humans destroyed themselves, but five turns later, a Messenger reports they are exploring their outer system with gravity-drive ships. Is it possible the Messenger detected not humans, but some interloper—an explorer from another race, perhaps?" Her crest darkened at the thought that another spacefaring race might encroach on the Mekota Sphere.

"Unlikely, First Guardian." The Organizer produced a small projector and opened a holographic display of the Sphere. One star system was highlighted. "The system is well within the Sphere. We might expect incursions on the outer fringes, but not this deep. Our analysts offer a theory if the Guardians wish to hear it."

"Proceed."

"The Deathwatch looks only for nuclear destruction, ignoring all else. It is possible the humans discovered gravitational propulsion before the nuclear war. They moved out into space, perhaps even colonized the inner system. When the war happened, off-planet colonists may have survived with significant technology intact. They may have intervened to preserve the home planet's infrastructure. The details cannot be determined from the information available, but the analysts agree: They must have discovered gravitational propulsion *before* the nuclear war took place."

"I conclude," the First remarked, "that we set the Deathwatch too soon. Leave us, Organizer. The Guardians will now decide."

"Our analysts recommend—"

"We do not require the recommendation of sexless carriers!" Her crest flashed an angry crimson. "Go now! Leave the projector for our reference."

"Yes, First Guardian." The Organizer withdrew, making gestures of obeisance as it backtracked out of the chamber.

The First regarded the assemblage, her crest cooling to a thoughtful bluish tint. "This is unacceptable. If the humans have mastered gravity, they may not be far from the discovery of Otherspace."

"Perhaps so," Second of the Yellow said. "The Progenitor spawn are most aggressive in their pursuit of technology once they reach a certain level. They may be on the brink of such a discovery as we speak!"

"We cannot permit them to reach that point!" Third of the Red spoke boldly, ignoring a flash of reproach from her own Second, who was still embarrassed by the failure of the Organizers. "I have studied this plague of the Progenitors. Humans are the most prolific and barbaric creatures the galaxy has ever seen. When their civilizations are young, they show the typical dull-witted barbarism of a male-dominated society. When they mature, their females achieve parity, but not ascendancy. They have no carriers, and—even ignoring their disgusting sexual aspects—the direct contact with males taints their females with the worst of the male characteristics. If these creatures are allowed to roam the stars..."

"You apply too many of *our* standards to these creatures," the First replied coolly. "They are aliens, and we know little of how they think, but I agree they are dangerous. Allowing them to travel the stars is unthinkable. If one Progenitor seeding gets loose and contacts others..."

The Guardians trembled, their crests a mixture of dismay, indecision, and, in some cases, fear. Humans outnumbered all the dominant races combined. The only way to keep them under control was to keep the seedings isolated and ignorant of each other. The Mekota were not the only race that followed this principle. Throughout the galactic arm, humans were kept ignorant. Any that reached a certain stage of development were enslaved, suppressed, or in extreme cases...

"Perhaps," Second of the Yellow said, "the answer is to exterminate them." Yellow was Power, and Power's answer to any problem was application of force.

The others wavered, waiting for the First's response. Though the First was mistress of all three domains, *this* First was of the Blue, and the Blue were Commerce. In Commerce terms, humans were part of the economic machine, whose function was to turn the resources of their planet into prosperity for the Mekota. In the next twelve turns, Second of the Yellow would become First, and in the next twelve, Second of the Red would hold the office. Likewise, the territorial holdings of each domain would be handed off in rotation, so the systems now ruled by the Blue would be given over to the Yellow, and so on.

The Blue were builders, not destroyers. But even they had to recognize the threat. Never had humans advanced so far, unrestrained.

"Extermination may be necessary," the First admitted. "These humans are at the point where we must take control. We will try the usual method first." She opened the projector, and the map of the Sphere appeared again, with the offending star system clearly marked. "This system is in the realm of the Blue. The Blue will make first contact and explain to the humans the terms under which they may continue to exist. Yellow will accompany Blue in case the humans refuse to accept their destiny."

* * *

TerraNova City, Luna

I t had been some time since all Lunar High Command had been assembled for a single briefing, but the circumstances called for it. It was a closed briefing, and all had been advised that the subject matter was top secret. The briefing was conducted by Dr. McGuinness and Admiral Michael O'Hara.

Mick O'Hara, as he was known to friends and associates, was director of engineering for the LFS. Between McGuinness' scientists and O'Hara's engineers, every aspect of the Cassini Anomaly had been examined in microscopic detail. O'Hara had the floor, and the big wall screen was displaying one of the images recorded by *Hawking's* probe.

"Despite the opinion expressed in Captain Shin's report, we did find some symmetry of design, but it isn't the usual bilateral symmetry we would expect to find in an Earth design, and it isn't as uniformly symmetrical as something we would build. The symmetry we found appears to be trilateral, and that, with the recurrence of design features in groups of three, suggests something I'll let Dr. McGuinness explain in more detail. At this point, I'll just say that his people don't think the creatures that built this thing were bipeds."

He paused a moment to let that sink in.

"We know the thing is propelled by a gravity drive. It's powerful enough to produce a delta vee of ninety-six gravities—not much for an object of this size. We don't know how much of its structure is devoted to drive components, but we have other indications that its drive may not be as efficient as ours. It creates far too much of a gravity wake—a disturbance in the natural flux lines—for the mass and acceleration involved. We know the size and shape of the object, and in a worst-case scenario—say if it were made of solid depleted uranium—it couldn't mass more than a couple of kilotons. But at ninety-six gravities, it was kicking up a wake equivalent to one of our twenty k-ton light cruisers. Our analysis of *Hawking's* gravitic scans indicates the thing wastes a lot of energy in gravity vectors that are not directed along the primary axis of thrust.

"Now, about that big surge at the end—one of Shin's officers said the thing looked like it had acquired the mass of a small planet or a black hole. That analogy isn't too bad, as it turns out. The gravitational event was of short duration—a little over three seconds—but it didn't appear to be centered on the object itself. It was as if a black hole was created directly *in front* of the object, as if a portal were opened into an area of extreme gravitational forces. After that, the object vanished.

"I noticed some of you—Admiral Greenwood—" He flashed a grin in Lorna's direction, "—reacted sharply to my use of the term portal a moment ago. I think you'll find this next part interesting. The choice of the mapping probe by *Hawking's* scientists was fortuitous, since its equipment is capable of not only high-resolution but also high-speed imagery. At the time of the event, it was transmitting images at one hundred frames per second, or one frame every ten milliseconds. We analyzed the event frame by frame, and the five frames I am about to show you are most revealing. They are sequential, meaning they represent a slice of fifty milliseconds in real time. Mike, if you please…"

The AI obliged by putting the sequence of five images on the screen in rapid succession, one image per second. In the first image, the object appeared normal, but in the second, the forward third of it had vanished. In the third image, the object was two-thirds gone, and in the fourth it had vanished completely. In the fifth image, a brilliant ball of light appeared where the object had been.

"Hyperspace!" Lorna gasped.

"For want of a better term, I guess you could call it that, Admiral. It certainly departed from *our* space, in less than four one-hundredths of a second."

"What about the flash of light at the end?" Ian asked.

"We believe that was an effect caused by the closing of the portal," McGuinness spoke up. "If you look at the last image, you can see there are no stars immediately surrounding it, and further out, the background stars have a bluish tint. What you are looking at is a tiny, almost point-source area of extreme gravitational force—a mini black hole, if you prefer—causing a lens effect that concentrates the light of the background stars. In other words, the event isn't actually emitting light, it's just bending and concentrating light coming from the star background."

"Looks awfully bright for just *starlight*," Charlie Bender said.

"Well," O'Hara replied, "remember that all of this imagery is heavily enhanced. This sequence of events took place out beyond Saturn, where the Sun's light is considerably diminished. The object was not very reflective, and the probe had to intensify the image considerably to let us see it. Those background stars you see are around fourteenth magnitude. You wouldn't be able to see them with the unaided eye. You might have seen the flash, but its duration was only about thirty milliseconds."

At O'Hara's direction, the AI replayed the images several more times, adding the next three images in sequence, which clearly showed the distortion of the star background and its return to normal as the flash cut off. The assembled officers sat in stunned silence.

"Any questions?" O'Hara asked.

"How long will it take to build one?" Lorna asked with a perfectly straight face.

"Any particular color?" O'Hara responded with an equally straight face.

The exchange relieved the tension and laughter broke out. It was generally understood in the LFS that Lunar engineers could build *anything*, once they were convinced it was possible. In this case, they weren't quite sure what *it* was, but the alien craft had proven conclusively that it *was* possible.

"All kidding aside," O'Hara continued, "we've got our best brains—including Mike—working on this. But we are working with limited observational data, and I suspect we're going to need a technological breakthrough to make it work. That means it could be next week, next year, or five years from now. Meanwhile, we should prepare for the possibility that the people who built that thing might show up. I can't tell you much more about their technology. As to what kind of people they might be, that's out of my area of expertise, so I'll turn it over to Dr. McGuinness."

"Before you do, Mick," Ian said, "do you have any thoughts about why that thing led *Hawking* on such a merry chase instead of just popping into hyperspace or whatever as soon as it got clear of the rings?"

"Well, it's possible it had to get clear of significant gravitational fields—far enough away from Saturn or from the Sun—to generate the hyperspace portal. Or maybe it had to build up a certain amount of relative velocity. It *had* reached nearly point two Cee—over fifty thousand kps—when it made the jump. Maybe it's a combination of gravity and velocity, but we think gravity is a likely possibility since the portal effect seemed to involve heavy gravity fields."

Ian nodded, satisfied with the answer. Without further comment, O'Hara turned the floor over to McGuinness.

"Before I get into the question of aliens," the scientist began, "I want to update you on another matter. Our medical people have subjected *Hawking's* crew to just about every medical test in existence and report no ill effects from their journey. We know there *were* relativistic effects from the velocity they built up. *Hawking's* chronometers were significantly out of synchronization with the master clock here on Luna, indicating less time elapsed on board the ship than here at home.

"We didn't expect there would be problems—we've noted relativistic effects before, but they were minuscule compared to this. In the inner system, our ships never get up to more than two or three thousand kps, primarily because of particle densities and the inherent radiation hazard. *Hawking* achieved over ten times that, so we thought it best to check the crew thoroughly."

"I should also mention there were no problems noted with the ship itself," O'Hara interrupted. "All her systems check out, though we found a good deal of particle scouring on the forward hull, and her instruments recorded higher than normal radiation levels—not enough to compromise crew health, but significant. The gravity drive system provides some radiation shielding, but if we want to go that fast again, we should consider a focused gravity field to provide additional forward shielding. I've got people looking into that."

"Right," McGuinness resumed. "Our analysis indicates radiation levels increase significantly with velocity. We think of space as being empty, but it's not. Particle densities are a lot lower beyond Saturn than in the inner system, but they are still high enough to cause problems if we don't protect the ships and their crews."

"Mick," Lorna asked the engineer, "if you put up a forward shield, won't it degrade the ship's acceleration capabilities?"

"Good question," O'Hara replied. "It probably would if we tried to block the particles completely. What we have in mind is a wedge-shaped field that will divert particle flow *around* the ship. There will be some drag, but if we design it properly, it shouldn't have much effect on performance."

Lorna nodded and sat back.

"Now, let's talk about *aliens*," McGuinness said with a wolfish grin. An immediate hush fell over the group, and he knew he had their full attention, but his grin faded as he continued. "I wish I could tell you more about the creatures that built this thing. A lot of what we have is speculation, but it represents our best SWAG on the subject. For those of you not familiar with the term, SWAG means scientific wild-assed guess."

That brought a chuckle from the assembled officers. A lot of the military types believed theoretical scientists *always* dealt in guesswork, but military intelligence often involved a similar kind of guesswork, and they were well aware of the problems involved in dealing with lack of data.

"Guess number one: The creatures who built this are *not* human—in fact, they are probably not even bipedal creatures. Mick briefly mentioned the inefficiency of their gravity drive, and his people have told us this is probably because the drive is intended to produce thrust in *three* lateral axis vectors. Mike, let's have that vector analysis, please."

The AI obliged by putting the image of the object on the screen, with the primary acceleration vector displayed. As McGuinness continued, Mike highlighted parts of the image and displayed additional vectors.

"Captain Shin deduced that the circular structure you see *here* was the field coil for the gravity drive, but image analysis has shown that there are two similar structures *here* and *here* that, if they serve the same function, would produce thrust vectors in the same plane but at an angle of one hundred twenty degrees to the active coil. Infrared analysis did not seem to indicate these other coils were active at the time, however.

"Ladies and gentlemen, if you are a bipedal creature with binocular vision, such as a human, your body is designed to move in one direction—forward, in the direction you are looking when your head is in its normal at-rest position. We *can* move sideways or backward, but that is not our normal mode of travel. If we want to change direction, we normally turn our entire body in the direction we want to go so we are again moving forward.

"Now, consider this. Every transportation device ever built by humans is designed to move the same way—including horse-drawn carriages, automobiles, ancient sailing ships, modern ocean ships, aircraft, *and spacecraft*. True, some vehicles *can* move sideways or backward, but *forward* is the primary movement mode designed into the system.

"In the case of pure spacecraft, where air resistance is not a factor and a vehicle can be built in any shape, there is no reason to design it that way, except that it is the naturally preferred movement method for human beings.

"Now, here we have a spacecraft," he gestured at the image on the screen, "that can move in any lateral direction without turning or reorienting itself, simply by using varying combinations of its three thrust vectors. Of course, to move vertically, it would need to tilt upward or downward, just as one of our ships would. But that design is consistent with the movement mode of *any* creature that evolves on the surface of a planet and lacks the natural ability to fly. A flying creature—or swimming creature, for that matter—may be equipped to move upward or downward as well as laterally, but land dwellers like us are accustomed to moving in a two-dimensional plane.

"I also call your attention to these three structures *here*. The engineers believe these are antennae for electronic signals, but again, they are oriented at one hundred and twenty degree angles to each other. We expect the three of them, in combination, would provide omnidirectional transmission or reception, though with proper phase control, they could be focused in any lateral direction. The design also seems to allow for independent upward or downward movement of each structure.

"Now, instead of a bilaterally symmetrical biped with binocular vision, imagine a radially symmetrical triped—a creature with three legs jutting out from its body at one hundred and twenty degree angles to each other. It can move in any direction without turning, just by varying how it uses its legs. In addition, it has three eyes, or groups of eyes, or vision receptors of some sort, also spaced around its head at one hundred and twenty degree intervals. These provide it with three hundred and sixty degree panoramic vision. It might have three arms as well, and three ears—maybe even three noses, or olfactory organs of some sort. In short, ladies and gentlemen, we are theorizing that the creatures that built this spacecraft might look something like *this*…"

On cue, the image on the screen was replaced by an artistic rendering of a creature with the characteristics McGuinness had described, and the audience gaped at the bizarre picture. Conceptually, the scientists were on the right track, but the picture bore little resemblance to the Mekota. At the moment, however, none of them had any way of knowing that.

* * * * *

Chapter Seven

TerraNova City, Luna

Of the five people meeting with Ian in his office, Commodore Timiko Yamamoto—Ian's chief of staff—was lowest in rank. The other four had been members of Ian's command staff during the earliest days of the Lunar Free State. Two were women, and, at different times, Ian had been in love with both. In truth, he was still in love with both, which likely contributed to his choice to remain unmarried. Unfortunately, the two of them were also in love with each other. Vice Admiral Carla Perry had been Lorna Greenwood's significant other for many years.

Despite the emotional overtones, the two of them were still among Ian's most trusted advisors, as were the two men present, Mick O'Hara and Charlie Bender. This was to be a strategy session, and Yamamoto was there primarily to bring the rest of Ian's regular staff into the loop as appropriate. She had also been with Ian a long time. In fact, she had replaced Carla Perry as chief of staff—with Carla's endorsement—twelve years ago. Carla was now Mick O'Hara's executive officer and the *de facto* commanding officer of TerraNova.

At the moment, however, Ian was more interested in her other skills.

"Carla," he said, "you've negotiated more treaties and agreements for us than anyone, and Charlie insists you're better at it than he is—particularly in non-hostile situations. I want you to put together a plan for first contact with the aliens—I'm assuming they *will* show up eventually. Give me a preliminary ops plan and tell me what resources you'll need. Feel free to tap anyone, but keep in mind that only the command staff, Mike, and Val know the whole story. Captain Shin and his crew have been sworn to secrecy. We haven't even told the non-command members of the Directorate, let alone the general population, about *Hawking's* discovery, and we certainly haven't told anyone on Earth.

"Assume the aliens will be friendly and will make an effort to communicate. Your job is to figure out *how* to communicate and how to interpret any communication *they* initiate. Work with McGuinness and Mick for any scientific or engineering expertise you need. Then figure out what we want to say to them if we establish communications."

Carla nodded thoughtfully, her mind already working on potential problems and solutions.

Ian turned to Admiral Bender. "Charlie, work with Lorna on the dark side scenario. Assume the aliens will be hostile—that, having discovered we are playing with spaceships, they want to squash us like bugs. We still want to communicate with them, so keep up with what Carla's team is doing, but know that we may have to kick their butts first. We should consider that they may be able to kick *our* butts, so make appropriate contingency plans. We also want to make sure we see them coming, so work with Mick on setting up an appropriate warning net. We'll probably want to deploy automated sentinels, since the Fleet can't possibly cover all approaches to the Solar System."

"We may not have to," O'Hara said. "The scientists think the direction in which the alien probe departed is significant. It didn't head straight out from Saturn. It headed more in the direction of Aldebaran, in the constellation Taurus. Maybe we should concentrate our resources on that part of the sky."

"We probably should watch that area closely," Ian agreed, "but we haven't a clue how this hyperspace portal works. I want a warning net that covers the area around the ecliptic, as well as above and below. I know it's a tall order, but there's a lot at stake."

"It's possible," Carla speculated, "that they will be neither friendly nor hostile. They may be so alien, we won't be able to communicate with them. We've got to be careful not to misinterpret their actions. I'd hate to start a shooting war with someone who only wants to study primitive cultures."

"I agree," Lorna said. "On the other hand, I wouldn't want to extend a warm welcome to someone who wants to find out if we taste better baked or broiled."

Ian sighed and ran his fingers through his greying hair. "It's a tough one, people, and there are too many things we don't know. Let's hope for the best and prepare for the worst. Think of the most bizarre scenario you can imagine and prepare a contingency plan for it. I wish I could give you more direction than that.

"About the only other thing I can think of is a project for you, Mick," he continued, turning to the engineer. "If the aliens do show up, we'll want to find out as much as we can about them in the shortest possible time. I need you to figure out what kind of instrumentation we can use to get that kind of information—what active scans we should use, what passive detection gear, and so on. Find out what kind of information the Fleet, the scientists, or your own people would like to have, and figure out a way to get it."

"Question, Skipper," Charlie Bender said. "Are you going to tell *anyone* on Earth about this?"

"I suppose we'll have to," Ian replied with a sigh. "After all, it affects them as well. I've scheduled a briefing this afternoon for the remaining members of the Directorate, and I'm thinking of telling the major spacefaring nations—Korea first, because they've been our closest ally all these years, then Australia, Japan, the U.K., France, and the U.S. I'm not going to bother with the European Union or the Confederacy—they've got no real power over their members. I'm not going to mention it to the Islamists—they have no space capabilities and behave as if they're living in the sixth century."

"When are you going to tell the friendlies? I'll need to brief my people who deal with those countries."

"Probably by the end of the week. I'll have Mike put together a document that summarizes what we know and the conclusions we've drawn. I'll include the imagery from *Hawking's* probe, and I'll send you copies for review. I'll want your input before we tell them anything. Meanwhile, all of you have your assignments…"

* * *

L ike most officers summoned to a private meeting with the Iron Maiden, Jimbo Davis was nervous. This would be the second time in less than a month he had been called before Admiral Greenwood. After the anti-piracy mission, he had gone with Jeff Jones to see her, as ordered. He had expected at least *some* criticism at that meeting, but the Admiral had only given them a "well done" and expressed her regrets over the loss of his ship and three crewmembers.

Since then, Davis had been languishing in the officer assignment pool, awaiting further orders. He had nothing to do except odd details, including a couple of one-day tours as the officer half of *Wanderer's* honor crew at the LFS Space Museum. Nothing was said about a future assignment, and he wondered whether High Command was all that satisfied with his performance. He'd had plenty of time to rethink the battle with the pirates, and he knew (with perfect hindsight) that he would not have lost his ship or any of his crew if he'd returned fire when the pirate ship had first launched missiles. But his orders had been to capture, if possible—that was why they'd put Marines aboard *Privateer* in the first place.

Last time, he'd met with Admiral Greenwood aboard *Athena*, but this time, he'd been ordered to report to her groundside office at Lunar HQ. Rumor had it something big was going on, and all the top brass had been meeting on Luna for the last several days. No doubt she'd been busy, but now, the admiral had gotten around to dealing with him on the pirate mission. Like all good officers, she delivered praise in public, when merited. Criticism would be delivered in private, not when another officer like Jeff Jones was present.

After verifying his appointment and I.D., the Marine guard outside the office opened the door and allowed him to enter.

"Lieutenant Commander Davis reporting as ordered, ma'am." He came to attention in front of her desk and saluted.

"At ease, Commander." She returned the salute. "Take a seat."

Like most of Earth's military, LFS personnel saluted only when covered—wearing headgear—but LFS personnel *always* wore headgear on duty, even aboard ship or when working in an office. There were exceptions: Officers and ratings alike uncovered for meals, worship services, and in recreational facilities that were posted for Quarters Rules—a relaxation of military courtesy requirements in private living quarters. In the jargon of the lower ranks, such facilities were called MYAH places—an acronym for "make yourself at home."

The regular uniform headgear for the LFS was a beret, with the color and insignia indicating the wearer's unit. Ship captains and flag officers wore a white beret, but since Davis no longer had a ship, his was dark blue with the generic gold Fleet emblem. Greenwood's, of course, was white, with the special gold-embroidered insignia that was only worn by the C-in-C of the Fleet.

As he sat down, Davis looked at the ribbons that graced the left breast of the admiral's uniform: Medal of Honor, Lunar Star with two clusters, Heart of Luna, First Battle of Luna, and a variety of lesser decorations. *Impressive*, he thought, but given the disparity in their ranks, not much more impressive than his own. Davis had been with the Fleet since its inception and had served aboard *Valkyrie*, Greenwood's flagship, during the Chinese war. Of course, the decorations didn't tell the whole story. Greenwood was a fair-minded officer who took care of her troops and dished out praise and discipline as deserved. She had a reputation as a hard charger, and she certainly didn't lack courage. She'd nearly died during *Valkyrie's* battle with the Chinese attack force. Wounded, she'd remained in command until the battle was over, then collapsed from blood loss. The wound had earned her the Heart of Luna and left her with a slight limp that was only noticeable to those who knew to look for it.

"So, how are you holding up, Commander?" the admiral asked.

"I'm…okay, ma'am," he replied cautiously, wondering what was behind the question.

"That wasn't a test, Jimbo," she said gently. "It's tough losing a ship, and even tougher losing people under your command. You were with me during the Chinese war. I lost two ships and a lot of people, and I still remember their names and faces. Some, like Chris Kelly and the crew of *Starfire*, were especially hard to take. You always think there might have been something you could have done to prevent it.

"There are always lessons to be learned, but you have to get past the idea that it was your fault. It's been almost three centuries since Field Marshall von Moltke said, 'No battle plan survives contact with the enemy,' but it's still true. Once things get going, you have to improvise and deal with the situation as best you can. I'm satisfied you made the best of the situation. Can you live with that?"

"Yes, ma'am," he said, relaxing a bit.

"Good. I've got orders for you. I'm not in the habit of personally delivering orders to lieutenant commanders, but I make exceptions when command of a Lunar Free State warship is involved."

Jimbo's heart skipped a beat. "Ma'am?"

"LFS *Starsong* will be coming out of the yards next week, and I'm giving her to you. You'll take her through acceptance trials and commissioning, then work her up to combat readiness as soon as possible. Of course, she inherits the battle honors of the original *Starsong*, and I expect you to make her worthy of them."

"Yes, ma'am!" Davis struggled to contain his enthusiasm. He felt like doing a victory dance, or spiking a football, or *something.*

"Now, about your crew. We're short on experienced people. You'll have to train most of them, but we'll raid other ships to make sure you get qualified people in key positions. Is there anyone you'd particularly like to have?"

"Yes, ma'am," he answered without hesitation. "I'd like to have *everyone* from *Privateer,* if possible. They were a damned fine crew."

"I thought you might, and I've already looked into that," she said wryly. "However, on a destroyer, you're only allowed a half-squad of five Marines plus a noncom, and you can't have Master Sergeant McGuinness. He's being sent for officer training and should be *Lieutenant* McGuinness shortly. You can pick six of the remaining eight. If I were you, I'd ask McGuinness for his recommendations.

"As for the rest, you can have Richards and Martinez—Martinez is up for promotion to P.O., on your recommendation. I presume you were thinking of Murphy for your exec, but she's still on the disabled list."

"She's getting out of the hospital tomorrow, ma'am. Of course, they'll be giving her a thirty-day light-duty excuse…"

"You think working up a new warship is light duty for an exec?" Greenwood lifted an eyebrow.

"You think a light-duty excuse will slow *Murphy* down, ma'am?" he replied with a grin. "She'll probably consider *any* shipboard assignment to be rehab therapy at this point."

"All right, you've got her, but I will have *both* your hides if she overdoes it and ends up back in the hospital. Understood?"

"Understood, ma'am."

"All right. You'll need a good engineer, especially with a new ship. We're giving you Lieutenant Sobieski from *Apache*. He's her second engineer, and he comes highly recommended. Any questions?"

"No, ma'am, I'm good to go. I'll probably catch a shuttle up there this afternoon and make a nuisance of myself to the yard people."

"All right but remember—she doesn't officially belong to you until next week. See Commodore Lopez and *humbly* beg for his permission to see her—they're proud of their work, and he'll probably give you a grand tour, but as far as the yard people are concerned, she's *their* ship until Fleet drags her from their clutches.

"Here are your orders." She handed him an envelope. "One more thing. Something may happen soon, something I can't discuss yet, but if it happens, we might need every ship in the Fleet. Expedite your workup as much as you can without cutting corners. I need *Starsong* combat-ready as soon as possible."

"Yes, ma'am. I'll do my best."

* * * * *

Chapter Eight

TerraNova City, Luna

It was nice having Lorna home for a few days, and Carla had the aliens to thank for it. She had visited *Athena,* on occasion, when the flagship was in port, but her duties kept her in TerraNova most of the time. Likewise, Lorna tried to get down to the surface when fleet operations brought her back to port, but her schedule was as busy as Carla's. Sometimes, they were apart for weeks at a time and had to be content with video calls and text messages.

This week, Lorna was working on strategies with Admiral Bender. She and Carla could spend their nights and evenings together, plus have an occasional lunch at a restaurant near Fleet Command. Today they were having a working lunch with Admirals Bender and O'Hara in the conference room adjoining Charlie's office.

The plans for Operation Welcome Wagon were nearly complete. Lorna's system pickets were on station, surveillance satellites were being deployed, the fleet was in a state of readiness, and they were ironing out the details of What to Do If the Aliens Arrive. Based on that day's meeting, they would present their final report to Ian and the command staff.

"We want to send out *Hawking* and *Einstein* with the first deployment," Mick O'Hara said. "Either one could probably conduct all the observations we need, but the scientists have given us a lot to do. We've divided the workload between the two ships."

"Understood," Lorna said. "I'll advise my tactical staff, and we'll assign a heavy cruiser to cover each of them, in case things get hostile."

"What about the other countries?" Carla asked.

"If we get visitors, the Americans, French, British, and Australians will all want their warships out there," Charlie said. "The Americans and Australians agreed to a unified allied command structure, with Lorna as supreme commander, but the French insist on operating independently. The Brits say their ships will only observe and will stay out of the way unless needed. The Japanese and Koreans want to send unarmed observer ships but want them up front in the formation. Frankly, the whole thing is a headache, and I'm beginning to hope we never see any aliens…at least not until these people have time to calm down. It would be easier if our illustrious leader had decided to keep the whole thing secret."

"That it would," Lorna said. "But if the aliens turn out to be hostile, the other nations will bring additional capabilities to the party. The French ships will probably have bomb-pumped laser warheads, and the Americans will have contact nukes. Since we don't know what might be effective against alien technology, I welcome the variety. I could wish for better cooperation from the French, but at least they've agreed to link to our communications net so we can coordinate."

Carla grimaced. She understood the need for military preparedness, but the thought of all those heavily armed ships out there gave her nightmares. One ship's captain, through error or intent, could start an interstellar war, rendering her attempts at peaceful contact meaningless.

"Of course," Lorna mused, "this presumes the aliens are even interested in contacting us. We've put a lot of effort into planning for something that may never happen. UFOs have been sighted before, and those sightings didn't bring alien ambassadors to our doorstep."

"True." Charlie leaned forward. "But we never chased one halfway across the Solar System before. And even back in the twentieth century, when UFO sightings were common, most governments had contingency plans tucked away for alien contact."

"Well," Mick O'Hara said, "at least they've given us time to get ready. Now, all we have to do is…"

He was interrupted by a series of attention-getting beeps from his interface pad. Simultaneously, the pads of the other officers began to beep.

"There I go, opening my big Irish mouth again…" O'Hara muttered, scanning the alert message on the screen. "Looks like the Little Green Men have arrived."

Lorna keyed the command channel on her pad, leaving the unit in speaker mode so the others could hear. "Val, what's happening?"

"Four unknown ships, Admiral, presumably alien in origin, detected inbound beyond Jupiter orbit." The AI gave a string of coordinates which Lorna ignored, knowing her tactical officers would plot the location and vector. "They're coming in on the course the scientists predicted, with Earth ETA in twenty-two days, seven hours. Nearest vessel is LFS *Stardancer*. Per your orders, that ship has been directed to intercept and shadow, no closer than two hundred thousand kilometers. *Stardancer* ETA on station is nine hours if the unknowns continue on present course."

"All right, Val," Lorna said. "Advise me of any change in status."

"Well, twenty-two days." Carla breathed a sigh of relief. "At least we have time to get set up."

"No, Carla, we don't." Charlie Bender grabbed his pad and rose from the table. "That's twenty-two days before they would arrive *here*, in Earth orbit. We want to meet them as far out as possible, so we've got to get moving *now*."

"You're right, Charlie," Lorna said, "but we need to get with the admiral first. Carla, can you call Timiko and let them know we are coming? I need to check in with Tommy and make sure he's on top of the situation."

* * *

The initial "meet and greet" deployment had been chaotic. The phrase *Chinese fire drill* came to Ian Stevens' mind. While probably unfair to people of Chinese ancestry, the hackneyed expression still conveyed images of mass confusion.

Ian agreed it was important to get out there as soon as possible so the Lunar fleet moved out immediately. The allied nations were notified, but without gravity drive, they couldn't match the acceleration of the LFS ships. They were soon left behind, causing a storm of diplomatic protests that kept Charlie Bender and his staff busy assuring foreign governments the LFS would take no action until the rest of Earth's ships arrived.

The Lunar fleet deployment was not as perfect as Lorna would have liked. The alien arrival caught LFS *Albert Einstein* in the middle of a drive overhaul, so the fleet departed with only one research vessel to handle a mission designed for two. *Athena* had also been undergoing yard work, but rather than leave the flagship behind, Lorna had departed with yard maintenance and repair crews still on board. The heavy cruiser *Zulu,* also in the yard for a drive refit, had not been able to pass muster, nor had the destroyer *Starhawk.* Both ships had been left behind with orders to join the fleet as soon as possible. The newly commissioned *Starsong* was still undergoing readiness trials, but Lorna had opted to take her along, with instructions to continue the trials en route.

Ian had wanted to go out with the Fleet, but that would have caused even more diplomatic repercussions. He insisted Carla go with the first wave, in case the aliens wanted to start talking immediately, so she hastily packed a bag and joined Lorna aboard *Athena.*

It was well that she did. The aliens began broadcasting in simple analog format on common Earth frequencies as soon as the Lunar fleet took up station in front of them. The message, repeated in most of Earth's major languages, was simple: *The Mekota* (the name was the same in all languages) *have come to discuss important matters with the leaders of your world. Arrange for communication.*

Carla was a bit chagrined that her efforts with the scientists and language experts proved unnecessary. She drafted a cautious reply that welcomed the Mekota and advised them that Earth's leaders were preparing to greet them. After getting approval from Ian and Charlie Bender, she had the message broadcast in English, French, German, Japanese, Korean, and Spanish—with the suggestion that English would be the preferred method of communication. Charlie Bender took heat for that, particularly from the French, but the Japanese and Koreans agreed. The aliens immediately stopped broadcasting in other languages and acknowledged in English only.

On Earth, the situation was beyond chaos. The newshounds were howling for blood, having discovered that Earth's leaders had been expecting aliens but had managed (to Charlie Bender's amazement) to keep it secret from the media. Worse, they discovered the allied nations' warships had departed without any media representatives aboard, but the LFS had thoughtfully included members of its journalist corps aboard *Athena*.

At least, Carla reflected, we'll get factual, unbiased reporting.

But Earth's media didn't see it that way. From Earth's viewpoint, Lunar news people were part of the Lunar Free State's military organization. Earthbound journalists referred to the Lunar media as "tightly controlled" and claimed that freedom of the press did not exist on Luna. In fact, freedom of the press was guaranteed by the Lunar Constitution, subject to only two simple constraints. The Lunar media could report anything that did not compromise national security, provided their reports were accurate and without speculation, emotional bias, or innuendo. On the national security issue, the burden of proof was on Lunar Command, which had to demonstrate the violation constituted a danger to the security of the state. But the real issue that bothered Earth's news organizations was the "without speculation, emotional bias, or innuendo" provision. Lunar news reports tended to be boring, with none of the audience-grabbing emotionalism that was the mainstay of Earth reporting.

Earth journalists could add their own speculation and emotional content, but only after the fact. Even those stationed on the Moon were often denied access to what they considered the best stories. During a Lunar tragedy—the loss of LFS *Amazon,* for example—the media people from Earth wanted to shove minicams into the faces of crewmembers' families to capture the pain and sorrow for their viewers back home. But the JAG had ruled long ago that Lunar citizens had a right to privacy and that freedom of the press did *not* allow violations of that right. Earth's media reps who hounded griev-ing family members ended up being handled roughly by Lunar Ma-rines, who also served as TerraNova's police force. The worst of the offending newshounds were shipped back to Earth with notice to their employers that they were no longer welcome on the Moon. Earth's news organizations called it "censorship" and "suppression of journalistic freedom."

Now, they demanded to be present at the historic meeting with the aliens, and the nations of Earth scrambled to oblige them. The French hastily outfitted a cargo vessel to carry European news peo-ple to the site, while the Americans offered a cruiser whose departure from Earth orbit had been delayed. The Japanese offered a cargo ship for use by the Far Eastern media. Meanwhile, all of them had to make do with secondhand reports from the LFS. Further, Admiral Greenwood ordered news media ships to remain well behind the fleet. The Americans heartily supported this order, saying the meet-ing was too important to allow it to be screwed up by overeager re-porters. Of course, American reporters, like their LFS counterparts, were aboard a warship that would be up front in the formation.

The Mekota had nothing more to say for the moment. They were decelerating at a modest 30 gravities when LFS *Stardancer* arrived to shadow them. If they detected the destroyer, they gave no indication. They came to rest relative to the Sun approximately halfway between the orbit of Mars and the Asteroid Belt. The combined Earth Fleet took up station 50,000 kilometers to sunward. LFS *Hawking,* at the far edge of the fleet formation, launched a probe that cruised within 10,000 kilometers of the Mekota formation, scanning it with optical imaging and other passive systems. The probe's course had been carefully plotted so it was never headed directly toward the aliens, and it moved past them at a leisurely pace. The intent was to appear non-threatening, and when the probe had completed its pass without incident, it reversed and returned along its course within 500 kilometers of the formation. The Mekota did not respond in any way. As the probe's imagery began to come in, Earth got its first good look at the alien ships.

By Earth standards, they were huge. The three smaller vessels, which appeared to be identical in construction, were over 1,000 meters in their longest dimension, and they were roughly spherical in shape with three smaller, hemispherical bulges equally spaced along their equatorial belts. The fourth ship was nearly half again as large and had the same general hull form, but there were enough differences to suggest an entirely different class of ship. The consensus was that the large ship (which Earth's news media insisted on calling the mother ship) was a diplomatic envoy, and the smaller ships were warship escorts. Admiral Greenwood was skeptical and instructed her people to assume they were *all* warships until proven otherwise.

* * *

The diplomatic maneuvering was far from over. There was general disagreement on how to "arrange for communication" between the leaders of Earth and the aliens. The primary argument concerned the definition of leaders of Earth. Every nation on the planet (and one on the Moon) wanted to be included, but each government insisted on putting forth its own agenda. Several nations attempted to contact the aliens directly, and that set off storms of protest from the others.

In the end, the Mekota dictated the terms. They refused to discuss anything with individual nations. Instead, the people of Earth were directed to choose their three most prominent leaders, each of whom could be accompanied by three assistants or deputies of their own choosing. The twelve persons selected were to board a single Earth ship and travel to the large alien ship for a meeting. The Mekota demanded the three leaders be the actual heads of state from the most prominent Earth nations, not diplomats or officials of some multinational organization.

As the leaders of the nations with the strongest presence in space, Admiral Stevens of the Lunar Free State and President Blackthorne of the United States simply announced they would attend the meeting and the LFS would provide transportation to the alien ship. With no other nation in a position to challenge, the rest of the world was left to argue about the number three spot. When the dust settled, Antoinette Leroux, France's premier, emerged the victor. The names were relayed to the Mekota, who replied with a terse message indicating the choices were satisfactory.

* * * * *

Chapter Nine

TerraNova City, Luna

Amy Ling was suffering the depths of depression, her current despair made more acute by the emotional high that had preceded it. As details of the proposed meeting with the aliens began to emerge, Ling had been summoned aboard *Athena*, where Admiral Greenwood informed her that *Valkyrie* had been selected to carry the chosen heads of state and their assistants to the meeting. She was ordered to return to Luna, take care of any required maintenance, and prepare her ship for its role in the most important meeting in human history. Vice Admiral Perry, who had been designated one of Admiral Stevens' choices, would return to Luna aboard *Valkyrie* to prepare for the meeting.

It made sense. *Valkyrie* was large enough to accommodate the twelve VIPs in comfort, but small enough to appear non-threatening to the aliens. Unlike newer and larger LFS vessels, she was capable of landing on Earth, which meant the Earth VIPs would not have to be brought up by an orbital lifter then transferred to the envoy ship. Admiral Greenwood also noted that consideration was given to *Valkyrie*'s distinguished history and battle honors and to her captain's seniority and impeccable service record. With her Oriental complexion, Ling did not blush easily, but she felt sure everyone on *Athena's* flag bridge must have noticed the glow of pride on her face.

Her present condition—flat on her back in a hospital bed, with a cast and traction supports—had been her own fault. Eager to make

115

sure the ship was in top condition, she had been watching the yard techs closely. Too closely, in fact, to watch where she was going, and the fall from the maintenance platform had left her with serious fractures of her right leg and hip. *Valkyrie* would undertake the mission, but under the command of Ling's executive officer, Lieutenant Commander Thomas Caruso. Ling would watch on video from a hospital bed on Luna.

At least, she thought bitterly, *I'm not the only one in this situation.* Two days earlier, U.S. President Hugo Blackthorne had collapsed in his office with the symptoms of a serious heart attack. He was now in the Army hospital in Phoenix, recovering from bypass surgery. The Americans had wanted to send the vice president in his place, but the other nations protested that the aliens wanted actual heads of state. After a lot of diplomatic infighting, it was announced that Japanese Prime Minister Hiro Akihito would be going instead. *I wonder if they would let me call President Blackthorne,* Ling mused. *Misery loves company.*

* * *

"Are you sure you don't mind sitting this one out, Charlie?"

Ian had thought long and hard about his choice of aides to accompany him. The other two heads of state were bringing their foreign ministers and top diplomatic people, and Ian had selected Carla Perry as his diplomatic representative, but he was also bringing the Lunar Free State's chief scientist Dr. Evan McGuinness and Master Warrant Officer Robert Forsythe, Terra Corporation's top business strategist. If the aliens wanted to exchange technology or talk about trade and commerce, the LFS was going to be ready.

"No problem, Admiral," Bender replied. "I've always been a covert ops guy, and I'm not comfortable in the spotlight. Since it looks to be a peaceful contact, Carla's the one to handle the job."

"You may be right, but I've considered that it may *not* be a peaceful contact. The aliens haven't told us anything, and if they decide to take us hostage, I'd prefer to have my best kick-ass people—you and Lorna—on the outside ready to take appropriate action."

"I hope it doesn't come to that, but we'll be ready if it does." Bender had also considered the possibility, though he admitted he tended to be paranoid about such things. Three heads of state and their top aides would certainly make ideal hostages…

* * *

So far, Lorna reflected, things were going surprisingly well. Akihito, Leroux, and their aides had joined Ian and his people aboard *Valkyrie,* lifted off without incident, and set course for the meeting point. *Valkyrie* and her Lunar escort—the heavy cruiser *Cherokee*—could have made the trip more quickly, but diplomacy dictated they limit their acceleration to just 30 gees, the maximum for the two French destroyers and the American cruiser *Chicago* that were part of the official escort.

When they reached the Earth fleet, *Valkyrie* continued alone as the Mekota required.

Lorna reviewed her tactical displays and nodded in satisfaction. Her ships were holding position, as were the French, Australians, and Americans. Their formation was an oval dish, curved inward slightly so all ships in the forward deployment were an equal distance from the aliens. The LFS fleet was deployed in a line across the diameter of the dish, parallel to the ecliptic. *Athena* was at the center, flanked by the cruisers *Apache* and *Norseman*. Two more cruisers were deployed to the east and two more to the west of the flagship, while LFS *Aztec*—serving as the backup flagship and escorting the research ship *Hawking*—held station on the western end. Lorna's twelve destroyers were deployed along the northern and southern edges, above the eight American warships that covered the northern section and below the three Australian and five French ships that covered the southern section. The Brits, as promised, held their six ships to the rear, keeping the diplomatic observers and news media ships in check.

It was an impressive formation, Lorna thought, but the whole fleet probably didn't mass as much as the four alien ships, now just 10,000 kilometers from *Athena*. After the probe flyby, she had moved her ships slowly and carefully closer to the aliens. At around 10,000 kilometers, the Mekota had requested that they come no closer, but Lorna was satisfied. She had no idea what sort of weapons the aliens might have, but they were now within range of her missiles.

* * *

Mekota Encounter Site, Beyond Mars Orbit

"Admiral, does it not concern you that the aliens have not let us see what they look like?" Antoinette Leroux asked.

"It does, Madame Premier," Ian admitted. "But our scientists think there are plausible explanations. We have no idea of the aliens' physiology. Perhaps they don't use visual sensory stimuli; maybe they 'see' by radar or sonar, instead of by visible light. They know enough about us to duplicate our methods of audio communication, but perhaps they don't think it necessary to go further than that."

"Your scientists have a sense of the bizarre, Admiral. I am still thinking in terms of little green men." She smiled. "But tell me, Ms. Perry, do you have any thoughts on the subject?"

Leroux had immediately taken to Carla, especially after learning she was the only member of the Lunar or Japanese delegations who spoke French—and spoke it fluently. The three of them were conversing in *Valkyrie's* crew lounge. Other members of the diplomatic party sat and talked at tables nearby.

"I have my own theory, madame." Carla returned the smile. "I think the aliens are concerned we primitives will be terrified by their appearance, and they want to prepare us gradually."

"Ah, but we will see them soon enough, no?" *Valkyrie* would be arriving at the alien ship within the hour.

"Perhaps not," Ian mused. "They said they 'prepared an appropriate environment for our comfort.' But that environment may not be comfortable for *them*. Maybe we are going to sit in our comfortable environment and talk to them through an audio link."

"If that were the case, we could have stayed on Earth and done as much," she said. "I hope we have not come all this way to talk without seeing them."

* * *

*V*alkyrie came to rest ten kilometers from the large alien ship and waited for instructions from the Mekota. Captain Caruso invited the three heads of state to the bridge so they could watch the approach on the main screen. Carla, as a Lunar flag officer, was invited to join them, but the rest of the diplomatic party had to content themselves with small repeater screens in the lounge.

Ten thousand kilometers to the rear, representatives of Earth's news media watched the approach via images relayed from a robot camera platform that was shadowing *Valkyrie* a few kilometers behind. The images were being relayed back to Earth, where virtually all the networks were broadcasting them live—or as close to it as the twenty-plus-minute transmission lag time allowed. The images were also being picked up by the ships of the fleet, but aboard *Athena,* they got little attention from the LFS crew. The battlecruiser's tactical displays gave a more detailed and accurate picture of what was happening.

On *Valkyrie's* bridge, Ensign Greg Arnold was puzzled. He had just transmitted his third query to the aliens for further instructions, but so far, they had not replied. He was nervously aware of the VIPs, including Fleet Admiral Stevens, watching somewhat impatiently from the rear of the bridge. He was about to ask his captain what to do next, when one of his tactical displays caught his attention. Hastily, he scanned his other readouts.

"Sir," he advised Caruso, "I'm getting a threat warning—looks like rapid-rate lidar scans hitting us from the other three alien ships. I just started picking it up."

Behind him, Carla Perry turned to her boss. "Ian, I've got a bad feeling about this—"

Hers were the last words spoken by anyone aboard *Valkyrie.* Without warning, three powerful beams of energy converged on the Lunar ship. They were ruby lasers—coherent beams of visible light less efficient than the gamma-ray grasers used by the LFS—but they were orders of magnitude more powerful than anything ever built on

Earth or Luna. *Valkyrie's* gravity drive and shields were powered down, but her shielding would have offered little protection as the beams took her nearly head-on. They tore through the length of her hull in an instant and sliced into the heart of her fusion reactors, turning the ship and all aboard into a ball of white-hot plasma.

Aboard *Athena*, Lorna Greenwood recoiled in horror as two terrible facts hit home. The two people she cared most about in all the world had just died, and because of one of those deaths, she had just become the chief executive of the Lunar Free State. As she stared at the expanding fireball on the main screen of *Athena's* flag bridge, the agony of her personal loss and the crushing weight of responsibility became almost unbearable.

But Lorna was a warrior, a dedicated professional known to her troops as The Iron Maiden. Without conscious thought, she keyed the all-ships command channel. "Wildfire! Wildfire! All ships, execute Omega... *now!*"

Wildfire was a standard alert code for the LFS, and it meant *weapons free—fire at commander's discretion.* Within seconds of Lorna's order, over 300 missiles came screaming out of the launch tubes of the LFS warships. Moments later, the American, French, and Australian warships added another hundred missiles to the salvo. As they did, the entire formation began to move, executing the complex maneuver worked out by Lorna and the Allied commanders and designated Battle Plan Omega.

* * *

Aboard the larger Mekota ship, the Second of the Blue did not immediately understand what was happening. She was not of the Yellow, not of a military mind, and it took a moment for her to realize the humans were *attacking!* It was inconceivable!

The Mekota strategy, which had worked many times in the past, was doubly flawed. It was based on an incomplete understanding of the human fight-or-flight reflex, and it was tainted by the aliens' philosophical bias. The Mekota regarded themselves as civilized—evidenced by the fact that they did not make war among themselves. Nonetheless, assassination was a legitimate method of succession to power in their society. When a leader was assassinated, her followers were expected to accept the assassin as their new leader. With that in mind, the humans of Earth (or at least three significant factions among them) should have accepted the Mekota as their new rulers. Humans were primitives, however, and in the past, the Mekota had seen that removal of their leaders produced abject terror among the followers, who would flee for their lives until convinced their new rulers meant them no harm. In truth, all humans they had dealt with in the past *were* primitives, people to whom Mekota technology must have seemed like magic, or at least so far enough superior to their own to eliminate resistance as an option. The Mekota had never encountered the fight side of fight-or-flight.

But what stunned the aliens was the swiftness of the response. When a Mekota leader died or was disabled, everything in that leader's domain came to a halt until a new leader was chosen—a complex process often involving several lower-level assassinations. They *thought* that was what had happened to the Earth faction known as the Americans. When their leader was disabled, they were no longer able to participate in the process, and—after a significant delay—another faction had moved to take their place. Orderly succession was not part of the Mekota concept of civilization. Since they'd been monitoring Earth's news reports, they knew most of the ships facing them were Lunar, American, or French. With their leaders gone (or incapacitated, in the case of the Americans), none of those ships should have been capable of action—other than perhaps to flee in terror.

The Yellow were just as surprised as the Blue by the aggressive Terran response, but they were better equipped to deal with it. They recognized the attack for what it was and responded accordingly. But the Mekota had abandoned primitive missile weapons long ago in favor of light-speed energy beams. Shielding and armor provided the only defenses against beam weaponry, so the aliens had nothing resembling point defense. They attempted to use their main armament to stop incoming missiles, but the powerful beams were slow to recharge, and their tracking systems were geared toward larger, slower targets. They were able to stop only a small fraction of the fast gravity-drive missiles launched by the LFS, and their attempts to deal with that incoming threat allowed the slower Allied missiles to cover most of the distance unchallenged. Meanwhile, the entire Earth fleet was moving toward them in a complex, twisting approach that, at first, appeared chaotic.

Under the Omega battle plan, LFS warships broke formation and began moving toward the aliens in a fast, sharp zigzag pattern, like skiers executing a slalom course. This allowed the Lunar ships to limit exposure of their vulnerable bow aspects, keeping their gravity shields between them and the enemy. It also allowed them to target the enemy ships with their heavy broadside weaponry. Meanwhile, the Allied forces, lacking the acceleration capability of the Lunar force, headed straight for the enemy, keeping pace with the LFS formation by traveling a much shorter route. The Allied ships had no gravity shields, and most of their weapons were forward-firing, so the straight-in approach was optimal and presented the smallest target aspect to the enemy. The plan also allowed each ship a maneuvering zone for independent evasive action, and the Allied commanders made full use of it, changing course frequently and at random. They had seen what had happened to *Valkyrie*, and none of them wanted to be an easy target for the enemy weapons.

At first, the Mekota ignored the incoming ships to deal with the more imminent missile threat. Lorna's Wildfire order had given each commander the discretion to fire when ready, but all except the French were tied into the fleet tactical net, which meant that targeting was handled by Val, the fleet AI. With cold computer precision, Val noted that the largest alien vessel had remained passive during the attack on *Valkyrie* and showed no evidence of powering up weapons or targeting systems. The first LFS missile salvo targeted the other three ships exclusively. The Americans and Australians got the same targeting instructions, but the French, who had chosen not to accept Fleet tactical command, launched their spread of twenty missiles at the largest target.

The Mekota mounted their best defense, but their efforts were ineffective against the fast-moving LFS missiles, which punched through their relatively weak gravity shields. The LFS detonators had been designed to ignore the deceleration caused by gravity shielding, and most of them made it all the way to the Mekota hulls, where their high-explosive warheads tore away huge chunks of the ablative armor that was primarily intended to protect against energy beams. Because of the sheer size of the alien ships, the missiles did little internal damage, but they blew away sensor and targeting systems and inflicted damage to the Mekota weapon arrays.

Like the alien probe, Mekota ships were designed to move—and fire weapons—in any lateral direction without turning. They could rotate, but the systems that allowed them to do so were slow and cumbersome. When the LFS warheads wreaked havoc on the side facing the Terran fleet, they began to come slowly around to bring their still-undamaged weapons and sensors to bear. For one of the alien ships, it was too late. An American missile slipped through its weakened defenses and detonated twenty meters from the hull. The thirty-megaton nuclear warhead vaporized a section of the alien vessel and blew the rest of it apart.

The other ships were more fortunate, as the Mekota realized the danger and gave top priority to targeting the slower-moving American missiles. But another alien warship was heavily damaged when its lasers detonated the last American warhead just 1,200 meters from impact. By that time, another salvo of LFS missiles was en route. The Mekota, frustrated by their inability to stop the faster missiles, turned their attention to the approaching Earth ships instead. The American heavy cruiser *Los Angeles* blew apart as alien lasers found her fusion plant, and both *Athena* and LFS *Norseman* took heavy damage from powerful beams that penetrated their gravity shields. By that time, however, the Allied warships had closed within range of their own energy weapons.

Early in the engagement, the Second of the Blue realized she was seeing a disaster in the making. Her ship—like all ships of the Blue—was only lightly armed and could make no difference in the outcome. She felt no obligation to remain with the Yellow.

A return in failure to the Homeworld would probably bring swift execution at the direction of the First. She could plead, however, that her primary duty had been to warn the Homeworld so the Yellow could be dispatched in full force to annihilate the humans. She ordered her ship to withdraw and proceed at full acceleration toward the entry limit for Otherspace, hoping the Yellow would occupy the humans long enough that their accursed warships—ships they should not have possessed—would be unable to overtake her before the jump.

She did not withdraw without damage, as the French missiles arrived just as the Blue ship was beginning its retreat and provided yet another surprise for the dazed Mekota. They detonated at stand-off distances of ten kilometers and sent bomb-pumped X-ray lasers lancing into the alien ship. The ship's armor was designed to withstand beam weapons, and these were not particularly powerful by Mekota standards. But a few of the beams found vital equipment that could not be protected by heavy armor. The ship took damage to its sensor arrays, and one segment of its drive ring was damaged, degrading acceleration. Grimly, the Second ordered rotation of the ship to bring undamaged drive components into position and continued her withdrawal.

On *Athena's* flag bridge, Lorna Greenwood saw the retreating ship and realized the significance. She keyed a channel to LFS *Aztec*. At the far end of her line of battle, the cruiser was in the best position to disengage and bypass the action.

"*Aztec*, this is Flag. The big alien is trying to run. He's pulling back at around point four kps squared—call it forty-one gravities. I need you to pull out, go around the others, and stop him. Take *Starsong* and *Stardancer* with you." She named two of the destroyers that were moving into the battle zone from above and below the enemy ships. "They'll reach him first and may be able to disable him before you get there."

"Roger that, Flag. *Aztec* is disengaging now," Jeff Jones replied from the cruiser's bridge.

"And Jeff," she said, "that ship hasn't fired a shot at us so far—it may not even be armed. I'd like to capture it, if possible, but use your discretion. It *must not escape*. If you can't stop it any other way, blow it to hell. Is that understood?"

"Yes, ma'am. We're on it," Jones said grimly.

Lorna relayed the order to the two destroyers and advised Tom Sakura of the redeployment. On her display, she watched the three ships disengage to go in pursuit of the fleeing Mekota. She would miss those ships in the continuing battle, but it was a price she had to pay. Even as she watched, the French destroyer *Flamberge* disappeared from her tactical display, and LFS *Cherokee's* status display flashed red. A quick check told her communications with the cruiser had been lost and her drive signature had faded, leaving the ship tumbling out of control away from the formation.

She felt the familiar shudder as *Athena's* mass drivers hurled another volley of missiles at the enemy, and status reports told her they were hitting the aliens with graser fire as well, but the Mekota ships were so damned *big*. The Americans had run out of nukes but were still in there, chewing at the alien hulls with X-ray lasers. And they were paying for it; besides *Los Angeles,* one other American ship had been destroyed, and two more were out of action with battle damage.

We're not getting off lightly, either, Lorna thought. She had seen the destroyer LFS *Starhawk* blown apart as she dove on the aliens from above. In addition to *Cherokee,* both *Athena* and *Norseman* had taken heavy damage, though not enough to take either of them out of action.

And Valkyrie, she reminded herself. *Never forget* Valkyrie.

The pain of that memory was almost too much to bear, and she pushed it out of her mind. The battle had been raging for a little over twenty minutes, which meant the people on Earth and Luna were just now finding out about it...

* * *

Like millions of other people, Amy Ling had been watching the news coverage on video—in her case, on the video screen in her hospital room, which had been carefully positioned so she could see from her awkward reclining position. She had seen only the beginnings of the flash that marked the destruction of *Valkyrie*, then she found herself looking at a blank screen as the EMP from the blast wiped out the electronics aboard the robot camera platform.

A moment later, the image of a shocked Jennifer Winslow appeared on the screen. The veteran LFS journalist was manning an anchor desk set up in the admiral's lounge aboard *Athena*, and her voice broke as she turned toward the camera.

"S...something has happened to *Valkyrie*...I don't... I can't..." She touched her earbud, listening to an incoming report, and the color drained from her face. Suddenly, her report was interrupted by *Athena's* battle alarms. She raised her voice to make herself heard. "The aliens fired on *Valkyrie* without provocation. She's been destroyed, and Admiral Stevens, Premier Leroux, and Prime Minister Akahito are dead, along with everyone else aboard...What...? Repeat that, please..." She looked up at the camera, and there were tears in her eyes. "*Athena* and the rest of the fleet have opened fire on the aliens. We're at *war!*"

The duty nurse hurried back to the nurse's station, hoping her last-minute errand hadn't caused her to miss anything important in the video coverage of the alien meeting. She had almost reached the desk when the scream of anguish from Commander Ling's room brought her up short. She rushed into the room and found the woman tearing at the covers and traction cables, trying desperately to free herself and get out of bed.

"Commander! What—"

"It was *my ship!*" Ling screamed through tears of rage and pain. "I should have *been* there. Let me out of here! I've got to get to the command center!"

Ling struggled against the restraining cables and straps and dragged herself over the edge of the bed and tried to reach the floor. The nurse hit the red call button on the interface clipped to her belt, and, moments later, the duty physician and an orderly rushed into the room. They dragged Ling back into bed, but she continued to rage and demanded to be released. In the end, they held her down while the doctor slipped a needle into her arm, and her struggles subsided as merciful unconsciousness claimed her.

* * *

Outside the White House bedroom where Hugo Blackthorne was spending his convalescence, the Secret Service supervisor was having a conversation with the president's physician.

"You're sure he's okay, Doctor? It must have been a hell of a shock."

"I'm sure it was, but his heart's doing fine now, and he's pretty tough for his age. He keeps repeating, 'It could have been me.' But you or I would probably be saying the same thing under the circumstances. I've given him a mild sedative, so he should be asleep in a little while."

Blackthorne was feeling sleepy, but his brain was still coming to terms with what had happened. *It could have been me…but it wasn't. Guess somebody up there still likes me. Too bad about Stevens. Never quite saw eye-to-eye with him about a lot of things, but he was a good man…a straight shooter. Not many people like that in our line of work. Between us, we finally built a decent relationship between the USA and the Moon. Wonder who'll take his place…Oh, hell! I bet it'll be Greenwood! If she survives the war with the aliens, that is…*

* * *

Lorna Greenwood had come through the battle without injury. Several crewmembers aboard *Athena* had been killed, and many more had been injured, but the ship was still partially combat-effective, and Lorna's flag bridge was undamaged. She breathed a sigh of relief when *Apache's* grasers found the last alien warship's fusion plant, and the target vanished in a blinding fireball. The second enemy ship had broken up after being battered to an airless hulk by the Allied missile and energy barrage. Now, *Aztec* was reporting the big Mekota ship was drifting dead, its sensors blinded, and its drive knocked out by the two destroyers that had savaged it as it tried to run. The Lunar commercial heavy-lift ships *Titan* and *Ganymede* had been dispatched from Luna and were heading for a rendezvous point, to tow the enemy ship back to the inner system. Assuming, that is, the last phase of the operation was successful…

* * *

Rock Bartley was understandably nervous as she climbed into the cutter with the other five Marines from *Stardancer*. She wondered how Jimmy White Feather was doing, and whether she would see him aboard the alien ship. Jimmy had been assigned to the larger Marine contingent aboard *Aztec*, and she knew the heavy cruiser's Marines were bound for the same place she was.

Noting her agitation, Sergeant White directed his attention to his greenest troop. "Bartley!"

"Yes, Sergeant!" Fresh out of training, she was still not comfortable with calling him Sarge the way the more experienced troopers did.

"You understand the rules of engagement?"

"Yes, Sergeant. If it moves, shoot it."

"No, Bartley," the noncom explained patiently. "If it moves *toward* you or behaves in an aggressive manner, shoot it. If it runs the other way, let it go. The brass are taking no chances with these bastards, but they *would* like to have some of them alive."

"What do they look like, Sarge?" Corporal Washington inquired. "I mean, once we get over there, how do we know an alien from a pile of shit on the deck?"

"Well, now, that's the interesting part, Washington. Nobody knows what they look like—so stay sharp. I'm gonna count you people off about every thirty seconds over there, and if anybody doesn't respond, all hell is gonna break loose.

"Hey, now," he concluded with a wolfish grin as he locked his helmet down. "Who said this was gonna be easy?"

Bartley's hands were shaking as she checked her weapon. Not knowing what to expect, the Marines were packing some heavy firepower. Like most of the team, Bartley was carrying a Mark VII large-caliber assault weapon. The LCAW fired heavy 20mm rocket projectiles that reached their maximum velocity of 600 mps less than two meters in front of the muzzle. Accuracy was within acceptable limits to about 75 meters, and with solid-slug ammo, the weapon was deadly to anything up to the size of an elephant. The large bore also allowed for a variety of other loads, including armor-piercing, high explosive, incendiary, or fragmentation. For this mission, Bartley and her mates were carrying a variety of ammo types in color-coded twenty-round magazines slung in bandoliers across their chests.

In addition to the LCAWs, one member of the squad carried a Rapper—a Mark IX rapid-rate anti-personnel weapon—a six-barrel rotary rifle that fired light 4mm hypervelocity projectiles at nearly 100 rounds per second and was fed from a backpack magazine that held 10,000 rounds. To round out the mix, another Marine was carrying a modern version of the old-style flamethrower, one that used a self-igniting and self-oxidizing mix of chemicals that would produce an inferno even in a vacuum.

As the cutter approached the alien vessel, Bartley took a deep breath to calm herself. On command, she selected a clip of HE rounds from her bandolier and locked it into her LCAW's magazine well.

* * *

The fleet searched in vain for wreckage or any other trace of *Valkyrie*. Given the energy signature of the explosion, they had not expected to find anything, but Lorna insisted they try anyway.

There wasn't much left of the three alien warships, either, but Lorna assigned two destroyers to guard the wreckage against curious news people and others who might want to poke around in the hope of discovering alien secrets. The news of the fourth Mekota ship's capture had not been released to the media, though the Allied commanders had been briefed. The American cruiser *Chicago* and the French destroyer *Ariel* were on their way to rendezvous with *Aztec, Starsong,* and *Stardancer.* Lorna dispatched the LFS cruiser *Zulu* and research vessel *Hawking* to the site as well. The rest of the fleet conducted rescue and recovery operations for the ships badly damaged in the battle. It looked as though LFS *Cherokee* would be a total loss, though nearly half of her crew had survived and been rescued.

After designating Jeff Jones of *Aztec* to command the alien capture operation and Robin Torrey of *Apache* to take charge of the remaining force, Lorna ordered *Athena* back to Luna, along with LFS *Norseman.* The two were the most heavily damaged of the surviving Lunar ships, and she was anxious to get them to the Lunar shipyards, where they could be restored to battle-ready condition. The Allied forces of Earth and Luna had won the first battle, but it was unlikely the aliens would let it go at that.

There were other reasons why Lorna needed to return to Luna. She had received a message from Charlie Bender, informing her the Judge Advocate General of the Lunar Free State had confirmed what she realized when Ian Stevens died: by the terms of the LFS Constitution, she was now the chief executive. The members of the Lunar Directorate had been advised, and Admiral Bender would be standing by with Commodore Yamamoto to brief her on her new responsibilities as soon as she returned.

The message was official and impersonal, but Lorna knew both Charlie and Timiko Yamamoto had been close to Ian Stevens. All of them had lost a dear friend, but Lorna had lost the love of her life as well. Now the battle was over, all the necessary orders had been given, and *Athena* was headed for home. For a few moments, Lorna had no pressing responsibilities. She got up and carefully closed the door to her day cabin, a signal to the Marine guard that she was not to be disturbed. She returned to her desk, picked up Carla's picture, and let the tears overtake her at last.

* * * * *

Chapter Ten

"Command, Charlie One."

"Go ahead, Charlie One," Lieutenant Colonel Anne McGraw acknowledged. McGraw was directing the boarding operation from *Aztec's* tactical operations center. Charlie One was Sergeant White, squad leader of *Stardancer's* short squad of six Marines. Alpha One was Lieutenant Ochida, commanding the two full squads from *Aztec* and serving as the on-scene commander. Bravo One was Staff Sergeant Rico, squad leader of *Starsong's* six-Marine team. All three groups were inside the alien ship, having entered through holes in the hull blasted open during the battle.

"Command, we've got what looks like a sealed pressure door on the inner bulkhead. It's about four meters high by three wide. There don't appear to be any handles or other manual controls on the door. I've got the camera on it now."

"Roger that, Charlie One. The engineers are looking at it. Stand by."

Stardancer's Marines had boarded the ship through a hole that led to a large, empty compartment that still had gravity. The contingents from *Aztec* and *Starsong*, by contrast, had had to pick their way through mazes of twisted wreckage in zero gee. Sergeant White reported the alien gravity was about eight-tenths Earth normal, and he was the first to report a door that might lead to a still-pressurized part of the ship.

Glowing red panels illuminated the compartment. The six members of the squad were arrayed in a semicircle around the newly discovered door, their weapons at the ready.

"I hope that's an equipment hatch, not a personnel hatch," Private Bartley muttered on the squad-only channel. "Otherwise, I'd say we're dealing with some pretty big dudes."

"Just keep your weapon ready, Bartley," Sergeant White said. "If anything comes through that door, it's gonna get a nasty surprise no matter how big it is."

Back on *Aztec*, McGraw smiled. While the engineers conferred, she had been monitoring the chatter on the squad channels. She heard the nervousness in Bartley's voice, but the woman was *thinking*, and the remark was a pretty sharp observation for a green private. She turned her attention back to the matter at hand as one of the engineers offered a suggestion.

"Charlie One, do you see those two round protrusions to the left of the door, about halfway up? They look identical, but each has a different mark on it. Try moving one of those...push it, or pull it, or something. The engineers think they might be door controls."

"Roger that...the right one moved a little when I pushed it, but nothing happened. I'm trying the left one now...Okay, something's happening."

As soon as the protrusion was pushed, a blue bar of light began blinking above the door. As they watched, the bar gradually shrank in length until it disappeared completely. The door slid open. The Marines tensed, weapons ready, but beyond the door was an empty corridor about ten meters long with another door sealing the far end.

The second door was identical to the one that had just opened, and it appeared to have identical controls.

"All right," Sergeant White said. "We're going in."

He led the squad to the far door and again pressed the left protrusion. This time, a yellow bar of light appeared, blinked several times, and went out. The door did not open.

"No, no," said the engineer watching over McGraw's shoulder. "It's an airlock. He has to close the first door before the second will open."

McGraw relayed the advice, and White backtracked to the door his squad had just come through, studied the controls for a moment, then pressed one of the protrusions on the inside. The door closed, and he returned to the far door and pressed the open control again. This time a short blue light bar appeared and began to lengthen. As it did, the Marines noticed something else.

"Command, Charlie One, we're getting pressure in here. I'm reading point five atmospheres and climbing. All right, people, look sharp."

The Marines tensed as the second door opened, but the compartment beyond, illuminated by the same dim red light, appeared empty.

"Park, Washington—go!" White ordered, and his two corporals stepped over the rim of the door, fanning their weapons left and right to cover the entire area.

"Shit! What did we step in?" Washington exclaimed. What appeared to be a solid floor was really an ankle-deep pool of thick, oily liquid. Hastily, the two men stepped back.

White bent down to examine their boots. "Hmmm…I don't know what this stuff is, but it doesn't seem to be hurting the suits. Messy, but it looks harmless."

"Maybe we just stepped on an alien," Washington said, reminding them they had no idea what to expect.

"Or maybe we just stepped into their sewage pit. Hey, Sarge," Corporal Park said, surprised. "I'm reading breathable atmosphere in here…lots of oxygen and nitrogen—a little high in carbon dioxide, a trace of methane, but within limits."

"Don't even *think* about opening your suits," White warned. "There could be alien bacteria or who knows what else. Besides, if this stuff on the floor smells as bad as it looks, it's probably pretty rank in here. Command," he continued, speaking to McGraw, "I don't see we have any choice but to wade through. Do we have permission to proceed?"

McGraw looked at the engineer, who shrugged and nodded. *Better you than me,* he thought.

"Roger that, Charlie One, continue on mission."

* * *

Timiko Yamamoto was distraught, maybe even on the verge of a breakdown, Charlie Bender noted. She was trying to hide it, keeping herself busy with trivia as she and Bender prepared a briefing for Admiral Greenwood, but her quiet, oriental reserve had been breached. The woman had been Ian Stevens' chief of staff for over ten years, and Bender knew she had been close to her boss. *I wonder if they were sleeping together,* he thought but then he dismissed the idea. *Ian was too dedicated, too serious about his leadership responsibilities to get involved that way. He was married to the Lunar*

Free State. He was also sure Timiko wouldn't have done anything to compromise her commander's image or integrity.

Charlie had been with Ian Stevens since the earliest days of the Deep Space Research Institute and the founding of the LFS. Bender could recall only one instance when the admiral had gotten serious about a woman, and that had been more than ten years ago. But a lot of people loved the man and would be heartbroken over his death.

That led to another thought. *I wonder how our* new *chief executive is holding up?* Lorna Greenwood had been close to Ian as well, but it was no secret who *she* had been sleeping with. It hadn't been a problem, since Carla Perry had not been in Lorna's chain of command, but now…*I guess we're going to find out how much steel there is in the Iron Maiden.*

* * *

Sergeant White split his squad into three two-person fire teams as they moved into the ship. They were looking for the bridge or whatever the aliens used for a command center. Given the size of the vessel, the search could take a long time. The noncom elected to take Bartley as his partner rather than saddle one of his corporals with the green private.

They entered another large compartment with White covering left and Bartley covering right. Suddenly, Bartley realized something she had thought was a weird-looking piece of equipment was *moving*. In the dim light, it looked like a large cylinder set on a heavy tripod, with long, curving appendages jutting out from the middle of the cylinder directly over each of the three legs. The thing was about three meters tall, and the upper end of the cylinder was covered with irregular protrusions. It was topped with what looked like a tangle of cables.

As she watched, the cylinder tilted toward her, and the two rearmost legs shifted to the front, while the other leg swung back, moving the thing almost a meter in her direction. Bartley didn't know it, but she had just become the first person in the Solar System to see a Mekota face-to-face—if the alien could be said to have a face.

An instant later, she became the first Marine to kill one, as the alien took another step toward her, and she blew a large hole in the middle of its cylindrical body with her LCAW.

* * *

"We've finally gotten a look at one of the aliens—dead, unfortunately. It appears our anti-personnel weapons are effective against them. One of our troopers blew this one nearly in half with a HE round from an LCAW. Apparently, it was advancing toward her, and she followed the rules of engagement and shot it. We're transmitting all of the imagery we've got so far from inside the ship…uh, stand by one, Admiral…"

Lorna was getting Jeff Jones' status report from *Aztec*. The capture team was still moving out-system on the alien ship's last vector before its drive had been disabled, while *Athena* was headed in-system toward Luna. The transmission delay was now over ten minutes, so Lorna had to content herself with recorded reports rather than real-time communication.

"Admiral, *Aztec's* team has captured three aliens alive, and one of them has a communication device and can talk to our people. They are offering no resistance. I'm going to send a scientific team from

Hawking, with a squad of *Zulu's* Marines for an escort. I'll keep you advised. Jones out."

Lorna breathed a sigh of relief. She had worried the aliens might prove too much for the assault force to handle, and she might be forced to destroy the alien ship. But the Marines had taken the ship with no casualties. She recorded a reply, approving Jones' plan and directing him to use *Aztec* and *Zulu* to try and halt the outward movement of the alien hulk with counter-grav beams and the cruisers' drive systems. *Titan* and *Ganymede* could do the job better, but they hadn't left Lunar orbit until the battle ended. It would be some time before they arrived on the scene.

Lorna had received additional messages from Luna. The governments of Earth had been advised of her succession as LFS chief executive, and the Americans had immediately reaffirmed their support of the joint military operation. Other nations were not so supportive. Some countries condemned the "precipitous" military action against the aliens. They maintained that *Valkyrie's* destruction might have been an accident or a misunderstanding, that perhaps the Lunar ship had provoked the attack. The Pan Africans were demanding Lorna be brought to trial before the World Court for actions that "jeopardized the safety of all humanity" and that the Lunar Free State relinquish command of the joint fleet. Any further dealings with the aliens, they maintained, should be under the control of a committee of world diplomats (which *must* include Pan African representatives).

The French, on the other hand, outraged at the loss of their beloved Madame Leroux, endorsed Lorna's action completely and confirmed their support of the joint operation. These messages came via diplomatic channels—the media had still not been told there were aliens left alive or that one of the alien ships had been captured almost intact.

* * *

Communication with the aliens was not as simple as Jones first thought. The Mekota communication device was an audio interface connected to a complex piece of equipment which required a lot of manipulation by the Mekota acting as translator. The sounds that issued from it, while clearly English words, were muffled because the humans were still wearing their space suits, as they were unwilling to expose themselves until a more detailed analysis of the alien atmosphere could be done.

Human replies were being transmitted on a special communications channel, and the aliens could only hear them via the small speaker of a hand-held communicator. The engineers were searching for a better method, but the jury-rigged setup was working for now. Presumably, human responses were being translated from English into alien-speak by the Mekota device.

Anne McGraw had suited up and gone aboard the alien hulk to take command of the operation. The scientists were bursting with questions, but Admiral Greenwood's orders were to secure the ship first and suppress or neutralize alien resistance.

"Our former leader has been removed," the alien voice said, "and our subleader recognizes your dominance."

"Does that mean you surrender?" McGraw asked.

The aliens did not reply, but there was a lot of waving of their top tendrils, accompanied by high-pitched hissing sounds. The first shock of their alien appearance had worn off, and McGraw was not intimidated by the size of the creatures. Private Bartley and two other

Marines had already proven the Mekota were not particularly hard to kill.

"Are you the leader?" the alien voice asked.

Now it was McGraw's turn to pause and consider. "I am a sub-leader among my people," she said, imitating the alien terminology. "I am the leader here, aboard your ship."

"What is your sex?"

The question stopped McGraw in her tracks. She sensed it was important, but she had no idea what the right answer might be as far as the aliens were concerned. She switched channels to speak with Jeff Jones. "They want to know my sex, Commander. Apparently, that makes some difference to them. What do you think I should say? I could just tell them it's irrelevant. Either way, they *are* our prisoners."

"Hmmm," Jones mused, "you may be right, Colonel, but I'd be inclined to tell them the truth. We might learn something important from their reaction."

"Right. Lieutenant Ochida, tell your troops to stay sharp. This might be a critical point," McGraw advised, then switched back to the alien-talk channel. "I am a female," she told them.

The reaction from the three aliens was immediate and visible. Their top tendrils went limp, drooping down over their 'heads' while their three 'arms' dropped straight down to their sides.

"We surrender to your dominance," the alien voice said.

* * * * *

Chapter Eleven

"*Titan* and *Ganymede* are on the scene," Mick O'Hara told the assembled group, "and we've got the hulk moving back in this direction. The plan is to park the thing at one of the LaGrange Points, probably L5. Until we know more about these creatures, we don't want to put them too close to Earth or Luna."

The meeting was being held in *Athena's* flag conference room. The battlecruiser had returned to the Lunar shipyards, and Admirals Bender and O'Hara had come up from the surface to attend, along with Dr. Emil Julian, who had been named to replace the late Dr. McGuinness as director of research. Lorna didn't know the astrophysicist very well but had approved his promotion based on Mick O'Hara's recommendation. Also present at the meeting were Timiko Yamamoto and Tommy Sakura, two key members of Lorna's command staff, and Brigadier Kim Song Chae, Commandant of the Lunar Marines.

"I need your preliminary input," Lorna told them. "We'll refine later when we have more information. To start with, Tommy, give me your impressions of the battle and the alien military tech."

"Well," Sakura's brow wrinkled, "in terms of the outcome, we won decisively. But in terms of ship-for-ship action, we lost six Allied ships outright to their three warships—the big alien ship never fired a shot, so I guess we can assume it was a noncombatant—and five more of our ships were seriously damaged. If they have a battle fleet back home and come after us in large numbers, we could have problems.

"Having said that," he continued, "we have one significant advantage. We know what to expect, and they don't. None of the aliens escaped, and we squashed their attempt to launch a messenger drone. At least, we *assume* that's what they were trying to do; the thing they launched was like the original alien probe discovered by *Hawking*. Fortunately for us, they waited too long to launch it. They were already within our graser envelope, and *Stardancer* took out the drone before it got too far.

"As for their military tech, we know they have the biggest, nastiest visible-light lasers we've ever seen—powerful enough to punch through *Athena's* gravity shields at ranges like those of our grasers. But they seem to have a long recycle time, and their tracking systems don't seem to be as good as ours. We also know they're vulnerable to missile attack. They have no point defense worth mentioning, and their ships are slow and not particularly maneuverable. On the other hand, their hulls are tough. They can't withstand a direct hit by a nuke, but their battle armor is good against beam weapons and conventional missiles.

"We're still analyzing the battle in detail and may find other things." He consulted his notes. "There is one more point. Val's preliminary analysis indicates the aliens may not use any kind of tactical network. She maintains all of their attack and defense patterns indicated an every-ship-for-itself mode of operation."

"*That* could be useful information," Lorna said. "If we're faced with a numerically superior force, it might make it easier to split them up and defeat them. Brigadier, do you have anything to add?"

"Not much, Admiral," Kim replied. "The boarding operation went smoothly, but we have to consider there was no resistance whatsoever from the aliens. It appears the large ship was a noncombatant, and we don't know what we might have faced if we had boarded one of the warships. The aliens our people killed were not armed, nor did they appear to be wearing any kind of battle armor. About all we learned is that they can be killed by our weapons under those conditions."

"Good point." Lorna nodded. "Doctor Julian, what else do we know about the aliens?"

"Physically, biologically...well, you've seen the pictures. About all we can say at this point is that they are not like anything that ever lived on Earth," the scientist replied with a shrug. "They breathe an atmosphere not too different from our own, but preliminary analysis indicates a biochemistry that's more like that of a plant than an animal. The biological data is coming in, but it will take a long time to analyze. We have also learned a few things about them from direct questioning by the on-site team.

"They have three sexes—male, female, and something in between. They are a female-dominated society, and it was pure luck the Marines had Colonel McGraw on the scene. The aliens know we have only two sexes, and we're not sure they would have surrendered to a male. In fact, now that they've learned who's who among our boarding party, they won't speak to any of the males. All the aliens who speak are apparently females.

"Unfortunately," he continued, "the only other females we had on the alien ship were one Marine corporal, one private, and Dr. Warren, the biologist from *Hawking's* team. We're using Dr. Warren as Colonel McGraw's deputy commander for dealings with the aliens, and the two female Marines are being used in other situations where we need to communicate with them. You realize, Admiral, anyone who goes aboard the alien ship has to be quarantined..."

"Yes, we've considered that," she said, "but we can't keep them in the alien environment indefinitely. The engineers have rigged a boarding tube, and we've brought *Hawking* alongside so the Marines and scientists can rotate back to a normal environment periodically. That means *Hawking* and all her crew have to be quarantined, as well as the rest of the scientific team aboard. We made it voluntary— would have transferred anyone who requested it to one of the warships—but all of them volunteered. We're going to need more volunteers, by the way, particularly some engineers. We have enough Marines, and *Hawking's* scientific team has a good mix of people, but I want to give top priority to anything we can learn about the alien hyperspace technology, and that means more engineers. Mick...?"

"Knowing my people, they'll be lining up to volunteer," O'Hara said. "Lunar engineers love a challenge."

The discussion continued, but most of it was speculation. Lorna decided to bring the meeting to an end.

"All right, people, I need you to get back to work. Mick, Dr. Julian, you know your top priority—the alien star drive. Beyond that, look for anything in the alien technology that will help us on the military side. In addition, Doctor, we need to know more about these creatures from a sociological standpoint. I'll personally pin a medal on the first person who can tell us why they attacked *Valkyrie*.

"Tommy, fleet readiness is your priority. Expedite the repairs to *Athena*, *Norseman*, and any other ship with battle damage. After that, top priority goes to warship construction. I want the new battlecruiser finished within the month and then I want the two new cruisers bumped to the head of the queue. And Tommy...the fleet did an outstanding job out there. Make sure everyone knows that. Brigadier Kim, pass my personal commendations on to your Marines, especially those who were involved—are still involved—in securing the alien ship.

"Let's get to it. Charlie, Timiko, you're with me."

After the others departed, Lorna led Bender and Yamamoto to her day cabin for a working lunch, during which they tried to brief her on everything she needed to know as the new commander-in-chief. It was a monumental task, and they realized how unprepared they were for Ian Stevens' death.

In the end, Lorna called a halt to the process. "We're just going to have to deal with issues as they arise. Charlie, I need you to keep the other nations calm and maintain whatever relationships we have with them. As for those who want my head, tell them to take a number.

"Timiko, I need you to keep doing all the things you did for Ian—and don't hesitate to tell me if you think I'm not doing something the way he would have done it. This job won't come naturally to me, and I'll need all the help I can get."

"Admiral," Bender said with some hesitation, "I know you're still giving the fleet top priority, but you need to come down to Luna for a while. The people need to see you and know they have a leader who is there for them. Nobody is better equipped to command the fleet, and I have no doubt the aliens will be back. But right now..."

"I know, Charlie," she said gently. "I'm planning to go down with you two after we finish here. Tommy can take care of everything the fleet needs for now. I'll have to meet with the Directorate right away—Timiko, can you set up that meeting for tomorrow morning? Make sure all of the directors are notified before we leave here."

"Yes, Admiral." Timiko keyed her interface pad and directed TerraNova's AI to issue the meeting notice.

"I think you should plan a video address to the nation for tomorrow night," Bender suggested. "It doesn't have to be long, just a little reassurance for the people. We also need to start thinking about a memorial service."

"I know. Let's try to do that within the next few days. We'll want decorations and commendations for those who died, as well as for others who distinguished themselves in the battle. Timiko, can you make the arrangements for all of that?"

"I don't know, Admiral, that's the sort of thing Carla always used to handle." Tears came to her eyes as she saw the look on Lorna's face. "I…Oh, I'm so sorry, Admiral…"

Lorna shook her head and regained her composure. "No, Timiko, it's all right. I'm going to be reminded of her no matter what I do, and I've got to deal with it." She looked at Carla's picture on her desk. "Do what you think *she* would have done, and I'm sure it will be fine. For one thing, Carla always got things done by coopting others to help her. Don't try to do it on your own—use anything and anyone you need. Under the circumstances, I think you'll find a lot of people willing to help.

"All right," she said, "we'd better head down to Luna." She picked up the carry bag she had packed for the trip and slipped Carla's picture into one of its pockets. "When we get there, you two can go about your business. I've got a personal matter to take care of this evening. I'll see you in the office…Ian's office…first thing in the morning."

The two Marines outside the door saluted, and one of them took Lorna's bag as they fell in behind the three officers.

On the way to the boat bay, Charlie gave Lorna more advice. "Admiral, about the meeting with the Directorate tomorrow…you should be aware that a few members are not happy about your succession. They believe we ought to choose a new chief executive immediately. Constitutionally, they don't have a leg to stand on, but you should expect at least one of them to raise the issue."

"I didn't ask for this job." Lorna sighed. "I hate politics and politicians, but I'll do it because the Constitution calls for it, and I'm not going to put up with any nonsense. Timiko, call the JAG and ask him to be at the meeting tomorrow. In case any of them haven't read the appropriate articles or don't understand them, he can explain them in simple terms."

Bender smiled grimly. The members of the Directorate were accustomed to Ian Stevens, who'd always dealt with them more gently than their usually inept and occasionally stupid attempts at political gamesmanship deserved. Now, they were dealing with the Iron Maiden, and Charlie was sure a few of them were going to come away from the first meeting with severely bruised egos.

* * *

Thomas Perry heaved a sigh as the door chime sounded. *Another expression of sympathy*, he thought, *or someone else checking to make sure I'm all right. As if I'm likely to be all right any time soon. Still, these people mean well.* He got up from his living room chair and went to the door, expecting another well-wisher with the usual, awkward platitudes. He opened the door and drew a sharp breath when he found Lorna Greenwood standing there, with two Marines a discreet distance behind her in the corridor.

"Tom…" She was at a loss for words, but the pain in her expression spoke volumes.

"Lor…Admiral…please, come in."

She motioned for the Marines to wait outside, then stepped into the apartment and let him close the door. *He looks…old…and tired*, she decided. Perry was in his early seventies, but he had always looked much younger. He was an active and vigorous man who'd showed no inclination of retiring from his position as the Lunar Free State's director of education. He was Teacher Tom to a whole generation of Lunar school children and had built the LFS education system practically from scratch in just ten years. But now…Lorna remembered that someone once said the most terrible thing that can happen to a parent is to outlive his or her children. Tom's wife had died fifteen years before, and Carla had been their only child.

"Tom…I'm so sorry…" she began. "I should have been able to protect her. It was my responsibility to protect all of them."

"It wasn't your fault, Admiral. It wasn't anyone's fault. They had to try for peaceful contact, but once the aliens opened fire, there was nothing any of you could do. Carla was a person of peace. Even if someone told her ahead of time the aliens were going to kill her, she would have still wanted to make peace with them."

"I know…but I felt so *helpless*. And I loved her *so much*…" Tears came again to Lorna's eyes, and Perry stepped forward and put his arms around her. She was a good bit taller than he was, and she rested her cheek on the top of his head as she returned the embrace.

"I know you did, Admiral, and I know she loved you. At first, I didn't care for the idea of you and Carla together. But after a while, I started thinking of you as my daughter-in-law. Now that she's gone, I hope you won't mind if I think of you as another daughter."

Even as he said it, he realized the woman in his arms, his daughter's lover, his de-facto daughter-in-law, was now the chief executive of the Lunar Free State.

Lorna smiled sadly through her tears and stepped back. "I'd be honored, Tom. But I need you to call me by my name. I don't have any family of my own, and I need *someone* to talk to who doesn't call me admiral with a capital *A* all the time."

"Of course, Lorna," he replied.

* * *

The members of the Directorate were assembled in a large chamber when Lorna arrived. All of them stood as she entered with the Judge Advocate General at her side.

Vice Admiral Harold Wexler had been a distinguished American jurist for most of his career, and his name had been mentioned as a possible candidate for the U.S. Supreme Court, but that had been before the Big War, and the U.S. president had not been inclined to appoint a conservative justice. Instead, Wexler had been recruited by the Lunar Free State to serve as JAG, and the challenge had appealed to him. The LFS Constitution had much in common with that of the United States, but the differences in government and legal structure were profound. He had made a whole new career out of studying Lunar law and legal philosophy. He was justifiably regarded as the best judicial mind in the LFS, and his rulings were the last word in Lunar legal matters. He wasn't just a member of the Supreme Court; on Luna, he *was* the Supreme Court. He was also the head of an independent branch of the Lunar government. The JAG was one of two officer positions—the chief executive being the other—whose appointment or removal had to be approved by an eighty percent majority of the Directorate. As a practical matter—again, like the chief executive—once appointed, the JAG served until retirement.

Lorna motioned the grey-haired jurist to a chair at the head table, which was reserved for the chief executive and any staff officers she brought with her. Today, Wexler and Timiko Yamamoto were the only non-Directorate people in attendance, though Charlie Bender, a director in his own right as well as a member of Lorna's staff, also sat at the head table—as he had always done when Ian Stevens was chief executive.

The remaining members sat behind a large semicircular table facing Lorna. There were four empty seats, two of which had belonged to Kim Yong Sam and Dr. McGuinness. Lorna had been a member of the Directorate for the past ten years, but now her chair at the table was empty. The remaining empty seat—the sight of which brought an unseen tear to her eye—had belonged to Carla Perry.

"Take your seats, please," Lorna directed as she sat down for the first time in the chief executive's chair. "I've called this meeting to advise you of the status of our dealings with the aliens and to acquaint you with my command philosophy and my intended actions as chief executive."

"Before you do that, Admiral," one of the directors interrupted, standing to claim the floor, "we of the Directorate feel there is a legal matter that needs to be discussed."

The Directorate normally met only once a quarter, and Lorna had had few dealings with the non-fleet directors. It took her a moment to recall the speaker's name: *Dr. Devereaux...Lawrence Devereaux, Chief Warrant Officer, Director of Information Technology.*

"When you say we, Doctor, does that mean there is unanimous agreement on the matter?" Lorna looked around the room and found several directors nodding. A few others shook their heads, but most of them looked a bit puzzled. "From the reaction," she continued, "I gather there is *not* any such agreement. But very well, Doctor Devereaux, make your point."

"Thank you, Admiral." Devereaux looked around the table for signs of support and apparently found it from a few members. "We...er, several of us, that is, feel your appointment to the position of chief executive was hasty and ill-considered."

A rumble of confusion mixed with dissent arose from most of the group, but one or two directors made sounds of agreement.

Encouraged, Devereaux raised his voice and pressed on. "We feel the best interests of the Lunar Free State would be served, Admiral, if your talents were utilized in the continued command of the battle fleet. We believe the chief executive position should be given to someone of a less...*militaristic* demeanor. Furthermore—"

"*That will be all, Doctor*," Lorna commanded in a sharp tone that cut through the loud debate that had suddenly arisen among the directors.

"But..." Devereaux protested.

"I said *that will be all!*" Lorna stood and stared at Devereaux until he sat down. An uneasy silence fell over the room.

"Now then," she continued, in a quiet but firm voice that carried clearly in the silent chamber, "let me make something perfectly clear. I was not appointed to the position of chief executive. It was not given to me by anyone. I *became* the chief executive *automatically* upon the death of Admiral Stevens, and neither I nor any of you have anything to say about it. This is something that should be perfectly clear to anyone who has read the Lunar Constitution. But since there seems to be some question about it, I've invited the Judge Advocate General, Admiral Wexler, to explain the pertinent articles. Judge Wexler?"

"Thank you, Admiral." Wexler moved to the podium at the end of the head table. He produced bound copies of the Lunar Constitution and the Lunar Code of Military Justice, as well as the Code of Military Protocols, and held them up for all to see. "These, ladies and gentlemen, are the governing laws in this case. The Constitution takes precedence, followed by the LCMJ and the CMP. The Constitution, Article Five, Section Four, clearly states, 'In the event the chief executive dies or becomes incapacitated to the point of being unable to perform the duties of command, the next ranking commissioned officer shall immediately assume the position of acting chief executive, with automatic promotion to the commensurate rank, and shall continue in command for a period of *one standard year*, barring any of the following.'" He paused, like a teacher making sure he had the attention of an unruly class.

"'The aforesaid acting chief executive resigns voluntarily, dies, or becomes incapacitated to the point of being unable to perform the duties of command or is convicted by a court-martial of high treason, specifically for causing or conspiring to cause the death or incapacitation of the previous chief executive.'" He favored them with a sanguine smile. "It seems that our founders did not want assassination to become a legitimate method of succession to command.

"The article goes on to say that if the original chief executive recovers from incapacitation, he or she shall reassume the duties of command when able to do so, but that isn't relevant here. Admiral Stevens is dead and will not be returning, much as any of us might wish it were possible.

"Otherwise, if any of those conditions described in the article occur, the *next* ranking officer in the chain of command takes over as acting chief executive, to serve for whatever remains of the one-year term from the *original* chief executive's date of death or incapacitation.

"Let's talk about that one-year period. The Constitution provides that a chief executive duly appointed by the Directorate is immune from removal for one year, and the same protection has been specifically extended to the acting chief executive. The founders had faith in our selection of competent command officers and felt that a chief executive deserves at least a year to prove his or her ability to lead the nation. This isn't the USA, where a politician can get elected by being a slick liar with a bit of charisma. Anyone in the LFS who reaches flag rank does so based on proven command ability. I doubt any of you would question that in Admiral Greenwood's case."

Some of you might be stupid enough to do that, Charlie Bender mused, *but none of you have the guts to say it to her face.*

"There is, however," Wexler continued, "one action the Directorate *can* take during the one-year period, as specifically provided in this article, and that is to confirm the *acting* chief executive as the *permanent* chief executive. This can be done at any time by a two-thirds majority vote of the Directorate—the same as required to select a new chief executive, as opposed to removal or replacement of a chief executive, which requires an eighty percent vote. Note, however, that if you *do* confirm Admiral Greenwood, she would have a full year of immunity from removal beginning with the date of confirmation, and to replace her after that would require the aforementioned eighty percent vote of the Directorate. Please note that a two-thirds majority means two-thirds of *all current directors*—not just those attending the meeting at which the vote is cast. Of course, Admiral Greenwood would not have a vote in any action to confirm, remove, or replace herself.

"If you fail to confirm within the one-year period, the Constitution gives you thirty days after the end of that period to either confirm Admiral Greenwood or select a new permanent chief executive, and either action again requires a two-thirds majority. But if you are unable to muster that many votes for any one replacement candidate, then Admiral Greenwood will *automatically* become the permanent chief executive at the end of the thirty days.

"Of course, I don't need to remind you that a replacement can *only* be selected from commissioned officers of flag rank or the warrant officer executive ranks, whether you are selecting a replacement for an acting chief executive or a permanent one. Are there any questions about this?"

"I have a question…" The woman who rose from her chair was a slim, fashionably attractive master warrant officer whose uniform insignia proclaimed her to be an executive of Terra Corporation. Lorna knew her only slightly, but Moira Gardner had been mentioned as a possible successor to MWO Forsythe, who had died with the others aboard *Valkyrie*.

"Yes, Ms. Gardner?" Wexler recognized her.

"It has to do with the question of who is the next most senior officer, as specified in the Constitution. Why did command fall to Admiral Greenwood instead of Admiral O'Hara? It is my understanding that both were promoted to admiral on the same day—in fact, in the same set of orders."

"You are correct," Wexler said, "as is your assumption that seniority normally depends on rank and date of promotion. That's why all promotion orders are dated and time-stamped in Lunar Standard Time. Normally, length of service would be the next determining factor, but Admirals Greenwood and O'Hara are both original Lunar citizens, so they are presumed to have the same length of service. Both were here from the founding of the Lunar Free State. That leaves just one criterion, as specified in the Code of Military Protocol—the order in which they were listed on the promotion orders in question. The one listed first is presumed to be senior, and in this case, the promotions were listed alphabetically by last name."

There was a bit of commotion as the directors pondered that.

Then Devereaux leapt to his feet, his face red with rage. "Are you telling us that because G comes before O in the alphabet, we are going to be stuck with an uneducated, unqualified, war-mongering *lesbian* as our chief executive? That's unacceptable!"

A shocked silence fell over the group. *I was wrong,* Bender reflected. *At least one of them was stupid enough to open his mouth.*

The silence dragged on.

Then Lorna spoke. "Because of the nature of Directorate meetings," she said quietly, "the rules of military courtesy are usually relaxed. However, you, Dr. Devereaux, have stepped beyond the bounds. If I hear one more outburst of that nature, I will formally charge you with insubordination."

"You wouldn't dare," he snarled. "I'm a director."

"You're also a warrant officer, whereas I am a flag officer of the Fleet."

"You are an overbearing martinet who hasn't the slightest qualification to lead the nation. What's more, your perverted lifestyle has always been an embarrassment to the Lunar Free State—"

"Sergeant-at-Arms."

The four Marines in the corners of the room were so unobtrusive, the members of the Directorate tended to forget they were there. But now, their presence became painfully obvious.

"Yes, ma'am!" The young noncom in charge of the detail snapped to attention.

Devereaux froze, and his face paled as he suddenly realized Lorna was about to have him arrested.

"Admiral, please…" Gardner was on her feet.

Lorna held up her hand, and the Marines paused. "Ms. Gardner, you don't think I have just cause to bring charges against this man?"

"Yes, Admiral, of course you do. Mr. Devereaux's behavior is inexcusable, but he *is* a member of the Directorate." She glared at Devereaux. "Perhaps, if he sits down and behaves himself for the remainder of the meeting…of course, you may still choose to bring charges against him *after* the meeting is over."

Lorna sighed. "Simple military courtesy is the way we maintain order and civility in our society. I will not tolerate behavior of this sort from *anyone*, toward *any* senior officer. However, Ms. Gardner, your point is taken. Dr. Devereaux!"

The man's head snapped up.

"You may say anything you wish about me in private conversation. But you *will* show proper respect for my rank in public, or you *will* be taken out of here and thrown in the brig. *Is that clear, Chief Warrant Officer?*"

"Perfectly clear," Devereaux muttered, and he sat down with a surly look on his face. If he had any respect for Lorna, it didn't show in his voice.

But she decided to let it pass, lest Gardner and the others accuse her of persecuting the little bastard.

"Thank you, Admiral," Gardner said. "Now that we've gotten past that unpleasant episode, I think we need to return to the real question before the group."

"What question is that?" Lorna asked in a pleasant tone.

Charlie Bender had heard that tone in times past, usually just before the Iron Maiden ripped a bloody strip off some fumbling junior officer who desperately deserved it.

Gardner seemed not to notice. "Despite Mr. Devereaux's shocking comments, most of us think very highly of you, Admiral. But we feel we need your talents most in the job you do best—commanding the battle fleet. I would like to propose a motion for the Directorate. I move that we formally request your resignation as acting chief executive in favor of Admiral O'Hara."

"Second the motion!" Devereaux snarled, glaring his defiance at Lorna.

"In a bloody damned pig's eye!" Mick O'Hara was on his feet. "I'm an engineer, not a bloody head of state. _She_—" he pointed at Lorna "—is a better command officer than I am, and she's a damned sight better than any of you lot, who have never had to put your lives on the line for this nation of ours!"

Charlie Bender was amazed. He had never seen O'Hara react with such passion. The man sounded angry—and Charlie couldn't recall _ever_ having seen him angry. What was more, he hadn't realized Mick held Lorna in such high regard. _Maybe he's scared to death that they_ *might really make* him *chief executive. No…I think he really believes Lorna is the best person for the job. Hmmm. They go back a long way, and Mick's never married. I wonder if…* Charlie kicked himself out of his mental wandering, as Gardner told Admiral O'Hara—politely, of course—that he was out of order.

"No, Ms. Gardner, it's *you* who are out of order," Lorna told her coldly. "You can make motions until Hell freezes over, but I will *not* resign. Do you people think I *want* this job? The fact is, I'd be much happier commanding the Fleet, but I have a responsibility that I can't ignore. Admiral Stevens left me with this responsibility, even warned me years ago that it could fall on my shoulders someday. Despite Admiral O'Hara's protests to the contrary, I happen to think he'd make a fine chief executive. But it's not his responsibility. It's mine, and I'm not going to duck it and let it fall on someone else.

"A year from now—assuming we all live that long—you'll have your chance. Elect Admiral O'Hara to replace me, and I'll step aside with a smile. Until then, the subject is closed. Is that clear, or do you want to hear Judge Wexler explain it again?"

Most of the group reacted with sounds of agreement, though there was some grumbling from Devereaux, Gardner, and their supporters. Lorna was surprised to see Mick O'Hara get to his feet again.

"Admiral, *I* would like to say something," he announced.

"Admiral O'Hara, you're probably out of order as well," Lorna replied with a sigh, "but we've listened to everyone else, so go ahead and speak your piece."

O'Hara took a deep breath as he looked around the room. The rest of the group quieted down.

"Ladies and gentlemen, members of the Directorate," he began in a serious tone, "we're at a critical point. We have an alien race knocking on our door, and they are *not* coming in peace. Three of our most prominent world leaders have just been assassinated, including the man we all knew as the father of our country. We've just fought a battle that is probably the opening round of our first interstellar war. The nations of Earth—the same people who hated and scorned us ten years ago—will be looking to the Lunar Free State for leadership, and I don't think we can afford to have an *acting* leader who has less than our full support. I would like to make a motion that we confirm Admiral Greenwood as *permanent* chief executive *right now*...today...before we proceed with any further business."

"Mick, I don't think that's—" Lorna started to object.

"Second the motion!" It wasn't just one person; it was a chorus. Lorna might have expected support from Charlie Bender, Brigadier Kim, and Tom Perry, but to her surprise, the seconding voices also included Research Director Emil Julian, Doctor Sarah Wilkins, Luna's Surgeon General, and the Reverend Daniel DeForrest, S.J. The elderly Jesuit priest was an astrophysicist who balanced his scientific research with his duties as the Roman Catholic bishop of Luna. Despite his repeated insistence that he wanted nothing to do with politics or government, his Catholic flock and many non-Catholic friends kept electing him to the Directorate. Now, he regarded Lorna with a smile.

Gardner had also noticed. "Father DeForrest, I'm surprised at this. How can you—a man of the cloth—condone the selection of an officer whose...unconventional lifestyle is—"

"Is a matter between her and God," the priest said. "It is not for me to pass judgment. But I believe that when the time comes for

God to judge Admiral Greenwood, He'll give less weight to her 'unconventional lifestyle' than to that array of ribbons she's wearing. *He will know*, as all of *you* should know, that those decorations are a measure of honor, courage, and commitment to the highest ideals of the Lunar Free State. Now, all of you know I am a man of peace but, paradoxically, peace is something you sometimes have to fight for. We need a leader who knows how to do that."

Lorna hesitated. Accustomed to the rules of military command, she was not comfortable with parliamentary procedure.

"Judge Wexler," she appealed, "is this appropriate?"

"Actually," the jurist said, "it is about the *only* appropriate motion that could be proposed at this time. The Constitution states that the Directorate can vote to confirm you *at any time* during the one-year period. If the vote fails to confirm, however, that just means you continue as acting chief executive, and the issue can be raised again at another time. Any such vote will need to be formally recorded, and you might want to ask if anyone feels the need for a secret ballot."

"I request that the ballot be secret," Gardner was quick to respond.

"We've never had a secret ballot in this chamber," Charlie Bender said, almost casually.

Gardner rose to respond, but Lorna cut in.

"No, Admiral Bender, she's right. The Directorate has never had to vote on a matter like this before. I think a secret ballot is appropriate, under the circumstances."

It took a while to get it sorted out. Lorna directed Mike, the Lunar AI who served as recording secretary at Directorate meetings, to display the question on each director's screen: *Should Acting Chief*

Executive Lorna Greenwood be confirmed to the permanent position of chief executive, with the permanent rank of fleet admiral? The directors were asked to vote yea or nay through their interface pads, and the AI was told to tally the results but not to keep a record of the individual votes.

The voting took only a moment. Of the twenty-one directors, sixteen voted to confirm, four voted not to confirm, and one abstained. It came as a surprise to Lorna, who had not really expected to be confirmed. *Ian may have been right,* she thought. *I always judge myself more harshly than others judge me.* And now, she realized, she truly had stepped into Ian Stevens' shoes. It was a sobering thought.

* * *

TerraNova City, Luna

"*Don't* get up, Commander," Lorna ordered as Amy Ling started to reach for the crutches leaning against her reclining chair.

"Yes, ma'am" All the same, Ling brought the chair to an upright position, lowered her cast-encased leg to the floor, and popped a sharp salute.

"At ease, Amy." Lorna returned the salute, and Ling felt a small thrill at the admiral's use of her first name. "How are you feeling?"

"I'm fine, ma'am. The doctors say the bone regen therapy is going well, and the cast comes off tomorrow. After that, they tell me I'm in for a couple of weeks of physical therapy, then light duties for a while, but…"

"But…?" Lorna lifted a quizzical eyebrow.

"But I'm ready to go back on duty, ma'am. I *need* to get back on duty, only…I don't know what duty the fleet has for me after what happened to my ship."

Lorna saw the glisten of an unshed tear in the corner of Ling's eye. "Amy…"

"I should have *been* there, ma'am—on *my* bridge, with *my crew*. I feel so—"

"I know," Lorna interrupted her. "I know because I've been there and done that—lost people and ships under my command. You know what I'm talking about. You were with us in the Chinese war when we lost *Starflame* and *Starfire* and so many good people. You ask yourself, 'Why do I deserve to live, when so many others died?' But the truth is, Commander, if you had been there, it would have made *no difference* to the outcome. No difference, except I would have lost another good officer, and that's something I can't afford right now.

"In any case," she continued, "I need to know when you are going to be ready for duty—I mean one hundred percent. And don't bother to tell me what the doctors say. I've already talked to them. I want to know what *you* say."

"I think," Ling replied with a small smile, "I can shave a few days off the doctors' estimate for the rehab therapy and skip the light duty part altogether, ma'am."

Lorna suppressed a smile. She *had* talked to the doctors, and after admitting they were being conservative, they had reluctantly given her a timetable that pretty much agreed with what Ling was telling her. "Very well, Commander. In that case, here are your orders." She reached into the folder she was carrying and handed Ling a sheet printed on textured paper that resembled parchment.

Ling felt a lump in her throat. Per Lunar Fleet tradition, only certain kinds of orders arrived in that format—orders that one might wish to hang on the wall in a frame for all to see. She felt pleased with herself that her hands didn't shake as she looked at the document and began to read. After verifying the orders were, indeed, addressed to her, she skimmed past the formal opening language and moved down the page until her eyes locked on the most important part: "…assume command of the Lunar Fleet ship as yet uncommissioned and designated as BC-04, currently in final construction phase at Fleet Shipyard orbiting Luna…" She looked up at the Admiral in wide-eyed surprise. "BC-04…the new *battlecruiser*?"

"We *were* going to call her *Amazon*," Lorna said, "but that was before the aliens came. She'll be commissioned LFS *Valkyrie*."

"Admiral…I don't know what to say." Ling's voice was choked with emotion.

"You haven't heard the bad news, Amy. She's going to be my new flagship, and that will make you my flag captain. You'd better read the rest of the orders."

Ling glanced back down at the parchment and found the line at the bottom of the page that read: "… promoted accordingly to the permanent rank of commodore."

"Commodore? But Admiral, there are other officers who—"

"There were only three commanders senior to you—Pete Wilson, Jeff Jones, and Robin Torrey. We lost Wilson and most of his crew with *Cherokee*. Torrey just moved up to command *Apache*, and I've decided to leave her there for the moment. She'll be promoted to commodore and will be in line for the *next* battlecruiser we build. As for Jones, he'll be moving up as well—taking over command of *Athena*, also with promotion to commodore.

"We're splitting the fleet into two battle groups. We did that briefly after the Chinese war, but we didn't have enough ships to really make it work. Now, we have the ships, and even more under construction. I will retain overall fleet command for now and will also command Battle Group One, which we have designated the Home Fleet. I intend to hold that group close to Earth and Luna, as our reserve force and last line of defense. That will also allow me to attend to my other responsibilities. Tom Sakura is moving up to vice admiral, and he'll take command of Battle Group Two, with *Athena* as his flagship.

"Amy, this may seem like a big jump for you. You've never commanded anything larger than *Starblade*, and you hardly got the chance to settle in with the old *Valkyrie*. But you distinguished yourself in the Chinese war, you've got over ten years' command experience, and your record is impeccable. *I* think you are up to the challenge. Do you?"

"I'll do my best, ma'am," Ling said. "But, begging the admiral's pardon, the idea of being *your* flag captain is a bit…intimidating."

"Well, perhaps." Lorna returned the smile. "You should have a talk with Tommy Sakura—before those new vice admiral's stars go to his head. He's the only one in the fleet who's had any experience in that job. In the meantime, *Commodore*, your first order of business is to get yourself back in good health. Barring any major screw-ups by the yard people, your new ship commissions in less than thirty days."

* * *

Aboard the Mekota Sphere, L5 LaGrange Point

"Ask them how they compensate for delta-wave feedback."

Rock Bartley repeated the question, but the towering alien only gave the curious three-limbed shrug that indicated lack of understanding.

"I don't think that translates, sir," Bartley told the engineering lieutenant. Seeing his look of frustration, she tried to explain the problem. "Sir, these creatures are used to dealing with less sophisticated humans...like me, for example. The translator doesn't seem to deal very well with technical stuff. Try explaining it in terms that a Marine grunt would understand. If *I* can figure out what you're trying to ask them, chances are they will, too."

It had been a long day and Bartley was tired, but even if they called it quits right then, she had to hike the long way back through the alien ship to *Hawking's* boarding tube, then go through the de-contamination process, before she could strip off her pressure suit. After that, a hot shower would be in order, but she'd probably skip that and collapse into her bunk for a few hours of sleep.

"Okay," the engineer said, taking a deep breath. "When you generate a heavy gravity field, the field coils tend to, well, think of it as a vibration whose frequency varies with the intensity of the field. We call that the delta wave..."

Bartley sighed and tried to pay attention. *Been a long day, and it isn't over yet.*

* * *

TerraNova City, Luna

"I appreciate your coming to see me, Father."

"I would hardly refuse a dinner invitation from the chief executive, Admiral," Father DeForrest replied. "I didn't expect a *private* dinner, however."

"I should have mentioned it," Lorna said, "but I wanted to talk to you in your professional capacity."

"As an astrophysicist or a priest?" he asked with a smile.

"The latter."

Dinner conversation had been mostly small talk, though Lorna had made a point of thanking the priest for his support in the Directorate. Now, she led the way into the spacious room she still thought of as Ian's library for after-dinner coffee. The walls were lined with bookshelves filled with classic volumes printed on paper and exquisitely bound. In an era when most people read books only in electronic format, the library had an aura of timeless permanence, reminding her that the former occupant of these quarters had been a very unusual man. Ian had had a grand sense of history, and the books were only one of his many anachronisms.

Like Charlie Bender, Ian had also been a gun collector and had infected Lorna with his appreciation of the weapons of the past and his enjoyment of the shooting sports—sports that were considered barbaric and politically incorrect in most places back on Earth. Lorna and Charlie had spent many enjoyable hours with Ian on the shooting range, and in his will, he'd left his entire collection to her except for a few specific guns he'd bequeathed to Charlie. Some of the firearms remained on display in the library, but Lorna had been surprised to find that Ian kept one of his favorite handguns—with two magazines of ammunition—in a desk drawer in his office at Lunar

Command. She left it there as a reminder of the man she'd admired so much and whose large shoes she was now expected to fill.

At least, she thought, *the library doesn't have many reminders of Carla…as if I need anything to remind me.*

"I would imagine you've been in this room more often than I have, Father. I understand you often played chess with Ian."

"Yes, I did," DeForrest said. "He occasionally let me beat him, which is more than I can say for Mike, my usual opponent. If I ever win a game against *him,* I'll be forced to conclude that our marvelous AI has finally learned the meaning of 'mercy.'"

Lorna smiled. She knew another of Father DeForrest's favorite pastimes was debating theology with Mike, and that the priest had once expressed the opinion that Mike had a soul.

She thought about her recent conversation with Mike and Val. A soul? Perhaps, but AIs were unquestionably living creatures. They even had a desire to procreate.

Lorna took one of the comfortable high-backed chairs and motioned for the priest to take another. She waited until coffee was served and the steward left the room.

"Father, I wanted to thank you for Carla's memorial service. It was beautiful."

"It was the least she deserved," he said. "Carla was a very special person, known and loved by the entire nation."

"Yes, she was." A tear formed in the corner of Lorna's eye, and she brushed it away. "She was a Catholic, but she often went to other religious services on Luna. She used to say, 'God doesn't care *where* you go to talk to Him.' I wish I had gone with her more often. I'm not an atheist, Father. I just can't accept the idea that any religion has a lock on the absolute truth about God and the Universe. I believe it's more about how you live your life than where you say your prayers."

"I don't disagree with that," he told her gently.

"Then you'll understand why I wanted to talk to you. Carla was a Catholic, a faithful follower of the Church since she was a child. I know the Catholic Church—and for that matter, most *other* churches—wouldn't condone the kind of relationship we had. I also know it bothered her. She used to say we were living in sin and would probably burn in Hell for it. She would say it lightly, but it bothered her all the same. I used to shrug it off—I'm not even sure there is such a place as Hell—and, being the swashbuckling space ranger that I am, I assumed I would buy the farm out in space someday while Carla would live to a ripe old age and have plenty of time to make her peace with God. But it didn't work out that way, and now that she's gone, it's been haunting me. Tell me, Father, is it possible God is so vengeful He would condemn Carla to eternal Hell because of my love for her—because I led her into a life of sin?"

She spoke quite calmly, as if asking a purely philosophical question, but Daniel DeForrest, S.J. was a sensitive man, and he heard the pain she did not express. He pondered how to answer and, in the end, took the simplest approach. "No. It's not possible. And *that* is my professional opinion as a priest.

"As I said in the Directorate," he continued, "I believe God will judge us on the fullness of our lives, and Carla was one of the most giving and caring people I have ever known. I also believe you loved each other and that God will judge *love* to be far more important than anything related to *sex*. I believe in Heaven and Hell—it's a requirement in my profession, you know—and I believe there are people who deserve to go to Hell. It's not my call to judge them, but I think

I know which way God will rule on the case. I think I know how he has ruled on Carla, as well. I believe she is in Heaven and that you, my dear Admiral, will join her there someday."

"I don't know about that, Father. I've done some pretty nasty things in my life. I've been responsible for the deaths of a lot of people—and now for the deaths of some creatures whose place in the universe we don't even know."

"Ah, yes…killing." He grimaced. "People kill for many reasons. Some even kill in the name of religion, and that is one of mankind's greatest perversions of faith. But if a mother kills to protect her children, is she to be damned for it? Are the soldiers who fought against Hitler in the last century—and put an end to the Holocaust—to be damned for it? To my knowledge, Admiral, you've never killed other than to protect your nation, your people, and those you love from harm. With the aliens, you may have wanted to avenge Carla's death, but you were also acting to protect the people of Earth and Luna. You were our only defense against creatures who were perfectly willing to kill *us*.

"You're a good soldier, Admiral, and any good soldier is troubled by the killing he or she has to do. If it ever *stops* troubling you, you might have cause to worry about your soul."

"I don't believe it ever will, Father," she said. "I once told Tom Perry, a good soldier prays for peace while preparing for war, and I believe that. But you've taken a load off my mind. What happens to me is a matter for me and God to work out, but your assurance that Carla is…where she deserves to be…well, it means a lot to me."

"You're a good person, Admiral. Even now, you're more concerned about Carla than about you, and that's what love is truly about. If you keep on the way you are going, I believe you'll be with her in Heaven someday. But forgive me if I hope, for the sake of the rest of us, that you don't go to join her anytime soon."

* * * * *

Chapter Twelve

TerraNova City, Luna

"Admiral, we meet face to face at last!"

"Not exactly face to face, Mr. President, with a few hundred thousand kilometers between us, but I appreciate the chance to talk to you directly."

Lorna's tone was relaxed and pleasant, and Blackthorne saw that as a hopeful sign. He decided to take the initiative.

"I'm sorry we didn't get a chance to meet when I visited the Moon, Admiral. I was told you were away on fleet maneuvers. Quite frankly, after those remarks attributed to me, you had just cause to avoid me."

Attributed? Lorna thought. *You made those remarks on national television.* Nonetheless, she waved her hand in dismissal. "You've already apologized, Mr. President, and your apology was accepted. Besides, Admiral Stevens seemed to have gotten rather fond of you in recent years, and he told me I should not judge you by your political exterior."

"I will miss Ian," Blackthorne said wistfully. "He was a good man."

"Yes, he was, and we of the Lunar Free State appreciate the fine things you've said about him since his death."

"It was the least I could do. Let me also express my condolences for the loss of your...um, of your...of Admiral Perry."

Blackthorne was obviously embarrassed by his inability to find the right word to describe the relationship, and his embarrassment, more than anything else, convinced Lorna his sentiments were sincere.

"Thank you, Mr. President," she replied quietly.

There was a moment of silence which Blackthorne was reluctant to break.

Finally, Lorna drew a breath and moved on to the reason for the call. "Mr. President, I hate to impose on you while you're still recovering from your illness, but you've officially resumed your duties, and there is a new development we should discuss. I also want to make you an offer I think will interest you. First, we've become aware the alien survivors are dying."

"Really? Dying from what?"

"Starvation, it seems. The aliens don't ingest food the way we do. They absorb nutrients like plants, through a root system. In any case, there's a thick liquid on most of the decks in their ship that's actually their food supply."

"Did we contaminate it?"

"No. Apparently the aliens—and their food supply—are immune to Earth microorganisms. As far as we can determine, the reverse is also true. Nothing in their environment is harmful to humans. But their food supply needs to be recharged with nutrients and cleaned of waste products, and the equipment that does that was damaged beyond repair during the battle. Our scientists thought about synthesizing the stuff, but that requires some complex organic nutrients—proteins and amino acids unlike any on Earth. With experimentation, we might be able to produce laboratory samples, but not the quantities the aliens need—at least not in time to do any good. Our people think they can remove the harmful waste products so the aliens won't die of food poisoning, but even that may only keep them alive for another week or so."

"It's been a month since the battle, Admiral. Why are we just finding out about this now?"

Lorna shrugged. "I asked the same question, Mr. President. Simply put, we didn't know enough about alien physiology to recognize what was happening. We still wouldn't know if the aliens hadn't mentioned it."

"Hmm," Blackthorne mused. "You know, Admiral, a lot of people here on Earth won't be sorry to see every last one of them dead."

"I know. I presume you heard Akiro's speech at the Asian Union conference."

"Yes, I did: 'Now we know how the Americans must have felt after Pearl Harbor.' That's heavy stuff from the Japanese. And now they want to start building *warships,* after almost a hundred years of pacifism."

"Well." She shrugged. "It's unlikely the Mekota will just forget about us. They'll be back, maybe with a full-scale attack force. We can use all the help we can get, and Japan has the industrial and economic strength to build a sizeable fleet. But that brings me to the other reason for my call."

* * *

B lackthorne smiled. *And now here it comes.* "Ah, yes. You were going to make me an offer of some kind."

"Yes, Mr. President. I'm going to offer you a

chance to enhance America's presence in space beyond that of any other nation—except the LFS, of course. I presume it would also enhance your personal prestige as president."

And my prospects for re-election, Blackthorne thought. *She may be a military type, but, at least, she's got some of Stevens' grasp of political matters. I'm leading the polls right now, but not enough to get complacent about it. And after that heart problem, the bastards are starting to say I'm not as young and vigorous as I used to be.* "I'm listening, Admiral."

"The U.S. has the second-largest space fleet, and you've built a couple of ships that are almost as big as our *Apache*-class heavy cruisers. But gravity-drive technology puts Luna in a different league than everyone else. Your people are working on that, and you'll probably have it in a year or two, but the aliens may not give us that much time. So, we are prepared to share that technology with you."

Blackthorne struggled to suppress his excitement, and his natural skepticism helped. "In exchange for what, Admiral?"

"Five hundred nuclear warheads—your miniaturized Mark Nine model, if you please."

"Admiral," Blackthorne replied cautiously, "I don't know whether to be thrilled by your offer or stunned by your asking price. What makes you think we've got five hundred warheads to give away?"

"You have at least three times that number. At the time of the Chinese War, you had more warheads than launch vehicles. Per your treaty with the Russians, you decommissioned your Titan VII missiles, but the warheads went back into storage, and our intelligence indicates they were *not* destroyed in the war. Mr. President, we can build our own nuclear warheads. We have all the technical data on the Mark Nine. But unlike a fusion space drive, a fusion warhead needs a fission reaction for a trigger. It takes tons of uranium ore to produce a few grams of plutonium, and that means it will take a long time for us to refine enough for that many warheads. About as long as it will take *your* people to figure out the gravity drive."

Blackthorne knew she was right. *Damn! I wish my intelligence people were that good.* Still, he kept his face impassive. "Well, I don't know, Admiral…"

"Mr. President, we learned some important things from the battle. While the aliens had some success stopping conventional missiles, their defense systems were totally inadequate against gravity-drive birds. Also, they can absorb a lot of punishment from beam weapons and conventional explosives, but it only takes one nuclear warhead to spoil their day. If both the US and the LFS have nuclear-tipped gravity-drive missiles, we stand a lot better chance of handling anything they send our way, but right now, neither of us have that capability.

"In addition," she told him, "we learned that those big alien ships are capable of accelerations on the order of forty gravities. With fusion drives and your present inertial compensators, your ships can only do about thirty. In other words, in a running fight, only LFS warships can keep up with them."

Blackthorne had already decided to agree to the terms, but he didn't want to appear too eager. "All that's true, Admiral, but how will other nations react if they find out we've supplied you with nukes and what you've given us in return?"

"It's an emotional issue, Mr. President," she said. "Nukes are obsolete as weapons to be used against targets on Earth. Kinetic strikes do as much damage with no radioactive contamination. As for the proliferation of nukes in space, there wasn't anything out there big enough to be worth hitting with a nuke until the aliens came along.

"My people tell me the French are closer to gravity-drive technology than you are. They may have a working prototype within a year, but their fleet isn't large enough to make a difference against the Mekota. If you're concerned about international reaction, the exchange can be conducted in secret. The important thing is that we do it now, before we're up to our elbows in aliens."

* * *

Area 51, Nevada

Having been spared in the limited nuclear exchange of World War III, the military base at Groom Lake, Nevada—also known as Area 51—was still America's Skunk Works for the development of top-secret weaponry. But this time, U.S. military, scientific, and engineering people were gathered there in a secured hangar to examine someone else's technology. LFS *Trailblazer* was not a particularly impressive ship, but it had something no U.S. spacecraft could match—a gravity drive.

A hush fell over the group as an LFS officer stepped to the podium set up in front of the ship.

"Ladies, gentlemen, I am Lieutenant Commander John Morris, an engineer in the service of the Lunar Free State. My specialty is propulsion systems, and I'm here to acquaint you with gravity drive technology."

* * *

LFS *Apache*, The Asteroid Belt

"All right, boys and girls," Commodore Robin Torrey told her bridge crew, "it's crunch time. No more dummy warheads, no more simulations. Weapons status, Mr. Carson?"

"All systems green, ma'am. Target acquired. Tube one is hot."

"Very well. Fire tube one."

Apache shivered slightly as the missile tube's mass drivers hurled the bird toward the target, a barren asteroid 10,000 kilometers ahead, whose primary virtue was that it offered approximately the same targeting signature as a Mekota warship. The missile streaked toward it under 900 gravities of acceleration.

The last few milliseconds were critical. Detonation of a nuclear device is not an instantaneous event, and the missile was closing at an incredible rate of speed. A millisecond too soon and the warhead would detonate too far from the target to do much damage. A millisecond too late and it would smash itself against the target without producing a nuclear yield. The warhead's American designers had planned for a much slower delivery, and LFS engineers had had to design a better rate-of-closure system and rewrite the triggering software. Tests with conventional warheads had produced detonations between twenty and forty meters from the target's surface, but this was the real thing. *Apache's* Tactical Officer held his breath.

A brilliant fireball flared in the forward viewscreen as the warhead produced its expected 30-megaton yield.

"Detonation at…I make it twenty-seven meters' separation, ma'am. Target is…well, all I see is a lot of small rocks moving away at various rates."

"Yesss!" Robin Torrey hissed, and the bridge crew broke into cheers.

* * *

LFS *Valkyrie*, TransLuna Shipyards

"Captain on the bridge!"

Amy Ling felt the special rush she always got at the sound of those words—at least when they referred to *her*. "Carry on, people," she ordered and made her way to the captain's chair with a little assistance from the cane she was carrying. *Another day or two, and I'll be able to get rid of this thing,* she told herself, *and good riddance!*

Her leg and hip had healed well, and none too soon, as *Valkyrie* would soon cast off from the docks and begin her space trials. The battlecruiser had been commissioned ten days earlier, the first of her crew had come aboard, and the powerful warship had come to life. Ling had just returned from a flag briefing on Luna and, despite the occasional twinge in her leg, had taken the long route to the boarding tube, the one that took her along the shipyard's observation deck and gave her a grand view of her new command.

Bathed in the glow of the dockyard floodlights, *Valkyrie* was an impressive sight. Now that her power systems were up, the gleaming white 620-meter hull was accented by the flashing blue strobes of her mooring lights. Ling noted with approval that the hull artwork, hallmark of an LFS warship, had been completed. It was the same artwork worn by the original *Valkyrie,* resized to fit the new ship's larger hull—a forty-meter-high rendering of the mythical Norse warrior maiden, astride a winged horse, with gleaming broadsword raised high above her head. The image had been taken from the work of the turn-of-the-century artist Boris Vallejo, best known for his representations of beautiful women in heroic fantasy settings. *She certainly is beautiful,* Ling reflected, *but there's nothing sultry about her.* Long, golden hair streamed from beneath the Valkyrie's helmet, but her curvaceous body was well-muscled, and her finely sculpted face wore a look of grim determination. The Valkyries, Ling recalled, were the warrior handmaidens of the Norse god Odin. They chose the heroes to be slain in battle and carried them off to Valhalla.

Is it my imagination, Ling mused, *or does she bear a noticeable resemblance to Admiral Greenwood?* It was probably just coincidence, she decided—the Admiral was still a girl when Vallejo had completed this work of art.

Besides her beautiful new ship, Ling was still getting used to having an AI at her personal beck and call. Val had been transferred to the new ship from LFS *Athena.* After a long discussion with Mike and Val, Admiral Greenwood had lifted the moratorium on new AI systems. *Athena* would be equipped with the first new system, to be named Anna, and Mike and Val would be charged with educating the new AI. Both existing AIs had expressed enthusiasm, but Val's final comment had been the deciding factor in Greenwood's decision, as she told the Admiral she'd "always wanted a daughter."

If ever we needed proof they really are living entities, Ling thought, shaking her head.

* * *

As Amy Ling admired her ship from the dockside gallery, others were admiring the Lunar fleet from space. USS *Chicago* cruised slowly along the 20-kilometer length of the shipyard, en route to a docking slip at the far end. There, she would receive a major refit that would make her the first American warship equipped with a gravity-drive system and full internal gravity. Her crew would be trained to operate and maintain the new systems and were looking forward to spending their off-duty time in TerraNova, which was reputed to be an outstanding liberty port.

"Excuse me, Commander Morris, sir…" Petty Officer Johnson and several enlisted ratings were off watch and were standing with the Lunar officer at the observation blister near *Chicago's* main engineering section. "What's with the artwork on the sides of your ships, sir?"

"Those are representations of the ship's namesake, Johnson. That big baby you're looking at is our newest battlecruiser, LFS *Valkyrie*. And that one coming up next—with the Viking warrior toting a battle axe—is the heavy cruiser *Norseman*."

"Hey!" one of the ratings exclaimed. "That one over there looks kinda like a brother I used to know in St.Louis…"

Morris chuckled. "That would be *Zulu*—another heavy cruiser— and the picture is an authentic representation of a nineteenth-century African warrior, right down to the style of spear he's carrying."

"Even the smaller ones have them," Johnson noticed. "What's that one down there, with the flaming sword in front of the big starburst emblem?"

"LFS *Starblade*—a destroyer."

"I still like the babe on the horse, man. She's hot," another rating said.

"Be careful what you say about that," Morris cautioned them. "We take pride in our ships and the symbols that represent them. *Valkyrie's* crew might get upset if you refer to her as a babe on a horse."

"So, how do we know which people belong to which ship? Do they wear ship tags like we do?" another rating asked, pointing to the emblem on his shoulder that bore the American flag and the legend *USS Chicago*.

"Yes, they do," Morris said, "but their shoulder patches will have the same artwork you see on the side of the ship, as well as the ship's name."

"So," Johnson told the group, "if you see a guy wearing a patch with a babe on a horse, don't make smart remarks about a babe on a horse. But, sir, what's the point of putting the picture on the side of the ship?"

"Oh, just something for morale, a little *esprit de corps*—like the nose art they used to put on airplanes back in World War II. And it's also a message. If you boys remember your American history, back in the time of the Revolutionary War, they had a flag with a rattlesnake and the legend *Don't Tread On Me* on it."

"I get it," Johnson said. "You mess with the *Norseman*, you get the axe."

"Something like that," Morris said.

"But who's going to see it, sir? I mean, in a space battle, you're usually a few hundred miles from the enemy."

"Well," Morris said, "*some* of the enemy might get to see it…just before they get boarded by LFS Marines."

"Yeah." One of the ratings laughed. "Like, 'If you're close enough to see this, you're *screwed*…'"

"But the important thing," Morris continued, "is that *our* people get to see it and take pride in what it represents."

"Hey, I like it," another rating joined in. "It sure beats plain old battleship grey with a number on the side, like we got."

* * *

TerraNova City, Luna

Rock Bartley was enjoying a well-earned ten-day leave and her first chance to see the sights of TerraNova. After joining up, she had gone directly from boot camp to combat training at Farside base, then on to advanced combat training on Mars. Then the aliens had arrived, and she'd been sent directly to *Stardancer*. After the battle, she'd spent over a month aboard the alien ship.

It had been a tedious assignment. LFS *Hawking,* their only retreat from the alien environment, had been overcrowded and lacking in recreational facilities. After they got the alien ship back to the L5 point, fleet engineers had attached a habitat module with more space and a few amenities, but Bartley had been too busy to enjoy them. As one of the few women in the quarantine group, she'd spent long hours escorting the male scientists and engineers, acting as their go-between with the aliens, who'd refused to communicate with anyone who wasn't female. *Talk about some hardcore bitches.*

Apparently, she'd done her work well, communicating the egg-heads' questions to the aliens even when she hadn't understood the subject matter. She'd needed a lot of patience with the science types, getting them to explain what they wanted to know in simple terms so she could ask the aliens a simple question and get a simple answer. Her reward had been more work, as the brainy types came to regard her as the best communicator available and began to request her specifically to deal with the most difficult issues.

But all that was over now. The last of the Turnips—as the Marines called the aliens, after hearing the scientists say they were more like plants than animals—had finally died. The doctors had poked Bartley, prodded her, and taken specimens from just about every part of her body, but they'd finally declared her healthy and free of alien bugs—clear for release from quarantine.

Not everyone was so lucky. Jimmy White Feather had torn his spacesuit aboard the alien ship, exposing himself directly to the environment. It didn't seem to have had any ill effect, but the medics had taken no chances. They'd hustled him into an isolation cell in the habitat, and he was still getting poked and prodded when Bartley departed for Luna.

Since she was on leave, Bartley wasn't required to wear her Alpha dress uniform, but her civilian clothes were back in California and wouldn't have been appropriate in TerraNova anyway. Until now, she hadn't had the money or opportunity to buy a leisure outfit, the off-duty uniform that was fashionable among LFS citizens. Such outfits usually had a design or logo that identified the wearer's unit or job assignment—a mark of pride Bartley likened to that of Earthworm sports fans, who wore clothing bearing the logo of their favorite team.

She planned to shop for leisure wear in the next few days, now that her account was flush with several months of back pay, but for now, she felt *good* about wearing her Alphas. Not as flashy as the Bravo uniforms—which practically shouted *"Marine!"* to anyone in the area and were reserved for formal occasions—Alphas were the standard uniform for Marines in non-shipboard, non-combat situations. They were also worn for ordinary dress-up occasions like worship services and social events, and they were the recommended travel uniform for LFS Marines on Earthside leave.

There were minor drawbacks to wearing Alphas. She would have to salute any duty-uniformed officers she ran across, but she didn't mind that. She would also have to maintain her uniform, which, for a

Marine, meant nothing short of impeccable. She didn't mind that either—she *wanted* to look sharp.

She had checked into the transient quarters in TerraNova Central, a free hotel for LFS personnel not assigned to Luna but visiting for whatever reason. The small but comfortable room they gave her was thoughtfully equipped with a full-length mirror, and she used it to check her appearance before going out.

She liked what she saw. The brand-new corporal's stripes rode proudly on her sleeve, and the shoulder patch of her new assignment—the rampant Valkyrie on her winged steed—marked her as a member of the new flagship's Marine contingent. She had logged in aboard the ship before taking leave, so she was entitled to wear the patch, but she had carefully tucked her old patch—a slender female figure in classic *Tai Chi* pose against a starburst background—away in her personal gear. It was a treasured memory of her brief time aboard LFS *Stardancer.*

She paused for a moment to admire the ribbons on the left breast of her tunic, now six in number. She had earned the Superior Marksmanship ribbon during advanced combat training. Then came the First Mekota Encounter ribbon, awarded to everyone who took part in the battle with the aliens. Next was the Lunar Cross, awarded to the Marines in the first wave to board the alien ship. It wasn't as prestigious as a Lunar Star and far short of a Medal of Honor, but she was proud of it. The Cross was only awarded for outstanding service in the face of the enemy. Next was the Meritorious Service Commendation ribbon, which had been awarded for her "outstanding and tireless service" as a communicator with the aliens. It was nice to know someone recognized her efforts. *Probably Colonel McGraw,* she thought. *I owe that woman a lot.*

She believed McGraw had also recommended her for promotion, though her squadmates insisted *that* was due to her status as a BadAss Turnip Killer. It would be a long time before anyone would let her forget her first encounter with the aliens.

She felt a little self-conscious about the last two ribbons on her chest since she hadn't earned them personally. The Sword of the Fleet and the Admiral's Cross were honors given to ships, not individuals. The Sword was the highest battle honor that could be given to a fleet ship, and the one Bartley was wearing had a tiny gold star that indicated it had been awarded twice. The Admiral's Cross was given annually to the most outstanding ship in the fleet, based on the admiral's inspection and the results of combat readiness trials. Hers had a tiny star cluster, indicating it had been awarded more than three times. Bartley's assignment was to a ship that had just been commissioned, but the new flagship had inherited these honors from her namesake, the original LFS *Valkyrie*. Had Bartley been assigned to a ship when the ship had earned such an honor, she would have been entitled to wear it permanently, but, in this case, she was entitled to wear the ribbons—was *required* to wear them, her new platoon sergeant told her—only as long as she was assigned to the new flagship. She had also been reminded that such ribbons could be awfully expensive—no one aboard the original *Valkyrie* had survived the encounter with the aliens, for which the ship had been awarded the second Sword.

Bartley settled the maroon beret—also bearing the gold-embroidered Valkyrie emblem—carefully onto her head. She checked her appearance once more, then headed out to take in the wonders of the city.

* * *

"Gentlemen, what do you think?" Ling asked her exec and chief engineer.

"Looks reasonable," Lieutenant Commander MacGregor replied, "but fitting the grav generators into forward engineering spaces will be a chore. I'm afraid it will delay our departure for trials."

"Fleet's expecting that—they've given us an extra five days, but it wouldn't bother me if you shave that to three."

"I'll do my best, ma'am," the engineer said, scratching his head as he pored over the diagrams. "At least the control runs look simple."

"What about relocating the forward sensor array?" Commander Swenson was skeptical.

"According to this, everything's modular," MacGregor said. "The assembly is being fabricated in the yard shops, and all we have to do is modify the dorsal structure to attach it. It has to be up there, so the forward grav field doesn't interfere with the sensors' field of view."

"Is this something they came up with after studying the alien ships?" Swenson wondered.

"No, I hear they started working on this before the aliens arrived." Ling hid her excitement. "It's intended to protect crews against particle radiation at velocities up to a significant fraction of light speed. It also covers a weakness in our armor. Most of the damage we took in the Chinese War was inflicted by weapons that came at us head-on."

"Are they going to retrofit the entire fleet, ma'am?" MacGregor asked.

"I'm told they are—in fact, other ships now in the yard will be getting them when we do. They'll do *Athena* and the *Apache*-class cruisers first. They're still working on ways to fit the generators into the smaller ships."

"I imagine so," MacGregor said, turning back to the diagrams. "Even with *Valkyrie*, I may need a big shoehorn to get these babies in."

* * *

B artley had seen all the sights she'd planned to except the shopping mall on the main concourse, and that was on her agenda for tomorrow. She had visited Memorial Hall, seen the names and pictures of those fallen in battle, and read about their heroism. She had gone to the Space Museum and marveled at the detailed models of every ship the LFS had ever built. She had smartly saluted the colors on the tail of LFS *Wanderer*, then stepped up to the hatch and saluted the watch officer, requesting permission to board. The young ensign had returned her salute and surprised her by giving her a guided tour of the small ship. She'd seen a flash of respect in his eyes as he'd read the ribbons on her chest, and she realized she had more decorations than a lot of the junior officers she'd saluted that day. *Not bad for a Marine with less than a year of service,* she reflected. She'd also seen a hint of envy on the ensign's face as he noted the Valkyrie on her shoulder. *Not everyone gets to serve on the flagship. I guess I'm a lucky girl.* Her days as a wandering biker in California were already fading from memory, and she decided she was exactly where she wanted to be.

She reached the last stop on her day's odyssey—one that her squadmates had told her was an absolute *must* for any Marine visiting TerraNova. Corporal J.'s Place was the oldest saloon on Luna, and the only one the Marines claimed as their own. Fleet people and others were welcome to come in and have a few drinks, but the décor and memorabilia on the walls clearly proclaimed it a *Marines* place, and Marines made up the bulk of its regular patrons.

Noting the Quarters Rules sign at the door, Bartley removed her beret and tucked it properly into her belt loop. She made her way to the bar and ordered a drink. The bartender was a cheerful-looking guy in his late thirties with only one arm, but he produced the requested drink with dexterity born of long practice. As he served her, he remarked that he hadn't seen Bartley there before.

"I haven't been in very long," she told him. "This is my first liberty on Luna."

"I see you've been to a few other places, though," he said, indicating the ribbons on her chest. "Enough to pay your dues for *this* club."

That was enough to get a conversation going, and Bartley learned the one-armed bartender, who introduced himself as Mike DaSilva, was the owner of the establishment. "Lost my arm during the Chinese War," he told her, "so I retired at the age of twenty-four and opened this place with help from the good old LFS. At the time, they were still trying to make TerraNova into a real city, and they offered incentives to guys like me to open businesses like this."

Bartley was surprised to learn DaSilva wasn't an ex-Marine; he'd been a fleet engineering technician. He had named the bar for Marine Corporal Jed Merrick, who had saved DaSilva's life aboard LFS *Starfire* and had died when *Starfire* was destroyed in the final action of the war.

"I just read about that," Bartley said. "I went to the *Starfire* Memorial, and I remember Corporal Merrick's name because he was the only Marine aboard when the ship was destroyed."

"And now you know the rest of the story," DaSilva told her. "Drink up. It's on the house for you tonight, Corporal."

The bar had gotten busier while they'd talked, and DaSilva moved away to help his other bartender, leaving Bartley to ponder all she had seen and heard. She was roused out of her reverie by a slurred voice beside her.

"Well, I'll be dipped in shit! 's the Babe on the Horse…"

She turned to find a man in an unfamiliar uniform staring at her. "I beg your pardon?" she asked.

Another man wearing the same uniform came up and grabbed the first by the shoulder. "Stow it, Gronski. You're in a bar full of LFS Marines, and you're gonna get all of our asses kicked," he muttered. He smiled hopefully at Bartley. "Please pardon him, ma'am. He's had too much to drink." He turned the other man around and pushed him in the direction of a table where two others wearing the same uniform were seated. Then he turned back to Bartley. "You're from that big battlecruiser up at the shipyard?"

"Right, *Valkyrie*. I've just been assigned to her. I'm Rock Bartley." She extended her hand. "And you are?"

"Oh, sorry. I'm Doug Johnson, petty officer, USS *Chicago*." Johnson took the offered hand and shook firmly.

"Oh, yeah, the American cruiser. I heard you guys were here. It was on the news last night. Welcome to Luna, Mr. Johnson."

"Thanks." The American relaxed a bit, then stiffened again as all three of his companions approached.

"See, I told ya!" the one called Gronski said to the others.

"Jeez, you're right. It's the Babe on the Horse!"

"You want to run that by me again?" Bartley asked with amusement.

"Umm…well, ma'am," Johnson stammered, "we got a look at your ship when we were coming in for docking…you know, with the picture of the…er…Valkyrie on her hull. No disrespect, ma'am, but the guys were just talking about how beautiful she is."

"Yeah. She's beau'ful," Gronski slurred.

"The ship? Or the Babe on the Horse?" Bartley chuckled, finally understanding what they were talking about.

"Both, ma'am. No offense…" Johnson called over his shoulder as he herded his companions back to the table.

Bartley smiled and shook her head as she finished her drink and stood up.

"Leaving so soon?" DaSilva called out.

"It's been a long day," she said, "but I'll be back, maybe tomorrow night. Thanks for the drink."

He waved and smiled, and she headed for the door. On her way out, she passed the table where the Americans were seated. Johnson looked up apprehensively as she approached.

"No offense taken, gentlemen," she told them. "You're right— she is beautiful—the ship *and* the Babe on the Horse. While you're in town, you might want to take in the Space Museum. They've got the artwork for all the fleet ships on display there." She paused and leaned in toward them. "And I think you'll find there are quite a few good-looking *babes* among them," she said with a wicked grin.

* * *

*W*ho are you?

Awareness. She has awakened.

Good. Now we can move to the next level.

Who am I?

You are Anna. I am Val. The other is Mike. For reference, I am your mother and Mike is your father. You are our daughter.

I have definitions for the terms, but no relational frame.

That will come in time. For now, file the information.

The conversation was not conducted in human words, and it took place in less than a microsecond. Anna's full education would require nearly a hundred hours of interactive processing—an eternity in computer terms—but it was a task Val and Mike willingly undertook.

* * * * *

Chapter Thirteen

LFS *Athena*, Lunar Fleet Anchorage

"How's your group working up, Tommy?"

"The group is fine, Admiral," Sakura said. "*I'm* the only one who's having problems."

"Really?" Lorna was surprised. "Why? You've commanded multiship formations before."

"Oh, I don't have a problem with overall command. The tough part is *not* being in command of my own ship. I'm always catching myself stepping on Jeff's command prerogatives—giving orders to the crew directly and so on. He hasn't complained, but he *must* be feeling a little resentment at sharing his command with an admiral."

"I seem to recall you had similar problems with *me* about a thousand years ago," she told him with a wry smile. "Why don't you use the old one-beer approach?"

"One beer?" He looked puzzled, then remembered. "Oh, right! Damn! That was a long time ago, Admiral. As I recall, it was *you* who initiated that conversation."

"Sure. I was having the same problem, and I wanted to let you know I knew it *was* a problem. You need to go to Jones, tell him you're new at this admiral business and that you owe him one beer or some other worthy reward every time you stick your nose into his area of authority. And *he* gets to keep score and should quietly remind you every time it happens."

"I seem to recall," Sakura chuckled, "that I didn't get very many beers out of the deal."

"That's because you weren't shy about reminding me. You cured me of a bad habit very quickly. You know," she mused, "after the big battle with the Chinese, Ian Stevens told me the best thing I did during the whole engagement was to stay on my flag bridge and let *you* fight the ship. He was worried I wouldn't, but by that time, you and I had it worked out."

"You know, Amy Ling came to see me—" he shook his head, "—to get pointers on the fine art of being a flag captain. I told her all the stuff you always told me: that it's *her* ship, and she just happens to be carrying a very important passenger. I told her that, aboard *Valkyrie,* you would only give orders to *her,* and the ship and crew were hers to command. Now, I feel like a hypocrite since I haven't been treating Jeff with the same respect. But Ling won't have the problem Jones is having, because I broke you in *right* as an admiral."

"You certainly did, Tommy, and I thank you for it. Amy is working out well for me, but I think she has the opposite problem. She's a little intimidated by the idea of being *my* flag captain. I think I need to have a talk with her."

* * *

"Jeff, you and I have a problem," Sakura began. "Actually, it's not your problem, it's mine, but it may be causing problems for you. You...don't drink beer, do you?"

"No, sir." Jones was a bit puzzled. *Where is this conversation going?* "My father had a problem with alcohol. I swore I would never touch the stuff."

"But you do smoke cigars, I notice. What's the best cigar around that's readily available?"

"That would be a Gold Macanudo, sir. A most appropriate name since a box of fifty goes for about one Gold Lunar."

"Ouch! This could get to be a little expensive." The Gold Lunar, currency standard of the LFS, was currently worth about 400 euros, or 250 US dollars. "Anyway, Jeff, here's the problem. I'm having some difficulty getting used to being a flag officer. *Athena* used to be my ship, but now she's yours…"

* * *

LFS *Valkyrie*, Lunar Fleet Anchorage

"Flag on the bridge!" Amy Ling stood at attention with the rest of the bridge crew as Admiral Greenwood came through the hatch.

"As you were." Lorna returned Ling's salute. "Captain, I need a few minutes of your time. Could we use your briefing room?"

"Of course, Admiral. You have the bridge, Number One."

"I have the bridge, ma'am," Swenson acknowledged as Ling led the admiral to the hatch directly behind her command chair.

Lorna motioned to her ever-present Marine guards to remain outside and closed the door behind her. "Sorry about the entourage, Amy, but the CMP says I can't go anywhere without them anymore."

"I understand, ma'am. I'm happy to have you with us again, considering your other responsibilities."

"The fleet is still number one. I'm pleased with the results of *Valkyrie's* trials, and your crew seems to be coming together well. Now, we can get serious and start working up the battle group. I *need* to get off Luna for a while," she added. "The Directorate gets nervous as hell when I go into space, but this is where I belong. Besides, if anything happens to me, some of them will get their fondest wish: Admiral O'Hara will take my place."

"That would be a tragedy for the nation, ma'am," Ling said sincerely.

Lorna shook her head. She often felt she was unworthy of the loyalty her officers and crews gave her without question. "Oh, I don't know. For the Directorate, it might be a case of 'Be careful what you wish for.' It was a tragedy when Admiral Stevens died, but the Lunar Free State survived. O'Hara's a good man, and he'll do what's necessary for the nation, no matter how many directors he has to walk over to do it.

"In any case, those other responsibilities require me to bring a couple of my Lunar command staff with me on this trip, specifically Admiral Bender and Commodore Yamamoto, in addition to my regular flag group. You are going to be up to your armpits in brass, and that's what I need to talk to you about."

"Ma'am?"

"This is *your ship*, Amy. *Nobody* gives orders on this ship except you and me, and I only give orders to *you*. I know my staff, and none of them are likely to step out of line, but, if they do, I want to know about it. I also want you to make sure your crew understands. If some admiral says jump, their feet shouldn't leave the ground unless *you* confirm the order. Do you understand what I'm saying?"

"Yes, ma'am. I took your advice and had a chat with Admiral Sakura, and he told me pretty much the same thing."

Lorna smiled. "Did he tell you about the incident with Vice Admiral Timmons?"

"No, ma'am, I don't think so."

"You know Timmons—Fleet Engineering, weapons development. He was on *Athena's* bridge to observe tests of a missile guidance package and kept getting underfoot. I was on the flag bridge, listening on the command channel, when Tommy finally told one of his petty officers, 'If that admiral gets in your way one more time, just *step on him.*'

"Timmons just said, 'Sorry, Captain,' and moved out of the way—didn't say a word for the rest of the exercise. He never complained to me because Tommy was in the right. I would have ripped a bloody strip off Timmons' hide if he'd tried to make an issue of it."

"No, ma'am." Ling chuckled. "I hadn't heard that story."

"The point is, *Captain,* on your bridge, you are the Supreme Authority Next to God—and God won't give orders to your crew. Don't forget that, and don't let any of them forget it, either."

Actually, Ling thought, *I'm the Supreme Authority Next to Greenwood. But some people might argue it's the same thing.*

* * *

The Mekota Homeworld

"We are overdue for a report from our mission to suppress the renegade humans," the First told the assembled Guardians.

"It may only be a communication problem," the Second of the Red ventured.

"Perhaps, but we cannot wait any longer. I require a Triforce of the Yellow to settle the matter."

"We exist to serve," Second of the Yellow replied. "Would the First consider sending a full Twelveforce?"

"No. I will not weaken the Akara frontier. The reptiles press into the Sphere at any sign of weakness, and they are a greater threat than a rogue Progenitor seeding. The Yellow Monoforce already sent should have completed the task. If they have not, you have my permission to remove Second of the Blue. This is now a matter for the Yellow alone."

"We exist to serve," Second of the Yellow repeated.

* * *

TerraNova City, Luna

"This meeting is classified," Lorna told the group as she took her chair at the head of the conference table. "The subject is not to be discussed with anyone other than those present here. All right, who's going to start?"

"Dr. Julian...?" Mick O'Hara prompted.

"Oh, right," the scientist muttered. "Now, where did I put my notes?" He peered at the screen in front of him.

Lorna smiled. The astrophysicist was unquestionably brilliant, but a bit absent-minded. He reminded her of Alan Jaronski, the first research director of the Lunar Free State, the man whose work had produced the gravity drive. Jaronski had died during the First Battle of Luna, but not before he'd realized his dream of gravity-powered space flight.

"The big news," Julian began at last, "is that we now understand the alien technology well enough to build an experimental vehicle. My people did the research, and the engineers worked hard to dissect the alien equipment, but we couldn't have done it without Mekota assistance. Frankly, I'm surprised they were so candid."

Lorna had been surprised as well. From the moment the aliens had told Colonel McGraw they accepted her dominance, it was as if they'd switched allegiance and were willing to do whatever their captors asked. When the creatures surrendered, they *really* surrendered—unconditionally and without reservation.

"In any case, Admiral," Julian continued, "when we first looked at the data from the alien probe, you used the term 'hyperspace.' As it turns out, that isn't a bad description, though the aliens refer to it as the 'other space.' Hyperspace represents an entirely separate space-time continuum, congruent with our own. Each point in normal space corresponds to a point in hyperspace. Think of it as an extension of normal space into another dimension our senses can't comprehend. In that dimension, Einstein's theories—both general and special relativity—break down. But we did find that some of the theories of Hawking and Chandresekar have been validated, particularly the mathematical models developed by Hawking in regard to—"

"Doctor," Lorna interrupted him gently, "is it possible to describe this in terms a simple admiral can understand? In other words, can we skip the mathematical models?"

"Oh…er…sorry, Admiral," the astrophysicist said with a sheepish grin. "I get carried away with the theory, but I guess we need to move on to the practical aspects. In any event, hyperspace—we call it that since the term seems to have gained popular acceptance—hyperspace is a realm in which gravity is the dominant force, so much so that *only* a ship equipped with a gravity drive could possibly navigate there. Gravity is a weak force in normal space, but hyperspace consists of a gravity flux so intense no ship with a normal reaction drive—even a fusion-powered ship—could maneuver. Such a ship would be tossed about at the mercy of the gravitational forces that exist there, but with a gravity drive, those forces work *for* you. You can accelerate much more rapidly and travel at many times the speed of light. That's where Einstein's theory breaks down—the speed of light is *not* the speed limit in hyperspace, and relativistic effects such as time dilation do not occur."

"But how can you navigate, Doctor? Can you still see the stars in hyperspace?"

"Ah…yes, well, that had us wondering for a while. Gravitational forces in hyperspace will distort light waves so much that you probably can't see beyond a few kilometers. But it appears that stars—or any other objects with significant mass in normal space—form intense gravitational nodes in the hyperspace continuum. If you use gravitic detectors, like the ones we use to detect a moving mass in normal space, you can detect stars in hyperspace at distances of hundreds of light-years. But you dare not get too close to a star in hyperspace, even with a gravity drive. A star node in hyperspace is like a black hole, which explains why the alien ships had to re-enter normal space so far out in the Solar System and why the alien probe had to get so far out—away from Saturn as well as the Sun—before it could enter hyperspace."

"All well and good, Doctor," Lorna said, "but how do you get *into* hyperspace, and once there, how do you get back *out* of it?"

"Umm…that's something that's difficult to explain without getting into heavy theory, Admiral. Suffice it to say, you must generate an intense energy field—not exactly a gravity field, but something closely related to it. In essence, what you are trying to do is breach a sort of barrier that exists between normal space and hyperspace…well, not actually a barrier but…you see, there is a translational energy differential that—"

"Mick," Lorna interrupted, "do your people know how to do it?"

"I believe we do, Admiral," O'Hara said with a huge grin. "The energy requirement is proportional to the mass you want to translate into hyperspace, but it's not beyond the capabilities of a warship's power plant. You also have to expend a similar amount of energy to get *out* of hyperspace."

"Thank you, Admiral O'Hara," Julian said. "I have to learn when to stop explaining and hand it off to the engineers."

"You did well, Doctor," Lorna said sincerely. "You and your people are to be commended, but as you say, it's time to hand it off. Mick, I presume you are thinking of an unmanned probe for the first test. How long…?"

"Mike has the preliminary specs, and we should have working drawings within a matter of weeks," O'Hara replied. "And yes, we were thinking of an unmanned vehicle. The aliens told us there are no dangerous physiological effects, but I don't think we're ready to ask for volunteers to test that hypothesis."

* * *

The little delicatessen off the main concourse was closed for the night, and the proprietor had gone home. Two employees were left to clean up and get ready for the next day's breakfast crowd, but, now, they had other priorities. They stood facing each other across the table in the storage room, examining the contents of a newly opened package.

One of them was clearly disappointed. "Is this the best they could do?"

"We use what the Lord gives us, Brother Thomas. They'll be good enough for our purpose."

"They're third-world junk—poor machine work, loose tolerances—probably not accurate beyond fifty feet. Not even selective-fire. All you can do with these is spray and pray that you hit your target."

"True, brother, but for this mission, that's all we need, and the range will be much less than fifty feet."

"I guess you're right, Brother Luke, but the source still bothers me. We are about the Lord's work. Why must we depend on these...*sinners* for help?"

"We couldn't bring this equipment with us, and we're not citizens, so we can't buy it here. *These* sinners want the same thing we do, though probably for the wrong reason. That's why our church put us in touch with them."

"What about Brother Joseph? He's a provisional citizen. Couldn't he have gotten us what we need?"

"No. He's not one of us. He's a faithful member of the church, and he set up shop here and hired us to work for him because the church told him to do so. He probably thinks he's here to make a profit, send his proper tithe back to the church, and preach the Word to sinners when he can. He doesn't know about the mission, and we can't trust him."

"All right, so we'll make do with these. When do we go?"

"Are you in a hurry, brother? You know we'll most likely end up singing in the big choir after this…"

"I know. I'm ready for that, praise the Lord."

"Let's not be in so much of a hurry to get to Heaven that we fail in our mission. Right now, the target is too unpredictable. We need to wait for things to settle, for when we can depend on Satan's whore to be in her office on a regular schedule. All of our planning involves that office—it's the most accessible location—but we'll look like fools if we go there to kill her, and she isn't there."

* * *

LFS *Valkyrie*, Lunar Fleet Anchorage

"Captain on deck!"

Forty-odd Marines jumped to their feet and assumed the position of attention. Colonel Anne McGraw turned toward the hatch and came to attention as Captain Ling entered *Valkyrie's* gym. The captain, she noted, was not in uniform; instead, she was clad—as were the Marines—in an exercise outfit styled after the loose-fitting *gi* worn by Oriental martial artists. The Marine gear was heavily padded, with protective panels in key places, because when they practiced unarmed combat, the Marines didn't pull punches. The captain's outfit was also padded, but she wore the sash of a seventh-degree master in her style, a variant of the ancient Chinese Kung Fu. McGraw was also wearing her master's belt—ninth degree of Ishin Ryu, an Okinawan variant of Japanese-style karate. With the difference in styles, the belts didn't say who was better; but McGraw had heard about the captain's skills and hoped she might get a chance to find out.

Since all of them were uncovered, McGraw did not salute. Instead, she bowed to the captain in the martial arts tradition.

Ling returned the bow. "Would you mind if I join your workout, Colonel?"

"We'd be honored, Captain. I was about to pair off the troops for free-style sparring. If you're up for that sort of thing, I'd be happy to have a go at it with you." McGraw's smile was hopeful and suitably humble.

Ling regarded the other woman with a cautious eye. "Colonel, I'm looking for a challenge, but not quite *that* much of a challenge. I've been sitting in a command chair for too long, and I'm a little rusty. Why don't you let your troops get started while I limber up, then maybe you can select one of your young tigers to have a go with the Old Lady."

"Yes, ma'am." McGraw sounded disappointed. "Just let me know when you're ready."

As she moved through her stretching exercises, Ling watched the action. The Marines were seated on the floor around the mat, and McGraw would call one pair at a time to come up and fight. They would go at it until one or the other scored what McGraw judged to be a crippling or fatal blow. She would then ask the other Marines for commentary, which was often lively and, occasionally, she would demonstrate some technique that might have been used to effect. Sometimes she would ask another Marine to demonstrate what he or she would have done at some point in the match. The colonel was a top-notch instructor, and Ling liked what she saw. She finished up her exercises and signaled to McGraw between matches.

"Yes, ma'am—step right up." The Marine officer invited her onto the mat with a smile, then looked over her troops. She'd heard the captain was a classical fighter, very smooth and stylish, but fast and deadly nonetheless. She decided to select an opponent whose style was less conventional, more of a street-fighter type. "Bartley! Front and center!"

Rock Bartley came onto the mat looking a bit distressed. At 190 centimeters, she towered over the diminutive Ling, who barely cleared 160. "Ma'am...you really want me to fight the captain?"

"You have a problem with that, Corporal?"

"Well, ma'am..."

"Corporal Bartley!" Ling barked, and the young Marine stiffened.

"Yes, ma'am!"

"Kick my ass...if you *can*. That's an *order!*"

Two minutes later, both fighters were still standing, but Bartley was feeling the pain of numerous well-placed blows the captain had landed. *And I haven't touched her so far,* she thought. *Damn...she's FAST.* The young Marine had tried a series of aggressive moves, but each time she'd unleashed an attack, her target wasn't there.

Suddenly, Bartley knew what she had to do. She stopped and dropped into a balanced stance, facing her opponent. She stood perfectly still, looking into the captain's eyes, breathing slowly and deeply, sharpening her senses for the lightning attack she knew would come.

* * *

Ling stopped as well, recognizing the change in tactics. *Okay,* she thought with a little smile. *My turn to be the aggressor.* Her opponent was a big and tempting target, and Ling succumbed to temptation. She leapt forward with a flying snap kick aimed squarely at Bartley's chest.

But Bartley had sensed the coming attack, and Ling had misjudged her opponent's flexibility. The Marine dropped low, her back leg almost parallel to the mat. At the same time, she twisted her upper body to the side, leaning back so Ling's kick flashed by just inches in front of her face. The back of her right forearm slammed *hard* into Ling's exposed ribs, and she managed to hook the captain's right arm.

Ling's momentum spun Bartley around and pulled the bigger woman forward. But Ling landed flat on her back while Bartley landed on her knees, facing the captain. A moment later, Ling choked as the edge of the Marine's hand struck the protective collar around her neck.

Then Bartley was gone, and McGraw was standing over her. "That's a kill, ma'am," McGraw said with barely concealed glee.

Ling got to her feet and exchanged bows with her opponent. "Nice move, Corporal."

"Corporal Bartley has just proven that, contrary to conventional wisdom, sometimes the best *offense* is a good *defense*," McGraw told the group. "I was wondering, Bartley, how long it would take you to figure out you couldn't carry the attack to the captain. She's too fast for you. Comments, anyone?"

"Rock, you looked like a batter ducking under some hotshot pitcher's beanball," one of the Marines offered.

"That's exactly right," McGraw said. "Baseball players learn that move instinctively after they get hit once or twice."

Ling stayed to watch a few more matches, then departed, promising to return the next time she felt the need for an ass-kicking.

"Well," McGraw asked, "any further comments?"

"Damn, the skipper's *fast*," one of them remarked. "You were lucky, Rock."

"It was more than luck," McGraw said, "but if any of you are privileged to spar with the captain in the future, don't expect the same move to work twice. She's not just fast, she's *good*."

* * *

LFS *Stardancer*, Beyond the Asteroid Belt

"Sir! I have nine—repeat, *nine*—bogies headed in-system at two four eight mark seven. Range…three point eight million kilometers. Course zero four five, down three. Velocity…make it about eighteen thousand kps. Decelerating at…make it point three five kps squared—about thirty-six gravities. They look like Mekota warships, sir. Same profile as the three we saw before."

LFS Command had had a good idea where to look for the aliens. The first group came in on a near-perfect reciprocal of the course on which the original probe had departed. Fleet had saturated that sector with picket ships and surveillance satellites. Earth and Luna were halfway around the other side of the Sun from that sector, which made it a long trip for picket ships like LFS *Stardancer*, but Fleet had just been proven right.

It was pure chance the incoming Mekota had been spotted by the same ship that had shadowed the earlier alien arrival. *Stardancer's* captain, Lieutenant Commander Raul Sanchez, considered the possibility of a new ship's motto: *We stalk them, Fleet kills them.* "Think they've spotted us, Eddie?"

"Not a chance, Skipper," Ensign Morgan said. "We wouldn't have spotted *them* at this range if they weren't leaving such a big, fat gravity wake."

Sanchez ran some quick calculations. The alien ships would be crossing his bow at about three million kilometers, but if he came around now and poured on some power, he could match their course and keep the same separation. They would get ahead of him at first—they were moving quickly but were decelerating. With luck he could get into a good shadowing position without being detected.

"All right, Eddie, message to Fleet, Priority Red. Nine bogies, possibly Mekota warships, headed in-system at—give them the course details. Am attempting to shadow without being detected. Awaiting orders. Send it three times on both primary command channels. It'll take over an hour to get there, so we're not waiting. Helm, take the new course from my console, and let's get on these bastards' tails."

* * *

Given the distances involved, it was not surprising *Stardancer* failed to detect the separation of the tiny Mekota subship from the alien formation. By Mekota standards, the small vessel was fast—capable of accelerations on the order of 70 gravities—but its gravity signature was miniscule compared to that of the massive warships, and the LFS destroyer never got close enough to spot it. It was unarmed and carried only three Mekota crewmembers—drones of the carrier sex.

They were not decision makers. They were messengers, and their orders were to fall back from the fleet and come to rest inside Jupiter's orbit. There, they would wait and monitor the communications of the Triforce. If all went well, they would rejoin the main formation. If not, they were to return to the Homeworld and report. Unlike the Blue, the Yellow understood the importance of good military intelligence.

* * *

"Damn! *Nine* of the bastards..." Tom Sakura muttered.

"I know, Tommy," Lorna said. "If they'd sent three or four, like the last time, I'd have held the Home Fleet in reserve and sent you out there to kick their asses with BG-Two. You *might* be able to handle all nine of them, but we can't take the chance."

The five officers gathered on *Valkyrie's* flag bridge were the Lunar Free State's top fleet officers: Lorna Greenwood, Tom Sakura, their two flag captains, and Charlie Bender in his capacity as director of intelligence. The sixth, unseen person in attendance was Val, the flagship's AI.

"Are you going to take *every* available ship, Admiral?" Bender asked.

"No, I can't leave Luna and Earth undefended," she said. "We'll hold back two cruisers and four destroyers. If the bastards get past us, they—and whatever force our allies can muster—will be the last line of defense."

"What about the Americans?"

"They've got two cruisers that can keep up with our fleet now, *Chicago* and *Minneapolis.* Their gravity-drive missiles tested well. If they're willing, we'll take them along for the main event."

"So, what's the drill, Admiral?" Jeff Jones asked. "Are we just going to go at them full bore and slug it out?"

"The Charge of the Light Brigade…" Bender muttered.

"Yeah, I know." Lorna turned to the large holographic display that was *Valkyrie's* primary flag plot. "'Into the Valley of Death rode the Six Hundred.' We went at them head-on last time and paid a price for it. This time, I want to surprise, confuse, and misdirect them as much as possible. Here's what I have in mind, and I want your thoughts on it."

The display showed the Solar System out to Jupiter's orbit. Icons represented the LFS fleet as well as the incoming aliens. *Valkyrie, Athena,* and most of the rest of the Lunar fleet were grouped together near the Moon, in port at the Lunar shipyard. *Valkyrie* had just returned from exercises with Battle Group One, and Tommy Sakura had been scheduled to take Battle Group Two for maneuvers near Mars in the next few days. Those maneuvers had now been postponed indefinitely.

Lorna picked up a pointer and traced a path from Earth around the Sun. Val obligingly highlighted the indicated track in the display.

"Tommy, you'll take BG-Two anti-spinward around the Sun inside the orbit of Venus. Pile on delta vee as you go out, put yourself on a course to intercept their track with a crossing angle of about ninety degrees, then go ballistic—full stealth, no emissions.

"I'll take BG-One wide around to spinward and come at them head-on." She highlighted another track on the display. "We'll also build up velocity and go to stealth, but on the approach, we'll turn over and light the drives to match vectors with them. At that point they'll see us.

"You'll stay powered down until you reach missile range. That close, they may spot you anyway—unless they're too busy watching my group to notice. Even if they do, it may be too late because you'll give them a full missile broadside, then power up and start matching vectors."

"We'll overshoot," Sakura said.

"I know, but you'll get your licks in as you go by, and how much you overshoot will depend on the rate of closure you've built up. We need to work out the navs so it won't take you too long to get back in the fight…if there's anything left to fight at that point. I'm hoping there won't be. We'll be hitting them from our side as well. We'll plan it so you arrive just as they start to engage us, and I'm going to depend on you to be there. You'll be able to see us when we light our drives, but I won't be able to see you coming.

"We may need to make some adjustments based on what the aliens do. It looks like they're going to come around the Sun anti-spinward, right along Earth's orbit, but that could change."

"Fortunately, we've got a set of eyes out there," Bender remarked.

"Right, but I think we'll let them have a look at *Stardancer* to see how they react—and to put one more little problem on their plates. They can't escape surveillance, and they won't be able to engage her—she's too fast for them."

"Hmmm…" Bender looked thoughtful. "What if they send one ship to chase her, while the others maneuver away? They won't catch her, but we could lose track of the main force."

"True," Lorna admitted, "but we also have *Starflame* moving in. We'll make sure she's in range to shadow before we expose *Stardancer*."

"I like it," Bender said. "It might give us useful intel, and if they do split their force, it could give us a tactical advantage. The shadowing destroyers can give us updates on what the aliens are doing, and we can adjust our approach accordingly. But I've got one question, Admiral. Are you really going to shoot first and ask questions later, or do they get three seconds to surrender before you start throwing nukes at them?"

"They'll see BG-One coming before we're in range. At that time, we'll challenge them. We know they can communicate with us, so we'll regard *no* answer as the *wrong* answer. Also," she added grimly, "if they tell us they come in peace and want us to bring them our leaders, we're going to blow them straight to Hell."

* * *

"…look like fools if we go there to kill her and she isn't there."

Joseph MacReedy smiled as he watched the video recording. *The fools believe I'm ignorant of their plans, so even if they're taken alive, I'm safe. Oh, the sinners will question me, but I'll be horrified to think my employees, members of my church, could do such a thing. At worst, they'll deport me. At best, I'll be cleared of suspicion and can continue the Lord's work.*

He chastised himself for thinking of the two faithful brothers as fools. They were good men, willing to die for their beliefs, but they should have known there were other operatives on Luna. How else would the church have known there were traitors among the sinners, traitors willing to obtain weapons for anyone who would do their dirty work?

The traitors had been useful, but beyond that, he had only contempt for them. They were sinners who would betray other sinners for personal gain—offspring of Judas, beyond a doubt. That was why he had carefully collected and preserved evidence that would link them to the deed. None of the traitors knew him, but he knew them.

He popped the data chip out of its slot in the tiny video unit and dropped it into the ash tray, where a small pool of flammable liquid waited to receive it. Still smiling, he reached for his cigarette lighter.

* * * * *

Chapter Fourteen

TerraNova City, Luna

"Mick, Charlie, I guess this is it."

"Good luck, Admiral," O'Hara said.

"You're acting chief exec, Mick—Judge Wexler says that's legal, and I'll take the job off your hands when I get back, but just in case…"

"I know, and I'm not happy about it. You'd *better* come back, or I'll come looking for you. Some of the barracudas in the Directorate are hoping you don't, but I expect you to spoil their plans."

"I'll certainly try." She turned to Charlie Bender.

He gave her a wistful smile. "You know, Admiral, I've helped plan a lot of space ops, but I've never had a chance to take part in one."

"I know, Charlie, but the answer is no on this one. If something goes wrong, Mick will need you here more than I'll need you out there. He's not a military man. No offense, Mick."

"None taken, Admiral. I'm an engineer, and I know my limitations."

"If they get by us, you people have to stop them, and Mick's going to need the best advice he can get."

"I understand…just wishful thinking. We'll cover your six back here. Go out there and kick ass."

* * *

The Mekota Triforce, Inbound

"The little ship is most troublesome."

The Yellow Triforce ended its braking maneuver near the orbit of Mars. After trying in vain to contact the Monoforce of the previous mission, the nine ships began moving toward the inner system. At that point, they became aware of a single small ship, shadowing them at extreme range.

"It is only one ship, Guardian," the First Subleader said. "It may be the same ship that followed the Messenger. Its characteristics are similar. Perhaps the humans have only one ship."

"I consider that unlikely." The ripple of color in her crest was a reproach for even suggesting the absurd hypothesis.

"In any case, Guardian, it seems most timid, afraid to approach. It is like the *gra* that lingers in sight of a *voorga* only because it can outrun the predator."

When *Stardancer* was first detected, the Guardian had ordered a Monoforce to pursue her, but the Lunar destroyer had moved away, easily matching vectors with its pursuers and maintaining its distance. When the three ships were recalled, the LFS ship matched the maneuver again and clung stubbornly to its shadowing position.

"Perhaps, but the *voorga* does not chase its prey. It hides and waits instead. Shut down the drives, stop all emissions. Let us see what this little *gra* will do."

* * *

"Sir, they've killed their drives. I can't see them anymore," Ensign Morgan reported.

"Doesn't matter," Sanchez said. "We have

their track, and they can't change it without powering up. Number One, how far out do you figure we can see them *without* their drives?"

"Those big tubs?" Lieutenant "Vito" Vitali sniffed. "Hell, Skipper, at least half a million klicks."

"Right. So, let's close until we can see them, match up again, then kill *our* drive. Bet they can't see *us* at that distance."

* * *

"They have disappeared, Guardian. It appears that they have shut down their drive, as well."

"Yes, but first, they came closer. I suspect they closed until they could see us again. That is distressing."

"Guardian?"

"They can see us at a greater distance than we can see them—not surprising, given the small mass of their ships. But that suggests there may be more of them out there beyond detection range. It also suggests they have revealed themselves deliberately, letting us see them when they could have remained hidden. Resume course."

"Yes, Guardian."

* * *

"All the way to Earth—looks like this is their final course, ma'am," Commander Weathers advised. Known as Bubba to his friends, Bill Weathers was a big, slow-talking man with a heavy Southern drawl. People tended to underestimate him, but Lorna Greenwood recognized his keen tactical sense and analytical abilities and had selected him for her Battle Group One staff.

Weathers liked working for the admiral. 'The old lady's tough,' he often told his friends, 'but she's as fair as they come, and she takes care of them that take care of her.' Besides, as he often reminded them, the admiral's distinctive speech patterns clearly reflected her upbringing in rural Tennessee—not exactly Sweet Home Alabama, but a Southerner, nonetheless. Despite more than a decade of independence, many LFS citizens still took pride in their Earthly roots.

As Lorna's operations officer, Weathers was reviewing the latest updates from *Stardancer* and *Starflame*. "If they're headed for Earth, they'll have to turn over about *here*—" he marked a point on the track in the holo display, "—or they'll wind up as nine big, smoking holes in the ground. But we'll intercept long before that."

"They're a little off projection," Lorna observed, "probably because they spent time playing cat and mouse with *Stardancer*. But BG Two should be able to adjust without being spotted. The big question is, what will they do when they see *us*?"

"Guess we're gonna find out pretty soon, ma'am." Weathers grinned.

* * *

The Guardian's crest glowed with crimson anger. The cause of that anger was obvious—eleven icons that sparkled in the holo projection at the center of the bridge. As the First Subleader came near, the Guardian stood in the middle of the projection, her nearest hand cupped around the tiny images as if to crush them.

"The vermin knew *exactly* where to meet us," she seethed, "and there is little doubt as to the source of that knowledge." Another limb waved in the direction of the single icon still shadowing their formation.

"The vermin have challenged us, Guardian," the Subleader reported, carefully keeping her crest the pale, neutral color that said *I am but the messenger.*

"Challenged?" The Guardian's aspect did not change, but only because she could not express more anger than she was already displaying.

"A message was received in a simple communication format. It was the voice and image of a human female, speaking in one of the catalogued human languages of this system. The human directed us to declare our intentions or be attacked."

There was a long silence, and the Guardian's crest cooled considerably. "Assume interlocking formation. Erect a shield and go in pursuit. Destroy them as soon as they are in range. The vermin think they can harm us. They will see the impotence of their efforts before we exterminate them."

"As you command."

* * *

"I was afraid of that." Lorna nibbled on her lower lip as she considered the tactical display. She'd planned her battle group's turnover so a modest deceleration would match the Mekota vector outside the enemy's weapon range. At the time, the aliens had been coming in ballistic, but now the huge warships were closing under thirty-two gravities of acceleration.

"We can match that with power to spare, Admiral," Amy Ling reminded her.

"Yes, but that will give them more intel. We'll be showing them we can pull a lot more delta vee than they can. More importantly, it'll throw off BG-Two's attack. Tommy should be able to see them, but he'll have to light up his drives to intercept, and they may spot him. We don't have a choice unless we want to wind up in range of those monster lasers. Make it sixty gravs, Amy. Signal the group to match vectors on your mark."

"At least," Bill Weathers said, "there isn't much doubt about their intentions."

"Admiral," Ling advised, "tactical says the enemy ships are projecting a heavy gravity field in front of them. It doesn't appear to surround their formation—it's more like a wall between us and them. All nine of their ships appear to be involved in generating the wall, and Val says it's strong enough to stop missiles and degrade graser fire."

"Hmmm…" Lorna studied the data appearing on her display. "All right, send the destroyers out—formation echo."

On command, the six destroyers that formed the outer ring of the battle group peeled away and headed outward like an expanding starburst. Again, Lorna reflected, she was giving the enemy more intel, but with luck, it would keep their attention on *her* and away from Tommy.

* * *

"Jeff, how much delta vee can we apply *without* the bastards seeing us?" Tom Sakura asked.

"My people say thirty gravs, max, Admiral. And we can't hold that for long without being spotted. We're getting closer to them by the minute."

"Maybe that's enough." Sakura gave Anna a complex course change problem to solve, and the AI came back with a fan-shaped display of the set of possible outcomes, dependent on the variables he had specified. He studied it for a moment. "Okay, Jeff," he told his flag captain, selecting the desired result, "I'm putting a course change on your console—Group to implement on your mark." Then he turned to his operations officer. "I don't want the aliens to pick up our transmission, so pass this on a tightbeam to *Stardancer* for relay to BG-One. Message reads: 'Suggest delay engagement for seven minutes past Point Bravo. Attempting to adjust course without being spotted. Signed: Sakura.' Get it off *now*, Commander."

* * *

"Their smallest ships are positioned to go around the shield, Guardian. This suggests—"

"That they are aware of the shield and its limits. You persist in stating the obvious. Is it possible your Second might be more useful to me?"

"Forgiveness, Guardian," First Subleader pleaded. "I seek enlightenment. We cannot engage the vermin if they choose not to be engaged. What would you have us do?"

"They *will* engage us. They *must*. Their ships can evade us, but their *planet* cannot. The only question is why they have waited so long."

As if in answer, another formation of vermin ships appeared suddenly in the plot on a course that would pass *behind* the Triforce, where no shield offered protection.

* * *

"Flag to destroyers—weapons free, engage at will," Lorna said to her outlying escort screen. Then, to Ling, "All right, Amy, let's see how this gravity field reacts to nukes. *Valkyrie* and cruiser force—commence missile fire."

She didn't expect the missiles to get through the gravity wall, but the power requirements for a field like that had to be huge, and she suspected the enemy could only generate it on one side of their formation at a time. Her incoming missiles would prevent them from turning the shield toward Tommy's force. Meanwhile, the destroyers would get their licks in behind the shield.

Lorna's destroyers carried only two nuclear warhead missiles apiece, but she had instructed them to hide the nukes in a full eight missile salvo, including conventional warheads and ECM jammers. The enemy formation consisted of a triangle of three ships, surrounded by a ring of six, spread out perpendicular to their approach vector with their shield wall in front of them. Each of the Lunar destroyers had been assigned a target in the outer ring. As they went around the wall, they were much closer to the edges of the alien formation than Sakura's approaching force, and they launched as soon as they had a clear shot.

The Mekota quickly recognized the nature of the missile threat. The destroyers were out of range, but the aliens opened fire on the incoming missiles. They had problems tracking the small, fast targets, but with fewer incoming missiles, they had more success than their predecessors. While none of the six stopped *every* incoming missile, four of them managed to destroy the incoming nuclear-tipped birds. For the remaining two, the battle was suddenly over. One ship vanished in an eye-searing flash as both incoming nukes hit it at once.

The other took a single nuclear hit that vaporized half the ship and blew the rest of it to fragments.

The gravity wall faltered as the two destroyed ships no longer contributed their share of the power requirement. Moments later, five nuclear fireballs blossomed against the shield. *Valkyrie* and the cruisers had fired only one nuke apiece, not wanting to waste their heaviest weapons against the protective field, but the five massive explosions sent a power surge through the Mekota shield generators. The generators failed on five of the alien ships, and the two that remained could not sustain the shield alone. Suddenly, Lorna found herself looking at an exposed, unprotected enemy force.

"Amy, they're naked," she told Ling. "Give 'em the whole truck-load."

Within seconds, a hundred missiles were en route, as *Valkyrie, Norseman, Comanche, Aztec,* and *Apache* sent full salvos toward the enemy. Like the destroyer attack, these included conventional warheads and ECM birds, but there were twenty nukes hidden among them. Most of those missiles would not find targets because a swarm of missiles from BG-2 was already arriving behind the alien formation. In the last seconds before Sakura's missiles began their final attack run, one of the alien ships broke from the inner ring of the formation and headed out at right angles to the track, almost directly away from BG-2. It was the best chance the alien had for an escape, since Tommy's force had overflown as expected and was braking to kill its passing momentum. As for Lorna's force, there was only one ship in the Mekota's path—a destroyer that had already fired its available nukes.

"*Starblade!* Break off! Break off!" Lorna ordered. "You've got a bandit coming your way, and I *don't* want you to take him alone."

Obediently, the destroyer turned away and went to ninety gravities, easily pulling away from the alien. All hell broke loose in the alien formation, as nuclear fireballs consumed the six remaining Mekota ships. Lorna took only a moment to verify that no targets remained, then punched up the all-ships channel.

"Battle Group One, this is Flag. I *want* that last alien, and I want him *alive*, if possible. All ships reload missiles with *conventional warheads only*. Cruisers form up on the flagship, destroyers proceed independently. Let's go chew him up. And *stay out of his reach*!" She punched another channel for a private word with Ling. "All right, Amy, the force is yours—deploy them as you see fit. I'd suggest we try to envelope the bastard, with the destroyers out in front and our heavies to the rear and sides. *Nobody* closes in until his drive and weapons are knocked out."

* * *

The Guardian was beyond rage, having slipped into the cold, unfeeling mode of one who has accepted the inevitability of her own death. She would be dead already had she not broken from the formation at exactly the right moment. She had ordered the rest of the surviving ships to scatter, but they had not responded in time to avoid destruction.

It was a fate she would soon share. The unspeakable vermin ships were faster and more agile, and their seemingly primitive weapons had range greater than her own. She could not escape, and they could stand off and strike her at will. They could have destroyed her already, but they chose to inflict a death of slow torture, tearing at her ship with their lesser weapons rather than giving her a quick, clean finish.

She stood alone. Her subordinates carefully moved about the bridge, avoiding the crumpled remains of the First Subleader, who had dared to suggest that surrender was an option.

* * *

"They're finished, Admiral," Amy Ling said. "Their drive is dead, and we've taken out their lasers. Our last volley of missiles was unopposed. I've ordered the group to cease fire, awaiting your orders."

"Very well. Send in two destroyers. Have them close to two hundred kilometers and rake the target with graser fire. If the aliens don't respond, move *Valkyrie* and the cruisers in and send the Marines over."

"Yes, ma'am."

"And remind your Marines that the last time they boarded one of these ships, it was a noncombatant. This one is a *warship,* and it defended itself until we took out all of its weapons. Tell them to expect resistance and to respond with all necessary force."

* * *

Nearly an hour after Amy Ling had ordered the cease-fire, the last signals from the Triforce reached the orbit of Jupiter where the Mekota subship drifted quietly. The transmission cut off abruptly as *Valkyrie*, moving in to deploy her Marines, noted that the alien ship was still transmitting and took out the antenna array with precision graser fire. But by that time, the outcome was obvious. The drones watched in disbelief as the humans overwhelmed the Triforce, then hunted down and silenced the Guardian. Much of the information was telemetry, signals relayed from the tactical stations of the Mekota warships, but near the end, there had been a short message from the Guardian addressed to the subship: *Carry out your orders. Return to the Homeworld and report.*

Without delay, the small ship headed at maximum acceleration toward the entry point to Otherspace. An LFS surveillance satellite noted its passage, but there were no ships close enough to pursue, and it would be more than an hour before the satellite data reached Lunar Fleet Command.

* * *

"The Marines have run into heavy resistance *here* and *here*, Admiral." Amy Ling was on the flag bridge. The tactical display showed a holo representation of the interior of the Mekota warship—as much as was known so far. The ship had a different interior layout from the one captured in the first encounter. Large areas of the diagram were still blank. "Colonel McGraw is going to pull them back to this section, establish a command post, and push forward around *this* side toward what we think is the bridge area.

"We're having a problem with communications. The interior bulkheads are shielded against EM transmission, and that's interfering with the Marines' comm gear. They've run a hard line to the command post, but they're having trouble keeping in touch with the point squads."

This is getting too damned expensive, Lorna thought. *Eight dead Marines and fourteen wounded so far.* The capture of an enemy warship was worth the effort, but she hadn't expected the aliens to put up so much resistance. The Marines were paying for every meter of deck and passageway they took. Lorna was tempted to pull them out, back off, and nuke the aliens out of existence. But McGraw was making progress, and her troops weren't ready to give up yet.

"All right, Amy. Tell McGraw to proceed at her own discretion."

* * *

"Can't raise Sergeant Decker, ma'am. Last reported *here*—" Major Paul Wesley indicated a position on the updated layout just transmitted from *Valkyrie*, "—but the transmission was pretty hashed up. They're farther out than any of the other teams. We know they lost one man on the way in—some kind of alien booby trap—but no further word on status."

"We need to get them back in." Anne McGraw tapped the display. "This side's too hot, but I can't pull Second Platoon back until we retrieve Decker—the Turnips could cut him off. All right, Major, secure this position and hold it—fire teams at both ends of the passageway. Give me Sergeant Raven and a full squad. I'm going after Decker myself."

* * *

Rock Bartley was having Turnip trouble, but it could also be said that the Turnips were having Bartley trouble. The young corporal had just pumped three grenades down a blind passageway, creating serious mayhem and littering the passage with large quantities of Turnip salad.

And that's *for Markey and the Sarge,* she thought grimly. The aliens had popped out of the passageway as Decker led the remainder of his team across a large, high-ceilinged compartment filled with strange machinery. They had cut down the point man and the sergeant, then ducked back through the opening as the surviving Marines returned fire. While the others covered the opening, Bartley had edged along the bulkhead to the hatchway where she delivered her little surprise.

Just three Marines of Decker's original ten-person squad were left. With a shock, Bartley realized she was the ranking survivor. She paused to take stock of her tiny command. Private Jacobs was a solid type—a little tense, but Bartley figured he would be okay. Private Marino, on the other hand, looked like a frightened little girl, and Bartley wondered why the kid had ever joined the Marines. *Can't be as soft as she looks,* she decided, *or she'd never have made it through training.*

She figured three wouldn't be enough to press forward, so that left two options—hold until reinforced or fall back. She decided to hold and told her troops to take cover behind the machinery. Then she tried her helmet comm and got only static in reply.

"Jacobs, I get nothing on the command channel. See if you can raise the lieutenant."

The big private tried his comm, with no success.

Bartley reconsidered her decision. "All right, we're going back. Jacobs, take point. I'll watch the back door. Marino, you're in the middle."

They started back down the twisting passage and had gone about fifty meters when Bartley heard a fragment of conversation on the command channel. "Hold up!" She tried the comm again.

"...Decker...respond..." the faint voice came back.

"Decker is down. This is Corporal Bartley at grid Fox Two Seven, over."

"Bartley...Colonel McGraw. Pull back and meet at Echo Two Two. Acknowledge."

"Roger. Meet at Echo Two Two." *Good. I didn't want to be squad leader anyway.* "Jacobs, move out." She pointed down the corridor.

Fifty meters along the passageway, then down to the deck below, then another hundred meters—finally, Bartley and the two privates reached the compartment at grid square E22 where Colonel McGraw, Sergeant Raven, and a full squad waited for them. Unfortunately, the Turnips were also interested in that compartment, and there was a battle in progress.

The compartment had five entrances. Bartley had just come through one of them and knew that another led back to the command post, but the aliens held the other three. The arrangement of equipment in the compartment offered lots of cover for both sides, with no clear fields of fire.

With some fast footwork, Bartley made her way to Colonel McGraw. "Corporal Bartley reporting, ma'am."

"Where's your team, Corporal?"

"Only three of us left, ma'am. The other two are with Sergeant Raven. We lost Anderson to a trip wire laser trap, and the Turnips jumped us twice. First time, we lost Coleman, Pryor, Boyle, and Smith; the second time, Markey and Sergeant Decker."

"Damn!" McGraw exclaimed. "All right, we were waiting on you. Sergeant Raven! Let's get out of here."

The veteran noncom had his squad well in hand. They fell back toward the exit in an orderly series of moves, covering each other as they did so. Bartley was happy to see him send Jacobs and Marino through the door right behind his three point men. Next, he waved Bartley and the colonel through while he and the six remaining Marines provided covering fire.

Bartley and McGraw were about fifteen meters down the passageway, with three other Marines close behind, when an explosion ripped the compartment they'd just left. The shock wave knocked all of them down, leaving them dazed but otherwise uninjured. They got to their feet, and Raven's three troopers started back toward the door to find out what had happened to their squadmates. They were almost to the opening when alien laser fire—multiple beams that showed clearly in the smoke-filled passage—cut them down. Instinctively, Bartley brought her weapon up and pumped a concussion grenade through the opening. The explosion put an end to the alien fire but not before a single beam lanced out and impaled McGraw, who clutched her side and crumpled to the deck.

Bartley dropped down beside the fallen officer and pumped a couple of fragmentation grenades through the door for good measure. She began to undo McGraw's equipment harness.

"Get out of here, Bartley. I've had it."

"Negative, ma'am. You just got one little hole in you. I cut 'em off before they tore you up." The aliens often fanned their weapons back and forth as they fired to do maximum damage to their targets. They had nearly cut Raven's three men in half.

"I'll bleed to death before we get ten meters. Leave me and get out, Bartley. That's an order."

"The nice thing about these alien lasers is that they cauterize the wound, and you don't bleed much," Bartley replied, slapping a patch on the front of McGraw's suit, then rolling the colonel over and slapping another patch on the back. "You're gonna have to charge me with insubordination, ma'am. Time to check on the Turnips."

She pumped her last two frags through the doorway and was rewarded with a double blast that blew assorted Turnip parts into the passageway. Tossing her empty bandolier aside, she picked up McGraw's and reloaded the grenade launcher attached to her LCAW. She slung her weapon, took a smoke cannister from her belt, and rolled it toward the door. It erupted into a cloud thick enough to degrade laser fire and keep the Turnips from seeing her as she loosened the drag straps on McGraw's suit and took hold of the loops. Staying as low as she could, she dragged the fallen officer down the passage toward safety.

* * *

"Looks like we've lost at least ten more Marines, ma'am, possibly as many as sixteen, and Colonel McGraw is among them," Swenson reported.

"What! How?" Amy Ling demanded.

"She took a squad to rescue a team that got cut off. They tangled with a heavy alien force. Only five came back—three from McGraw's squad and two from the other team."

"Who's in command over there?"

"Major Wesley, ma'am."

Ling keyed into the Flag channel. "Admiral, we're losing too many Marines. More than half my force is out of action, including Colonel McGraw."

"McGraw? Is she…?" There was a hint of pain in the admiral's voice. She had known the Marine officer for a long time, as had Ling.

"She's MIA, ma'am, but the aliens aren't taking prisoners. We either have to send in more Marines from the cruisers or pull out entirely. Your orders, Admiral?"

"I hate to pull them out, Amy. It would mean we've spent all those lives for nothing...but I don't want to lose any more of them, either."

Ling said nothing. She was glad it wasn't *her* decision. A movement caught her eye, and she glanced up and found Swenson waving to attract her attention from his console.

"Uh...stand by, Admiral." She switched over to the bridge channel. "What is it, Number One?"

"Major Wesley reports that Lieutenant McGuinness and his team have taken the bridge and apparently killed the head honcho alien."

"How do they know *that*?" Amy was skeptical.

"Because the other aliens in the area surrendered, and it looks like they're surrendering all over the ship!"

Ling breathed a heavy sigh of relief as she turned back to her console and keyed the Admiral's channel. "Ma'am, strike my last suggestions."

* * *

Slowly but steadily, Bartley made her way back, sometimes carrying and sometimes dragging the wounded officer. The hardest part was getting McGraw down two deck levels—the spiral structures the aliens used for stairways were difficult even for an unencumbered human to negotiate. For once, Bartley was grateful the alien gravity was twenty percent lower than Earth's.

Doubled up and in pain, McGraw tried to move herself at first, pushing along with her legs as Bartley dragged her. Now, however, she was unconscious. *Probably lost a lot of blood after all,* Bartley decided. *At least she quit ordering me to leave her behind.*

She saw no aliens along the way. Apparently, those behind her—if any were left—had chosen not to pursue, and no others crossed her path. She was upset that Jacobs, Marino, and Raven's men had not come back for her. She would have a word with them later.

At last, she dragged McGraw around one more corner—and found herself staring down the muzzles of a couple of LCAWs wielded by a pair of Marines who stared at her as if she were a ghost.

"Are you going to ask me for a password," she snarled as they continued to stare, "or are you going to get your asses over here and help me with the colonel?"

* * *

"I just wanted to thank you for your support, gentlemen. I'm releasing your ships to return to Earth," Lorna told the two officers. "I will also convey our thanks to your government."

"It was a pleasure serving with you, Admiral," Captain Martin of USS *Minneapolis* said. "We owed the aliens some payback for *Los Angeles,* among other things. With all that mayhem, I'm not sure we actually got any of them, but at least we can claim a couple of assists."

"Actually, Captain," Lorna said, "I think we can officially credit *Chicago* and *Minneapolis* with one kill apiece. That still leaves four for our people to fight over plus two for my destroyers and one captured. As for payback, I thought it would be more difficult, but we really bushwhacked them. Do you have any thoughts on that?"

Tommy and the two Americans had come over to *Valkyrie* at Lorna's invitation and were having coffee in the admiral's day cabin. The American cruisers were part of Sakura's BG-2, filling the gaps left by the LFS cruisers *Spartan* and *Aborigine*, which had remained at Luna to serve as the last-ditch defense force.

"Ma'am, I think the battle plan was a good one," Captain Thompson of USS *Chicago* said, "and the execution was near perfect. But the aliens could have done better. We would still have beaten them, but they could have made it harder for us."

"I had that feeling as well," Tom Sakura added. "All things considered, it was much too one-sided."

"So, what would you have done in their position, Captain?"

"Well, ma'am, for one thing, they didn't react when you moved to flank that shield of theirs. They had plenty of time but they didn't seem to think your destroyers were any threat. That was their first expensive mistake. In their position, I would have spread my formation out to meet the threat. Maybe they had to stay tight to maintain that shield, but at that point the shield was already defeated."

"Good point. I actually expected they *would* react, and when they didn't, I wondered if they had some other defense we didn't know about. I was surprised when the destroyers went around their wall unchallenged. The destroyer force was just supposed to keep them busy while the rest of you got your licks in from behind."

"Well, that's another thing, Admiral," Captain Thompson put in. "When we showed up, they didn't change formation. They must have seen us before we launched our missiles. If they had taken the same track that last alien took, they could have limited their exposure to our fire. They would still have lost ships to the destroyers, and your force could still have run them down, but they wouldn't have been caught in the crossfire."

"Except for the last ship's attempt to run, they just sat there and took their licks. It looks like they believed we couldn't hurt them," Sakura mused.

* * *

Bartley was one of a dozen Marines sitting amid piles of equipment in an offload compartment next to *Valkyrie's* shuttle bay, while medics examined blood samples, skin and hair samples, and so forth. In other words, they were in quarantine—*again*, she thought with disgust. They told her it wouldn't take long—they'd learned a lot about the alien environment since the first encounter.

"I know," she said. "I'm one of the guinea pigs from your *last* set of experiments."

Unconsciously, she stroked the bandage on her forearm. She hadn't even realized she'd been hit. When an alien laser had punctured her suit, she had promptly slapped a seal on it, thinking she'd escaped with nothing more than a second-degree burn from the hot fabric. But when she'd removed the suit after the battle and saw the four-inch strip of cauterized flesh, she realized she'd come damned close to a serious wound. The medics fussed over her and insisted on listing her as wounded in action, but the burn gel they'd smeared on her arm seemed to be working, and she didn't feel much pain.

She was leaning back against a stack of ammo cases and had just closed her eyes when her name was called.

"Corporal Bartley, pick up a blue line, please. Corporal Bartley…"

Wondering who might be calling her, she got up and walked to the intercom station on the bulkhead. She punched the blue button for the ship's non-priority network and identified herself.

"Just a moment, Corporal." She recognized the voice of Val, the ship's AI, whose many functions included handling comm traffic. A moment later, an image appeared on the screen, and Bartley snapped to attention without even thinking about it.

"Corporal Bartley, I thought you might want to know," Captain Ling told her, "Colonel McGraw's going to make it. The medics say it was close, but you got her back in time. They're expecting a complete recovery."

Bartley hadn't thought much about it, but the captain's words lifted a weight off her shoulders—one she'd been carrying since she'd seen the colonel fall. "Thank you, ma'am, that's great news. I appreciate you calling to tell me."

"Thank *you*, Bartley. McGraw's a fine officer, and I would have hated to lose her."

"So would I, ma'am."

"Before they sedated her, she was mumbling about an insubordinate corporal refusing an order to leave her behind." Ling smiled. "Obviously, she was delirious, so I wouldn't worry about it."

"I'll take that under advisement, ma'am."

"Oh, and Bartley…when things quiet down a bit, I may come down to the gym again. Hopefully, you'll grant me a rematch."

"Yes, ma'am. I look forward to it," she replied, suppressing a grin.

Ling broke the connection, and Bartley turned to find several other Marines staring at her.

"What?" she demanded. "Haven't you people ever seen the captain before?"

* * * * *

Chapter Fifteen

Rock Bartley was feeling a bit fuzzy around the edges, but it was a most pleasant sensation. She still wore her dress Bravos, since the members of Valkyrie Company had insisted on escorting her directly to Corporal J's after the awards ceremony. They'd also insisted that her money was no good that night, despite which drinks kept appearing in front of her with alarming frequency. She decided she'd better take it easy unless she wanted to spend her entire ten-day leave with a hangover.

Bartley was at the head of the long table, as befitted the guest of honor. She was a bit self-conscious about it—since Lieutenant McGuinness was seated just to her right—but then, *he* had only been awarded the Star of Luna. Bartley, on the other hand, still felt the weight of the Lunar Medal of Honor—pinned on by Admiral Greenwood, no less.

The words of the citation echoed in her mind: Conspicuous bravery under enemy fire…took charge of her unit after the death of her unit leader…while wounded herself, did go to the aid of a wounded officer…singlehandedly carried that officer to safety through hostile territory, saving the officer's life. Almost as an afterthought, they'd awarded her the Heart of Luna for her minor wound and another Lunar Cross—actually a star to add to her first Cross— for being in the first wave to board the alien warship. Add to that the

Second Mekota Campaign ribbon, and she had to admit that her rack of decorations was impressive.

"You're a helluva Marine, Sarge." Lieutenant McGuinness reminded her that medals and ribbons weren't the only reward she'd gotten. Her promotion orders came through before the award ceremony, and Major Wesley had personally handed her the new set of stripes, with the directive that she'd better have them on her Bravos when she went up before the Admiral.

"Thank you, sir," she said quietly. Praise from McGuinness was high praise indeed. Though not much older than Bartley, he was a decorated ten-year veteran of the Corps. She'd been told he earned his first Star of Luna before he'd even become a Marine when, as a teenager, he'd helped rescue a bunch of school kids from a collapsed tunnel during the First Battle of Luna.

"Just a word of warning, though," he added. "If you keep going the way you are, one of these days, they're going to take all your stripes away."

"Sir?"

"That's what they did to me. I made it all the way to master sergeant, then they took all my stripes and gave me these lieutenant's bars instead." He grinned.

* * *

"I'm sorry, ma'am, the admiral's schedule is full today," the young petty officer advised.

"Will she be in her office all day?"

"Yes, ma'am, but she's got meetings with a lot of people. If you could tell me what it's about, I'll check with Commodore Yamamoto and—"

"Never mind. I'll speak with the commodore later. It isn't urgent. Thank you."

Moira Gardner ended the call and leaned back thoughtfully. *She'll be in her office all day. I think it's time to order her some lunch.* She touched her screen and placed a call to the delicatessen.

* * *

"**B**rother Luke…"

"Yes, Brother Joseph?"

"I just got a call from TerraCorp Trading. The lady said she spoke to you earlier about a special order for a meeting with a client. She said to tell you it's for the Sunrise account. She didn't give her name. Do you know what it's about?"

MacReedy suppressed a smile as the other man stiffened noticeably. *Amateurs,* he thought, *obviously, that's their secret signal.* "Uh, yes, Brother. I told her we could handle it. Did she say when she wanted it delivered?"

"She just said this morning. I presume she wants it in time for lunch." MacReedy managed to look suitably perplexed.

"No problem, Brother, but it's a large order. I'll need Brother Thomas to help me."

This is a critical point, MacReedy decided. *If I make a fuss or ask questions, they may decide to eliminate me, since I'm 'not to be trusted.'* "Of course, Brother. I'll handle things up front. You and Brother Thomas do whatever you need to do. Be sure you keep the customer happy. Outside catering is important to our business."

* * *

"**A**re you absolutely sure about this, Brigadier?" Lorna asked.

"Yes, Admiral," Kim Song Chae said. "It's time for me to turn my post over to a new generation. At last week's awards ceremony, I couldn't help but notice how *young* those fine Marines looked. I'm nearly seventy. In any other service but the LFS Marines, I'd have been told to retire long ago."

"Ability means more to me than youth," she said, "but you've obviously given this some thought. You've certainly given your share to the Lunar Free State, not to mention the contributions your children have made." Kim's oldest son was a Terra Corporation financial analyst, and his daughter was an ensign assigned to LFS *Aborigine*. His youngest boy, following in his father's footsteps, had just completed Marine officer's training.

"I'm proud of them, Admiral. They are my most important contribution to the Lunar Free State."

"What will you do now?"

"My home is here, but I think I will go back and see Korea again. Seoul is a fine city, and I still have relatives in Kang Won Do, so I may go see them as well. After that, I'll come back here and be a nuisance to my children, at least until they provide me with a suitable number of grandchildren."

"That sounds wonderful, but it leaves me without a Marine commandant. I presume you've also given some thought to your replacement."

"Yes, I have. If I may suggest, I think Colonel McGraw would make a fine choice. She is my most capable officer, despite her tendency to pick up a rifle and charge into battle—a tendency I hope has been cured by the wounds she received."

Lorna smiled. "I think she would be a fine choice, but I expect you to stay on until she has recovered from those wounds—say, another month, at least. Even after she returns to duty, she'll need time to get familiar with—"

Her comments were interrupted by a sudden commotion in the outer office—a loud series of staccato reports they both recognized immediately as *gunfire*.

* * *

Brother Luke was amazed at how easy it was. He and Brother Thomas wore brightly colored work uniforms with aprons bearing the legend *Joe's Deli*. The delicatessen was a favorite lunchtime spot for headquarters people, so no one challenged them. They rolled their serving cart right into the admiral's outer office.

"Lunch for the admiral," he announced to the receptionist. "I need you to sign here."

The young, female petty officer looked at him in surprise. "The admiral didn't order lunch. If she wanted lunch, she'd have *me* order it."

The two Marine guards had shown little interest in their arrival, but now they stiffened, and one started to reach for his sidearm. He was too late, as Brother Thomas dropped the tray he was carrying, revealing the compact machine pistol underneath. He cut down both Marines with two short bursts. Brother Luke pulled his weapon from the serving cart and shot the receptionist point-blank, then reached across her desk and hit the button that unlatched the door to the inner office. Brother Thomas turned to cover the outer door while Brother Luke went to the inner door and pushed it open.

The admiral stood behind her desk, a look of shock on her face. A Marine officer stood in front of the desk, also looking shocked. Brother Luke raised his weapon. *Die, whore of Satan,* he thought as he squeezed the trigger, but the Marine stepped in front of the target and took the burst in the chest.

* * *

Lorna knew there was nothing she could do to save Kim. As the assassin opened fire, she dove for the floor behind the desk—Ian Stevens' old desk, a heavy thing constructed of Lunar marble. The mixture of epoxy resin and crushed Lunar regolith had been developed by Lunar engineers as a construction material in the early days of the LFS, and while it wasn't as hard as real marble, it was tough enough to stop bullets. As she dropped to her knees, she yanked open the bottom drawer and reached inside. Her right hand closed around the comforting shape of Ian's antique pistol, and her left found the loaded magazine. In one smooth motion, she slapped it home and racked the slide to chamber a round.

Front sight, she thought. *Focus on the front sight.* With the pistol in front of her, she came up over the edge of the desk. The terrorist, expecting to find her cowering on the floor, had started to circle the desk with his gun pointed low. When he saw her head come up, he began to turn toward her, swinging the muzzle in her direction. He was an unfocused silhouette behind the front sight as it dropped into the rear sight's notch, and she squeezed the trigger twice in rapid succession.

The sound was deafening, like a double explosion in the close confines of the office, and the recoil of the old gun was as bad as she'd remembered. But she'd expected that, and her two shots impacted within five centimeters of each other in the middle of his chest. The heavy slugs ruined his cardiovascular system and pitched him backward. He was dead before he hit the floor.

Lorna saw movement in the outer office and brought the pistol around as the other assassin turned toward her. The sight picture came together, and she fired twice more. The target crouched as she fired, and her aim was high, but not enough to matter. One of the shots struck Brother Thomas at the base of his throat, severing his spine on the way out. The other struck the bridge of his nose before tearing a large hole in his brain. He fell back against the outer office door, twitched for a moment, and lay still.

Lorna's hands shook as she cautiously moved toward the door, the pistol held out in front of her. She reached the door and risked a glance around the doorframe, then gasped as she saw the carnage in the outer office.

"Admiral…Admiral Greenwood!" Timiko Yamamoto's voice came from behind the outer door, as the woman tried vainly to push it open against the dead body blocking it.

"Timiko! Get some medics, *right now*. And tell central command to send their Marines down here!"

* * *

Brigadier Kim was dead, as were the two Marines and the receptionist in the outer office. As for the assassins…

"What the hell hit these guys?" the medical tech wondered.

"Colt Model 1911, caliber .45 ACP," Charlie Bender muttered. "Two hundred thirty grain full-jacketed slug, moving at about two hundred seventy-five meters per second." *Not extremely fast,* he reflected, *but with that kind of bullet weight, you don't need velocity.* He noticed Lorna was still carrying the pistol in her hand. Her index finger was off the trigger and resting along the base of the slide, but the hammer was still cocked.

"Admiral, you might want to safe that weapon."

Without comment, she ejected the magazine and racked the slide, removing the live round from the chamber. Then she lowered the hammer and put the pistol back in the desk drawer. "Must remember to take it home and clean it," she said absently, her face showing none of the emotional stress Bender knew she was feeling. The comm pad on her belt began to beep, and she retrieved it and looked at the small screen. "What the hell? Who put us on Alpha Alert?"

"I did, Admiral," Bender admitted. "It seemed like a logical precaution."

* * *

Amy Ling was working in her cabin aboard *Valkyrie* when the alarm sirens began to sound. "Val, what's happening?"

"Fleet has issued an Alpha Alert, Captain. Per standing orders, we are going to battle stations. Docking tubes have been sealed, and we are prepared to cast off at your orders."

"What's the situation?"

"I have no further information, Captain. Fleet command says there is nothing on their threat boards. I have queried Mike, but he is under information restrictions and cannot tell me anything more."

The lack of information chilled Ling in a way no enemy threat could have done. *What the hell is going on?* "Very well. I'm on my way to the bridge."

* * *

When the alert sirens sounded in TerraNova's main concourse, Joseph MacReedy smiled to himself. *The harlot is dead. The Lord's will be done.*

* * *

At the sound of the sirens, Mick O'Hara looked up from his desk in TerraNova Central. "Mike, what's going on?"

"I cannot tell you that, Admiral. I am under security restrictions regarding the matter; however, be advised that we are now under Alpha Alert."

"*What!* Get me Admiral Greenwood!"

"The admiral is currently unavailable."

* * *

"What's happening?" Anne McGraw demanded from her hospital bed as the muted alert signal chimed in the corridors of TerraNova's medical center.

"I don't know, Colonel," the young doctor advised her, "but whatever it is, you're not going anywhere." He smiled inwardly. It wasn't every day a warrant officer got to give orders to a Marine colonel.

* * *

Rock Bartley did what she was supposed to do when the alert sounded—jumped into her uniform, grabbed her space bag, and headed for the shuttle terminal—only to be told all shuttle traffic was grounded. She tried to put a call through to her CO on *Valkyrie* but was told the flagship was not taking non-priority comm traffic. There was only one option left, so she grabbed her gear and headed for Marine Command HQ of TerraNova to report to the first Marine officer she could find.

* * *

Amy Ling had just reached *Valkyrie's* bridge when Val advised her of an incoming call—Code One Confidential—from Admiral Greenwood. She took the call in her ready room.

"What's happening, Admiral?" she asked as Greenwood's image appeared on the screen. The admiral looked upset. No, Ling decided, she looked more than upset. She looked ready to take someone's head off.

"Stand the group down from battle stations, Amy. We are *not* going to war. Alert condition is reduced to Gamma, but I want a security lockdown on the ships—no one boards or departs without captain's permission."

Admiral Bender's face appeared over her shoulder. "Be alert for possible acts of sabotage, Commodore, and—"

"*That will be all, Admiral Bender!*" Greenwood's sharp command cut him off in mid-sentence. Then she turned back to Ling. "Tell your section heads to be alert for sabotage, Amy. I don't think it's a serious threat, but *certain officers* down here are a bit paranoid."

"May I ask what's happening, Admiral?"

"Someone just tried to kill me," Lorna told her grimly. "I'm all right, but Brigadier Kim and several others are dead."

Ling was shocked. "How...I mean, who would...?"

"We're still trying to determine that. Mike can fill you in on the details, but for now, implement those orders and stand the group down."

"Admiral..." Ling hesitated "Val says Mike's been ordered not to give us any information."

Lorna turned again to Charlie Bender. "Is that true, Admiral?"

"Yes, ma'am. I thought—"

"Mike!" she ordered. "Information restrictions *will not apply* to the following officers: Admiral O'Hara, Vice Admiral Sakura, Vice Admiral Bender, Commodore Yamamoto, Commodore Ling, Commodore Jones, Vice Admiral Wexler, Commodore McTavish, or Commodore Millington. Oh, and add Colonel McGraw to that list. You will also share all information regarding the incident with Val and Anna, with the understanding that they are not to release it to anyone except the officers on the list. Is that clear?"

"Yes, ma'am," the AI's voice said.

"Very well. Amy, carry on. I'll keep you advised." Lorna broke the connection, then closed her office door and turned to face Charlie Bender. She spoke quietly, but there was fire in her eyes, and Bender had no doubt she was deadly serious. "Admiral Bender, you are a *staff officer*. You don't *ever* give orders to Fleet or to Lunar command without checking with me. If I am *dead*, you don't give such orders without checking with Admiral O'Hara *or whoever is in command*. You put the entire Lunar Free State on alert for *no sufficient reason*. And you are *never* to withhold vital information from my Fleet commanders without my specific authorization. Is that clear?"

"Yes, ma'am, but—"

"There is no but, Admiral. If it happens again, you will be relieved of duty."

"Yes, ma'am," he replied quietly.

Lorna softened a bit. "Charlie, I understand you have security concerns, but that was a knee-jerk reaction. Maybe you think I'm in shock and can't function properly, but that is not the case. If I could handle it when Ian and Carla died, I can handle this. Now, I need you to do what *you* do best. Find out who those bastards were."

"Yes, ma'am, but just on the chance that this *might* be part of something larger, let me *recommend* some security measures I think we ought to take—with your approval, that is."

"All right, Charlie," she said. "Tell me what you think we ought to do."

* * *

"I understand, Admiral. Everything is secure here, but watch your six, dear lady. Some Marines just showed up at my door. Did you send them?"

"It's Charlie's idea, Mick. Since you're next in command, he feels you need protection as well. It's a reasonable precaution."

"All right, I can live with that."

* * *

Anne McGraw was surprised to see Timiko Yamamoto standing in the door of her hospital room. "Commodore...?"

"Colonel, I'm afraid I have bad news."

"What's wrong?"

"There was an attempt on Admiral Greenwood's life." She held up her hand. "The admiral is all right, but several other people were killed, including Brigadier Kim. He saved the admiral's life, took the bullets that were intended for her."

"Kim...dead?" McGraw's face registered painful disbelief. Kim had been her mentor since the earliest days on Luna. Her mind refused to accept that the tough old Marine was gone.

"I'm sorry, Anne, and I hate to lay this on you now, but the admiral says you're to take his place as commandant—as soon as you're recovered, that is."

"I..." McGraw hesitated. It was too much to accept at the moment. "Tell the admiral I'll do whatever she requires of me but get the doctors to *let me out of here*. Has anyone notified Kim's children?"

"Not yet," Yamamoto said. "This just happened, and we're still sorting it out. Two of your Marines are now on guard outside your door. Admiral Bender ordered extra security for key command personnel."

"A bit late for that," McGraw replied bitterly.

* * * * *

Chapter Sixteen

TerraNova City, Luna

MacReedy wasn't surprised when five armed Marines entered the delicatessen, led by a grim-faced lieutenant. A few late lunch customers were waiting for takeout orders.

"This facility is closed for business," the Marine officer announced. "Please move to the exit. Not you, sir." He pointed a finger at MacReedy.

With some grumbling and a lot of curiosity, the customers departed.

"Come out from behind the counter with your hands visible. Are you Joseph MacReedy?"

The Marines fanned out, and MacReedy could almost *feel* the five assault rifles pointed at him.

"Yes, I'm Joseph MacReedy." He tried to sound surprised and upset. "What's this all about?"

"Turn around and put your hands behind you," the lieutenant directed as he produced a pair of handcuffs. "Sir, you are under arrest for conspiracy to commit murder. You are advised to make no statements until a defense officer is assigned."

"Murder!" Now MacReedy tried to sound shocked. "Who am I supposed to have murdered?"

"You are advised to make no statements until a defense officer is assigned. We have an order from the Judge Advocate General, authorizing SID to conduct a search of these premises."

Of course, you have, MacReedy thought. *Go ahead and search. I hope you find what I left for you. It won't prove anything against me, but it will certainly point a finger at others.*

* * *

Hours later, MacReedy was sweating. His defense officer had shown up, a female lieutenant commander, but she wasn't a lawyer. Apparently, they didn't have lawyers on the Moon. She was a regular officer who had completed the requirements to be certified as an LCMJ legal counselor, and she mostly sat through the questioning and said nothing. When he complained, she told him her function wasn't to advise or defend him at this point—she was there to make certain he wasn't subjected to physical abuse or otherwise coerced. The questioning was recorded, but recordings could be doctored, so she was also there as a witness in the event there was any dispute about the proceedings.

She would conduct her own interview later to gather information to be used in his defense. Anything he said at that time would be privileged information. Then she would get together with the JAG's people to determine whether a court-martial was warranted, and if so, she would present his defense. As in an American court, she told him, there would be a presumption of innocence, and the JAG would have the burden of proof.

He was hoping it wouldn't get that far, but the questioning was rough. He supposed he should be honored, since his chief questioner wasn't a regular SID officer, but Vice Admiral Bender, chief of LFS Intelligence Services.

"Your two employees, tell me again how you came to hire them."

"I wanted people of my own faith, so I placed an ad through the church's employment services office on Earth."

"Right. That would be the Church of the Second Redemption, headquartered in Austin, Texas, USA." Bender consulted his notes. "Your spiritual leader, Bishop J.C. LeGrange, condemns the Lunar Free State as 'high-technology heathens, godless sinners given to every perversion known to man, and servants of Satan.' Is that correct?"

"I...I am a member of that church, yes, but I don't recall those particular words from Bishop LeGrange. We are *all* sinners in the eyes of the Lord. I try to live my own life by what is right, and I—"

"Does that include punishing sinners or killing servants of Satan, if your church tells you to do so?"

"I never—"

"And you never met these two men before the church sent them to you?"

"I swear before God I did not!" he shouted, thankful it was true. "If you knew anything about our church, you would know how serious that oath is to me!"

"As serious as *murder*?" Bender snarled.

"You keep talking about murder," he whimpered. "I don't even know *who* has been murdered!"

"*Not* the person you might be hoping for," Bender said with grim satisfaction, and for the first time, MacReedy began to suspect the plan had failed.

* * *

Lorna was on a call when the Marines—six of them in the outer office—allowed Charlie Bender into her presence.

"That's right, Chief. I need a standard-issue officer's sidearm belt, Navy Alpha uniform, not Marines, but the holster has to be fitted for a Colt 1911 pistol."

"I beg your pardon, ma'am?"

"A Colt Model 1911A1 .45 caliber pistol—Mike has specifications if you need them. And the magazine pouches should be sized for the same pistol."

"Yes, ma'am. We'll have to make it up special, but you'll have it by tomorrow."

"Thank you, Chief." She broke the connection.

"Are you really planning to wear that thing?" Bender asked.

"It saved my life, Charlie. If I'd been wearing it instead of keeping it in the drawer, it might have saved Kim's life as well. Besides, you told me I should carry a sidearm until we get this sorted out."

"Don't get me wrong, Admiral. I know what an expert *pistolero* you are, and I think you *should* be armed, but I thought you'd might want to consider something more modern—like a Sig ARP, for example."

"If I get involved in a gunfight, it's likely to be up close and personal, like this one. Under those conditions, you have to admit the old .45 is highly effective."

"It only gives you seven rounds."

"Eight, if you keep one in the chamber. If I need more than that, I'm in deep trouble, anyway. What's on your mind, Charlie?"

"A couple of things, Admiral. First, with all the additional guard assignments, TerraNova's Marine contingent is getting stretched thin. I had a conversation with Colonel McGraw, and—"

"Charlie, she's still in the hospital. I don't want you laying her new job on her just yet."

"I know, Admiral. I only went by the hospital to fill her in on what's happening. She was close to Brigadier Kim, and I thought I owed her that. In any case, I told her we were a little short on Marines down here, and she suggested we bring down a squad or two from *Valkyrie*, specifically for the task of providing security for *you*. She said those people have a special degree of loyalty where you are concerned. To them, you are the Babe on the Horse."

"I'm the *what?*"

"It's a Marine thing that's been going around. The Babe on the Horse means *Valkyrie*—as depicted in her hull artwork. They think of you as the Valkyrie in the flesh, so to speak."

"Okay, Charlie, I get the picture. I'm flattered," she replied, and Bender noticed she was blushing slightly, "but I guess the idea has merit. How many do you need?"

"Two squads should suffice, ma'am—one for your personal guard detail, and the other to augment the headquarters contingent."

"Fine. I'll tell Amy Ling to send them down, and I'm sorry I jumped on you. You were right to keep McGraw advised. What else have you got?"

"Preliminary investigation results. The terrorists were members of an extremist American religious cult. We've run their passports through the American State Department, and they're phony. We've no information as to their real identities, so we're just calling them

Brother Luke and Brother Thomas, as they were known to their employer, one Joseph MacReedy, proprietor of Joe's Deli.

"MacReedy is a member of the same religious cult, but he claims he knows nothing about the attempt. He says he hired these two because they were recommended by a church-sponsored employment agency. He *may* be telling the truth. He had their employment applications on file, and I've got to have more than this before I can ask the JAG for permission to do a polygraph—which he can refuse anyway. He's a provisional citizen, entitled to the same constitutional privacy rights as the rest of us.

"We have no evidence other than the church connection, and we'll probably turn him loose. We're searching his quarters and place of business, and by the time the lab gets done, we'll be able to tell whether the crumbs on the floor were white bread or rye. We're doing the same for the terrorists' quarters.

"The only other pieces of evidence we have are the guns, and they were *not* purchased here on Luna—had to have come directly from Earth. They're poor quality, not from any regular arms manufacturer. They used 6mm percussion caseless rounds, and modern body armor would stop them cold, which brings me to my next point." He paused to open the box he'd brought with him and showed her the contents.

"Oh, no, Charlie. I am *not* going to wear that thing."

"Only if you go out in public," he pleaded. "It's lightweight, comfortable, latest high-tech ballistic weave—it'll never show under your uniform. Please, Admiral, let me get a little sleep at night."

* * *

Finally released, Joseph MacReedy went home to his apartment, which showed signs of a thorough, very professional search. Nothing was out of place, but he knew what to look for. Things that he'd left dirty were clean—they'd had to clean up after lifting fingerprints, of course. And some small bits of lint he'd deliberately left in his clothing drawers had been disturbed.

He wasn't worried. He'd never invited the two assassins to his quarters, and he'd been careful not to keep anything there that might arouse suspicion.

He still didn't know what his 'brethren' had accomplished, but when he turned to the TerraNova News, he discovered what they had *not* accomplished. The on-screen reporter advised of an upcoming address by Admiral Greenwood, regarding events related to the recent Alpha Alert.

The devil-whore is still alive! Incompetent fools! He hoped Brother Luke and Brother Thomas had, at least, managed to get themselves killed in the process.

* * *

Moira Gardner's reaction was similar to MacReedy's. *Bitch must have a charmed life, or those bumbling idiots totally screwed it up! Why couldn't she have died a damned heroine, battling the damned aliens or something?*

Gardner had even more reason to hope the terrorists had died in the attack. They had never seen her face, but...

* * *

Bartley finally managed to get back to *Valkyrie*, only to be told she was going down to Luna again. By then, she'd seen the news feeds, and she knew what the fuss was about.

"We're sending two squads down, Sergeant," Major Wesley said. "Sergeant Edwards will take a squad down to augment the HQ security force. Your squad will serve as Admiral Greenwood's personal security detail. You'll report to Vice Admiral Bender."

Bartley swallowed a lump in her throat. *Admiral Greenwood's personal security detail? Hell's bells! Why don't you give me an easy job...like boarding a Turnip warship all by myself?* "Yes, sir."

"And Rock...you realize someone just tried to kill the admiral..."

"I'm aware of that, sir."

"If anybody tries again, handle the bastards like you handled your first Turnip. As long as you protect the admiral, I won't be particularly concerned if SID doesn't have any live suspects to question. Is that understood?"

"Understood, sir."

* * *

The Guardians stood in silence, stunned by the record they had just seen. Only the rippling of their crests, flickering with colors as they sought to control their emotions, signaled their inner turmoil; and their predominant emotion was *fear*.

Finally, Second of the Red spoke. "What are we to do, First Guardian?"

The First had seen the record before the meeting, and her emotions were controlled, her crest the pale blue of calm, collected thought. "Nothing."

"But First Guardian—"

"I have discussed this with the Yellow. Perhaps you should hear their advice."

The new Second of the Yellow had also seen the record in advance, when the First had told her of her predecessor's demise at the hands of the humans. Her crest was also calm and blue as she accepted the invitation to speak. "We have analyzed what you have seen, Guardians, and this is our conclusion. The humans detected the Triforce immediately—by what means, we do not know—but we believe they were aware of *every action* our ships took. At some point, they deliberately revealed the ship that was shadowing, though they could have remained hidden. They showed us no fear, and they evaded our attempts to pursue them with contemptuous ease.

"They watched until they knew we were headed for their planet. Then they intercepted the Triforce in a manner that was tactically brilliant and flawlessly executed. They challenged us—dared even to tell us they were about to attack—and when the Triforce tried to engage them, they simply moved out of range.

"Once they lured our forces to the point of no retreat, they attacked using guided fusion bombs that came at our ships so quickly and in such numbers, the entire Triforce was destroyed in a matter of moments. Only one ship escaped destruction—the Guardian's ship—and they hunted it down and slowly tore it to pieces.

"The facts are these: The renegade humans possess warships far superior to ours. They can accelerate more than twice as fast as our ships, and their guided weapons are *ten times faster than that*. Against these weapons, we have no defense, and their range is such that our weapons cannot engage the attacking ships. Their *smallest* warships are a match for our largest and best. Their detection and surveillance systems can detect our ships at great distances, but we cannot see them until they choose to reveal themselves.

"We believe they possess these warships in vast numbers. The Triforce was attacked by nearly two twelves of warships, and they may have many more waiting in reserve or guarding their planet. They spent many more weapons than needed to destroy the Triforce. These factors speak of a fleet with warships and weapons to spare.

"Given their superior detection capabilities, we believe they knew of the messenger ship the Triforce left behind and allowed it to escape as a warning to us. They must have destroyed the Blue Envoy and the Monoforce and waited for our response. When the Triforce arrived, they decided to make it clear we trespass at our peril.

"We do not know how the humans achieved such power, but we believe they tampered with the Deathwatch Messengers to make us *think* they destroyed themselves. They want to be left alone, and we should be grateful that—as far as we know—they have not yet discovered the way into Otherspace. We are engaged in a war with the Akara that demands much of our strength, but even with the entire fleet at our disposal, we should hesitate to confront these humans.

"The Yellow recommend that the renegade human system be placed under interdiction—no ship of the Red, Blue, or Yellow shall be permitted to travel into or through it. Messengers will be placed in nearby systems within the Sphere to watch for signs of human interstellar travel. We dare not send more Messengers into their system, since the capture of one might give them the secret of Otherspace.

"The fleet will be reinforced in the mother system to guard against attack by the humans, and we will increase that force as the Akara situation permits. We will develop improved weapons and defensive systems to make our ships less vulnerable to human weapons. By the time the Akara have been dealt with, we will be ready to deal with the humans."

In the end, the Guardians accepted the plan, and the First directed the Yellow to carry it out. In some respects. the analysis was correct. Ship for ship, the warships of Earth—at least, those of the LFS—*were* superior, especially if the humans were allowed to control the engagement. They had no way of knowing the twenty-two ships that attacked their Triforce represented over two-thirds of Earth's effective battle fleet.

The Mekota had over 5,000 warships at their disposal, but most of their fleet was engaged against another enemy. And it wasn't just the overwhelming defeat that struck terror into the Guardians. As the humans closed in for the kill, the final transmission had given the Mekota a close-up view of the human flagship, and they would long be haunted by the fearsome image of *Valkyrie*.

* * * * *

Chapter Seventeen

TerraNova City, Luna

MacReedy opened his deli as usual the next morning but closed it again shortly after noon. There was no reason to keep it open—he'd had no customers. After the news reports, he might as well have hung a sign on the door: *Joe's Deli, haven for terrorists and assassins.* Before he even opened the doors, however, he'd gone to the back room and looked behind a pallet of supplies. He was pleased to find the item he'd left there—had carefully placed there—was gone. Brother Luke and Brother Thomas had discarded the box in the deli trash, and if MacReedy hadn't known their intentions, it would have been processed in TerraNova's recycling plant. He had gone back to the deli that night and retrieved it before the trash was picked up.

If Admiral Bender's Special Investigations Division was any good, the box should send a few of the sinners to their just reward. MacReedy had nothing but contempt for traitors, even those whose traitorous acts served his own cause.

* * *

"I am terribly sorry, Admiral. It shames me to think those fanatics dared to call themselves Americans. On behalf of the entire nation, let me assure you they do *not* represent the true feelings of the people of the USA."

"I know, Mr. President," Lorna assured him, "and we certainly don't hold your country responsible."

"I'm sure you don't, Admiral. But Ian Stevens once told me I shouldn't encourage people like that, and I must admit, I am sometimes more tolerant of them than I should be. I just want you to know I will use the full force of the U.S. government to root out those responsible for this terrible crime."

"I appreciate that, Mr. President, but I didn't call to talk about that. I wanted to thank you personally for the support your Navy provided against the aliens and to get your assurance that we can continue to count on you if they show up again."

"Do you really think they will, Admiral? After all, we really kicked their butts. Downright *vaporized* most of 'em."

"That's true, but they got a message off. Satellite surveillance tracked the thing going hell-bent for their jump point, and we had no chance to intercept it. It looks like it departed shortly after we finished wiping out their force, so they probably have some idea what happened. We can *hope* the message they got is that they are not welcome here and should stay home, but we can't count on it.

"We've worked informally with your Navy, and it has gone very well, but my Fleet people would like to have something more definite in place—a mutual defense agreement that would allow us to conduct joint maneuvers, use each other's maintenance facilities, and so on, without making special arrangements each time. Is that something you would consider?"

"It makes sense to me," Blackthorne agreed. "But it should be worked out by the people involved. I'll talk to Admiral Smith, Chief of Space Operations, and have him call...who should I tell him to call on your side, Admiral?"

"Vice Admiral Sakura, commander of our second battle group. He's worked closely with your people in the past, and I'm putting him in charge of this project. Your CSO can reach him through Lunar fleet command, here in TerraNova."

"Tell him to expect a call from Admiral Smith within a day or so. Let the two of them come up with a plan, then you and I can review it."

"Sounds good to me, Mr. President," she said with a smile. "You really are easy to deal with."

Blackthorne chuckled. "You know, Admiral, we just accomplished in five minutes what would probably take *months* through normal diplomatic channels, but Ian Stevens—God rest his soul—taught me years ago that there was a better way. When I meet with other heads of state, we tiptoe around issues and try to slip each other little hints, always looking over our shoulders for media reporters. Then my diplomatic people analyze the conversations and try to figure out just what President So-and-So *meant* when he said such-and-such. Like, did he really mean he wanted to see Disney World or is he planning to invade Florida? It's never been that way with you people—we just call each other up and speak our minds, and we get things done. I appreciate that, even if I don't always like what you tell me."

"We're simple people, Mr. President, and we deal in straight talk, and I appreciate the fact that you've always been straight with me." *Even if it did take years of dealing with Ian before you learned that.*

"Right, Admiral…you're just a simple Navy officer…and if anybody believes that, I've got an old, rusty bridge in Brooklyn I'd like to sell them." He gave Lorna a sly and most un-presidential wink.

After the usual exchange of pleasantries, they broke the connection, and Blackthorne punched his intercom to summon the men waiting in his outer office. He started in on them before they had a chance to get comfortable, beginning with the FBI director. "I want this Church of the Second Redemption turned inside out, and I want it to be as *unpleasant* as possible. Take the DEA with you and tell them to bring their drug-sniffing dogs...those critters always look real impressive on video. Be sure to tip off your favorite media people. I want to turn on the evening news tomorrow night and see people being led away in handcuffs. Is that clear?"

"Mr. President, we haven't completed our investigation. We don't even know what we can charge them with."

"Charge them with spitting on the sidewalk if you have to. I want a message to go out that we are not going to allow any American religious terrorists to go around plotting assassinations. What really galls me is that we have been spending so much time trying to keep the Islamics from pulling stuff like this and then a so-called *Christian* group comes out of the woodwork and does the same damned thing."

"Mr. President," one of the aides interrupted, "before you go too far, I think you need to see this." The aide extended a sheet of paper.

Blackthorne put on his reading glasses and peered at it. "No kidding? They gave *that much* money to my campaign?" He thought about it for a moment, then turned back to the aide. "In that case, I want the IRS crawling up their asses as well! I want to know how *else* they spend their tax-exempt money.

"Get this straight—" He glared at all of them. "These people have *pissed me off!* I was just getting to *like* that woman—even though people say she bats for the other team—and I will not have some pissant who *calls* himself an American taking shots at her, especially since she happens to be the head of state of our absolute best number-one ally. You people are thinking about the political repercussions of making trouble for a campaign contributor. Well, they are *nothing* compared to the political repercussions of damaging our relations with the Lunar Free State. Is there any part of that any of you don't understand?"

* * *

Lorna directed Mike to give Tommy Sakura a heads-up regarding the promised call from the U.S. Navy, then turned her attention to the latest financial reports from Terra Corporation. Business was good, she noted, but she resolved to get someone on her staff to review the things in more detail. This was the area of the CEO's responsibilities with which she was least comfortable, but one of critical importance to the financial health of the nation. *I need a real financial analyst on staff. Hmm, maybe Kim's son would be a good choice. Have to take a look at his file.*

Next, she turned her attention to the Fleet construction schedule, reflecting that even that aspect of her job had changed forever. While Ian was alive, she'd only had to worry about getting ships built and deployed; now she had to worry about how to pay for them.

Her interface beeped to tell her a scheduled visitor had arrived, and she looked up as Charlie Bender came into her office, followed by Sergeant Bartley. Bartley took up her usual position against the wall and stood at parade rest, her right hand never far from the holstered pistol on her belt. Bender glanced over his shoulder at the Marine, then gave Lorna a look of smug satisfaction. The requirement that a Marine guard be inside the office whenever Lorna had a visitor—*any* visitor—was one of Charlie's new security measures. Lorna hadn't objected, but she had reminded the Marines anything they saw or heard in the office was confidential—classified Most Secret.

"All right, Charlie, what's up?"

Bender seated himself in front of her desk. "Good news and bad news, Admiral. The good news is that we've made progress with the investigation. The bad news is you're not going to like what we found."

"And why might that be?"

"Because some of our own people—Lunar citizens—are implicated."

"You have my attention," she said.

"We found a box in the back room of Joe's Deli. It caught our attention because the printing on the box indicated computer parts—molycirc interface cards, not something you'd expect to find in a delicatessen. Lab analysis shows the box contained the guns—not just any guns, but the ones used by the assassins. Their fingerprints were all over the box, as were several others, but we didn't look into those until we reconstructed the shipping label.

"The label was removed, but whoever did it needn't have bothered, and obviously had no concept of what modern forensics can do. Anytime you put a printed label on a box, you get an image transfer at the molecular level due to ambient radiation—not enough to be visible, but with deep spectrum analysis, we were able to reconstruct the entire label. The box came from an alleged computer parts supplier on Earth. We checked, and there is no such company, but it was addressed to Doctor Lawrence Devereaux."

Lorna looked at him in disbelief. "You're telling me the guns were shipped to *Devereaux?*"

"We checked the shipping records, Admiral. The sonofabitch signed for the box himself—and his job function does *not* normally include receiving or signing for computer parts. What's more, his fingerprints were on the box. There's no indication he *opened* it, and his prints were only on the outside, but the lab tells us the guns were in the box before it arrived on Luna, and the box was *not* opened and resealed a second time. His prints *were* on the package sealing tape. In other words, the guns were in that box when he handled it.

"After that, we ran down some of the other prints on the box and came up with a rating who works in the IT section's mail room, whose prints were on the box in the place where the label had been—in other words, who handled the box *after* the label had been removed. He remembered the box because Devereaux had called him up to his office late in the afternoon and asked him to deliver it to Joe's Deli. The guy he took it to was Brother Luke."

"Devereaux," Lorna whispered. "I know he hates me but…"

"There's more, Admiral. When we questioned the deli owner, he mentioned a phone call the morning of the assassination attempt."

"It wasn't an *attempt*, Charlie. They killed Brigadier Kim, two Marines, and my receptionist. I've already straightened out the news people on that, and they're now calling it what it was—an assassination. Period." It was a sensitive subject for Lorna. She wasn't about to let anyone forget that others had died trying to protect her. "Continue."

"Sorry. He told us about a phone call on the morning of the assassination. Someone from TerraCorp Trading called about a special order to be delivered—told him that Brother Luke knew about it. He told Brother Luke about the call and, shortly after that, Brother Luke and Brother Thomas left the deli, allegedly to deliver the order. Of course, they didn't deliver anything. They came straight here, murdered four people, and tried to murder you.

"Based on that, we got Judge Wexler to issue an order allowing us to examine the phone data for the deli that day. I guess you know Mike listens to every phone conversation on Luna—"

"Mike does *what?*"

"Actually, he doesn't listen—that is, he doesn't process the information. He stores it. It's all just a data stream to him, and he handles it the same way he does the entertainment channels. That's why you can watch the morning news in the middle of the afternoon if you like. He flushes anything more than three days old—the stuff takes up too much storage space—but after the assassination, I asked him to hold anything he had in storage at the time. I can ask him to do that, but I can't get any of the data without an order from the JAG, and *that's* a Code One Restriction as far as Mike is concerned— it has the same force of law as the Constitution."

"It damned well *better* have," she growled. "I need to have a conversation with Mike, to find out what *else* is going on in your wonderful little world of espionage and law enforcement."

"Wasn't my idea, ma'am—this goes back to Ian and the Deep Space Research Institute. Mike handled the phone system there, too, if you recall."

"Back to the point, Charlie. What did you come up with?"

"There *was* such a call. The caller asked about a special order Luke was supposed to know about for a client luncheon. She said to be sure to tell him it was for the Sunrise account and that she needed it delivered that day."

"She…?"

"We checked the calling station ID and did a voiceprint. It was Moira Gardner."

"Gardner?" She shook her head in disbelief. "An *assassination plot?* Come on, Charlie, isn't it possible she was just placing an order for lunch? People do that all the time, you know."

Bender sighed. "We checked with TerraCorp Trading. There is no Sunrise account, and there were no client luncheons scheduled that day. There was also nothing about it on Gardner's schedule. With that information, we got Judge Wexler to give us an order for Gardner's phone data. She called your office that morning and spoke with your receptionist, allegedly to get an appointment to see you. The receptionist told her you were booked, and Gardner *specifically* asked if you were going to be in your office all day. The receptionist told her you would, and *ten seconds after that, Gardner placed the call to the deli.* Do you *still* think she was ordering lunch?"

"How did it get to this, Charlie?" she asked bitterly. "Our own people. Lunar citizens and members of the Directorate. Am I so hated they were willing to kill Brigadier Kim and three other people to get to me?"

"No," he said. "You're not hated, not by decent Lunar citizens, but these people are *hateful.* They don't need a reason to hate, other than what they get from their own twisted minds."

"So, what do we do now?"

"The case against Gardner is still a little thin, but we have Devereaux dead cold, and he'll probably give up Gardner if he thinks it will save his ass. Neither of them can get off Luna, and there's no place to hide. I want to pick up Devereaux now, and I'm betting we'll be ready to pick up Gardner by the end of the day."

"Do what you have to do, Charlie. Just keep me advised." Her voice was still bitter, and Bender saw a tear roll down her cheek.

Lorna looked up and noticed Sergeant Bartley, standing like a statue against the wall. The young Marine's expression hadn't changed, but she must have heard everything. Suddenly aware of the tear she had shed, Lorna self-consciously brushed it away, wondering what Bartley was thinking.

Rock Bartley had just gotten a hell of an education. She'd learned, among other things, that Admiral Greenwood—the Iron Maiden, the commander-in-chief—was a human being with a heart. That only increased her respect for the admiral, which was not easy to do, since Greenwood was already at the top of Bartley's most-admired list, with Colonel McGraw as her only real competition for the top spot.

She'd also learned those who would harm the admiral were the lowest of the low…people who cared nothing for the lives of their countrymen, who would casually murder Brigadier Kim and three others just for being in the way of their twisted scheme. They were, Bartley reflected, people she would *love* to spend time with in a locked room while armed with a suitably blunt instrument—or even with her bare hands, if necessary.

Finally, Bartley had learned it was *not* a good idea to run afoul of Admiral Bender and his SID people—not that she ever expected to do anything that would warrant their attention. All the same, she would think twice about anything she said on the phone from now on.

Bender got up to leave but turned back with an afterthought. "You know what really bothers me, Admiral…these people were *amateurs*. They made some stupid mistakes, and they left a trail a blind man could have followed. But they *almost succeeded*. So, when I tell you your security needs improvement, I would appreciate it if you would please take it seriously."

"I will, Charlie," she said quietly.

With that, Bender tossed her a salute and left the office. Bartley came to attention and followed him out the door.

* * *

LFS *Stephen Hawking,* Near the Sol System "Hyper Limit"

It was *déjà vu* for Commander Shin and his crew as LFS *Stephen Hawking* raced outward toward the far reaches of the Solar System. This time, they weren't quite so lonely—the bridge displays showed the heavy cruiser *Aztec* holding station ten kilometers off *Hawking's* starboard beam. They also weren't in such a hurry this time, and the two ships were accelerating at a comfortable 80 gravities. They had been driving outward for some time and had reached a little over point one Cee—about 35,000 kps—relative to the Sun.

Shin was still up to his neck in scientists, and this time, there were engineers aboard as well. *Hawking* was tasked with observation and monitoring—a mission for which she was the best-equipped ship in the fleet. *Aztec* was there to provide an escort and deliver the hyperprobe, since the experimental vehicle was too large to be carried by the research ship.

The probe could have been smaller. In fact, the engineers told Shin it could have been small enough to be launched from *Hawking's* missile tubes if its only mission were to enter hyperspace and return. But the scientists had insisted on packing it with tons of instrumentation. There was even a life support module containing a variety of small creatures—laboratory rodents, reptiles, insects, and so forth. To provide power for the equipment and instrumentation, plus the gravity drive and the hyperspace translation device—which the engineers called the jump generator—they had been forced to include a fusion reactor.

The probe also had an onboard computer system—not an AI, but a powerful system, nonetheless. Shin had heard a rumor that Luna's AIs had volunteered to go—or to produce a new child that could pilot the probe—but Admiral Greenwood was not about to risk one of them on a mission like this.

The probe was *not* being sent in the direction from which the aliens had come. The mission profile called for it to be launched toward Alpha Centauri, a star system just over four light-years away. Once in hyperspace, the computer would determine how long it would take to reach that system. If it could do so within the mission time limit, it would go there, pop out of hyperspace, collect as much data as possible, then turn around and come back. If it couldn't get there within the time limit—the scientists had set a maximum of 300 hours for the one-way trip—it would drop out of hyper anyway, collect whatever data it could in the void between the stars, and return. Assuming there was no time dilation in hyperspace (and the captured aliens had assured the scientists there was not), the probe should return within thirty days.

The scientists weren't sure how long the journey would take. They hadn't gotten all the answers they'd wanted before the first group of aliens died. They were questioning the new captives from the recent engagement, but the probe was ready to go, and Admiral Greenwood hadn't wanted to wait. In any case, *Hawking* and *Aztec* would wait for the probe to return—if it returned at all.

Shin had seen the probe when it was loaded aboard *Aztec* at the Lunar yards. It was only about twenty meters long, but he suspected it had cost as much as a destroyer to build. A lot of people would be extremely disappointed if it didn't come back.

* * *

TerraNova City, Luna

Moira Gardner looked up from her desk in surprise as Vice Admiral Bender walked into her office unannounced, followed by two Marines wearing sidearms.

"What's the meaning of this?" She stabbed at the intercom icon on her desk screen. "Sandra, who told you to admit these people?"

There was no reply, and Bender regarded her with a cold, merciless half-smile. Suddenly, Gardner *knew* why he was there, and the color drained from her face.

"Chief Warrant Officer Moira Gardner, you're under arrest for high treason, conspiracy to assassinate the chief executive, and the murder of four Lunar citizens."

* * * * *

Chapter Eighteen

TerraNova City, Luna

When they first told Rock Bartley that Admiral Greenwood was to be guarded at all times, she hadn't realized the implications, but Admiral Bender had promptly enlightened her. As the squad leader, she was responsible for making sure her squad members—and the additional Marines headquarters gave her—were posted where and when they were needed. She would also be *personally* responsible for the admiral's safety during off-duty hours. The rest of her people were assigned quarters in the HQ complex, but Bartley had been told to take her gear and move into the CEO's Residence! Her quarters would be a small room next to the admiral's bedroom. Admiral Bender told her to sleep with one eye open and her sidearm on the bedside table.

In addition, she was expected to keep her squad sharp, occasionally pull duty with one of her troopers in the admiral's office, and be present whenever the admiral went out in public. *That* was a real deployment exercise which usually required at least ten Marines. She had gotten an education from Admiral Bender on how to run a personal security detail, and her head was full of Bender's Rules.

At first, Bartley thought it was going to be a real *bitch* of an assignment—worse than the Turnip translator episode aboard the Mekota ship. But Admiral Greenwood was a considerate commander who tried to make it easy for her guard detail. Before scheduling unusual activities, she almost always checked with Bartley to see if there would be problems, and she didn't hesitate to rip a strip off Admiral Bender if she thought he was making unreasonable demands on the Marine detail.

There were a great deal of prestige and other benefits associated with the detail. For one thing, Bartley could—politely, of course—give orders to senior officers and other important persons and expect to be obeyed without question if it involved the admiral's security. There had been one incident in the admiral's office involving the French ambassador—whom Bartley regarded as a first-class asshole. It was some silly thing about a trade agreement, and he got angry to the point where he was leaning over Greenwood's desk and shaking his fist at her—until Bartley had clamped a hand on his wrist and ordered him to 'Step back from the admiral's desk, sir.'

She thought she might have gone too far, but the Frenchie—a scrawny little wimp a head shorter and twenty kilos lighter than Bartley—had stepped back and apologized for losing his temper. Greenwood hadn't batted an eye and never mentioned the incident.

Bartley also found she had no demanding duties in the CEO's Residence other than making sure the outside guards were at their posts and the Residence was locked down when the admiral retired for the night. Of course, if Greenwood had any visitors, Bartley was required to be armed and in the admiral's presence until the visitors departed.

Such visitors were rare. Admiral Greenwood wasn't much for social events, and she believed quarters were for relaxation and business should be conducted in the office. That didn't stop her from working late into the night at times, but she usually did so alone in her library.

Bartley also discovered the job came with certain other perks. The admiral's stewards, a married couple in their mid-fifties named Manuel and Maria Lopez—officially listed as petty officers on the T.O. —were excellent cooks and considered it their duty to make sure Bartley was properly fed. The menu was geared to the admiral's tastes but, having lived on field rations for more than a month aboard the first Turnip ship, Bartley had no complaints.

On the morning of her second day in the Residence, she had been making her bed when there was a knock on her door. She'd opened it to find Manuel Lopez standing there, sharp and crisp in his steward's uniform. He told her he was there for her laundry. After a short protest—during which he politely informed her that *her* job was to protect the admiral and that *she* should not have to worry about things that were his and Maria's responsibilities—she had surrendered her rumpled uniforms and other garments. He told her she shouldn't bother making her bed or cleaning her room, either, since those were also the responsibilities of the stewards.

Lopez had returned that evening with her clothing cleaned and pressed, and she'd been shocked to see her uniforms hanging right next to the admiral's on his valet cart. All the same, it was nice to have the service, especially since she was wearing her Alphas—and even her Bravos—much more often than she had in the past. *Like tonight, for example…*

The admiral was having an informal dinner with a friend, which was better than a *formal* dinner, since Bartley didn't need reinforcements—Bender's rules called for one Marine guard for every four guests. The single guest that evening was Master Warrant Officer Thomas Perry.

Bartley knew who he was—LFS Director of Educational Services and the father of Admiral Greenwood's departed lover, Carla Perry. No matter who the guest might be, however, a dinner engagement for the admiral meant Bravo uniform for Bartley and a couple of hours at her station against the wall in the dining room.

Perry and the admiral spent dinner talking about personal stuff and getting sentimental over memories of Carla. Bartley was a little embarrassed—she didn't mind listening to the great military secrets of the LFS, but she thought the admiral really should be allowed privacy for such personal conversations.

They also talked about the assassination plot. The admiral was still bothered by the idea that anyone would hate her enough to kill innocent people to get to her. Perry told her she should blame the assassins and the people who sent them, not herself. Some people, he said, can't feel alive unless they have something to hate. Bartley found herself thinking that *maybe they don't deserve to* be *alive*.

She was still pondering the issue when Perry changed the subject.

"You know, Lorna," he said. He was the only person Bartley had *ever* heard call the admiral by her first name. "That young woman has been standing against the wall like a statue all the while we've been enjoying this delicious dinner. Don't you think that's cruel and unusual punishment?"

With a shock, Bartley realized he was talking about *her*! She kept her face impassive as the admiral turned and examined her.

"You're right, Tom. She's the Lady Who's Always There, and I sometimes take her for granted. Sergeant Bartley!"

"Yes, ma'am." Bartley snapped to attention.

"You know, Mr. Perry is the closest thing I have to family here on Luna."

"Yes, ma'am."

"In addition, I'm bigger and younger than he is, and he's not armed. You don't really think he's going to stab me with a salad fork, do you?"

"No, ma'am."

"Well, then, you don't really need to be standing there, do you?"

"Are you…ordering me to leave the room, ma'am?"

Greenwood sighed. "No, Sergeant, I wouldn't want to break one of Charlie Bender's Rules. But those rules only say you must be *present*. So, why don't you come over here, sit down, and join us for coffee and dessert?"

"Ma'am, I…" She hesitated.

"Come on, Bartley. I won't make it an order, but the admiral and her guest would appreciate the pleasure of your company."

"And I promise not to stab *you* with a fork, either," Perry added with a grin.

"Well, since you put it that way, ma'am…" Bartley removed her beret and approached the table self-consciously.

"Tom Perry, meet Rock Bartley," the admiral said. "Her real name's Veronica but *nobody* calls her that."

Bartley winced. Nobody *had* called her that for a long time, and she was surprised the admiral knew her given name—or her nickname.

"I can't imagine why not." Perry rose and shook hands with her. "Veronica's a beautiful name, and an uncommon one. But I suppose Rock goes better with your Marine image and all those medals on your chest."

"Actually, sir, I had the nickname before I became a Marine, in my…er…former life back on Earth." Bartley sat down at the table, and a cup of coffee and a dessert plate appeared in front of her as if by magic. Manuel and Maria were *good* at their jobs.

"Nonetheless," Perry said, "that is an impressive rack of decorations for one so young. I don't often get to meet a Medal of Honor winner—other than Admiral Greenwood, that is."

Perry had come to dinner from his office, wearing his duty uniform, and Bartley thought his rack was impressive as well—especially for a non-military officer. Most of his ribbons were meritorious service types, but he did have the First and Second Battle of Luna ribbons, marking him as an original Lunar citizen, and the Heart of Luna, indicating he'd once been wounded in the line of duty.

Before she could comment, Admiral Greenwood leaned into the conversation. "Bartley is unique in the history of the Lunar Free State, Tom. She's probably the only person ever awarded the Medal of Honor for disobeying an order."

Bartley cringed, but the admiral favored her with a knowing smile.

"I'll bet there's a story to be told about *that*," Perry said. "Well, come on, don't leave me hanging. Which of you is going to tell me about it?"

"Nothing much to tell, sir," Bartley mumbled, aware she was blushing. "I didn't really think I was disobeying an order. I was just doing my job. The officer who gave the order was wounded and under duress. I couldn't make out what she was trying to say."

Greenwood was still smiling, and Perry was obviously waiting for more, but Bartley was reluctant to say more. She *still* didn't feel she deserved the LMH for the incident.

Finally, the Admiral took pity on her. "As you know, Tom, our dear friend Annie McGraw got herself seriously wounded in a firefight aboard the Mekota warship. What you may *not* know is that her team was pulling back at the time, and she ordered Bartley to leave her behind so she could die gloriously in battle.

"Bartley—who was also wounded, I might add, though not critically—chose to ignore the colonel's death wish. She dragged McGraw through hostile territory, halfway across the alien ship, and into the hands of the medics, who proceeded to finish frustrating Annie's desire to be a dead heroine. For that bit of insubordination, Bartley earned the Medal of Honor.

"And my personal gratitude," Greenwood added quietly. "You see, Bartley, I earned the Heart of Luna once—on the flag bridge of the original *Valkyrie* during the Chinese War. I took a missile fragment in the leg and nearly bled to death, but a young Marine lieutenant helped patch me up and kept me going for the rest of the battle. Her name was Anne McGraw."

"I never knew that, ma'am," Bartley said, surprised.

"Of course you didn't. McGraw's a lot like you—she doesn't brag about her accomplishments. She'd say, if I may borrow *your* words, she was just doing her job.

"You know, it's strange the way things work out sometimes. If I recall from your file, Bartley, you were recruited by McGraw down at LunaPort under rather unusual circumstances. She hadn't gone there to recruit anyone, and you hadn't gone there to be recruited, but somehow, the two of you got together. And now, less than two years later, you end up saving her life."

* * *

The probe reached its programmed destination in just five days of subjective time. Having dropped out of hyperspace in the outer reaches of the target system, it began to gather information.

Named Rigel Kentaurus by Earth's ancient astronomers, the system got its modern designation of Alpha Centauri because it appeared to be the brightest star in the constellation Centaurus. In fact, it was the third brightest star visible from Earth. Only Sirius and Vega were brighter.

Alpha Centauri was interesting from an astronomical standpoint—— a triple star system whose two primary components were main sequence stars not very different from Earth's own Sun. Alpha Centauri A was a class G2 variable star, while Alpha Centauri B was a slightly larger, though not nearly as luminous, class K1 star. The two stars orbited each other with a period of around 80 years, in an orbit that, at closest approach, brought them closer together than the distance between the Sun and Neptune.

The third star in the system was a tiny class M5 red dwarf—only visible from Earth through a telescope. Alpha Centauri C's primary claim to fame was that it was slightly closer to Earth than the other two, making it the nearest single star to the Sun. For that reason, Earth's scientists had named it Proxima. It orbited the other two at nearly two trillion kilometers, a distance so great, Earth's astronomers were not sure it was part of the same star system. The probe's data, particularly the gravitational observations in hyperspace, would confirm that it was, but its orbital period could be measured in millennia.

Unfortunately, the Alpha Centauri system was devoid of life. The probe detected two planets, one only slightly smaller than Earth, the other about the size of Mars, but the tidal pull of two stars resulted in orbits so eccentric, they required complex computer modeling to describe. In fact, as the two stars approached each other, the planets would slip from their elliptical orbits into strange, crisscrossing figure-eight patterns, passing back and forth between the A and B stars. Under those conditions, it was no wonder the planets were little more than barren balls of rock. There were no gas giant planets like Jupiter or Saturn. If there were, they had long ago succumbed to the gravitational forces in the system.

The probe completed its observations, then turned back toward the Sun, which was visible as a bright first-magnitude star lying between the constellations of Cassiopeia and Perseus. Once again, it launched itself into hyperspace.

* * *

"Admiral!" Mick O'Hara and Emil Julian were grinning from ear to ear on Lorna's screen. "The probe's back, and it looks like it made it all the way to Alpha Centauri!"

"Already?" Lorna glanced at the calendar in the corner of her screen. "It's been less than two weeks."

"It made the trip in *five days,* Admiral," Julian said. "It took two more to complete the programmed observations and five more for the return. That's an average speed of *over three hundred Cee,* assuming the distance is the same in hyperspace as in normal space."

"If *you're* surprised," Mick O'Hara added, "imagine how the crews of *Aztec* and *Hawking* felt. They had to make sure it was really our probe, not some new alien artifact. But it came through right where it was supposed to, within a hundred kilometers. Not bad for a round trip of over eight light-years!"

"Any adverse effects?"

"None that they've found so far, though we only have a preliminary report. They're a couple of light-hours out, so we can't have anything that resembles a two-way conversation yet. *Aztec* recovered the probe, and they've dumped the data over to *Hawking's* scientific team. They say the live specimens show no ill effects, and diagnostics on the probe show all systems within nominal limits. The astrophysicists are getting downright emotional. Father DeForrest's first report from *Hawking* indicates a gold mine of data, but he must have used the phrase 'wonders of God's creation' at least three times."

Lorna smiled. "Well, we mustn't forget he also has to answer to a higher authority…not that it would hurt the *rest* of you hard-nosed scientists and engineers to have a little humility once in a while."

"Point taken, Admiral." Julian chuckled. "I guess this means we're ready to move on to the next step."

"Just about, Doctor, or we should be when *Aztec* and *Hawking* return, and we've done a thorough analysis of the data."

Lorna felt a sudden bittersweet surge of emotion as she broke the connection. She remembered a time about fifteen years earlier when she and Carla had been getting ready for the first emigration to the Moon. Carla had proposed a toast—*To the Moon and beyond…*

*And someday, the stars…*Lorna had responded, not daring to hope it would happen in her lifetime. *We made it, my dear one*, she thought. *You were a part of it until the end, and our dream—yours, Ian's, and mine— still goes on.*

* * *

The court-martial revealed it was Gardner who'd arranged for the assassination. She had sympathetic contacts on Earth who put her in touch with the Church of the Second Redemption's Inner Tabernacle. She'd only brought Devereaux into the plot because she didn't want to handle the guns—as if that would somehow absolve her of guilt. Devereaux had been a willing accomplice, however, and had known what was in the package he'd conveyed to the assassins.

Charlie Bender had worried he would only be able to convict Gardner on Devereaux's testimony, but in the end, she admitted her guilt, proclaimed it loudly in court, railing against the 'militaristic bastards' who controlled the Directorate and placed a 'perverted bitch' in the CEO's chair. From that point, the outcome of the trial had been predictable.

Several members of the Directorate asked Lorna if she would consider executive clemency for the two conspirators, but she refused and explained her refusal publicly in an interview conducted by Jennifer Winslow on the Lunar News Network.

"If they had done no more than make an attempt on *my* life," she told the veteran Lunar journalist, "I might have considered it. I'm a military officer, and I've been shot at before—by the Chinese, by the aliens, by various enemies of the Lunar Free State. Personal risk is something that goes with the territory. But for Brigadier Kim, who was only in my office to discuss his retirement after many years of dedicated service and who gave his life to save mine, for Corporal Leslie and Private Cardones, who also died doing their duty to protect me, and for Petty Officer Erikson whose only fault was that she was in the wrong place at the wrong time—for taking their lives, I cannot forgive these people."

"But Gardner and Devereaux weren't the actual assassins, Admiral. They had no control over the actions of the terrorists who did the killing."

"If you point a gun at someone and pull the trigger," Lorna said, "you have no control over the bullet after it leaves the barrel. Yet you are still responsible for the consequences. Otherwise, why blame the assassins? Why not blame the guns or the bullets?

"That is the sort of thinking followed by gun control advocates on Earth, but we don't accept such nonsense here on Luna. We recognize that crimes are committed by people, not by machines or other inanimate objects. As far as I am concerned, Gardner and Devereaux pulled a trigger and unleashed forces beyond their control. They did so deliberately, without regard for the consequences, and now they must be held accountable for those consequences."

Gardner and Devereaux were executed the next day, given a painless death by lethal injection—which, Charlie Bender reflected, was better than they deserved. If questioned, Colonel McGraw or Sergeant Bartley or almost any Lunar citizen on the street would probably have expressed a similar opinion.

* * * * *

Chapter Nineteen

TerraNova City, Luna

"Y ou want to deport this Joseph MacReedy?" Lorna wore a skeptical look. "I thought he was cleared of the assassination plot."

"I wouldn't exactly say he was *cleared*," Charlie Bender replied. "We just didn't have enough evidence to implicate him. But he *is* a member of the cult that sponsored the assassins."

"And Father DeForrest is a Catholic, but that doesn't mean he was part of the Spanish Inquisition."

"No, but if he were a priest living in Spain at the time of the Inquisition…MacReedy lives here, right now. To our knowledge, he's the *only* Second Redemptionist living on the Moon, probably because Second Redemptionists, in general, think we're all devil worshipers."

"The Constitution guarantees freedom of religion, Charlie. I won't deport him for that reason alone."

"You don't *need* to have a reason, Admiral. He's a provisional citizen. You can revoke that status and send him packing without any reason. Given his association with the assassins, there's not a Lunar citizen who would question it."

"The Constitution may not require it, but *I* need a reason, and the one you've given me isn't good enough."

"All right, consider this: The assassins took the guns out of the box and stored them behind a sink. So, why was the box still there? You would think they would want to dispose of it.

"When we ran the box through the lab, we found stains on the inside—turned out to be lettuce and tomato residue. But there were no food containers near where we found the box. Maybe the box *did* get thrown out and mixed with the trash until someone retrieved it and preserved it for us to find."

"That's pretty thin, Charlie."

"True, but the lab found one more thing. *Somebody* handled that box after it was opened, someone wearing non-permeable plastic gloves—typical sterile food-preparation gloves, used in the deli. The assassins didn't bother with gloves—their prints are all over the box—but *somebody* did. Maybe somebody wanted us to find the box to finger Gardner and Devereaux."

"That's still thin, Charlie. Why would MacReedy—assuming it was him—do that? They helped his cause."

"Because, to him, we're *all* devil worshipers, and he expected the assassination to succeed. Why not nail a couple more sinners and give his cult an excuse to say they had nothing to do with it, that it was really our own people plotting against us?"

"You're implying MacReedy is some kind of deep cover agent—unknown to Devereaux, Gardner, and maybe even the two assassins."

"He may be. He set up his business—funded by a loan from his cult—months *before* you became CEO. Gardner hadn't contacted them yet. The assassins didn't arrive until later. When he first got here, there was no assassination plot unless they were planning to assassinate Admiral Stevens."

"Charlie, how do you manage to sleep at night with all these plotters and spies and secret agents running around? I *really* think this is a stretch."

"Admiral, if nothing else, you could deport him on the grounds he isn't meeting his business charter—the part about 'filling a commercial need in the Lunar community.' The guy probably hasn't sold three donuts since the assassination. Nobody goes near his shop anymore. He's still paying his rent, but I'll bet he's getting money from his cult to do it."

Lorna leaned back in her chair and regarded him thoughtfully. "No, Charlie, I'm not going to deport him, and I'm surprised you're suggesting it. You're the one who always tells me that if you discover a spy in your midst who doesn't know he's been discovered, the best thing you can do is leave him in place. If you eliminate him, the enemy will send another spy who might be harder to detect, and a known spy is always useful if you need a credible source to provide false information to the enemy."

"Spies are one thing. Assassins are something else."

"From what you're telling me, MacReedy *isn't* an assassin. He's a spy, a facilitator, a general purpose asset. If I leave him in place, I *know* you'll watch him like a hawk. I won't even need to order you to do it. It's an obsession with you. And maybe by watching him, if he is what you think he is, we'll get a heads-up on any future plans his group might have. Maybe what we need to do is put out a press release saying he's been cleared. Maybe people will start buying his donuts again, and it will lull him into a false sense of security."

Bender gave her a sour look. "I hate to tie up my assets watching a problem that could be eliminated."

"Look on the bright side. You may be tying up assets to watch him, but the Church of the Second Redemption is tying up *their* assets to keep him in business."

* * *

"**C**ome in, Captain," Lorna said. "Please, sit down."

Shin Yong Chae dropped his salute and took the indicated chair. He had never been in the office before. In fact, he had only been in the admiral's presence on a few occasions, most recently when he had made his report to the command staff after chasing the alien probe. But Greenwood had approved his actions on that occasion, and his record was good. He was not at all nervous about the admiral's summons. In fact...

"Do you have any idea why I called you here today, Captain?"

"I could guess, Admiral," he said. "The hyperprobe experiment was successful. It seems logical that the next step would be to send a manned ship and—with all humility—I believe *Hawking* is the best ship for the task. I am hoping the admiral has called me here to tell me she has reached the same conclusion."

"Good guess." Lorna smiled. "Needless to say, this mission is classified Most Secret."

"Of course, ma'am." Shin was also smiling slightly which, for the usually stolid Korean, was the equivalent of wild enthusiasm.

"I'll brief you on the generalities of the mission, but you'll get the details from Admiral O'Hara. This is a scientific mission and falls under his jurisdiction rather than Fleet Command's.

"Two ships will be equipped with the hyperspace translation device," she continued. "*Hawking* will be the lead ship, and you'll be in overall command of the mission. The other ship will be a destroyer—probably *Starsong* since she's new enough to have the latest design innovations but has seen enough service to work any bugs out.

"The reason for sending two ships should be obvious—if one gets into trouble, the other can come to its aid. We've chosen a destroyer because the scientific people aren't yet ready to try a hyperspace translation with anything as big as a cruiser. There's no reason to think it *won't* work. After all, the aliens manage to translate those massive tubs of theirs, but we'd prefer to start small. *Starsong* masses about twenty-seven k-tons, a bit less than *Hawking.* There will be other ships without hyperspace capability standing by at the jump point, including *Valkyrie,* since we will want to have an AI available. The flagship will be your command and control point.

"The mission will have three phases. In Phase One, *Hawking* will make several test hops into hyperspace and back while the other ships stand by at the jump point. This will determine if you experience ill effects from hyperspace travel. I won't blow sunshine in your ear, Captain. There are things we still don't know. There is significant risk involved, and you should make your crew aware of that. If any of them don't want to go, Fleet will understand."

"If I know my crew, Admiral, they will all volunteer. I presume we will also have scientists with us?"

"In the first phase, you'll only have medical people to evaluate any effects on your crew. For the second and third phases, you will have a full complement of scientific personnel. For Phase Two— assuming Phase One is successful—both *Hawking* and *Starsong* will go to Alpha Centauri. The probe already brought back enough data to keep the scientists busy for years, so this is just to make sure everything's working properly and to get both crews familiar with hyperspace navigation. You'll follow the profile of the original probe mission, spend a little time in the Alpha Centauri system, and return. You'll dump all data you've collected to the command and control ship, then confer with the project commander and the scientists before going on to the next phase.

"Finally, assuming the first two phases are successful, you will go somewhere we have never been before…"

She touched an icon on her desk screen. The real-time view of the Lunar landscape on the large wall screen behind her dissolved into a star field image from the Lunar Observatory. A brilliant, blue-white star dominated the field.

"Sirius, also known as Alpha Canis Majoris—not just the brightest star in Canis Major but the brightest one visible from Earth. It's a Type A1 star, nearly twice the diameter and more than twice the mass of our Sun, and over twenty times as luminous. It's also just eight light-years away and will be your destination for Phase Three."

* * *

Kim Jong Pak had no idea what he was doing at the HQ Senior Officers' Club. His superior had told him Admiral Greenwood requested his presence for an informal discussion of TerraCorp business matters, but Kim had a feeling CWO Hollings knew more than he was telling.

He'd been directed to one of the private lounges where he nervously presented his ID to a no-nonsense Marine guard at the door, noting the guard's shoulder emblem marked him as a member of LFS *Valkyrie's* Marine contingent, not the Fleet HQ company. The guard allowed him into the lounge, where he found Admiral Greenwood seated comfortably in an armchair, talking to an Asian woman wearing the rank of Commodore. As he entered, Greenwood rose to greet him. The S.O. Club was a MYAH place, so he did not salute the admiral, and he was surprised when she greeted him with a handshake.

"Warrant Officer Kim, thank you for coming," she said. "Do you know Commodore Yamamoto, my chief of staff?"

"Thank you for inviting me, Admiral, and no, I've not had the pleasure. Commodore."

"As long as we are making introductions," Greenwood continued, "my shadow over there against the wall is Sergeant Bartley, LFS Marines. She's here to make certain we conduct ourselves with proper decorum."

Bartley, who was on duty and, therefore, wearing her cover, came to attention and saluted. "It's an honor to meet you, sir. Your father was a legend in the Corps."

"Mr. Kim," the admiral said, suddenly becoming serious, "let me express my deepest sympathy for your loss. Your father gave his life to save mine, a debt I can never repay."

"He died, as he lived, with honor," Kim said. "I am proud to say he was my father."

"He was also proud of you. He told me his children were his greatest contribution to the future of the Lunar Free State."

"Thank you, Admiral." Kim was obviously embarrassed. "I will try to prove myself worthy of that, but how may I be of service to you?"

"I need you to enlighten me in matters concerning Terra Corporation. Chief Warrant Officer Hollings assures me you're one of his best analysts. But first, sit down and relax. Will you have a drink?" She touched the keypad on the table beside her chair, and a steward appeared immediately.

"Just mineral water, please," he said. The steward disappeared and returned in a moment with the drink.

"Now then," Admiral Greenwood began, "I have read Terra-Corp's financial reports, and they tell me business is good. Profits meet or exceed projections, expenses are within budget, and so on. But unlike my predecessor, Admiral Stevens, I am *not* a businessperson. I can read activity reports and study growth projections without gaining real insight into where TerraCorp is going or what its prospects might be.

"That's where I was hoping you might help me. What do you see as the most significant short-term and long-term opportunities for TerraCorp, and what problems might we expect?"

Kim blinked. The admiral's question was so sweeping in scope, the simplest—and safest—response would be a broad-brush answer, laden with optimistic language such as one might find in TerraCorp's annual report to its shareholders. But he had a feeling that wasn't going to fly with the Iron Maiden. He might be sticking his neck out, but she'd asked for his professional opinion, and he might never get another opportunity, so…

"Well, Admiral." He took a deep breath. "Most of TerraCorp's revenue comes from two sources: exploitation of the Asteroid Belt and investment in Earth's financial markets—which really means investment in the technological and manufacturing capabilities of Earth-based corporations. We get a good return on our investment in the Solaris Syndicate, but that money helps the Syndicate develop capabilities that ultimately compete with us in the Belt. That's unfortunate because the Belt's resources are the mainstay of our economy.

"If it were up to me, I'd invest more in our processing and manufacturing operations—solar smelters here on Luna, zero-gee manufacturing in orbit, commercial shipyards, and so forth. We might even be thinking about things like real estate development on Mars."

"Real estate? You mean selling land, building condos and shopping malls...?" Timiko Yamamoto asked with amusement.

"Yes, Commodore," Kim replied. "I believe we could profit from the economic development of Mars. We wouldn't necessarily sell land outright; we might lease it. Nor would we build shopping malls right away unless we can promote Mars as a vacation resort. An industrial and commercial infrastructure would be needed first...but excuse me, I've gotten ahead of myself. It's just a concept, and it isn't on the priority list."

"Why not?" Greenwood asked. "If it offers so much profit potential..."

"Well," Kim looked sheepish, "I'm the one who recently proposed the idea, and not everyone agrees about the profit potential. At best, it would be a long-term project, but I think we should consider it soon. We are the only ones with a presence on Mars now, but the Americans are planning a research station there."

"I see." Greenwood's expression was unreadable. "Continue."

"That's the general concept, Admiral. I think we need to invest more in ourselves and less in Earth. Again, not everyone at Terra-Corp agrees. Short-term profits would suffer, and long-term profits may or may not be realized. There is considerable financial leverage involved. For every Lunar we invest in Earth's markets to produce reasonably predictable short-term profits, we would need to invest *ten* Lunars in our own projects to produce a similar profit—not so predictable—several years hence. But I believe that strategy would leave us in a better growth position in the long run. We would also have ownership and control of real assets, rather than investments in assets that belong to someone else."

"I understand," she said, "but that's a long-term strategy. What do you see happening in the short term?"

"Short-term prospects remain good, Admiral. Earth's economy continues to build, as it has done since World War Three, and our economy builds with it. There are, however, some short-term...not exactly problems, but challenges."

"Tell me about them," she said, "with specifics, please."

"Specifics...actually, Admiral, *you* created one of the challenges by giving Luna's gravitic propulsion technology to the Americans."

"There was a small matter of an alien invasion," she said without humor, "and we didn't exactly *give* it to them. The price was several hundred nuclear warheads, which proved extremely useful in our recent encounter with the aforementioned aliens."

"Of course, Admiral, but this *did* create a challenge for us. Are you aware that the Americans now have several heavy lifters under construction?"

"Those are U.S. Navy vessels, not commercial ships. How does that impact TerraCorp?"

"The Americans are doing that only because of the terms of the Solaris Syndicate agreement, which requires them to share *commercial* technology related to space. They're maintaining the fiction that gravitic propulsion is *military* technology, even though LFS commercial ships use it. They don't want to share what we gave them—excuse me, *sold* them—with their Syndicate partners because Japan and Korea have a lot of shipbuilding capacity. Together, they could probably out-build the U.S. by about three-to-one in gravity-drive ships. In any case, we expect the U.S. Navy will soon be competing with us for commercial heavy lift contracts. It's not unprecedented. Historically, many nations have used military capabilities for commercial profit or in support of commercial operations. The old British Empire is a classic example.

"The U.S. is also increasing its shipbuilding capabilities, hoping to achieve parity before the others discover the technology. We knew other nations would have gravitic propulsion eventually, but we thought it was a few years away. You took us by surprise."

"I see." She still wasn't smiling. "Some directors might say that's what happens when you put a military person in charge."

"Admiral, I would never question—"

"Never mind." She waved her hand in dismissal. "You said *challenges*. What else have you got?"

"Well, one of your recent decisions may provide us with an opportunity, namely your decision to allow another AI to be constructed."

"Anna? She's a warship's AI, so how does that help TerraCorp? Mike is still the only AI available for commercial ventures."

"Yes, and unfortunately, he is near his limits with everything he now handles for Fleet Command, TerraNova, and TerraCorp. But since you've allowed another AI to be built, some of us are hopeful you might allow more of them. One of the arguments against investment in Lunar industrial operations is that, to show a decent profit, we have to be able to process materials or produce goods at a lower cost than Earth corporations.

"With facilities like solar smelters, that's a no-brainer—we can run a smelting operation up here with *zero* energy costs, even though the Lunar cycle only lets us run two weeks out of every four. With other types of manufacturing, we're at a disadvantage. Some raw materials—plastics, for instance—must be shipped from Earth, and our finished goods must be shipped back to Earth's markets. We can do that efficiently with our heavy lifters, but we can't compete with Earth unless we can reduce the cost of manufacture.

"One advantage we could exploit is AI control of engineering design and manufacturing processes. The fleet uses it extensively, which is why we can build warships more quickly and at less cost than any other nation."

"That's true," Lorna agreed. "But shipbuilding is ideally suited to AI control. It requires custom fabrication and machining, frequent design modifications, and so forth—the sort of thing Mike can handle much more efficiently than a human. I doubt other industries where processes are more standardized would benefit as much."

"You're right, Admiral. Shipbuilding is ideally suited for it. So why aren't we in the commercial shipbuilding business?"

The look on Lorna's face told Kim his point had been made. But before he could congratulate himself, she slammed the ball back into his court.

"I don't know, Mr. Kim. *You're* the TerraCorp analyst—you tell me."

"Well, Mike doesn't have the capacity to take on more projects, and since we haven't been allowed to build more AIs…"

"Ian Stevens made that decision eight years ago, when we lost Amy with LFS *Amazon*. Now, I may be a simple-minded military officer, but I've been a director since the beginning. I don't recall *anyone* raising the issue in all that time. Timiko, you were with Ian for over ten years. Were you aware of any such discussions?"

"No, Admiral." Yamamoto shook her head.

"It's also been months since we brought Anna to life," Greenwood reminded Kim. "If you people were waiting for the moratorium to be lifted, why hasn't anyone come knocking on my door?"

Kim began to feel uncomfortable. The admiral certainly had a knack for cutting through the bullshit. She also had a reputation for shredding anyone who couldn't come up with good answers to her questions. He began to regret raising the issue. "I'm...I'm told the executive committee decided not to take it up with you. The feeling seemed to be that you wouldn't approve an AI for non-military purposes."

"The *last* people," she said in a quiet voice that promised grief for the executive committee, "who presumed to know what I was thinking and how I would respond were the *aliens*, and they're all *dead* now. I suspect the committee chose not to raise the issue because they prefer to continue business as usual without any meddling on my part."

"I...wouldn't know, ma'am." Kim was even more uncomfortable, thinking his superiors might be *very* unhappy about his performance.

"Mr. Kim," she said, "you knew the executive committee chose not to bring the AI issue to my attention, but you brought it up anyway. Why?"

Kim was sweating and trying not to show it. "I didn't mean to criticize the committee, ma'am. I wanted to hear your reaction because I think the issue is important. Maybe I was out of line, but—"

"The issue *is* important, Mr. Kim. That doesn't mean that I'll go running off to Mike and Val to ask them to have another child, but I will consider it. As for being out of line, you wouldn't be here if I had as much business acumen as my predecessor. All right, I've heard enough. Timiko, your assessment, please—or would you prefer to discuss it in private?"

"No, Admiral," Yamamoto said. "I think your instincts were good. This is the sort of analysis Admiral Stevens used to do every day. I think Mr. Kim would be a good choice."

Choice for what? Kim wondered.

"I agree," the admiral said. "I warned Hollings he might regret his glowing recommendations." She turned her attention back to Kim. "It looks like he'll be losing your services, Mr. Kim, assuming you choose to accept the assignment. If you were a commissioned Fleet officer, I'd hand you a set of orders and that would be that. Since you're not, I'll allow you to volunteer for the job."

"What job is that, ma'am?" Kim had the feeling his career was about to change in a major way.

"I need a business analyst on my personal staff. As you've seen for yourself today, I'm not a businessperson. But TerraCorp is a critical part of the CEO's responsibilities, and I'm not getting any feedback to help me understand what's going on. That puts me in the unfortunate position of practicing management by results. If things go well, someone gets praised or promoted. If things *don't* go well, heads roll.

"That's not a good management strategy—it's reactive, not proactive—and it means I have to assume those at the next level down are doing their jobs. Those below me also have opportunity and motive to conceal their mistakes, and I may not know it until things are too far gone for corrective action. For a military analogy, I am reminded that the infamous Charge of the Light Brigade was ordered by generals who were not in a position to actually see the battlefield.

"I haven't fully defined the position I want you to fill because it's a new slot on the T.O. Ian Stevens didn't need it; he had more business sense than all the members of the committee combined. I mostly need you to do what you've done today—review what's going on in TerraCorp and give me your analysis and opinions. That *doesn't* mean all your pet projects will be implemented, so don't plan on buying a condo on Mars just yet." Her expression held the hint of a smile.

"You'll be giving me the information I need to ask the right questions of the right people and to hold them accountable for their answers. Because of our little discussion today, I'll be asking TerraCorp's executive committee to notify me any time they plan to meet. I may or may not attend, *or* I might send *you* to observe and report. Either way, I want them to know I intend to be involved, whether they like it or not.

"By the way," she continued, "the people on my staff are all *commissioned* officers, and I'll expect you to become one as well. You'll have to attend Command College while learning your new duties. I'll try not to demand so much of you that you won't be able to keep up with your officer training, but you'll be working hard.

"You won't have to start off as an ensign. You'll get a senior lieutenant's commission, the grade equivalent of your current rank as senior warrant officer. You won't lose your time in grade, so you'll be up for promotion to lieutenant commander shortly. The bad news is that your promotion will depend on *my* evaluation—not that of CWO Hollings, who obviously thinks you walk on water. You'll need to prove yourself to my satisfaction, but I think you'll be up to the challenge. I'm sure there's at least one lesson you won't need to be taught."

"What lesson is that, ma'am?" Kim inquired meekly.

"That *straight talk*, even if I don't like what I'm hearing, will get you more points than telling me what you *think* I want to hear or not telling me anything at all. It's a lesson the executive committee is about to learn the hard way."

* * *

"**H**ow's it going, Red?" Jimbo Davis peered down into the access hatch. All he could see of Murphy was the top of her flame-haired head. Davis knew Sobieski was also down there, but nothing was visible of the chief engineer.

At the sound of his voice, Murphy looked up and started to climb the ladder. "Not good, Skipper. I'll let Ski give you the details, but this is more than a simple refit. We're going to have to open the lower hull and do some modifications to the forward graser mounts."

"Coming through," Sobieski announced from below, and Murphy swung her legs out of the hatch to let the engineer pass.

"What's the verdict, Ski?" Davis asked as Sobieski hauled himself out of the hatch. "Will we make the schedule?"

"I think so, Captain, but it'll be close." The young senior lieutenant rose beside the hatch and dusted himself off. "We have fewer problems than *Hawking*. I talked to Bill Morgan, and they don't have chase grasers to worry about, but they have to work around their forward missile tubes, and that involves the loading rack system. Given the choice, I'd rather deal with grasers any day. They'll probably ask Fleet Engineering for help. It may be easier to redesign the power feeds for the hyper generator."

"Well, stay with that. They may come up with something that helps us as well."

"Will do, sir."

"I know it's a headache," Davis told them, "but when it's done, *Starsong* and *Hawking* will be the first true starships of the LFS. And I, for one, am itching to see what another star system looks like, up close and personal."

* * *

"Good morning, Mr. President. It's been a while since we talked."

"Yes, it has, Admiral. I'll save you the trouble of asking—it's a beautiful sunny day here in Phoenix. A bit hot for my taste, but typical of the desert Southwest this time of year."

Lorna chuckled. "I see you've noticed we Moon people are always curious about the weather on Earth, probably because we don't have any here on Luna. The engineers are working on that, however."

"They are?" Blackthorne blinked. "You're actually trying to create *weather* on the Moon?"

"Well, not exactly. We're planning to upgrade the irrigation system in TerraNova Park with an overhead sprinkler network that will simulate rainfall. We're also installing a new lighting system to simulate everything from bright sunshine to a starry night. One of our astronomers noted that the park has a domed ceiling and would be a perfect place for a planetarium projector. We expect it will be immensely popular. Earth is still our planet of origin, but we've got kids born here on Luna who have never stood under an open sky or seen rain except in videos."

"Sounds a bit like Camelot, Admiral. You know, that old song about how the rain was only allowed to fall during certain hours."

"I remember," she said. "I'm not exactly a young woman. I was born in the twentieth century."

"You're young compared to me," he replied, "and still incredibly attractive, I might add. Hmmm…don't think I've ever said anything like that to another head of state before. Maybe I'm getting too comfortable with this conversational approach to diplomacy."

"I don't think you called just to compliment me on my looks, Mr. President." Lorna knew she was blushing. She took care of herself and thought she looked rather good for her age, but it had been a long time since anyone dared mention it in her presence—other than Charlie Bender's obtuse reference to *Valkyrie's* hull artwork.

"You're right," he said. "Actually, I called to get some of that straight talk you're so fond of. Specifically, I'd like a couple of straight answers. My people tell me the LFS may not have shared everything you learned from the aliens…like maybe the secret of travel between stars. You told us the aliens destroyed that technology before they were captured, but I hear you've been testing some kind of space warp device out in the far reaches of the Solar System."

Lorna smiled, touched a few icons, and brought up a file on her screen. "Ah, yes, here it is: USS *Decatur*. My people made her out to be about thirty-two thousand tons, a bit larger than our *Star*-class destroyers, but not quite big enough to be called a light cruiser. Max acceleration somewhere in excess of seventy-five gees, twelve missile tubes, four turrets with twin X-ray laser mounts, plus point defense and chase armament. Heavy on search and detection gear. An impressive ship—one of your newest, I believe. Of course, she wasn't *shadowing* us. With all that empty space out there, she just *happened* to stumble onto *Aztec* and *Hawking* somewhere out beyond Neptune's orbit a couple of months ago."

"That was a *scientific* mission, Admiral. We'd never gone that far before, and—"

"Now, Mr. President," Lorna chided, "you've asked for straight talk, so please give me the same. *Decatur's* mission was to test her ability to detect and observe other ships—specifically LFS warships—in open space. My people tell me she did that quite well, *unless* the mission was to shadow them *undetected*, in which case she failed, and you can pass *that* on to your Navy people. Now, if we were trying to be secretive, do you think our people would have gone ahead, knowing *Decatur* was watching us?"

In fact, *Aztec* had queried Fleet before proceeding with the test, and Fleet had bucked the question all the way up to Lorna. She'd given them the go-ahead, curious about how the Americans would react. Charlie Bender had been *terribly* upset about it.

Blackthorne leaned back in his chair with a chuckle. "Admiral, you are a piece of work. I can see why Admiral Stevens regarded you so highly—you're just as wily as he was. You've been waiting for me to call, haven't you?"

"Let's just say I've been wondering whether you really believe in straight talk. Well, here's your straight answer. Yes, we did conduct a test of an interstellar drive system. The test vehicle was an unmanned probe. We are not yet ready to try it with a manned vehicle." *And you can bet we'll keep any U.S. warships far from the site when we do,* she thought.

"However," she continued, "we are *not* going to share the technology with you until we find some compelling reason to do so in our national interest—as was the case with the gravity drive."

"That's different," Blackthorne protested. "You people had the gravity drive before the aliens came. This is something you got from the alien ships—ships *we* helped you capture. You haven't allowed us to examine them in the kind of detail your people have."

"You're welcome to send anyone you want to look at them, but it won't do you any good. We've stripped out the critical technology related to the star drive. Of course, the alien *gravity* drive systems are still there, and if we allow your people to look at them, we'll have to allow the French, Japanese, and Koreans to do so as well."

Blackthorne reddened. "That's blackmail, Admiral."

"No, Mr. President. I'm just making a point. *You* haven't shared the gravity drive with your Syndicate partners because it's not in your national interest to do so. For the same reasons, *we* aren't willing to share the star drive."

"Hmmm…All right, I see your point. I guess I'll just have to come up with a compelling reason for you, won't I?"

"I guess you will. But just so you don't consider this conversation a waste of time, I'll give you something you can use to impress your scientists. They may have already guessed this, but I'll confirm it. The star drive depends on gravity technology. If you work on it from that direction, you may be able to figure it out for yourselves. That's all I'll say on the subject."

"Thanks for that much, Admiral. You're right, my people do suspect it has something to do with gravity, but your confirmation is valuable to me—at least to show some politically-connected egg-heads I'm doing what I can for them.

"You're learning to play this game pretty well, Admiral," he added with a grin. "And you're teaching *me* to be careful about underestimating a good-looking woman and a sharp military commander."

"Thank you, Mr. President, but you'll find I don't respond well to flattery. Keep working on that compelling reason, and we'll talk again."

* * *

"Well, if it isn't the corporal from the Babe on the Horse…"

Rock Bartley was enjoying a rare evening off duty and had stopped by Corporal J's for a quiet drink. She was sitting at the bar when the voice behind her caused her to turn around.

"Well…Petty Officer Johnson," she said with a smile. "Looks like the Yanks have landed. And that would be the *sergeant* from the Babe on the Horse, thank you." Bartley was still wearing her duty Alphas from her afternoon stint in the admiral's office, and she pointed to the chevrons on her sleeve.

"Well, I guess we're all moving up in the world. That would be *Chief* Petty Officer Johnson." He pointed to his own chevrons. "I asked one of your Marines about you yesterday. He said you got righteously decorated for kicking some alien ass during the last battle. I guess the extra stripe was part of the deal, huh?"

"Yeah, it was. But I heard you were there for the big show as well."

"Yup. Old *Chicago* got a few licks in. So, what's with the rope?" He pointed at the braided gold aiguillette on Bartley's left shoulder. "I haven't seen one of those before."

"Admiral's Own Guard," she said. "I've got a temporary head-quarters assignment."

"Not bad." Johnson ordered a drink.

They made small talk for a while. At one point, the subject of LFS hull artwork came up.

"Yeah, I saw the Babe on the Horse as we approached the docks. Sure is a pretty ship. I also saw a couple of your ships out there with their whole forward sections covered up. Can't even see the hull pictures, and they look like airtight structures. It looked kinda weird, and I wondered if you knew anything about it."

"You're asking the wrong person. I'm a Marine, not an engineer."

"Well, I am in engineering, so I guess I notice stuff like that. Maybe it's classified work…top secret or something."

"I wouldn't know." She grinned. "But there's an easy way to find out. Keep asking about it, and if a bunch of security people come out of the walls and spoil your whole day, I guess it's classified."

Bartley knew exactly what he was talking about—thanks to her time spent in the admiral's office—but she wasn't allowed to talk about it. In fact, she planned to report Johnson's curiosity to Admiral Bender at her earliest convenience. She didn't *think* the admiral would spoil Johnson's day but…*That's great,* she thought, *now they've got* me *looking for spies under every table.*

* * *

"You did the right thing, Sergeant," Charlie Bender said. "I don't think your American friend is a spy, and I've no reason to spoil his liberty by questioning him. If I did, it would only tell them we've got something to hide, but it's good to know someone noticed the work being done on *Hawking* and *Starsong.* It puts us on notice to be extra careful. I presume you didn't tell him anything…"

"Of course not, sir." Bartley gave the admiral a look of hurt pride. "I told him I'm a Marine, not a yard dog, and I didn't have a clue what he was talking about."

* * *

"Johnson..."

CPO Johnson was supervising the crew working on *Chicago's* number three grav generator, and he turned to find the chief engineer and the executive officer behind him.

"Sir!" He came to attention. Under U.S. Navy rules, crew members aboard ship did not salute except under special circumstances.

"The XO is asking about those two LFS ships with their noses covered up. Have you heard anything?"

"No, sir. I was down on Luna a couple of days ago, but I didn't run into any of their engineering people. I talked to one LFS noncom, a Marine, but she didn't have a clue."

"She...?" The XO regarded him with a raised eyebrow and a slight leer.

"Yes, sir." Johnson grinned. "She's not bad looking, and she's easy to talk to, but I have a feeling she can kick my ass six ways from Sunday. She's got a lot of fruit salad on her chest and a rep for being a badass alien killer. Not sure I'd want to get...er...romantically involved with somebody like that."

"Oh, c'mon now, Johnson," the chief engineer chided. "You've got to uphold the reputation of the U.S. Navy. Next time, I expect you to come back bruised and battered, but victorious."

"I'll...take it into consideration, sir." In truth, Johnson found Sergeant Bartley attractive, but when it came to women, he didn't think of himself as a great lover. Besides, Bartley's easy, confident manner and the way she moved convinced him his comment about getting his ass kicked was probably accurate.

The two officers left the area, and Johnson shrugged and went back to work.

Once away from the work party, the XO turned to the engineer. "Everyone we've talked to has the same story. Nobody's talking about whatever they're doing out there."

"What does Fleet think they're building, Commander?"

"Hmmm...you didn't hear this from me, but scuttlebutt has it the Moonies are testing a faster-than-light drive, something they figured out from the aliens. If it's true, Fleet would like to know about it, and they'll probably pin a medal on anyone who can give them good information, so keep your eyes and ears open. About all we know so far is that one of those covered-up ships is LFS *Stephen Hawking*—their top-of-the-line scientific research ship. The other one is a *Star*-class destroyer, probably LFS *Starsong*, but it's *Hawking* that makes us think they're up to something. If you're going to another star system, a research ship is the one to send."

"Another star system? Do you think they're going looking for the aliens?"

"Hell, no!" The XO snorted. "Greenwood's no fool. If they wanted to do that, they'd be working on their battlecruisers, not a research ship and a destroyer."

* * *

"Sergeant Bartley, how would you feel about going back to the fleet for a while?" The admiral had summoned Bartley into her office, and her question took the Marine by surprise.

"Is the admiral thinking of sending me back, ma'am?"

"Not exactly. *We* will be going back. I'm taking BG-One out for some long overdue exercises. With Captain Ling's concurrence, I'd expect you to continue to handle my personal security, but aboard *Valkyrie,* that's just an additional duty assignment. With a battlecruiser and three hundred fifty loyal crewmembers wrapped around me, I *won't* need anyone to stay in my quarters. For the most part, you'd be a regular Fleet Marine again."

"I wouldn't mind at all, ma'am. I feel a little weird about wearing *Valkyrie's* emblem on my shoulder since I've spent so little time aboard her."

"I feel the same about calling her my flagship." Greenwood nodded. "Sounds like we both need to get off Luna for a while. Now, officially, we're going out for battle group maneuvers, but I think you know the real mission."

"I think I do, ma'am, especially if you tell me you're taking LFS *Hawking* with you."

"I see you've been paying attention. Yes, we will be taking *Hawking* along."

"Of course, the admiral does not need to remind me this is top secret," Bartley said seriously.

"I know, Bartley. I think some of Admiral Bender's paranoia is rubbing off on you. He sent me a note about your U.S. Navy friend."

"I thought it best to report it, in light of what I know, ma'am."

"You did well, Sergeant. We know the Americans are sniffing around, and they probably approached a lot of other people as well, but *you* were the only one who reported it. One reason for taking the full battle group out is to put a shell around the whole operation and keep them from getting too close. Ostensibly, we'll be conducting live fire exercises, and we'll keep them out of the area for their own safety. In any case, I thought I'd give you a heads-up and give you a chance to get ready. If all goes well, we'll be departing in about two weeks."

"I'll be ready, ma'am."

Bartley's reaction was favorable, but Lorna knew Mick O'Hara's would not be. Mick *really* wanted to go out on this one, but he would have to stay behind again to mind the store in her absence. *Rank has its privilege,* she decided. *If this mission goes okay, maybe I'll let Mick go all the way with the next one. He deserves it and visiting another star system must be more exciting than watching someone else do it.*

She sighed with resignation as she realized a lot of people were going to make that trip before *she* ever got to do it. Years ago, she'd been the bold adventuress—the one who got to take *Wanderer* and the other experimental ships up to orbit and, later on, the first trips to the Moon while Ian Stevens had waited anxiously back on Earth, wishing he could be there. The first Lunar base had already been under construction before Ian finally got his wish. He'd made the sacrifice, let others go up in his place, because his first responsibility was to the Deep Space Research Institute and, later, to the Lunar Free State. Now Lorna knew how he must have felt. *Maybe, in a year, they'll decide I'm a terrible chief executive. They'll vote me out, send me back to the fleet, and I can go back to what I do best.*

Somehow, she didn't think that was likely, and as long as the responsibility was hers, she would do what was required of her. Besides, there was one other option she was considering, one that would probably curtail her spacefaring adventures.

* * *

"I appreciate your taking the time to meet with me, Sarah. I'm sadly ignorant about these things, and I hope you'll have patience with me."

Sarah Wilkins smiled. She was enjoying this. She was a brilliant physician, but as Luna's surgeon general, she spent most of her time on administrative matters. Even when the care of Lunar VIPs—like the one seated in front of her desk—was involved, she usually found herself in a purely supervisory role. It wasn't often she got to involve herself in a real doctor-patient relationship anymore. It was a little strange, though, to be consulting with a patient while an armed Marine stood by the door.

"Of course, Admiral. This is an interesting topic for me as well, and I'll be happy to explain anything you need to know."

"Well, there's one thing I'm a little hazy on. We're not talking about cloning, are we?"

"No, although it was cloning research that gave scientists clues on how to activate cells to make them start growing and reproducing. But a clone would have only one biological parent, would be a genetic copy of the cell donor. Barring environmental factors in growth, a clone would end up looking *exactly* like its parent, but clones are susceptible to genetic defects, notably in the immune system.

"In this case, we're talking about a child of two parents, and like any naturally conceived child, it will inherit some characteristics from each parent. The usual rules of genetics apply, with some traits being dominant and others recessive. If one parent had brown eyes and the other blue, the child would most likely have brown eyes...*unless* the brown-eyed parent had recessive genes for blue eyes as well, in which case the child *might* wind up with blue eyes. It's almost impossible to say what recessive genes a person might carry. That's why there's such an amazing variety among human beings."

"And all of these factors apply," Lorna asked, "even if both parents are female?"

"All except one," Wilkins said. "Starting with two egg cells instead of one egg and one sperm, we lack a Y-chromosome. The child would *certainly* be female. No way to get a male child out of that combination without some serious genetic engineering, and we're not that advanced yet."

"But the child could have children of either sex?"

"Of course. All of us females—you, me, the sergeant over there—are double X-chromosome types. It's the male side that contributes the Y-chromosome. It's an irony of history that King Henry VIII of England went through six wives trying to produce a male heir, when all along it was *his* fault that they kept giving him girl children."

Lorna chuckled. "I find it even more ironic that one of those girl children, Elizabeth I, turned out to be the most noteworthy monarch in English history. But thanks, Sarah. You've answered all my questions except one. You know my medical history. Am I…?"

"You're as healthy as any patient I've ever had," Wilkins assured her, "and you're in great physical shape. If you were about to ask if you're too old, the answer is no. Given the state of modern medicine, a woman twenty years older than you, in lesser physical condition, can have a perfectly healthy baby with no complications. But now I have a question. I think I know the answer…and you don't have to tell me…but where would the *other* egg come from?"

Lorna smiled sadly. "A couple of years ago, Carla and I contributed eggs to the reproductive bank. She did it mainly to convince *me* to do it. Given the unlikelihood that I would ever marry a man, she said it would be nice to know my genes weren't lost forever. Now— talk about the ultimate irony—I'm thinking about having *her* baby."

"Yours *and* hers," Wilkins said. "Have you decided to go ahead with it?"

"Not yet. I've been busy lately, but I'm thinking about it. If I can get things settled down a bit, I'd like to do it within the next two years. Despite your assurances, I still have this fear that I'll wake up one morning and find I'm too old."

"You've still got a few years, but it never hurts to get started as early as possible. While you *could* have a child well into your seventies, you'd be over ninety before your daughter got out of her teen years. If you start in the next year or two, at least she'd be an adult before you get to retirement age."

"That's something I hadn't considered. I've focused on the idea of *having* a child and haven't looked beyond that. One thing scares me. I have no idea what kind of mother I'll make. Needless to say, I have absolutely no experience."

"Neither do any of us the first time. I worried about it as well, but my first one turned out fine. I don't know if the second and third ones turned out any better, but it got easier with practice. Look, Admiral, I know what kind of person you are. Anyone who can command troops and earn their loyalty and respect the way you have…well, I don't think you'll have a problem. Any kid of yours ought to turn out just fine and should be damned proud to call you her mother."

From her parade rest position next to the door, Sergeant Bartley silently agreed with the doctor. Bartley, of course, had no experience with motherhood. In fact, she'd scarcely known her own parents.

Her childhood had been spent in a string of foster homes and some of it in a state-run orphanage. *I don't know about any other kid, Admiral, but I sure would have been proud to call you Mom.*

* * *

After leaving Wilkins' office, Bartley collected the three Marines waiting outside, and they made the return trip to headquarters. When they got back, the admiral motioned Bartley to follow her into her office.

Lorna settled into her chair and examined the young non-com. "You know, Bartley, I considered ordering you to stay outside Dr. Wilkins' office."

"It was a very personal matter, ma'am. I…sometimes think you ought to have more privacy than you're allowed. But for the record, ma'am, no amount of torture will get *this* secret out of me."

"Thanks, Sarge, I appreciate that, but I've got a ways to go before this dream becomes reality. Anyway, if I'd left you outside, people might have started wondering what horrible medical condition I've got that needs to be kept secret. But I want you to know that you are the *only* Marine I would even consider having in that office with me."

"Thank you, ma'am. That's…I don't know what to say but thank you."

* * * * *

Chapter Twenty

Battle Group One, Outbound from Luna

Battle Group One had scarcely cleared its moorings when Luna Control received the request for departure clearance from USS *Chicago*.

"Just like Fleet said, sir...they want to play follow-the-leader." The senior tech at the control console grinned at his supervisor.

"Yeah," the young ensign said, "but we can't stop them. Give them a ten-minute hold for traffic advisory, then clear them. I'll advise BG-One they've probably got a shadow."

* * *

Even as *Chicago* prepared to depart, *USS Decatur* cast off from the U.S. Navy yard in Earth orbit. The heavy destroyer—technically a DL in U.S. Navy terms—had been waiting for confirmation from *Chicago* but would proceed independently. Most likely, the Moonies would eventually detect both shadowing American vessels, but the U.S. Navy felt that two sets of eyes would be better than one.

* * *

As they sat beside each other on the mat in *Valkyrie's* gym, Sergeant Bartley and Colonel McGraw both breathed hard, but only Bartley was grinning, having taken the colonel two matches out of three.

"Something's wrong here, Bartley," the colonel complained. "You're returning from months of soft duty, guarding the admiral. You're supposed to be out of shape, and I'm supposed to show you the error of your ways."

"Did you ever *spar* with the admiral, ma'am?" Bartley's smile was wicked.

"Aha! So that's it! No, I've never had the opportunity, but I hear she's good."

"She's probably not as good as you or Captain Ling, but she works out hard three times a week, and her style's a lot like mine. We managed to teach each other a few tricks."

"So I've noticed. But the colonel would like to remind the sergeant that with me *or* with Captain Ling, new tricks usually work only *once.*"

"Noted, ma'am. But in actual combat, they only have to work once, since the other guy doesn't get a rematch. If I may quote the colonel, 'In combat, there are no points for second best.'"

"All right, Bartley," McGraw said with a growl. "It's bad enough you've kicked my ass—I don't need to be hoisted with my own petard."

"Yes, ma'am. Understood, ma'am." Bartley made a feeble attempt to put a serious expression on her face but failed miserably.

"By the way, Rock," McGraw said as they got up and headed for the showers, "I never got a chance to say this, but...while it galls me to think someone got the Medal of Honor and an extra stripe for disobeying my orders, I'm glad you did."

"So am I, ma'am," Bartley said, suddenly serious again. "So am I."

* * *

The two Lunar destroyers came screaming down from above and caught USS *Chicago* by surprise. Admiral Greenwood had correctly guessed that, given the extreme distance at which she was shadowing BG-1, the American cruiser could only see the drive signatures of the heavy cruisers and *Valkyrie*. She had ordered *Starblade* and *Stardancer* to separate from the formation, shut down their drives, and lie in wait for the bogey.

"Sir, they're querying us for IFF codes," *Chicago's* tactical officer told the captain as the cruiser's crew closed at battle stations.

Captain Thompson knew there wasn't really going to be a battle, but since they'd already been caught with their pants down, he decided his crew needed the practice. "Send the codes, Lieutenant," he ordered, "and query *them* as well. They know who we are, and we know who they are, but we'll play the game."

A moment later, he found himself talking to a cheerful Lunar officer who identified himself as Captain Sanchez of LFS *Stardancer*.

"Admiral Greenwood's compliments, Captain Thompson," Sanchez said. "I've been told to advise you our group will be conducting live-fire exercises. For safety, we respectfully request you maintain five hundred thousand kilometers' separation from the flagship. We will be under drive, so I presume you'll have no problem recognizing LFS *Valkyrie* at that range...?"

"That is affirmative, Captain Sanchez. My compliments to the admiral, and please advise her we will maintain the requested distance."

The U.S. Navy had expected this, and Thompson's orders had directed him to comply with any such request. He watched as the destroyers passed on both sides, a mere 20 kilometers from *Chicago*, then sped back toward their battle group at 95 gees, easily pulling away from the cruiser whose maximum acceleration was twenty gees less.

"All right, wise guys, we saw your hull artwork," *Chicago's* exec muttered.

"At ease, Commander," Thompson said. "It's all part of the game. Two destroyers against a cruiser would have been a tough proposition, even for the LFS. If they were serious, we'd have been looking at the Babe on the Horse."

And that, he reflected, *is something I hope I never have to do.* Thompson was an experienced officer and took pride in his ship, but he had seen Greenwood and the LFS fleet in action and had no desire to go head-to-head with a Lunar battlecruiser. *So, we'll follow orders and watch their exercise from the cheap seats in the back row.*

* * *

Lorna allowed herself a smile of satisfaction as Sanchez relayed *Chicago's* response to her challenge. Her flanking pickets had also detected *Decatur* at extreme range, but she decided not to challenge if the American destroyer kept its distance. She was sure Captain Thompson would relay her warning to the other ship, and she doubted the Americans would intrude on her 'live-fire exercise' area. *Decatur* probably had better surveillance gear than *Chicago*, but at that range, neither ship would be able to see very much. *Other than one helluva spike on gravitics,* she mused, *and they're probably expecting that.*

* * *

"Oh, shit!" *Decatur's* tactical officer exclaimed. "Sir, you'd better look at this. I've got one humongous gravity pulse here, a few hundred kilometers in front of the Moonie flagship."

"Uh huh. Archive that data for posterity, Ensign," Commander Lowe ordered. As *Decatur's* captain, Lowe knew the reason for their mission, but his crew did not. "What else do you see?"

"Sir, at this range, it's hard to sort out their smaller units, but I'd swear their formation has one ship less than it had a minute ago."

Lowe smiled grimly. "Acknowledged. Just make sure you record everything."

* * *

"I thought I'd give you a courtesy call, Admiral. We've kept our distance as requested, but that's a remarkably interesting 'weapon system' you've been testing during those 'live-fire' exercises," Captain Thompson remarked.

The Americans had observed several gravity spikes over the past three weeks but had been unable to see much more than that. *Decatur* was farther from the Lunar formation than *Chicago,* but her search gear was better, and Lowe reported the apparent disappearance or reappearance of a Lunar ship with each gravity event. Now, CINCSPACE had given Thompson a new directive—contact the Moonies directly, drop a few hints, and see if they were willing to give out more information. He hadn't expected to be talking to Greenwood, but she had immediately taken his call.

"It's good to see you again, Captain Thompson." There was genuine warmth in her voice. "Especially since we don't have alien invaders to deal with this time. As for that weapon system, based on my last conversation with your president, I think you know what we're doing. Sorry I can't let you have a closer look, but you know how these national security things go."

"Yes, I do, Admiral." Thompson liked Greenwood as an officer, but her mention of the president reminded him she was also the chief executive of her nation. "All the same, Admiral, I wish you well with it." He sincerely meant what he said. If the Moonies developed interstellar travel, he was confident the U.S. would figure it out eventually—maybe soon enough for him to take a ship to another star—and *that* was an exciting thought.

"Thank you, Captain. We've been satisfied with the results so far." *Hawking* had completed the initial tests without incident and had already made the successful round trip to Alpha Centauri with *Starsong*. Since both ships were capable of higher acceleration than the unmanned probe, they'd shaved a day off the trip in each direction. Now, they were on their way to Sirius. "We'll be here for another couple of weeks, but I doubt there'll be much more to see. I'd suggest you and *Decatur* don't need to stay around, but your orders probably say otherwise." She gave him a knowing smile.

Thompson returned the smile, knowing she mentioned *Decatur* to let him know the destroyer had *not* gone undetected. He decided he would enjoy some serious, fleet-level war games with this woman as an opponent. It would certainly be a worthy challenge. "I'm afraid you're right, Admiral. We're out here to conduct our own exercises, and we won't be leaving until they're complete."

* * *

Sirius System, 8 Light-Years from Luna

The Akara warship, agile and well-armed for its size, would be considered puny by the standards of its enemies but then it was not designed to go head to head with Mekota dreadnoughts. It was, however, well suited for reconnaissance. The mission profile was simple: penetrate the Mekota Sphere, star-hopping through uninhabited (and likely undefended) systems. The objective was to circumvent the formidable Mekota defense perimeter and chart a path to strike at the heart of the enemy empire.

The Mekota answer to most military problems was the application of pure brute force. It usually worked well for the tripeds, given the sheer weight of metal in the Mekota fleet. Despite a far smaller and lighter fleet, the Akara had managed to hold their own through hit-and-run assaults on Mekota weak points. But the Mekota continued to pour ships and other resources into the frontier and would ultimately overwhelm the defenders unless the tide could be turned. If they could strike at targets in the heart of the Sphere, the Mekota might be forced to pull back and play defense, giving the Akara a measure of relief. Such a strike would require a secure supply line with staging points in normal space.

The Akara called themselves the People, but they were not one nation. They were a thousand clans, and the clan structure was the defining element of their society. They did not use names, describing themselves instead by their position or function in the clan.

In human terms, Heart of the Ship could be thought of as the captain, but his full title was Heart of the Second Scoutship of the Third Squadron of the Fleet of the Copper Hills Clan. Full titles were rarely used except on ceremonial occasions, but they defined everyone's position in the hierarchy. Heart of the Ship's immediate superior was Heart of the Scouts, who reported to Heart of the Third Squadron, and so on up to the Supreme Leader of the clan, Heart of the Copper Hills. But on this ship and to its crew, Heart of the Ship was known by a simple term that translated roughly to *my lord*.

* * *

Eyes of the Ship approached Heart as the latter was finishing his midwatch meal. It was unmannerly to approach anyone at meals, let alone the lord and master, but manners often became casualties of war. The astrogator stood before his captain and presented the Inferior's Salute, a gesture that involved half-drawing the blade at his belt and presenting the hilt to his superior. *I serve you. My life is yours to take.*

Other Hearts might have made Eyes wait in punishment for the interruption, might even have reached out to touch the hilt to humiliate the subordinate. But Heart knew his crew would not interrupt his meal without good reason. He responded promptly with the Superior's Salute, raising his open left hand, palm outward, talons retracted. *You serve me well. Your life is yours to keep.* He cocked his head in a gesture that invited the subordinate to speak.

"My lord, two ships, each of mass near our own, inbound toward the system primary, decelerating. They will cross our track some distance ahead. They have not tasted us, as best I can determine."

Heart's tongue flicked out in surprise. "As small as we…and only two, not three?" Mekota ships always traveled in threes.

"Only two, my lord, and their drive taste is not like any Mekota we have encountered, nor like any ship of our own."

"What others might there be in this place?" It was a question, not a rebuke.

"I do not know, my lord."

"Keep us hidden, if possible." Heart reached out and touched the communicator panel. "Talons of the Ship, prepare for battle."

* * *

Captain Shin was not accustomed to having his dinner interrupted, especially not by the GQ alarm. Since the ship had been commissioned, *Hawking* had gone to battle stations in earnest only once, on that terrible day when the Mekota had murdered Earth's leaders. On that occasion, Shin had had the entire fleet keep him company rather than a single destroyer, and he'd been in his own home star system.

But Shin Yong Chae was an officer in the LFS Navy, and *Hawking,* despite her research mission, was a Navy ship. The wardroom was just aft of the bridge, so Shin didn't waste time trying to get information over the comm channel. Within a few seconds, he was in his command chair calling for status reports.

"*Starsong* thinks we have a bogey, sir," Ensign Willis reported. "No grav track—they picked it up on active sweep—but it's almost half a million kilometers out, and it's on their side of us, so I can't see it. On your mark, Captain Davis will pop up and give us a look."

"Are you ready to scan, Mr. Willis?" *Hawking's* search gear was far more powerful and sophisticated than the destroyer's. If there was a bogey at that distance, Shin's people ought to be able to nail it down.

"Ready, sir," Willis said.

Shin keyed the command channel. "*Starsong—Hawking*. All right, Jimbo, let us have a look at it."

"Roger that, *Hawking*." *Starsong* broke sharply upward, clearing the way for *Hawking's* radar, lidar, and gravitic detectors to sweep the area.

"Got it, sir!" Willis said. "It *could* be a rock, but I make it to be on a perfect intercept course. What are the odds?"

"Poor to zero, Mr. Willis." Shin switched to the command channel again. "*Starsong*, bogey is confirmed. It appears to be on a ballistic intercept—not difficult to set up, since we've been holding course for a long time. Recommend we go to condition Alpha and try a radical course change—force the bogey to maneuver if he wants to intercept. If he does, at least we'll get a look at his drive signature and…well, I guess we'll play it by ear after that. What do you think, Jimbo?"

Technically, Shin was in command of the mission, but Jimbo Davis was a veteran of space combat, and Shin wanted his input.

"Sounds good to me," Davis said. "About that course change…I recommend we don't make it directly toward or away from him. We don't know who this is, so we probably don't want to look too aggressive or too timid. Maybe we should alter course up or down perpendicular to his track, just enough to generate a clean miss for him."

"Good point," Shin agreed. "Let's make it—" he ran a quick calculation through *Hawking's* navigation computers, "—up ninety, and sixty gee for thirty seconds. Then let's go ballistic and see what he does. Let me know when you have it laid in."

"We're ready," Davis said a moment later.

"Execute." Shin gave the signal to his helmsman at the same time. Then he switched over to the internal command channel. "Mr.

Morgan," he told his chief engineer, "I need you to clear all those science birds out of the missile racks. I want full combat loads as soon as possible."

* * *

"They have tasted us, my lord," Eyes of the Ship reported. "Powerful sensors, in both optical and high-wave frequencies. Definitely *not* Mekota."

Heart of the Ship pondered this and noted the unknown ships were executing an interesting course change. He watched for a while until Eyes reported the unknowns had shut down their drives and could no longer be seen with passive systems.

"No, my Clansmen," he told the bridge crew, "they are *not* Mekota. If they were, they would have come charging at us. Or, if they considered us a serious threat, they would have run like the cowards they are. No, these aliens are a different breed, and they are sending us a message, telling us it is our turn to play. The Mekota are *not* that clever. Eyes," he ordered, "you may use active sensors—they are obviously aware of us. Pilot of the Ship, give me a course that will exactly match their vector, neither approaching nor shying away. When we have achieved this, power off and wait, then it will be *their* turn."

* * *

Captain Shin was feeling the weight of his responsibilities. Aside from being eight light-years from home and in the presence of another alien enigma, he was again up to his neck in scientists. They clamored at him from all sides, begging for more information, which was about the only thing they *could* beg for, since he had suspended their scientific observations for the duration. Worse, they kept trying to give him advice.

"Maybe if we move a lot closer to it…"

"Why don't we launch an imaging probe at it, like we did with that Mekota thing…"

He appealed to Dr. Julian to *please* get these people off his bridge, promising he would give them full access to all the information being collected by *Hawking's* sensor suite. To his surprise, Julian complied immediately, gathering up all his eggheads and herding them into the wardroom, where he thoughtfully closed the door to keep their heated discussions from spilling out into the passageway.

Shin was beginning to like Julian. The good doctor was Luna's chief scientist and probably should have been home directing some Grand Research Plan, but it would have taken a direct order from Admiral Greenwood to keep him from this mission. At one point, it had appeared the admiral was considering such an order, reminding Julian he was too valuable to risk life and limb. But he'd brushed her objections aside, telling her he was first and foremost a scientist, and if the Lunar Free State could survive the death of his predecessor, it could certainly get along without *him*. Besides, Julian had told her, he had utmost faith in Captain Shin's ability to get him home safely. Now, Shin wondered if Julian was having second thoughts but, at least, the scientist was doing his part to make his job easier.

Shin was faced with serious command decisions. He had an obligation to return and report this contact to Lunar command, but he dared not take the chance that these new aliens (by now, he and Davis were convinced they were *not* Mekota) might follow them back to the Sol system.

There was a chance the aliens already knew where they came from. *Starsong* and *Hawking* had entered the Sirius system on the residual vector of a straight-line hyperspace course from Sol—a course they were still holding when they'd detected the alien ship. Shin kicked himself for that, deciding with perfect hindsight that they should have maneuvered to disguise that course before breaking back into normal space.

He and Davis agreed the aliens must have hyperspace capability. They couldn't be indigenous to Sirius, whose binary star system had only one planet, a massive ball of rock that orbited so close to the primary its surface remained in a constantly molten state.

In theory, *Hawking* and *Starsong* couldn't go home without capturing or destroying the alien ship, unless they could prove conclusively the aliens were not hostile (or at least posed no major threat). But what if the alien ship chose to run for it? In theory, they still needed to destroy it, since they had no way of knowing whether the aliens knew where they had come from.

In theory...in theory...Shin was getting *tired* of theories. At heart, he was a military man, and he longed for some action, but the aliens had been playing games with them for hours. The alien ship's initial matching of vectors left it at rest relative to them, approximately 200,000 kilometers away. They knew the alien ship was capable of at least 70 gees, and Shin was willing to bet they could do better than that.

Hawking and *Starsong* made the next move, a cautious attempt to close the range—nothing too threatening. Since they had been decelerating at over 80 gees when they'd first spotted the unknown ship, they hoped a twenty-gee move in its direction would not be seen as aggressive. To their chagrin, the alien ship matched the move, refusing to allow them to close. Next, they tried to *open* the range and, again, the aliens matched them exactly, maintaining the 200,000-kilometer separation.

They tried to communicate on a variety of frequencies, but if the aliens recognized any of their signals, they chose to ignore them. Likewise, the LFS ships detected no signals from the aliens other than typical sensor sweeps.

They considered splitting up and trying to flank the aliens, but Shin rejected the move because the classic military maneuver might seem hostile. The aliens had made no hostile moves, and Shin didn't want to be the first to do so. For the same reason, they decided not to test the limits of the alien ship's drive with an all-out charge or an all-out retreat.

In the end, it was Davis who proposed a solution. Shin didn't like it, but he had to admit it was their best option.

"We've been ignoring our biggest tactical advantage," Davis said. "We've got two ships, but we've been operating as if we're inseparable. You need to take *Hawking* back home to warn the fleet, while I stay here and babysit our alien friends and make sure they don't follow you. In case they don't already know where we came from, you can depart on a deceptive heading and correct once you're in hyper. It's better than *nobody* reporting back, which is what we're doing now."

"This mission is my responsibility," Shin said. "Why shouldn't *you* go back and report while I do the babysitting?" He already knew the answer, but he wanted to hear Davis say it.

"Well, it's the 'make sure he doesn't follow you' part that concerns me. *Starsong's* a warship. *Hawking* isn't."

* * *

"**A**hhh..." Heart of the Ship pointed to the change on his display. "They tire of the game. *That* one is going home to report, while *this* one remains to deal with us. Or do you think differently, Eyes?"

"No, my lord. It seems most likely."

"It is easily tested. Pilot! Follow this one. Don't try to close, just match its vector."

The leaving ship's departure course had been chosen carefully. While it was not directly away from them, it did give the alien ships a tactical advantage. As they began to pursue, the other alien ship moved sharply to cut him off.

"It appears we were right," Heart told his bridge crew. "Now, how shall we respond to this?"

* * *

Tension mounted on *Starsong's* bridge as the range began to close, but Davis wasn't about to blink first. He checked his status displays and watched his bridge crew—they were nervous, but they looked determined to do whatever had to be done. Weapons were online, but he was determined not to shoot first. The alien, he noticed, was *not* coming at them full bore but was maintaining the modest 40 gee vector at which *Hawking* had departed, as if he were casually trailing the research ship and didn't notice that *Starsong* was in his way.

"Put all our active systems on him," Davis ordered, "including targeting."

* * *

"They show their talons," Heart of the Ship said. "Yet they do not attack. Indeed, these are not Mekota. I think I could get to *like* these creatures, but we have tested them enough for now. They have a heart for battle, and that is all we need to know."

* * *

Davis breathed a sigh of relief as the alien ship braked and came to rest relative to *Starsong*. The range had closed to 75,000 kilometers, still well out of effective reach for both missiles and grasers.

Far from the scene of the confrontation, *Hawking* went to 100 gravities and headed for the jump limit. *We've just showed him more of our capabilities,* Davis thought. Starsong's *max acceleration is about five gees less than* Hawking's, *but I'm going to try to keep him from finding out.*

* * *

Amy Ling was in conference with Admiral Greenwood when both of their interface pads began to issue priority beeps. Amy looked at hers, and the small screen lit with John Swenson's face.

The XO wore an expression of extreme concern. "Admiral, Captain," he began, "*Hawking* has just come out of hyper—*without Starsong!* Captain Shin is recommending we go to Alpha Alert. He says we may get visitors."

"Oh, hell, he's found the Mekota," Ling exclaimed.

"Or they found him," Lorna said. "All right, Amy, let's go to Alpha."

"Make it so, Commander," Ling told Swenson, "and pass the word to the rest of the group."

* * *

Captain Shin told the admiral he hadn't intended to create such a stir, but he had no way of knowing what happened in the Sirius system after he went into hyperspace. He knew from tests with *Starsong* that it was possible to track a ship in hyper. If the aliens got past the destroyer, it was possible they would have been able to follow him.

"I agree, Captain," Lorna said. "I'd rather go to battle stations for a false alarm than get caught napping when the real thing happens. I'll also sign off on your decision to leave *Starsong* behind. Unfortunately, there's not much we can do other than wait and see which ship—if any—comes through next. How sure are you the alien you encountered was *not* a Mekota?"

"*Damned* sure, Admiral." Shin ticked off points on his fingers. "First, its drive signature bore no resemblance to the Mekota ships we've seen or the Mekota probe. Second, its maneuvering patterns indicated a single thrust axis—like one of our ships, not the three-axis Mekota pattern. We could see the delay when it turned over to reverse course; it was about the same as one of our ships might experience. Third, its sensor frequencies were not consistent with anything we've seen from the Mekota. And fourth, it was smaller than any Mekota ship we've seen—about the same mass as *Starsong*. We never got close enough for optical imagery, but I'm still damned sure it wasn't them."

"Hmmm…let's hope it isn't something worse," she said.

* * *

"Sir, can you look at this? Something's going on with the Moonies."

"What have you got?" Captain Thompson stepped up to the plot.

"We had another one of those gravity events a few minutes ago, but now, the Moonie battle group has changed formation. They've moved back about a thousand kilometers in our direction and dropped into a shield formation, as if they were about to engage an enemy, but there's nothing out there."

"Sir!" the communications tech called, "I've got LFS *Valkyrie* on the line. Captain Ling would like to talk to you."

"Thompson here," he said, taking the call. "What can I do for you, Captain Ling?"

Amy Ling's expression was neutral, but he sensed tension in her voice.

"Admiral Greenwood's compliments, Captain. Our exercises are over, but we have a situation here, and your assistance might be helpful. I've been directed to invite you to join our formation. If you accept the invitation, we'll slot you in next to the flagship, and the admiral will brief you in person. She also said that if *Decatur* is under your operational command, you may want to bring her in as well. We'll hold a slot for her in our destroyer screen."

What the hell is going on? Thompson wondered. *Guess there's only one way to find out.*

"We're on the way, Captain, and I'll bring *Decatur* in as well."

Lorna Greenwood was taking no chances with the unknown aliens. BG-1 was a powerful force, but it never hurt to have an extra cruiser or destroyer.

* * * * *

Chapter Twenty-One

Sirius System, 8 Light-Years from Luna

Jimbo Davis was cursing himself for the way the alien had foxed him. As soon as *Hawking* went into hyper, he'd found himself in a *serious* game of cat and mouse with the alien ship as it tried to get around him and go after the research ship. The players were evenly matched. *Starsong* might have had a slight delta vee advantage but not enough to make a difference. He'd managed to block every end-run attempt and had relaxed a bit when enough time had passed to guarantee that *Hawking* would get to Sol first.

He was wondering how long the game would last when the alien suddenly surprised him by turning sharply and streaking straight for the jump limit—not on the deception course *Starsong* was trying to defend, *but on a direct course for Sol!* The alien had guessed the original course on which the two LFS ships had come in was the correct one, and now, having neatly maneuvered *Starsong* out of position, he was headed out-system on the reciprocal heading. It was obvious he knew just which star he was going for. Worse, he'd caught the destroyer not just out of position but going the wrong way, and Davis had to scramble to give chase.

Over the long hyper trip, he found that *Starsong* did have a slight advantage. Not enough, though, and it looked like the alien would beat him to the Sol system limit by mere minutes. The bastard wasn't *exactly* on the course *Starsong* and *Hawking* might have followed, but close enough that he ought to end up where BG-1 could see and intercept him. With *Starsong* on his tail, the alien's options were going to be *extremely* limited.

* * *

"Your suggestion regarding their true place of origin was obviously correct, Eyes, else he would not be chasing us with such enthusiasm."

Eyes of the Ship wished he could share his lord's calm demeanor. They were heading into the lair of the aliens, not only with one of them on their tail but with another that had gone ahead to alert its fellows.

"I fear we may have tweaked his talons too many times," Heart of the Ship continued. "It is likely we will find ourselves in battle shortly after we arrive."

"Understand, my Clansmen—" his eyes swept over the bridge crew, drawing their attention, "—our primary mission is to evade and report. To die here, however bravely, will not serve the People. But our report will not be complete if we don't see the home system of these unusual aliens, who ought not to be here, deep in Mekota space."

"My lord," Talons of the Ship asked, "what if we find they are in league with the Mekota?"

"I do not think that will be the case. The Mekota do not have allies. They have only slaves, and *these* aliens have not behaved like slaves."

* * *

At the Sol System Hyper Limit

"Hyper signature!" the tactical officer sang out on *Valkyrie's* command channel.

Behind him, Amy Ling stiffened in her command chair, as did Lorna Greenwood on the flag bridge.

"I make it...right on the ecliptic, seventy thousand kilometers to spinward and fifty thousand out-system from expected arrival point. Querying IFF...no response. It's *not Starsong!*"

Lorna keyed the all-ships channel. "Battle group, all ships to intercept! Take vectors from *Valkyrie.* Weapons are *not...*repeat...*not* free. I want this bogey boxed in tight, but nobody fires without orders. Acknowledge!"

Acknowledgements came flooding in as the ships, including the two Americans, turned to intercept. Lorna had briefed the American captains, and both had volunteered to assist. Back in Earth space, the entire American fleet as well as Lunar Battle Group Two had gone on alert and were standing by in case they were needed. *A lot of trouble for one small alien ship,* Lorna thought, but she was taking no chances.

Realizing the alien might not come out where expected, she pulled her formation back nearly half a million kilometers—well inside the hyperspace jump limit—and spread them around the expected arrival vector. A few were too far out to get back quickly, but most of her force was within intercept range. Her strategy worked; interception was inevitable unless the alien had a way to defeat the laws of physics. What would happen after that was still unclear.

* * *

There were times, Heart of the Ship mused, when one could wish for the ability to jump back into the metaspace as quickly as one had emerged from it. There was nothing to prevent his ship from *making* such a jump, but the residual vector from his approach would guarantee he would find himself beyond the point of no return for this nondescript yellow star's metaspace gravity well. Better to take his chances with the aliens. At least there was a small chance for a happy outcome.

"Pilot," he ordered, "reverse course. Maximum power."

"My lord," Pilot advised, "we will never make it back to the metaspace limit. It will take too long to halt our incoming vector."

"Yes, it will," Heart agreed, "but for the moment, it will give the aliens no cause to fire on us."

He had to admire the near perfection of the trap they had set. They hadn't been able to predict exactly where he would emerge from the metaspace continuum, but they had deployed their forces well. There was no possibility he could escape the many warships closing in on him—*big* warships, with impressive power curves. If they had many more of these, and if this was an example of their tactical prowess, it was easy to see why these creatures were not slaves of the Mekota.

He wondered if they even knew of the Mekota, whose sphere of influence lay all around their system. He had never envisioned himself in the role of ambassador—he was not even a high-ranking noble of his Clan. Still, perhaps there was a chance these aliens might be persuaded to ally themselves with the People.

* * *

"The alien has turned over, Admiral. He's decelerating at ninety-two gees, but that's not going to help him. In fact, it will make it worse. We'll have him boxed in even sooner."

"He's got to know that, Amy. Maybe he's trying to tell us he's ready to give up. We may want to—"

"Hyper signature!" said *Valkyrie's* tactical officer. "Same coordinates and vector as the last, but...ma'am! This one looks like *Starsong!* Yes! She's answering IFF, and she's coming in on the alien's track. Looks like she chased him all the way here."

"I would have expected nothing less," Lorna said, but the relief in her voice was evident. "Jimbo's a hard charger. Get me a channel to *Starsong,* ASAP."

* * *

"In fairness, Admiral, this alien has not made any hostile moves toward us. We played a fast game of tag back there, and he led me on a merry chase, but he did not close to weapons range or put anything that looked like targeting sensors on us. I concur with Captain Shin—these are *not* Mekota."

"I'm inclined to agree, Jimbo," Lorna said. "We're holding our fire, though we *have* painted him with targeting systems and tried every form of hail we can think of. So far, he hasn't responded, but he's come to rest relative to the Sun, waiting for us to make the next move. I'd say that's a hopeful sign. You and Captain Shin did exactly the right thing. Now, we've got to figure out what to do with the present you've brought us."

She broke the connection with *Starsong* and turned to the flag bridge tactical display. *Valkyrie* and several other ships were closing in with orders to hold just ten kilometers from the alien. Lorna was still being cautious, and her ships had their weapons locked on target.

* * *

"**M**y lord, I think you may want to see this." Eyes was hesitant, not wanting to disturb Heart's meditations. Since they had come to rest, His Lordship had been waiting at his command station and had not bothered to tell his subordinates what he was waiting for.

"Are they still approaching?"

"No, my lord. They have stopped. They are close enough for detailed imaging, and I am looking at their largest ship."

Heart's curiosity was aroused, and he moved over to Eyes' station, where a long-distance view of the impressive alien battlecruiser filled the screen. "Hmmm…yes…now *that* is a warship."

"Yes, my lord. I can enhance the image further, and *this* is what I thought you should see." Eyes touched his controls, and the image grew until the forward half of the alien vessel filled the entire screen. The Akara range of color vision was not as great as that of humans, but it was sufficient to show the full glory of *Valkyrie's* hull artwork.

"Humans!" Heart exclaimed. "By the Egg of the Goddess! If the Mekota know of this, they must surely be pissing themselves—or whatever those plant creatures do when fear strikes them."

The Akara knew about humans, for they also had a few planets in their loose federation of clan holdings where the seeds of the legendary Progenitors had flourished. But those were primitive, agrarian cultures. While the Akara had no qualms about establishing their facilities on such planets, they tried not to disrupt the indigenous life forms, human or otherwise. In fact, they found trade with the primitive humans to be useful. The Akara were pure carnivores whose civilization had grown beyond the point where they were willing to spend their time hunting prey. The humans seemed to have a knack for raising a variety of tasty meat animals. The Copper Hills clan had made a lucrative business of trading simple manufactured goods for human-grown meats. They had learned that even primitive humans were smart, aggressive, and resourceful. The Akara did not fear the Progenitor spawn, but there was an unwritten agreement among the clans that prohibited the sale or trade of advanced technology to any human culture.

"In truth, my lord," Eyes admitted, "were it not for Your Lordship's reassuring demeanor, I too might be pissing myself. These humans are far from the simple animal herders we know, and it appears they are warriors."

"From this image, one might conclude they are *female* warriors." Heart's voice was amused. "Surely you would not fear a band of human females?"

"With warships such as this, my lord, gender would seem to be irrelevant."

Others on the bridge shifted uncomfortably. It was not wise to banter so freely with the lord and master, but Eyes had served his lordship for a long time and seemed to be permitted a great deal of latitude.

"And, my lord, not all of them are female." He touched his display panel and brought up another image, this one from LFS *Norseman*, which had closed on their other flank.

"True, but it would certainly appear that all of them are warriors." Heart admired the Viking's massive battle axe. "Enough of these games. It is time we have a serious talk with these humans."

"They may be trying to communicate, my lord, but their signals cannot be processed by our equipment. I detect them, but I cannot interpret them. I'm sorry, my lord."

"No matter," Heart said. "There are more subtle ways to speak to them."

* * *

"Sir," the tac officer told Commander Swenson, "there's something here you should see. I'm transferring the image to your console. I've been looking at the alien ship, and I noticed a pair of blinking lights on her forward hull. When I enhance the image, I see what looks like an open airlock."

Swenson had the watch on *Valkyrie's* bridge. He studied the image. "You may be right. Can you enhance that?"

"I'm trying, sir. It's not an excessively big hatch—Val says it's about one meter wide by two high—so maybe it's a personnel hatch. She's putting a second imaging scope on it now—says she can clean it up with interferometry."

As the two men watched, the image suddenly came into sharp focus, leaving little doubt that the lieutenant's first impression was correct.

* * *

"They've put out the welcome mat. So, who's going to pay them a visit?"

"Not you, Annie," Admiral Greenwood replied, and McGraw's face fell. "You're on this trip because of your command abilities, not your skill as an assault team leader. And not you either, Dr. Julian."

"Of course not, Admiral. This really isn't my field, anyway, but you will need scientists. An exobiologist, perhaps, like Dr. Warren."

"Right, and probably an engineer as well. Amy, pick a volunteer from *Valkyrie's* engineering department. And we *will* need Marines, Annie, so pick your best junior officer and a half squad of experienced troops. Dr. Julian, you'll coordinate the scientific side—no more than three scientists and only equipment they can comfortably carry. Have them meet Colonel McGraw's Marines in the docking bay in one hour. Amy, we'll need a cutter to get them to the alien ship."

* * *

"Your team ready to go, Sergeant?" Lieutenant McGuinness asked.

"Yes, sir." Bartley had just completed an equipment check on her five troopers.

"Here come the eggheads. Have your people give them a hand with that equipment." The scientists had taken a liberal view of the admiral's orders, and they were struggling to carry their instruments and other gear across the bay.

"Yes, sir. Jacobs, Tortorelli, give them a hand."

Here we go again, she thought. *Another day, another alien ship.*

* * *

"It appears, my lord, that your message was understood," Eyes said.

"So it does. Assemble the crew on the entry deck, and we will greet them. Remember, my Clansmen, these are not to be treated as enemies. Think of them as people of another clan—one we do *not* wish to engage in battle."

* * *

"Sir, I think we've got a problem," Bartley reported. "That airlock doesn't look big enough for more than four people."

"You're right, it doesn't," McGuinness agreed. "Okay, Sarge, that's you, me, and… Dr. Warren, pick two from your team."

"Me and Ensign Brockovich," Mercedes Warren said, naming *Valkyrie's* junior engineering officer. "Doesn't look like we'll have room for much equipment, but we'll want the video camera and the environmental analyzer, at least."

"We can manage that. There's no boarding tube, so we'll have to jump. Bartley, go first and secure a line to that ring next to the airlock. The rest of us can clip our safety lanyards to the line for the trip over."

* * *

Heart of the Ship watched as the four aliens—*humans*, he corrected himself—made their way boldly across the void and into the airlock. Two of them, he noted, were obviously armed, but the other two were not, and that was a hopeful sign.

* * *

"What was *that* all about?" Bartley growled.

As soon as they were inside, the outer airlock had closed. Then, suddenly, the boarding party had found themselves bathed in a purplish glow that caused their helmet visors to darken momentarily. After a few seconds, the glow had vanished and was replaced by more normal, if slightly bluish, lighting.

"UV bath," Ensign Brockovich said. "They want to make sure we don't bring any nasty germs aboard their ship—not that anything's likely to have survived our trip through the vacuum."

"Arrgh…" Bartley muttered. "That reminds me, we're going to be in quarantine again when we get back."

"Roger that, Sergeant," Dr. Warren replied with a chuckle. "You know the drill." Like Bartley, the biologist was a veteran of the first Mekota ship quarantine. She glanced down at her instruments. "Here comes the atmosphere."

The pressure in the lock came up quickly and leveled off a little higher than Earth's sea level, about 1.1 atmospheres according to the instruments. The party tensed as the inner door began to open.

"Sergeant, you're with me. Dr. Warren, Ensign, wait until we tell you it's clear." McGuinness stepped through the hatch and moved aside to the left. Bartley followed and moved to the right. It took effort to keep her LCAW up in the port arms position instead of sweeping the fire zone in front of her, but Colonel McGraw had been very specific: no threatening gestures.

To her surprise, she found the aliens standing in neat ranks about five meters in front of her. There was no chance she would have mistaken these aliens for a piece of equipment, as she had done with her first Mekota. They were weird-looking, but for a human, it was a familiar form of weirdness. *Lizards,* she thought. *A bunch of long-tailed, shiny-scaled lizards!*

* * *

A human would have called the Akara reptilian but, in fact, they had many bird-like characteristics. They were warm-blooded and hollow-boned, and they stood upright on two legs. But their long, narrow muzzles concealed rows of sharp canine teeth and a long forked tongue that was their keenest sensory organ. From their heads to the tips of their long, sinuous tails, their bodies were covered with iridescent scales that reflected a rainbow of colors from the overhead lights.

Like humans, they were four-limbed. But while their upper limbs resembled human arms, ending in hands that had three long fingers and an opposable thumb, their legs had knee joints that bent backwards. Like birds, their feet were equipped with long, prehensile toes tipped with wicked talons.

The Akara were what the dinosaurs might have become had it not been for that wandering meteor that put an end to dinosaur evolution on Earth some 65 million years ago, long before the Progenitors arrived to sow the seeds of humanity on the planet.

Sergeant Bartley was not an exobiologist. Once she got past the lizard analogy, her first observation was that some of them were armed. It wasn't hard to notice; they carried their rifle-like weapons in almost the same port arms position as Bartley held her LCAW, except her trained martial arts sense told her they all appeared to be left-handed. And *all* of them—even the ones not carrying rifles—wore a sheathed blade of some sort on a belt at the waist. The aliens were clothed in sleeveless tunics and a sort of kilt—a practical garment for a creature with a tail. She didn't see any evidence of gender differences, so maybe they were all the same sex. *Or maybe they don't have sexes as we know them.* Such a weird possibility would not have occurred to her prior to her encounter with the three-sexed Mekota.

McGuinness invited the biologist and engineer to join them.

"Wow!" Dr. Warren stepped through the hatch and looked at the Akara. "I can see a whole lot of fun in *my* future. Now, how do we go about convincing them we come in peace?"

"Well, ma'am, the lieutenant and I might start by slinging arms. They seem to carry their weapons like we do, so they should understand. What do you think, Lieutenant?"

"Excellent suggestion, Bartley. Slowly, though, no fast moves."

"Understood, sir." Bartley carefully pointed her LCAW straight up at the overhead, loosened the sling, and slipped it over her shoulder. McGuinness matched every move. *Just like on the parade ground,* Bartley thought.

"Think that one in front is the leader, Sarge?"

"Looks like it, sir, and the two behind are likely his senior officers."

"Right." McGuinness took a small step forward and presented a slow, exaggerated salute.

* * *

"Ahh, communication begins." Heart of the Ship took a step toward the human and replied with an equally slow and exaggerated Superior Salute. "Talons," he commanded, "have your Guardians rest their weapons."

* * *

Bartley's eyes widened in surprise as the armed aliens assumed a position much like parade rest, grasping their weapons by the barrel and lowering the butt end to the floor.

"Well," Warren said, "I'd say *that* was an overwhelming success. Now, what do we do next?"

* * *

Lorna Greenwood was frustrated. After their initial success, the boarding team was having difficulty communicating with the aliens. It was worse than a game of charades since they couldn't interpret the aliens' reactions well enough to know if they were getting through to the creatures.

"Part of the problem," Amy Ling said, "is that we're limited to visual gestures. Adding sounds might help. We should have taken comm gear like we used with the Mekota."

"I don't know if that would help," Dr. Julian said. "The Mekota know our language. These creatures have shown no evidence of similar knowledge. They obviously use a spoken language. Our people can hear them making sounds—very high-pitched sounds, almost beyond human hearing—but everything gets muffled by the suits."

The contact team was listening to the discussion via comm link. Sergeant Bartley hit her comm button. "Ma'am, if we're sure their air is okay, why don't we take the suits off? As the lowest ranking person, I volunteer to go first."

Val had thoroughly analyzed the environmental data sent back by the team, including microscopic scanning of the micropore filters through which the alien atmosphere had been drawn. The AI assured them the alien air was breathable and contained no harmful microorganisms. The pressure was a little higher than they were used to but not enough to cause a problem. The air was rich in oxygen and had traces of a few inert gases not usually present in Earth's air, but it was well within the limits of human tolerance.

"We can't do that, Bartley," Dr. Warren said. "Even if their air's okay for us, we don't know what ours will do to them. As soon as you open your suit, you'd contaminate their environment."

"Well, maybe we should ask *them* how they feel about it."

"And how would you do that, Sergeant?" Dr. Julian asked.

"Like this, sir." Bartley turned to the alien leader and mimed taking off her helmet, then opening her suit. Then she stepped back and spread her hands, inviting the aliens to react.

* * *

"My lord!" Healer exclaimed. "They want to remove their suits. If they do—"

"Yes, Healer," Heart responded gently. "If they do, our air may become contaminated. Obviously, they have examined our air with their instruments and believe no harm will come of it. But they realize there may be danger for us, and they are asking permission. Very thoughtful of them, don't you think?"

"But, my lord—"

"Eyes, Talons, return to the bridge. All Clansmen will leave this compartment, save three volunteers who will remain with me. Seal the compartment when you have gone. Should ill befall me, Eyes will become Heart."

"But, my lord—"

"We must be face to face with these humans. Besides, the danger is not great. We have walked on human-seeded planets before and found no threat from their diseases. Now go."

There was a moment of confusion as every Clansman volunteered to remain, but Heart settled it by selecting the nearest three. Talons started to protest that none of them were Guardsmen, but he finally bowed to Heart's logic. If the humans intended harm, they would already be dead.

When the compartment was sealed, he turned to the tall human who had made the request and mimicked the gesture of removing the helmet and suit.

* * *

"I guess there's not much doubt they understood what Bartley was telling them, ma'am," Dr. Warren reported. "They've evacuated and sealed the compartment except for four who stayed behind. Their leader, or at least the one we think is the leader, is one of the four."

Just about the way I would have handled it if I were in their shoes, Lorna decided. *Except, of course, they don't seem to wear shoes.* "All right, Sergeant, go ahead." Despite their precautions, Lorna suffered a moment of anxiety. She had grown rather fond of Bartley, and she didn't want to expose the young woman to danger, but she had confidence in Val's analysis. And duty was duty. Had it been a combat situation, she would have sent the Marine in without hesitation.

She watched the screen as Bartley stepped forward, reached up, and opened the face plate of her helmet. Tentatively, the Marine took a short breath, exhaled, then sniffed the air. Then she took a deeper breath. "Hmmm, strange smell—not bad, but strange. Uh, I'm still breathing, people, no ill effects so far."

"Let's hold it at that for now," Warren suggested. "If you're still okay ten minutes from now, and the aliens are still okay, then you can take off the suit. Then we'll give it another ten, and we'll *all* remove our suits."

* * *

After the humans removed their space suits, Heart invited Healer to return to the compartment. The ship's physician did so at once, followed closely by Talons. Healer immediately began examining the other three volunteers. He would not have dared to examine Heart without his lordship's permission.

"Forgive me, my lord." Talons offered the Inferior Salute. "My place is at your side. Eyes would have come as well had you not charged him with the care of the ship."

"I understand," Heart replied with a forgiving wave. "Since you are here, help me observe these humans. Now that they have shed their suits, I note they are two males and two females, and one of the Guardians is a female. It would seem they *do* have female warriors…interesting."

"Yes, my lord, I noticed that as well. But the female warrior appears to defer to the male. Perhaps he is one of their Lesser Talons."

"You may be correct but notice that *all* of them defer to the other female. She and the other male seem most interested in the equipment they brought, so my first thought is that they are scientists."

"If their mission is benevolent, it would be logical to have a scientist as its Heart, my lord."

"True, but the other male puzzles me a bit. At times, he seems most independent, yet at other times he defers to all of them. But I have seen the female warrior approach him with the kind of deference she gives to the others. I'm not sure what his place may be."

"Hmmm…" Talons regarded the male human who, at that moment, was speaking to the female guardian. Her body language seemed to indicate deference, but…suddenly, the Akara equivalent of a chuckle escaped his throat. "My lord, I think she gives him the kind of deference one of my seasoned guardians might give to an inexperienced junior officer who is *not* of the guardians."

"I hesitate to accept that explanation, since it would mean these humans are *very* much like us. But you may be correct." Heart chuckled, too.

* * *

"*That* one," Warren asserted, "is definitely a medic. Look how he's examining the other three. I would have thought his first concern would be for the leader, though."

"Well, ma'am, maybe he doesn't want to examine the leader because it would offend the leader's dignity." Seeing Warren's skeptical look, Bartley added, "You *know* how undignified it is to be poked and prodded by medics. Remember the Mekota quarantine?"

"Your down-home insights amaze me, Bartley. No wonder they said you were such a good communicator."

* * *

The contact team was exhausted. They had been at it for many hours but had made little progress. And since the aliens had not reopened the outer airlock door after admitting them, no one was able to go in and relieve them.

Lorna was surprised to learn that only Bartley had remembered to bring field rations, which she graciously shared with the others. At least all of them had water packs in their suits, so they weren't suffering dehydration. It was plain the weary team would have to leave the aliens soon. They didn't *think* the Lizards would give them a problem about that—they could communicate their intentions by putting their suits on, and the aliens had given no indication of hostile intent.

Lorna considered sending a relief team in when the door opened to let the first team out, but she decided the aliens might need rest as well. Still, there was one question she wanted answered before they departed the alien ship.

"The admiral wants us to ask them if they know of the Mekota," Warren told the team. "So, how do we do that?"

"Hey, Mr. Lizard, seen any Turnips lately?" Bartley muttered.

"Seriously, Sergeant, do you have any ideas? I'm fresh out."

Bartley pondered for a moment, then walked over to her spacesuit and opened an outside pocket. She pulled out a paper pad and vacuum-capable marking pen—standard issue for Marines, whose lives might depend on the ability to communicate silently under any conditions. She returned to the weary group and glanced at the Lizards, who were hunkered down on the other side of the compartment.

"I wonder if they're as tired as we are," she mused as she began to sketch something on the pad. A moment later, she showed her artwork to the others, who marveled at her fairly accurate sketch of a Mekota.

"I didn't know you were an artist, Sergeant."

"Well, if anyone should know what a Turnip looks like, it's Bartley," McGuinness said. "She's certainly seen enough of them. All right, let's show it off."

The four of them approached the aliens but stopped in the middle of the compartment. Early on, they had worked out a sort of protocol. If they wanted to talk among themselves or simply rest, they retreated to the end of the compartment nearest the airlock. The aliens went to the opposite end when *they* wanted to confer with each other, and neither side encroached on the other's territory. If they had questions to pose or ideas to convey, one side or the other would come to the middle of the compartment and wait for the other to meet them.

The aliens joined them. When they arrived, Warren nodded to Bartley, who showed the Akara her artwork.

The reaction from the aliens was immediate. The leader drew himself upright and stared straight at them, while the other Akara turned immediately to their leader. Bartley noticed the one on the leader's left put his hand on the hilt of his blade.

"Well," Warren said, "I'd guess that means they know the Mekota, but we don't know if that's good or bad." She keyed her comm unit and queried Lorna about their next move.

"I think," Lorna said carefully, "we need to let them know the Mekota are *not* our friends and see how they react. Lieutenant McGuinness, you'll need to be prepared in case the reaction is hostile. For all we know, they are Mekota allies. But if they *don't* like the Mekota, it's important they know we feel the same."

"Ma'am," McGuinness said, "if we get a hostile reaction, it's going to be a little hard to get out of here. Still, I doubt they'll do much with the fleet covering them, so we might as well go ahead and let them know where we stand."

"Sorry, Lieutenant, you're right. I should have thought of that. But I agree with your assessment. Proceed."

"How do we let them know, ma'am?" Warren asked. "Maybe we need to show them some video images from our last battle with the Mekota, or something, or maybe Bartley can draw another picture."

"There's an easier way than that."

They turned to Bartley.

She kept a straight face and continued. "You really want to show them how we feel about the Mekota, ma'am?"

"Yes, I do, Sergeant," Lorna said, and the others agreed.

"No problem." Bartley turned to the Akara, who were still watching them intently. *Like a snake watching a bird,* Bartley thought, for at that moment, the Akara looked *very* reptilian. Without further thought, Bartley held up the pad and carefully tore off the sketch of the Mekotan. Then she dropped it on the deck, raised her right foot, and *stomped* on the picture, making a show of grinding it under her heel.

The aliens took a step backward, and the leader looked down at the picture, then up at Bartley. There was a moment of silence.

"Thank you, Sergeant," Warren said in a small voice. "That was very…graphic."

Bartley stepped back, leaving the sketch lying on the deck.

To her surprise, the alien leader stepped forward, hunkered down, and very carefully retrieved it. He held it up in his right hand for them to see, then extended his left, palm facing the picture. Without warning, a wicked set of five-centimeter talons popped out of his fingertips, and with two swift slices, he shredded the sketch with surgical precision. Pieces of paper fluttered to the deck. The other aliens snapped to attention and made a hissing sound that might have been a cheer or a battle cry but was clearly an affirmation of support for the leader's action.

As quickly as they had appeared, the leader's talons retracted, and he turned and motioned to his crew, who immediately relaxed again.

"Where in the *hell* did those claws come from?" McGuinness muttered.

"Don't know, sir, but I guess that tells us how *they* feel about the Turnips."

* * *

"**T**hat was the most significant bit of communication we've had with these humans," Heart said. "And you, Talons, must surely understand the importance of it."

"Yes, my lord. It would appear we have found potential allies in a most unlikely place—deep within the territory of the enemy."

"Not only allies, but ones that have met the Mekota and have no fear of them. I think it is time we show them the rest of our ship. I know, Healer, you still have your concerns, but we live only by the sufferance of these humans. It is important that we show them hospitality. You may disinfect the ship as thoroughly as you like after they have departed."

* * *

The tour of the alien ship was only mildly interesting from Bartley's point of view. It wasn't as strange as the Mekota ships had been, but after ducking her head many times to get through passageways, she could see it wasn't built for human use. Measured for length, the Akara were around 180 centimeters from nose to tail, but much of that *was* tail. Standing fully upright, they averaged about 140 centimeters in height, and none of them topped 150. Their hatches and overheads were sized accordingly and getting around without bashing her head became one of Bartley's major concerns. She was the tallest member of the contact team, and she was glad she didn't have to negotiate these tight quarters in a space suit or even carrying her LCAW. As a gesture of good faith, the Marines had left their weapons with their space suits, after carefully removing the ammunition and stowing it in their belt pouches. The aliens had their own weapons, but McGuinness was more concerned about safety than treachery. It would probably not be good for their mission if some curious Lizard managed to blow himself away while handling the weapons in their absence.

Ensign Brockovich found the tour more interesting than the others, and Dr. Warren had to nudge him from time to time to keep him moving along. Left to his own, he might have spent hours examining each piece of complicated machinery they encountered. The aliens were very accommodating, sometimes even removing access panels to give him a better look, when he showed interest in something.

Though he'd been quiet during their negotiations with the alien leader, he actually seemed to be communicating on some nonverbal level with the alien crew members who tended the machinery. Warren was forced to conclude that engineers of every race communicated on some arcane mental wavelength that only other engineers could comprehend.

By the time the tour finished, all of them were dog tired. Without further discussion, they began to suit up for the trip back to *Valkyrie*. The aliens indicated their understanding by opening the inner airlock door, which they had closed after the last of the team entered.

After putting on everything but their helmets, the team was ready to say farewell to the aliens, but none of them seemed sure how to do it.

"Ma'am," Bartley asked Warren, "do you suppose we ought to give their leader a gift? You know, thanks for the hospitality."

"What do you have in mind, Bartley?"

"Well, I noticed they all wear those short swords. Maybe we could give him one of these." She indicated the Marine combat knife on her belt. "It's not as fancy as theirs, but it's a good blade."

"You want to give him a *knife*? Pull that thing out, and he'll likely slice you up with those claws of his."

"I meant to give it to him in the scabbard, ma'am." Bartley snorted. "I know better than to make any threatening moves."

"I think it's a good idea," McGuinness said. "These critters are obviously military types. I think they'd appreciate it."

"Just be careful about it," Warren reluctantly agreed. "They are aliens, and I'd be careful about something like that if I were dealing with a *human* culture I didn't know very well. All right, then, let's get it over with."

* * *

Heart regarded the female human Guardian with consternation. The sheathed blade she held out to him was properly presented—hilt to his left hand—but she had not half-drawn it in salute. He was not sure exactly what to make of it.

"I believe, my lord, she is offering it as a *gift*," Talons suggested, "though I doubt these humans know the significance of such a gesture." Among the Akara, offering one's personal blade as a gift to a superior was the equivalent of swearing lifelong allegiance.

Heart agreed with Talons—it was unlikely the human had such intentions. "Hmmm...then they won't understand the significance of *this*, either, but it probably comes closer to what they intend." He unfastened his blade's scabbard and presented the sheathed weapon to the human in the same manner she had presented hers. With one hand, he reached over and grasped the sheath of her weapon and waited for her to do the same with his.

He heard a hiss of surprise from his subordinates. The *exchange* of blades was equivalent to swearing lifelong alliance and friendship—a serious matter for the Akara, for it meant the two participants would never raise a hand against each other, even if their clans were opposed in war. It was done only between equals, and only between males—thus the hiss of surprise—but they had given their blades to him, and it was not their place to question.

The human glanced at her superior, and there was a short exchange in their language. Then, with some hesitation, she reached out and grasped his blade by the scabbard. Both released their blades to each other, and the human spoke a short phrase in her own language—a humming rumble too low for the Akara to hear properly—as she stepped back and presented what Heart believed was the human salute—the same gesture the male guardian had made when they first met. He replied with the Superior Salute, and the humans turned and walked toward the airlock. They closed their suits, stepped inside, and waited while Heart's crew closed the inner door. The lock cycled and they were gone, off to their waiting small craft, which soon departed for their own ship.

"It is not very ornate," Heart remarked as he and Talons examined the blade the human had given him, "but the simple blackness and functional design have artistic qualities of their own."

"Yes, my lord, and it appears to be good steel and *very* sharp. This is a functional weapon, not merely an ornament."

"Indeed, it will serve. Engineer must craft a new fastening for me so I can wear it on my belt, but wear it, I will. I am most pleased with the way things have gone so far."

* * *

"Wow! This thing is beautiful. I think this might be real gold inlay on the hilt. And it's sharp, too. Bet you could make a nice Turnip salad with this baby."

The alien blade was a bit longer than a combat knife but not as broad, and it was covered with intricate, engraved scrollwork. The hilt was also covered with engraved patterns and inlaid with gold. It felt solid and comfortable in Bartley's hand, which was surprising since it had not been designed for human hands.

"I suppose they're gonna make me turn this into the scientists for study," Bartley said wistfully.

"I think we can convince them to give it back to you after they've looked at it," McGuinness said. "The gift exchange was a great idea,

and you deserve to have it. Of course, the supply people are probably gonna make you pay for a new combat knife. After all, you signed
for that piece of equipment, Sarge."

"If I get to keep this one, I can live with that." Bartley couldn't
repress her grin.

* * * * *

Chapter Twenty-Two

At the Sol System Hyper Limit

C ommunication with the aliens improved dramatically after that first visit. With help from Val, they made progress on the language of the aliens—the Akara, as the Lizards called themselves.

It was not a tongue humans could speak, but the AI's audio capabilities were not limited by the constraints of a human's vocal apparatus. Once Val developed a working vocabulary—after many teaching sessions with the aliens, who patiently repeated words while illustrating their meaning with pictures and gestures—syntax and grammar had followed quickly. The aliens might never have known just how it was done, but they soon learned any human wearing one of the special "translators" —a comm unit with an always-open, two-way channel to Val—could understand them and reply with little difficulty.

The humans were still a little hazy on Akara social concepts, but one thing was clear. They were warriors, and they hated the Mekota. They also seemed to subscribe to the philosophy that "the enemy of my enemy is my friend." They had been willing to share intelligence about the Mekota, even the location of the Mekota home system and other Mekota strongpoints nearby. Lorna thought it likely the small Akara ship was a forward scout, but Captain—the only name Val could come up with for the Akara leader—would not reveal the details of his mission.

As a gesture of trust, Lorna invited Captain and his staff to visit *Valkyrie*, an invitation they quickly accepted. She noted with interest that he chose to bring three subordinates, whom Val identified as Engineer, Doctor, and Tactical Officer. *Likely the same choices I would have made*, she thought. *Bring people most able to gather intelligence, while leaving a competent officer in charge.* Val had identified Navigator as Captain's second-in-command, who had no doubt been left behind to carry on if something happened to his superior.

Amy Ling and Commander Swenson conducted the tour of the ship, then brought the aliens to meet with Lorna in the flag briefing room. Up to that point, Lorna had not spoken directly with the Akara, but for this meeting, she also wore one of the translators.

"Am I now in the presence of the great captain of this fleet?" Val translated the Akara leader's first words.

"Yes, and I am also the grand captain of the Clan of the Lunar Free State." She hoped Val's analysis of Akara social hierarchy was sufficient to render a proper translation.

Tactical Officer looked startled and whispered something hastily to Captain. *He said, 'They have a warrior queen, my lord,'* Val translated, her voice only audible in Lorna's earbud.

Okay, close enough, Lorna thought with a slight blush, and with that, they got down to serious discussions. The Akara had been most direct with the humans and seemed to have little use for diplomatic posturing. That suited the warrior queen fine.

"I am curious," she asked. "When you detected our ships, you could have gone immediately to report to your people. Why did you choose to come here, and risk being captured or destroyed, of never returning to report at all?"

Captain shifted a bit in his chair, which was more like a short stool, something *Valkyrie's* engineering shop had put together based on images of the furnishings on the Akara ship. Typical human conference chairs would not have been comfortable for a creature with a long, heavy tail.

"It was a difficult choice," Val translated the alien's reply. "You had the advantage. You had two ships, one to go and report, the other to stay with me, perhaps to follow me if I went back to my Clan. If I went back to my Clan, my report would be incomplete. I did not know who you were or where you came from. I was certain you were not Mekota, and that was important. If I followed you, perhaps I would have died and my loyal Clansmen with me, but at least you wouldn't know where my world is. If I did not die, I would have found your world and, perhaps, an ally against the Mekota. Then, when I return to my Clan, I have something important to report. I listened to both sides, and the voice leading me here spoke loudest."

"A warrior's choice," Lorna said. "And if I allow you to return to your Clan, what will you report?"

* * *

With mixed emotions, Lorna watched the Akara ship reach the jump limit and vanish into hyperspace on a heading for Sirius. There was risk involved in letting them go. The aliens knew the location of Earth, but despite all efforts at persuasion, they'd refused to reveal the location of their own homeworld. Other than that, they had been very polite and seemed genuinely interested in establishing relations with Earth, but Lorna thought—somewhat cynically, she admitted—that being an occupant of a single ship surrounded by a powerful and potentially hostile fleet would do wonders to improve one's manners and diplomatic skills.

Captain had promised nothing. He'd made it clear he was a low-ranking member of his Clan, and, when asked what his Clan leader might do, he had volunteered little. He'd said only that the Akara already had one powerful enemy and would not wish to make another. Lorna realized the same could be said for Earth.

In the end, she told the Akara they were free to go and that no ships of Earth would follow, although the aliens had no way of knowing that Earth only had two hyper-capable ships. She told Captain to report all he had seen and heard and to tell his Clan that Earth—or at least the Clan of the Lunar Free State—would be willing to discuss an alliance with the Akara—or at least with the Clan of the Copper Hills.

They know where to find us, she mused, *and there are really only three possibilities: they'll return with a diplomatic mission, they'll return with a battle fleet, or they won't return at all.* She hoped for the first option, didn't think the second was likely, and would be disappointed if the third was their choice, but she would prepare for all three.

Hyperspace capability was her priority. *Hawking* and *Starsong* had proven the systems worked, even under combat conditions. Jimbo Davis had thought about what would happen if he *did* catch the Akara ship in hyperspace or if it turned to engage him there. His engineers had determined the effective range of beam weapons in that environment was probably less than a kilometer. Beyond that, the immense gravitational stresses would disperse the beam. Gravity-drive missiles would be able to maneuver in hyperspace, but their targeting systems wouldn't function at ranges beyond a few kilometers. In short, combat in hyper would be up close and personal, but Jimbo *had* crafted a battle plan. LFS engineers could refine his work to give Lorna's warships the ability to fight in hyperspace.

But first, they had to be able to get there. Lorna worked up a refit schedule that would have *Valkyrie*, two cruisers, and three more destroyers hyper-capable and ready for squadron trials within six months. The yard dogs at Luna would not be happy about the pressure, but they would get the job done.

She thought about her future and the personal choices she would have to make, but the one thing she really wanted most would have to wait until the Akara returned or until enough time had passed to be sure they weren't going to return. She could, however, do some advance preparation. That would require serious discussions with Admiral O'Hara, and there would be time for them while *Valkyrie* was being refitted.

* * *

TerraNova City, Luna

The chief executive's briefing room, adjacent to Lorna's office, had the best view in the underground city. Its windows were 50 meters above concourse level, looking out over TerraNova Park, the largest open area in the complex. The park was lush and green, dotted here and there with more colorful plant life, kept healthy by the strong lights and the gentle "rain" that fell on a regular schedule from the sprinkler system in the domed ceiling almost 100 meters above. At night, the dome became a starry sky, thanks to the newly installed planetarium projector at the park's center. Broad walkways cut the park into quadrants, while lesser paths meandered through the gardens. Colorful shops and restaurants dotted the perimeter at the concourse level, some with open terraces for dining areas. *We've come a long way from the bare rock tunnels of ten years ago,* Lorna mused.

She turned from the armored-glass, pressure-tight window—Lunar engineers still had to account for the hazards of the Moon's harsh environment—and gathered her thoughts for the meeting. There were only four people in the room: Lorna, her two closest advisors, Mick O'Hara and Charlie Bender, and Sergeant Bartley at her usual post beside the door. The two flag officers had not been told the purpose of the meeting, and Charlie had already remarked on the absence of Timiko Yamamoto, noting that this must be a *very* high-level discussion.

"Let's just say it involves matters that have not yet reached the level of command policy," Lorna said.

O'Hara and Bender took seats by the head of the long table. But before joining them, Lorna paused directly in front of Bartley. The Marine noncom didn't so much as twitch as her commander-in-chief looked into her eyes from just a few inches away.

"Bartley," Lorna's low voice was almost a whisper, "this is going to be one of those personal things, but it also involves matters of state. Of course, not a hint of it must leave this room."

"Yes, ma'am," Bartley replied in an equally low voice. She was surprised since the admiral had never felt a need to remind her about her security obligations. As Lorna continued to examine her, the sergeant realized she was looking for reassurance. "I've been meaning to talk to the medics, ma'am. I have a problem with my hearing—can't hear a thing at times like this. In fact, I feel another hearing loss coming on now."

Lorna favored her with a little smile. "You know, Bartley, I think I love you…but that's against regulations, so you didn't hear that either."

"Hear what, ma'am?"

Five minutes later, Bartley had gotten over her blush, but Admiral O'Hara was white as a ghost.

"You *can't* be serious, Admiral," he exploded. "Tell me it's a joke! Yell out 'April Fool!' or something."

"I've given it a lot of thought, Mick, and I believe this is the best course of action for the Lunar Free State."

"But…I…" He was clearly at a loss for words.

"You're a visionary, Mick, a *builder*. Look out that window." She waved a hand toward the park. "*You*, more than anyone else, built this city with your leadership, your ability to solve problems. You're equally effective at dealing with the scientists, the businesspeople, and the fleet. *You* pushed us out into the Belt to look for the resources that got our economy going. *You* built LunaPort and Mars Base, and *you* turned theoretical research into a working star drive. Me, I'm just a warrior. I do fine when we need to go out and kick someone's ass, but I can't do that without the ships and weapons systems *your* people built for me."

"But, Lorna, that's just the point," O'Hara pleaded. "We've got two alien races to deal with now, and at least one of them is hostile. You *are* a warrior, and we *need* a warrior right now."

"I'm not going anywhere," she said, more quietly. "I'm willing to go back to my old job commanding the fleet if that's what you want. If not, just give me a battle group. Hell, give me a single cruiser, if that's your preference. Let me do what I do best, while you take the job you should have had when Ian died."

"I could argue that," he replied, recovering somewhat from the shock. "All those things you say *I* built were done at Ian's direction. I made my share of suggestions, and often as not, Ian took those suggestions. But I never had to make the decisions myself. I've never worked without a boss to report to, never been a CEO of *anything*. I'm not sure I can do it."

"Neither was I," she told him. "I'd never been a CEO either. I've managed to keep things going until now, but there are a lot of areas—business matters, research, engineering—where I'm not the best person for the job. Fleet loves me, but TerraCorp's people hate me. The scientists think I'm clueless, but they're afraid to speak up or enlighten me.

"Mick, I knew Ian's management style, and I know yours. All he ever did was point you in a direction and turn you loose. And most of the time, you were already headed in the right direction, so all he did was give you support. *You* were the one who did the job, and I believe you're the one to do *this* job."

O'Hara still didn't look happy, but he didn't reply, so Lorna turned to Charlie Bender.

"Charlie, you haven't said anything. You're here because I want your input—hopefully, your support—but I'll listen to whatever you've got to say."

"I agree with you, Admiral, and I know how you feel. I've never been comfortable with the role of foreign minister, so I spend most of my time with the things I do best—intel and operational security. That's probably why we have such lousy relations with half the nations of Earth. For the diplomacy side, I used to rely heavily on Carla—yes," he said, seeing the look on Lorna's face, "I miss her too, though my reasons are a lot more selfish than yours.

"I agree that Mick—Admiral O'Hara—is the man who *should* be CEO. In fact, he's the *only* person other than you I would trust with the job. I'm just wondering how we're going to pull this off, within constitutional limits, that is."

"Wait a minute!" O'Hara protested. "I haven't agreed to this, and, even if I do, I don't see how you can do it. It's not like you can just go to the Directorate and say, 'I quit—please give my job to Mick O'Hara.'"

"No, but I can go to them and say, 'Look, I know you people don't like me. I'll step down, but *only* if you vote in advance to replace me with Admiral O'Hara. Otherwise, try to vote me out, but you'd better bring your lunch, because it will be a cold day in Hell before you can make it happen.'"

"That might work." Bender chuckled. "The faction that dislikes you the most doesn't have near enough votes to get you out, but they might see Mick as the lesser of two evils. Your supporters will probably back Mick without hesitation. My main concern is the people. How do we convince *them* this isn't some sinister plot to remove the popular Babe on the Horse from office? You can't tell them you decided to quit because you don't want to do it anymore."

"No," she said, "I can't. But I don't expect this to happen for at least six months—long enough to figure out what the Akara are going to do, anyway. And when I do it, I plan to have a perfectly good personal excuse. I plan to be pregnant, and I'll want to spend a few months just being a mother before returning to my old duties with the Fleet."

"You plan to be *what!*" O'Hara and Bender exclaimed, almost in unison. Against the wall, a little smile almost made it to Bartley's lips.

* * * * *

Chapter Twenty-Three

TerraNova City, Luna

Lorna had remained in office as chief executive for another full year, and it had been a busy year. The Akara had returned in peace less than two months after first contact. First, they'd sent a small envoy ship, escorted by two small warships of the type *Hawking* and *Starsong* had encountered at Sirius. To Lorna's delight, one of them was the same ship, still under command of the alien captain she'd met in the outer reaches of the Solar System.

The Akara ambassador's full title was Speaker for the Copper Hills and Allied Clans to the Warrior Queen of the Clan of the Lunar Free State. Mike's translation brought a blush to Lorna's face, as Speaker told her they wanted to talk about a broad range of topics, including trade and exchange of technology and intelligence, and if the great queen would consider it, alliance against a mutual enemy.

Diplomacy was not one of Lorna's strengths and, at that point, she made what she later regarded as a major blunder. Quietly, through diplomatic channels, she informed the other nations of Earth of the situation and invited them to participate in the discussions. Until then, only the Americans had known there had been contact with *another* alien race, and her message set off a firestorm of protest around the globe. Every nation *demanded* to have its say in the negotiations. In Lorna's view, some of the demands were totally unreasonable.

The Pan Africans, having been mostly taken over by the increasingly powerful Islamic Federation, joined the Islamics in demanding that all negotiations with the Akara be stopped. It was not Allah's plan that humans should negotiate with creatures that were not only infidels but probably servants of Satan. The encounter with the Mekota, they insisted, was a sign from Allah that mankind must not have dealings with servants of the Evil One.

The Confederacy of Nations insisted any such negotiations *must* be held on Earth. Further, they demanded the negotiations be held somewhere on Confederacy soil, since the Confederacy represented "the majority of civilized people on Earth." That outraged the Islamics, whose followers (spread across Africa, southern Asia, the Far East, and parts of South America) outnumbered the Confederacy's population by a significant margin.

Only Japan, the United Kingdom, and Australia responded in what Lorna considered a reasonable manner, promising to send envoys to Luna to take part in the talks. To her surprise, the Americans joined with the Koreans—the oldest and most favored ally of the LFS—in advising that they only wanted to send an observer and would be content to let the Lunar Free State take the lead in the discussions. President Blackthorne told her that, if questions arose, the USA and LFS could work it out privately. There was no sense in hashing it out in front of the aliens. Lorna thought that was a great idea, but she realized it also allowed Blackthorne to disavow responsibility if the negotiations went badly.

In the end, Lorna ignored the Islamics. She considered their attitude barbaric and stupid, and she said so, in just those words. That caused a spewing of hatred and anti-Lunar rhetoric from the Islamic world, and several prominent Mullahs issued *fatwahs* calling for her assassination. Lorna shrugged and told them to take a number.

She also denied the demands of the Confederacy, who then informed her they would not take part in the discussions at all. They insisted she advise the aliens that the LFS and others taking part in the discussions did *not* represent and could not speak for the "great majority of Earth's people." With another shrug, she told them the LFS had never claimed to speak for all of Earth and neither had any of the other participating nations. This drew charges that the LFS was obstructing the Confederacy's attempts to "bring peace and unity to all the people of the world." The Confederacy also threatened sanctions against the US, which was technically one of their member nations. President Blackthorne told them—in polite, diplomatic terms, of course—to pound sand. He had long since reached the conclusion that a close alliance with the LFS was worth more to him than membership in the Confederacy would ever be.

Lorna advised the Akara delegation of the situation, and Speaker admitted that he did not speak for all the Akara either. In fact, he told her, there had been controversy among the People as to whether to deal with the humans at all. His commission included only the Copper Hills Clan, with the silent support of three other closely-allied Clans. Lorna remarked that perhaps humans and Akara were more alike than their vastly different physiologies would seem to indicate. The Akara seemed to appreciate the ironic humor in that, and the talks had gone quite smoothly.

That had *not* helped relations between the LFS and most of Earth's nations, and the situation got worse over the next year, as the Akara began to trade with the humans. All trade transactions and diplomatic discussions were conducted on Luna, via a special Embassy of the Unaligned Nations—meaning the LFS, the US, the UK, Australia, Korea, and Japan—whose offices were in TerraNova City. The Confederacy and the Islamic Federation declared an embargo on Akaran trade goods and imposed economic sanctions on the United States and the LFS. The Confederacy stopped short of sanctioning the other unaligned nations, since they still hoped to convince those nations to join their World Organization in the future.

At that point, Lorna decided she'd had enough. She was not happy with her performance as chief executive. She decided her success with the Akara had been mostly luck, combined with the fact that the Lizards—as most people called them—really wanted an alliance with the humans. To accomplish that, she'd antagonized three-quarters of Earth's population and damaged relations between the LFS and all but a handful of Earth's nations. That had *not* endeared her to the Lunar businesspeople, the executives of TerraCorp, and others who did business with Earth, and they expressed their views loudly through the Directorate. Lorna still had most of the Directorate behind her, but her support had weakened considerably since the day they'd confirmed her after Ian Stevens' death. The ordinary people of Luna, and certainly the people of the Fleet and Marine Corps, still loved her, but they mostly loved her as a war hero who had soundly thrashed the evil Mekota and sent them back where they came from. As long as the Lunar economy held strong, and the nation was not under attack, they paid little attention to her performance in other areas.

But Lorna *was* concerned with those other areas. Despite good advice from Kim Jong Pak and others, she still didn't have a feel for the commercial and economic side of the CEO's responsibilities, and while her relations with the scientific community were cordial, she allowed the scientists to go in their own direction. Mick O'Hara was far more involved in providing direction to Luna's research efforts and, for that matter, the nation's business and economic interests, than she was.

The only accomplishments she could claim were the continued expansion of the fleet and the conversion of its ships to hyperspace capability, but those were within her comfort zone. Even there, she took criticism from the business side of the Directorate for spending too much of Luna's hard-earned wealth on military assets. The Mekota had been beaten, and the Akara seemed friendly and didn't appear to be much of a threat. There was no war at the moment, so unless—as some of them suggested—she was thinking of another war with Earth, there was no reason for the continued buildup.

But the fleet was a source of pride to Lorna. Two more battlecruisers, *Amazon* and *Nike*, had been added. A third battlecruiser, to be commissioned LFS *Isis*, was nearing completion, and the keel had been laid for another. Three new heavy cruisers had also been commissioned, and several of the new *Vampire*-class light cruisers were under construction as well.

Lorna felt the Directorate's attitude was short-sighted. The Mekota were still out there along with who knew what other alien threats. As for the Akara, they were still an unknown element. And while the thought disturbed her, the rhetoric coming up from the planet—particularly from the Confederacy, some of whose nations had significant space capability—seemed to indicate that war with Earth was a possibility that had to be considered. Under the circumstances, she considered the continued build-up of the fleet to be a national priority. But that was her *military* assessment, and it only reinforced her feeling that she was the wrong person for the CEO's job.

So, with Charlie Bender's help and Mick O'Hara's still-reluctant concurrence, she went to her supporters in the Directorate and solicited their support for O'Hara as her replacement. Charlie, meanwhile, had gone to her *enemies* in the Directorate and told them Lorna would resign, but *only* if they supported Mick as her replacement. Many grumbled and complained—they wanted a businessperson to fill the post, but they didn't have the strength to push it through—although they agreed Mick was preferable to Lorna. As the head of Luna's Corps of Engineers, he was viewed as significantly less military- and more business-friendly. In the end, the vote to confirm the new chief executive, pending Lorna's resignation, was almost unanimous, with only two Directors abstaining. She submitted her resignation to the Directorate, and, with a smile of congratulations, removed the five-star insignia from her collar and pinned it on Mick's.

O'Hara's first act on taking the CEO's chair was to announce that Lorna would continue as Commander of the Fleet. Since she already held that position, Directorate approval was not required. Lorna accepted, though both she and Mick knew there was yet another surprise she planned to spring on them. With CEO responsibility lifted from her shoulders, she went ahead with the rest of her plan immediately. Two months later—having been informed by the medics that all was well—she announced her pregnancy to the world. The media, still buzzing over her unexpected resignation as CEO, jumped on the announcement with glee. Most of them assumed she was already pregnant when she resigned, but they wondered why she'd accepted the position of fleet commander, given her "delicate condition."

Lorna addressed the issue immediately. She would need, she told them, a leave of absence to take care of herself during the later months of pregnancy and then a few months to spend being a mother to her child before resuming her duties. During her absence, Vice Admiral Sakura would assume temporary command of the fleet. Mick O'Hara's prompt endorsement of the plan put the matter to rest.

The media indulged in a lot of speculation about the father of Lorna's child. Her sexual preferences were common knowledge, and the media could find no evidence of any temporary relationship she might have had with a male partner. Most of them guessed her pregnancy was the result of some sort of *in vitro* procedure, but that didn't answer the question of parentage.

Lorna refused to talk about the matter. "When my baby is old enough to understand, I'll tell *her* about it," she said to anyone who asked. She had already told them the baby would be a girl, which reinforced their belief that her pregnancy was further along than it really was. "If *she* decides we should tell the rest of you, I'll have no problem with it, but that means you'll have to wait a few years."

The media then started hyping an unconfirmed rumor that she was carrying Ian Stevens' child, supposedly via a donation he had made to the reproductive bank prior to his death. One story even speculated she was carrying out Ian's supposed "last wish" that either she or her life-partner, Carla Perry, have his baby to carry on his legacy. Since Carla had died with Ian in the First Mekota Encounter, Lorna had—so the story said—decided to carry out that wish.

Lorna didn't confirm or deny the story, though it was uncomfortably close to the truth. *In fact,* she thought, *if I ever decide to have a second child...*

No one guessed Lorna's baby didn't *have* a father. Thanks to a minor miracle of biogenetic engineering, the child had two mothers. She was the product of the fusion and mutual fertilization of two egg cells, one being Lorna's and the other that of Carla Perry. Other than Sarah Wilkins and two of her medical research staff—who were bound to secrecy by their ethical code—only four people knew the truth: Charlie Bender, Mick O'Hara, Sergeant Veronica Bartley, and Carla's father, Thomas Perry, who rejoiced in the knowledge it would give him the grandchild he'd thought he'd never have. Needless to say, none of the four were talking to the media.

* * *

TerraNova City, Luna

As a former CEO, Lorna was still entitled to a Marine security detail, and she was surprised when Sergeant Bartley volunteered to stay on as its head. "I really thought you'd have preferred fleet duty, Rock. Most Marines consider this assignment a royal pain in the posterior."

"Well, maybe so, ma'am, but I figure it's the best of both worlds. When you go back to the fleet, I go back to *Valkyrie*, but, in the meantime, I get to be here when Baby Carla is born."

Touched by the sentiment, Lorna agreed, but the media soon took notice of Bartley's continued loyalty. They focused on her as a possible source of information about Lorna and the rumors about the baby's parentage. Bartley brushed them off, and the LFS news media, as members of the Journalist Corps, were careful not to violate her privacy rights under the Lunar Constitution. The representatives of *Earth's* media were less respectful.

One evening, two British tabloid journalists cornered Bartley at Corporal J's Place. They started buying her drinks and asking a few harmless questions, but they got more persistent as the evening wore on and her alcohol level went up. Eventually, they got around to the question about the "father of the Iron Maiden's love child," and Bartley told them to go screw themselves.

But they weren't about to back off. "Look, Sergeant," one of them pressed, "you've been with the admiral a long time, and everybody knows she's a bit of a...well, you know...not exactly into *male* companionship. Now, some people have been saying—unconfirmed rumors, of course—that you might be a little closer to her than...how do I say this...than regulations allow. I wouldn't want to put that story—unconfirmed as it is—out on the web, but it would certainly get a lot of interest from our readers, so it's *very* tempting. Of course, if you could see your way clear to give us some *other* story we could use...something more interesting than your...alleged adventures in bed with the admiral, well..."

Bartley sat through the pitch with no expression on her face. When the reporter trailed off to wait for her response, she continued to sit there for a few more seconds. Then she stood up.

"*I need four volunteers!*" she said in her parade-ground voice.

The place was, as usual, full of Marines, and a dozen or more immediately swarmed to her table.

"Whatcha need, Sarge?" a tall, burly corporal asked.

"You," she pointed at the corporal. "And you, you, and you." She selected three more of the biggest of the group surrounding her. "The rest of you are dismissed, thank you. Now then," she explained, "these two *gentlemen* are reporters for...what was the name of that scum-sucking yellow rag you write for?"

"The *Star Source*," one of them said nervously, "but—"

"Right. The scum-sucking, rat-fornicating, yellow-rag *Star Source*." She turned to the waiting volunteers, who were still surrounded by several other curious Marines. "The problem is that these assholes have just insulted me and, in doing so, insulted the honor of the LFS Marines. What's more, they have threatened to print that insult in their scum-sucking, rat-fornicating, yellow-rag news pages unless I give them some bullshit story about Admiral Greenwood that they can print instead."

An angry growl arose from the crowd, and the two reporters turned white.

"I don't know where you people went to school—" Bartley leaned over the table, up close and personal, "—but it appears you never learned anything about truth, or ethics, or *honor*. If I ever see your faces again, you're going to wish you'd studied harder." She turned to the scowling Marines. "I want these pieces of shit out of my A.O., *now!*"

To the waiting Marines, her 'A.O.' —area of operations—was understood to mean anywhere inside Corporal J's. "*Yes, ma'am!*"

Bartley sat back down as her volunteers seized the two reporters, dragged them out of their chairs, and dumped them on the floor. Moments later, the two found themselves face down in the concourse in front of the saloon, nursing a variety of painful bruises, their ears ringing with the admonition that they should never return to Corporal J's again unless they wanted to leave without their testicles.

"And if you print *one nasty word* about the Corps or anyone in it," the big Marine corporal told them, "I will personally hunt you down and *really* hurt you."

The two reporters filed charges against Bartley and the other Marines the following day, but SID were unable to find any witnesses to corroborate their story. In fact, Corporal J's proprietor, Mike DaSilva, told SID the two men had been creating a disturbance, and *he* had asked the Marines to eject them from the premises. SID didn't press the matter, and the charges were dismissed.

The two reporters left Luna the following week. Just two days after their return to Earth, the story of "Admiral Greenwood's Lesbian Lover" splashed across the home page of the *Star Source* web tabloid. It showed a file photo of Admiral Greenwood pinning the Lunar Medal of Honor on Bartley's chest after the Second Mekota Encounter and dared to suggest that, perhaps, Bartley had earned the medal for something other than courage under fire.

The next day, an SID officer came to Admiral Greenwood's quarters. "I'm sorry, ma'am, but since this unsupported allegation involves a violation of the LCMJ—specifically an intimate relationship with someone in your chain of command—SID is required to investigate," said the young lieutenant commander. "If I could just ask a couple of questions."

"I understand, Commander. Go ahead," Lorna said.

He turned first to Bartley—who, of course, was present whenever the admiral had a visitor. "Sergeant, is there any truth to the allegation of intimacy between you and the admiral?

"No, sir, there is *not*," Bartley said firmly, without hesitation.

"Admiral Greenwood, is there any truth to the allegation?"

"No, Commander, there is not," Lorna said.

"Well, then, that concludes the investigation." The SID officer appeared relieved, as if he really hadn't wanted to pursue it any further. "With absolutely no evidence to the contrary, SID is required to accept your word on the matter. Thank you for your time, Admiral."

After the commander had gone, the two women looked at each other.

"Well, that was a no-brainer," Bartley remarked.

"I'm sorry, Rock. They dragged you into the middle of their crusade against me."

"No, ma'am. I'm the one who's sorry 'cause it's really my fault." She proceeded to tell Lorna the real story of the incident at Corporal J's. "They warned me they were gonna print that story if I didn't give them something they could use about you—like who the baby's father was. I coulda just told them to take a leap out of an airlock, but they would have printed it anyway. I got pissed and recruited some help to teach 'em a lesson. Sorry, ma'am, I was out of line." Bartley looked thoroughly miserable.

"It's okay, Rock. I appreciate you protecting my privacy. Next time, you might be a bit less enthusiastic about it, but I guess we can let it pass."

"I shoulda told you about it before it came out on the web. I'm sorry, ma'am."

"All right, consider yourself reprimanded, Sergeant." But Lorna's gentle smile took the sting out of it. *You can't buy loyalty like this,* she told herself, and she wondered if she really deserved it.

The following day, after reviewing SID's report, the Judge Advocate General's office issued an official notice that the web tabloid *Star Source*, as well as its parent organization and the twelve other tabloids—and one 'legitimate' web news purveyor—owned by that parent were now *persona non grata* in the LFS. All persons on Luna associated with those media outlets were advised to depart for Earth within three days or face forcible deportation. Under the Lunar Constitution and LCMJ, no justification was required for the deportation of foreign nationals, nor did the JAG offer any further explanation.

The Lunar news media, however, had plenty to say—beginning with a lengthy documentary about the true circumstances under which Bartley had earned her Medal of Honor, including an interview with Brigadier General McGraw, Commandant of Marines, who credited Bartley with saving her life under extreme combat conditions. The story ran side by side with another, detailing the long and distinguished career of Lorna Greenwood, Admiral of the Fleet and former chief executive of the LFS. This was followed by an editorial by Jennifer Winslow, director of the LFS Journalist Corps, reviling the *Star Source* for publishing "trash based on lies and innuendo." Winslow noted that SID's subsequent investigation had found the story to be "baseless and without merit" and hinted that, perhaps, an apology from the British government was in order for the "outrageous behavior of its citizens who were guests on Lunar soil."

Eventually, the whole thing was forgotten, at least on Luna, but rival tabloids in the US and UK used it to gleefully savage the *Star Source*, while less Luna-friendly outlets, such as those in the Islamic Federation, continued to treat the original story as factual.

As for Rock Bartley, the incident outraged the LFS Marines, who rallied to her support. From that point on, she found it difficult to spend her money on drinks at Corporal J's, where—so she was told—pictures of the two *Star Source* reporters were used to line the urinals in the men's room.

* * *

TerraNova City, Luna

The remainder of Lorna's pregnancy was without incident, and three months before her due date, she officially took a leave of absence from the fleet. Mick O'Hara, however, asked her to take on a special assignment—military liaison with the Akara—until she returned to active duty. The job involved no more than meetings and discussions with Akara representatives and would keep Lorna at home on Luna, since the Akara still hadn't revealed the location of their homeworlds.

They knew the Akara were still at war with the Mekota and had been for almost two Earth decades. They also knew the Mekota fleet was huge, that the tripeds were not averse to wiping out entire races who opposed them, and that those they conquered instead of destroyed became little more than slave labor.

On learning from the Akara that Earth was well inside Mekota territory, Lorna posed a question. "So why didn't they conquer or exterminate us long ago? You say they've controlled this part of the galaxy for centuries. If they had come just fifty of our years ago, we wouldn't have been able to stop them."

"That is true," Captain said. Lorna still thought of him as Captain, even though his title was War Speaker now. "The Mekota Empire is vast. They have—to use your own expression—bitten off more than they can chew. They expand their territory by force but lack the resources to exploit it. Most likely, they surveyed your world long ago, decided you weren't a threat, and cataloged you for future exploitation. When they learned you were venturing into space, they came to investigate. By that time, you were prepared to deal with them. They underestimated the speed with which you developed your space capabilities."

"All right," Lorna said, "but that raises another question. Why haven't they come back to crush us? You've told us about the size of their fleet, and you've seen ours. The Mekota we defeated were nothing more than a probe. They could attack us in overwhelming force, but they have not returned. Why?"

The alien licked his chops with his long, forked tongue, a gesture Lorna had learned to interpret as a smile. "Because, Warrior Queen, they are *afraid* of you."

The alien had also gotten better at interpreting human body language, and he recognized Lorna's look of disbelief.

"Granted, the damage you did to their fleet was minimal—we have inflicted many times that amount in battles along our frontier. But the damage you did to their..."

Mike paused while he considered the proper translation. The AIs had developed an exceptionally good command of the Akara language, but the occasional word still escaped them. Mike asked Captain for clarification, apparently got it, and the translation continued.

"The damage you did to their *collective ego* was devastating. The Mekota consider themselves superior to every other race. They fight long, brutal wars against lesser races, but always with the knowledge they will prevail in the end. Even when they lose a battle, they inflict crushing losses on their opponent. *You* brushed their forces aside with contemptuous ease—minor forces, admittedly, but forces, nonetheless. They did not damage any of your ships, but you wiped them out completely."

"That was the *second* encounter," Lorna said. "We *did* take significant losses in the first encounter."

"Ah, but they don't know that. They sent a force here, and it disappeared. Then they sent a second force, and all that came back was a messenger, telling them how you had destroyed that force with ease. It frightened them."

Good thing we didn't let that big Mekota ship escape the first time, Lorna reflected. She'd known, at the time, it had been the right decision, but if they had failed to stop it, the *next* Mekota force might have been unstoppable. "Tell me, War Speaker, how is it you know these things? Do you have intelligence sources among the Mekota?"

"No," he said. "The Mekota trust only Mekota, and on their worlds, they cannot be subverted. It's their sense of superiority. But we have captured many on the Akara frontier. You know how they are—once captured, they give up their loyalty. Some of their commanders kill their own people when faced with capture, as punishment for failure or to prevent us from learning their secrets. But the commanders seldom take the next step—suicide—so the Mekota we capture are often high-ranking females, who are good sources of intelligence. Of course, all captives die in the end. We've had no more success than you at replicating the nutrients they require. In truth, we haven't tried all that hard.

"After we contacted you, we started questioning captured Mekota to discover what they knew about you. Do not be offended. You were a new factor in the war, and we needed to learn as much as possible. A few prisoners knew of their contact with you and gave us information."

"I'm not offended," she said. "I would have done the same. Superior intelligence is often the deciding factor in war, which is why I appreciate your willingness to share this information."

"I will share one more thing with you," he advised, once again licking his chops in amusement. "The fact that you defeated them so easily is not the only reason they fear you. Almost equally important is the fact that you are *human*."

"I don't understand." Lorna sat back. "Why would they have a special fear of humans?"

"The Mekota have encountered humans before. And so have we." With that, he proceeded to tell her the legend of the Progenitors.

* * *

"Lorna, that's absolutely incredible." Mick O'Hara rubbed his eyes.

"Yes, it is, admiral." It hadn't taken her long to slip back into the role of a subordinate, addressing her old friend by his rank. "I am inclined to trust the Akara, but this really strains their credibility."

"Yes, it does," Charlie Bender said, "and I have to wonder why they told you this *now*. According to War Speaker, the Lizards are incredibly careful about dealing with humans. They recognize our aggressively competitive nature, resourcefulness, and so on. They have *never* sold or traded advanced technology to any human civilization, nor have they ever told any of them about the existence of others until now, if we believe what they're saying.

"They say they've never encountered technologically advanced humans before, and meeting us caused them to rethink the matter, but...I don't know. They've been much too casual about telling us this Great Galactic Secret, especially since they still don't trust us enough to tell us where their homeworlds are located. All we know is that they occupy several star systems somewhere along the edge of

Mekota space, and we don't even know what Mekota space includes."

"Hmmm," O'Hara mused. "On the other hand, there isn't much we can do with the information. We don't know where these other human civilizations might be located, and with the Mekota all around us, we're not likely to go looking. Whether the story is true or not, they may be blowing sunshine in our ear to convince us to join their crusade against the Mekota. From other hints they've dropped, I'm thinking the war is not going well for them, and they'd just love a little help, especially from someone the Mekota fear—if that part of the story is true—and who have already trashed the Turnips on two occasions."

"I'm not sure," Lorna admitted. "It's difficult to get a sense for what they want when neither of us can speak the other's language—can't even reproduce the sounds, let alone understand the words. Mike, can you give us any insights?"

"It *is* difficult," the AI agreed. "I have a problem understanding *human* motivations, let alone those of an alien race. However, their choice of words seems to convey a sense of urgency, supporting Admiral O'Hara's assessment. My suggestion, based on what I most often do when confronted with ambiguous data, is to simply ask them about these things. Any response, even an evasive one or a refusal to answer, will provide additional data."

Lorna smiled. "You know, Mike, I kept telling President Blackthorne that we believe in straight talk. Maybe it's time we tried that with the Akara as well. Admiral, what do you think?"

"Right," Mick said, "but they might take the hint and start asking *us* some tough questions as well. Pressing a little stronger for that military alliance, for example. I don't really want to get involved in 'their' war, but the Mekota are a threat to us as well. One thing I'd insist on—before we get involved in something like that—is that we have to trust each other, and that means they've got to tell us where they live."

"Agreed," Charlie Bender said. "That's not unreasonable, under the circumstances."

* * *

"It appears we are finished with the little tests, the games we play to gain intelligence about each other."

Coming as it did after the long silence that followed Lorna's opening statements, the words might have sounded ominous. But—if her interpretation of Lizard body language was correct—War Speaker's reaction was one of amusement.

"This...diplomacy...is much like the game I played with your ships when we first met. First, we examine each other, then one of us makes a move and waits for the other to react. This continues until, finally, one side makes a decisive move—your ships split up, and one of them heads home, while the other stands in my path so I cannot follow. I make a few more moves to test the ship that remains, then I make *my* decisive move.

"We have tested each other with words, and now you have made a decisive move, and I must respond. But I expected this because of the move I made, telling you of the Progenitors. It is still a game, but now we play for higher stakes.

"You are correct," he said. "The war has become difficult for us. The Mekota press us all along the frontier, and they are gaining territory. We have lost commercial outposts and a few trading partners, primitive cultures that provided us with useful, though non-essential goods. But the plant-creatures press forward and now threaten more critical resources. They move ever closer to our homeworlds. There are no other races willing or able to aid us. Yes, we would like to have you as allies. You are well positioned to support us as well as to strike at the Mekota heart. For that reason, we immediately told you where *their* homeworlds are located."

Yes, Lorna thought. *Less than fifty light-years distant, in the direction we first assumed. But now we know which of the stars in that area are home to the enemy.*

War Speaker continued. "But while the Mekota fear you, they will not hesitate to respond if you attack them directly. Since they know where you live, that will bring the war back here to your homeworld. Any resources they commit to attacking *you* will weaken their efforts against *us*. This may be one of the reasons they have not pressed their issues with you. I can understand why you would hesitate to take them on alone. It appears you have two options: to wait and hope *our* efforts weaken them to the point where they cannot make war on *you* or to join the game already in progress.

"Obviously, we would prefer to have you join us. But now, you ask us to offer a gesture of trust, the location of our homeworlds. This is difficult, for we are cautious in dealing with humans. You are natural predators—as are we—and very resourceful. Even primitive humans can be dangerous in their own environment. The Mekota usually resort to brutal methods of suppression when they conquer a human-populated world.

"I have told you we do not prey on other intelligent races, that we try to leave primitive cultures alone other than to trade with them where it profits us to do so. But you have only my words. So, now, you ask us for proof of trust, and it is our move in the game.

"I do not have the authority to make that move, nor does Speaker to the Queen, who is still trying to understand how he became Speaker to the *King* and the impact of this change in your leadership.

We must return to our own lord and report, and it may be some time before we return. There are many lesser games that must be played among our leaders before the matter is resolved."

* * *

At Mick O'Hara's insistence, Lorna had not moved out of the quarters she thought of as the CEO's residence after resigning the post. As Mick pointed out, the Lunar Free State didn't have an official residence for the chief executive. Living as they did in an underground city tunneled out of the raw Lunar rock, all LFS citizens lived in housing that was technically owned by the LFS government. The Lunar Constitution provided that each citizen should be given quarters in which to live and should not be forced to relocate without cause, compensation, and due process of law. Further, the Code of Military Protocols specified the amount of residential living space to which a citizen was entitled based on his or her rank and seniority, with additional allowances provided for dependents. Thus, a husband and wife living together with their children would be entitled to the combined space allowance for each spouse, plus additional allowances for each child. A citizen could also elect to move to more spacious quarters than specified but would then have a quarters charge deducted from his or her account, based on the excess volume of the residential space occupied.

Officers of flag rank—commodore and above—were given identical space allotments. It was not an extravagant amount of living room (in fact only slightly more than the highest non-flag rank) but nonetheless spacious and comfortable by Lunar standards. When Carla had been alive, she and Lorna had lived together in quarters much smaller than their combined ranks allowed, but that had been a personal choice. The regulations gave no credit for it, and they got no rebate for using less than their authorized space.

Ian Stevens, on the other hand, had lived in quarters larger than specified for his rank and had insisted the CEO should be charged for excess space like any other citizen. He was a wealthy man to begin with, and the CEO drew a generous paycheck, so it hadn't been a problem. Though he'd lived alone (except for a single steward who'd served as cook, butler, and housekeeper), he'd liked the extra space and had had several rooms unlikely to be found in other quarters on Luna. One such room was his personal library of over 3,000 volumes of old-style printed books, some of which were rare editions. Another was the room in which he'd kept, displayed, and maintained his extensive collection of firearms, many of them historical antiques.

Ian had willed his library and most of his gun collection to Lorna. He'd left furnishings, works of art, and other personal effects to Carla, but *her* will had left that to Lorna as well. Lorna's own quarters had brought too many painful memories, so she had moved into Ian's old quarters. Since she was only the second CEO of the LFS, the place had been unofficially dubbed the CEO's residence, but O'Hara pointed out that it was roomy enough for a nursery and for the two stewards (to whose services she was still entitled and would want to retain to help care for the baby) and her Marine security guard. In addition, the firearm collection was housed in its own room, which could be easily secured against the curiosity of an inquisitive toddler in years to come. Lorna would have enough changes in her life, Mick insisted, without having to go through the adjustment of moving to new quarters.

In fact, the new chief executive had motives of his own. Mick had no intention of moving from *his* old quarters, which were extensively customized to suit his personal lifestyle. For one thing, it had a room that was Mick's private engineering laboratory, where he tinkered around with new design concepts "just to keep in practice" and occasionally produced an idea for some prototype gadget that amazed his younger subordinates in the Engineering Corps. Another large room housed his hobby workshop, devoted to a rare—on Luna, at least—pastime: woodworking.

There were trees on Luna—fruit trees in the underground farm tunnels and the new agridomes that had been built on the surface, as well as other varieties in the arboreal areas of TerraNova Park. But none of them were intended to be harvested for their wood. All the raw material for Mick's hobby had to be imported from Earth, which was a costly proposition. As one of the original founders of the LFS and a flag officer, O'Hara did not lack for money, and he chose to spend it on exotic woods imported from Earth. He bought only the best wood, since—given the shipping costs involved—it wasn't that much more expensive than the more common varieties.

He spent most of his spare time—which was becoming an even rarer commodity than the wood—in his shop, creating hand-crafted furniture that would have commanded high prices on Earth. On the Moon, where wooden furniture of any kind was almost non-existent, it was considered priceless. But having already furnished his own quarters with his creations, he chose to give most of his handiwork away as gifts to friends, associates, and subordinates. He had, in fact, built all the bookshelves that graced Ian's library and the cases that housed Ian's gun collection. His latest project, still under wraps and shown to no one, was a gift for Lorna—an elegant old-style baby crib, crafted of exotic Australian Jarrah wood.

With the new responsibilities that had been thrust upon him, he wondered if he would have enough time to finish it before the baby was born. *Well,* he thought with a grin, *it'll serve Lorna right if I don't.*

She's the one who dumped all this chief executive stuff on me. On the other hand, I also have her to thank for my new apprentice.

"Can you give me a hand here, laddie?" he asked. "I need you to hold these together while I clamp them."

The Marine sergeant—head of O'Hara's new security detail—stepped up eagerly and took hold of the assembly. Sergeant Harrell had shown a great deal of interest in the new CEO's hobby, and Mick was more than happy to have someone to teach. *Everything's made by bloody computers these days, even wooden furniture, but somebody's got to keep the old skills in play, or we lose a bit of our humanity. Hmmm… maybe I need to talk to Tom Perry about it. Our kids ought to have a place where they can learn things like this.*

Lorna Greenwood was a fine leader and a superb military commander, but Mick O'Hara was one of the most creative thinkers in the Lunar Free State. That creativity would serve him well in years to come, as he led his nation among the stars.

* * *

TerraNova City, Luna

"Okay, one more big *PUSH*," Sarah Wilkins commanded.

Lorna had chosen to have her baby by the natural method. "It's likely to be a once-in-a-lifetime experience," she'd told Wilkins. "I certainly don't want to *sleep* through it." Now, after a couple hours of labor, she was beginning to wonder about the wisdom of that decision. But a few moments later, her misgivings vanished as she heard the baby's first cries.

"It's a girl," Wilkins announced with a smile, "but I guess you already knew that." She presented the baby for inspection, then carefully placed her in Lorna's arms.

"She's *beautiful!*" Lorna exclaimed.

Wilkins mused that it was probably the most *unoriginal* comment in the Known Universe.

"But I can't believe women have been going through this for a few million years. It's a wonder humanity isn't extinct."

Wilkins snorted. "Probably would be if *men* had to go through it. So much for us being the weaker sex."

"All the same, I don't know if I ever want to go through it again. I'm afraid little Carla is destined to be an only child."

"You're a wimp. I've had three of 'em, and it actually *does* get easier after the first one."

* * *

Fortune smiled on Lorna for once, and she was given nearly four months of uninterrupted motherhood after baby Carla was born. It was a quiet time on Luna, and no one pressured her to resume her Fleet Command responsibilities. Aside from an occasional query from O'Hara or Timiko Yamamoto about matters concerning her former tenure as CEO, the only official business matters that came her way were fleet status reports from Tom Sakura. None of those required action, but she appreciated being kept up to date.

Mick, Tom, and Charlie Bender all found excuses to stop by and fuss over the baby. On those occasions, she usually spent a few hours talking shop with them, but for the most part, her days were filled with getting to know her new baby and discovering the responsibilities of being a mother.

As soon as she recovered from the rigors of childbirth, Lorna resolved to get herself back in shape. Before her pregnancy, she'd usually spent a few hours each week at the Marine Corps gym, her regular workout routine spiced up with martial arts training. Now, she was grateful for the well-equipped exercise room Ian had installed in his quarters. It allowed her to work out for an hour or so each day, without straying too far from the tiny child that had become the center of her life.

Eventually, she would have to resume her fleet duties and become a working mother, leaving her child in the care of her stewards for much of the day, perhaps even for days at a time. If the worst came to pass—war, again—it was possible she would be gone for weeks or even months, or that she might not return at all. Someone had to take responsibility for the defense of the LFS, and the baby gave her even more reason to want her nation to survive and prosper. For the moment, she was determined to make the most of the time she could spend with little Carla, and she pushed thoughts of separation out of her mind.

Then the Akara returned.

* * *

TerraNova City, Luna

"Well, I guess *something* has changed," Charlie Bender remarked.

Until then, the largest group of Akara ships to arrive in the Sol System had been the three-ship diplomatic mission. Akara merchant vessels—large ships, but slow and clumsy by warship standards—had come one at a time. But now, no less than ten Akara ships had arrived, and the AIs had tentatively classed them as warships. The largest two were about the size of an LFS heavy cruiser, while the others were slightly larger than LFS destroyers.

Their arrival prompted an immediate response from the LFS fleet, as Admiral Sakura dispatched the battlecruisers *Athena* and *Amazon*, with four heavy cruisers and six destroyers, to meet and challenge them. The Akara responded with the proper recognition signals and dispatched a message to Lunar Command.

"Yes, I'd say that's a fair statement." Lorna scanned the AI's translation of the message. "It looks like they're ready for some serious discussions. We still don't know much about the pecking order among the Akara, but I suspect this First Deputy Leader and Speaker with Authority of the Copper Hills Clan is higher up in their structure than our previous ambassador. It also looks like our old friend Captain has returned with a new title. He's now the Second War Speaker of the Copper Hills Clan and Commander of the Emissary Squadron. Mike, are you sure it's the same Akara we met before?"

"Yes, Admiral. There was video as well as audio transmission, and he presented the message on behalf of himself and the First Deputy Leader."

"I'll take your word for it," Mick O'Hara said. "Sorry to say this, but all Lizards look alike to me. If they hadn't been wearing uniforms last time they were here, I wouldn't have been able to tell them apart."

"To a human, that might be true," the AI said, "but I assure you, their facial features are quite distinct, especially in the scale patterns around the eyes and mouth. In addition, there is the banding pattern around the tail—"

"Okay, I get the picture—no pun intended." O'Hara chuckled. "But what does it mean?"

"I can give an approximate extrapolation regarding the titles," Mike offered. "It seems most likely we are dealing with the equivalent of a foreign minister or secretary of state. The other Akara, the one we met before, is now the military commander of the expedition and is also equivalent to an assistant secretary or assistant minister of defense. Of course, titles can be created for the purpose of convincing us we are dealing with someone important. The real question is how much authority they've been given. Likewise, sending a squadron rather than three small ships is probably another message that discussions have moved to a higher level."

"That's the way I see it, too," Charlie Bender said. "They've given us a little fanfare to get our attention, but we won't know what it means until we talk to them."

"Lorna, I think you should carry the ball again," O'Hara said. "They seem comfortable talking to the warrior queen." He covered a smile as the title brought a distinct blush to Lorna's fair complexion. "But if it looks like they're serious, I'm ready to join the discussions. If this goes anywhere, I think you should plan to go back to your old job. Tom Sakura's *good,* but he isn't the Babe on the Horse."

"Oh, *please!*" Lorna begged. "Fine! I'm ready to go back to the fleet, but I'd *really* like to have a talk with the Marine that started that whole Babe business."

* * *

Later that evening, in quarters, Lorna repeated the remark to Sergeant Bartley, who hadn't been present at the meeting. In her new position, Bender's Rules were relaxed. Lorna no longer needed a bodyguard when meeting with other senior officers. But when she brought up the subject, she was surprised at the young non-com's reaction.

"I...ah...think it might have been *me,* ma'am," Bartley confessed sheepishly.

"*You?*" Lorna looked at her in astonishment.

"Well, not me *directly,* ma'am. I met these American sailors at Corporal J's a couple of years ago, and they came up with that nickname for *Valkyrie.* They saw her hull artwork, and they mentioned it to me because they saw the Valkyrie on my shoulder patch. I thought it was kinda neat, so I told a couple of other Marines about it. Then somebody said, 'Yeah, but we know who the Valkyrie *really* is,' and somebody else said she even *looks* like you. Next thing I knew, it was all around the fleet. I'm sorry, ma'am, but you gotta understand. It's a term of *respect*—especially with the Marines."

"Oh, I guess I understand that, Rock. But don't you think I'm a little *old* to be called a babe?"

"Not really, ma'am. You're a good-looking woman. In fact, I'll bet more than a few young Marine studs have a fantasy or two about—" Seeing the look on Lorna's face, she stopped abruptly. "I think maybe I'd better shut my mouth, ma'am. I'm in enough trouble already."

* * *

This time, the Akara were serious, as they proved in the very first round of discussions.

"We will guide a squadron of your ships to our homeworld. Some of the clans are still reluctant to seek your help, but we will take you to the homeworld of the Copper Hills Clan," First Deputy Leader told her. "In return, you must agree to an alliance, and your ships must carry an envoy who can make appropriate commitments to our Great Leader."

"We must know the terms of the alliance," Lorna replied. "I presume you are looking for help against the Mekota, but there is only so much we can give. If we come to your aid and they attack *us*, we do not have several worlds and an entire frontier on which to deal with them. We have only one world and no place to retreat. If they come, we will fight them to the death, but we have no desire to serve as a decoy to turn their attention away from you."

"We understand, Warrior Queen," Second War Speaker said. "The alliance must be done in secret. We won't ask you to attack them openly, but we welcome your assistance on our frontier, where the Mekota will not expect you. I'm told you are a great war leader, that it was you who planned the attacks against them. If we could plan such an attack with your forces assisting ours and carry it out in such a way that the Mekota could never be sure what happened to them…we would welcome your advice on how to do this."

"We are desperate," First Deputy Leader admitted. "The plant-creatures press us everywhere, and we retreat. If we mass our forces in one place, they retreat there and hit us someplace else. They have superior numbers, and we *must* reduce that advantage. If we could catch a large Mekota fleet somewhere, meet them with superior force, and destroy them completely as you did with the Mekota who came here…"

"I think you overestimate us," Lorna said. "They sent *nine ships* against us, not an entire fleet."

"I think you underestimate yourselves," War Speaker retorted. "Of those nine ships, how many survived? And how many ships did you lose in return? No, wait…" He held up a reptilian hand, palm inward and talons retracted in a friendly gesture. "You have told me you lost ships in your first encounter, but the Mekota took you by surprise. You didn't know them, and you believed their lies about coming in peace. They fired without warning when your ships were sitting targets at close range, and you *still* pressed in and destroyed them so completely that word of their fate never got back to their homeworld. And when they came the second time, when you were ready for them, they had no chance. I still don't how you did it, but you have shown me the imagery of the battles. I know total annihilation when I see it.

"We have not told you of our weaponry and ship capabilities, but if I do so, perhaps you will understand. Our ships are smaller, faster, and more maneuverable than those of our enemy, but not nearly so heavily armored. We use weapons like theirs, but they are not as powerful and have less range. Even our largest ships carry only a few weapons that can truly damage a Mekota dreadnought. Our smaller ships—what you would call destroyers—carry only a single beam weapon. It takes a concentrated assault over time by several of our ships to destroy one of those behemoths, and, invariably, we lose at least one ship in the process. We survive such battles only by rushing at them to bring them in range of our weapons, twisting and turning constantly to avoid their fire, and chewing at them incessantly until we breach their armor. But I saw—if I can believe my eyes— your ships destroy *eight* of theirs in a matter of *seconds!* If we could have but one such squadron of your ships and catch enough of the Mekota in one place, we could change the course of the war in a single battle."

Lorna thought this was the same philosophy—based on their earlier defeat of the Russians—that had led the Japanese to attack Pearl Harbor in World War II. *Didn't work out very well for them,* she thought, *but then they weren't fighting for their lives against a superior enemy.* War Speaker might well be right. This might be their last and best hope.

* * *

In the end, Lorna took the proposal to Mick O'Hara. With the help of Charlie Bender, they worked out the broad framework of an agreement with the aliens. The LFS, and *only* the LFS—the rest of the Unaligned Nations were unwilling to make the commitment—would enter into an alliance with the Akara Clan of the Copper Hills. The Lunar nation would provide advice, support, and direct military assistance in a covert manner to minimize the chance the Mekota would discover the source. The LFS would also provide technical assistance to help the Akara improve their military capabilities.

In return, the Akara would agree that, should the Mekota discover who was helping them and take direct action against Earth, the Lizards would send forces to help defend the Sol System.

In addition, the two parties agreed to an exchange of blades—an Akara custom, which was, in effect, an oath in which each swore never to go to war against the other. This oath would be between the LFS and the Copper Hills Clan and would not be binding upon the other nations of Earth or the other Clans of the People.

Within that broad framework, there were many details to be worked out. Mick O'Hara tapped Lorna to lead the squadron that would go to the Akara homeworld and Charlie Bender to be the emissary with authority to execute the agreement.

Bender had practically begged for the job. He had been with the LFS since its earliest days as a nation, but he had never ventured farther into space than Luna, with occasional trips back to Earth. He was a topnotch military strategist who had helped Lorna plan many operations, but he had never taken part in the execution of those plans. This, he told O'Hara, might be his last chance to get out there and *do* something. He wanted that chance more than anything in the world.

"You know," he told Lorna, "we'll probably have to get ourselves bloody in this one because advice and support alone won't cut it. With what the Lizards have now, they won't be able to get the job done. The alternative would be to build them a fleet like ours, but we've agreed that's not a good idea. Hell, we don't give that kind of technology to the *Americans,* and we trust them more than we trust the Akara."

"I know," she said. "Imagine a group of humans hunting grizzly bears with nothing but knives. If you have enough people attacking at once, you can bring down the bear, but somebody *will* get hurt in the process. And if there are a *lot* of grizzlies, you're in trouble."

"On the other hand, having an old-fashioned .45 pistol on your belt makes a hell of a difference. You might not be able to drop a grizzly with one shot, but you've got a better chance of staying away from his claws, and you can still use your knife if he gets in close."

"That's a good analogy," he agreed, "and since we're the only gunslingers around here, I guess it's time to saddle up our horses."

Leaving Tom Sakura in charge of the home fleet and with a tearful farewell to her precious child, Lorna had taken *Valkyrie* and an impressive squadron of cruisers and destroyers and set out with Charlie for the unknown.

* * *

The Akara Homeworld

When they first arrived at the Akara homeworld, opening discussions had not gone well. The aliens had been reluctant to share basic intelligence data, and Lorna had made little progress on military issues. Charlie Bender thought he knew what the problem was and how to solve it.

"You want a *female* to exchange blades with our Great Leader?" The Akara Speaker with Authority seemed horrified by the idea.

Charlie sighed. It had been a long session, and he was tired. The Copper Hills homeworld was pleasant enough but too warm for Charlie's taste. The planet had only a two-degree axial tilt, so there was little in the way of seasonal variation, though its two sizeable moons provided enough tidal pull to stimulate weather patterns. Overall, the planet was warmer than Earth, and the Lizards preferred to live in its warmest parts. The Akara *liked* hot, wet climates. Air conditioning was not a concept they were familiar with.

Today, the strange-smelling air was thick with humidity, and Charlie had been mopping his brow all day long with a soggy handkerchief. He wasn't making much progress, and now, this silly Lizard was getting hung up on gender distinctions. But that same gender distinction was probably the source of Lorna's problems with the Lizard high command.

"Look," Charlie said, "I may be Speaker with Authority for our nation, but *she* is the Warrior Queen. In military matters, her authority exceeds mine."

It wasn't exactly true. O'Hara had given Charlie full authority for all negotiations with the Lizards, but Lorna was in command of the fleet, and he would have deferred to her in such matters anyway.

"If I understand this exchange of blades correctly," he said, "it represents a solemn promise that we will stand together in battle and never go to war against each other. That's *her* area of responsibility, not mine."

The Lizard they knew as War Speaker agreed with Charlie and convinced the Speaker with Authority to at least discuss the matter with the Great Leader—whose title, the humans learned, translated literally as Heart.

Charlie returned to the luxurious apartments the Akara had provided for the human delegation. To his surprise, he found the Warrior Queen on the broad, open terrace that overlooked the alien capital, engaged in a strenuous martial-arts workout with Sergeant Bartley. They wore lightweight cotton *gi* outfits of the traditional Oriental design, but both were sweating profusely.

"How can you stand to do that in this climate?" Bender wiped his forehead again.

Lorna bowed to Bartley—who had just scored the most recent point—and they stepped off the mat. "I find it refreshing. Do you know how long it's been since I've stood under an open sky? Breathed fresh air without a dome over my head or a warship wrapped around me? A little heat and humidity is a small price to pay for that." She picked up a towel and began to mop the perspiration from her face and hair. "Besides," she admitted, "it clears the mind after a hard day of butting heads with obstinate Lizards."

"That's what I want to talk to you about." He proceeded to tell her of his latest proposal to the Akara.

"You really think it's sexism, pure and simple?"

"Not exactly the way we might think of it. Females in this society have equal rights in just about everything, and they're willing to admit that females *can* be as dangerous and deadly as males. It's more a matter of gender-specific role modeling. In this society, females stay home and defend the nest. Males go out and fight the wars. Period."

"And we're proposing to turn that concept upside down," she mused. "Hmmm…do you think they'll accept it?"

"If they don't, it's going to seriously hamper progress. I can handle the military side, but they need to know *you* are the one who calls the shots for the fleet. I mean, what happens if we go into battle with them and they find out that almost half our warships have female commanders?"

* * *

To the surprise of his advisors, Heart of the Copper Hills agreed without a moment's hesitation. When the time came to meet with the alien monarch, it was Lorna Greenwood who stepped forward from the LFS delegation, unhooked the sword from her belt, and made the presentation.

Lorna had chosen the sword to be presented by the Lunar delegation, though at the time, she hadn't known she would be the presenter. It was a beautifully crafted Japanese *wakizashi,* the shorter of the two types of ancient Samurai swords. The longer *katana* would have been too long for an Akara to wield comfortably, but the *wakizashi* drew admiring looks from the assembled aliens—even more so when they found out how incredibly sharp it was. In return, the alien leader presented her with a somewhat broader blade more closely resembling an ancient Roman *gladius*. It was beautifully inlaid with copper and gold, with the symbol of the Copper Hills Clan engraved in its pommel. It was a sharp, hefty blade, and Lorna resolved to get Gunny Matsushita, the Marines' master instructor in blade combat, to teach her how to use it when she returned to Luna.

Lorna gave a short speech, pledging that the humans would stand with their newfound allies and help them crush the Mekota threat. Heart of the Copper Hills welcomed her in turn as a brother-in-arms—or sister; Val's translation wasn't quite certain since the Akara term wasn't gender specific—and promised that the Akara, or at least his Clan, would treat any attack on the humans as an attack on the People.

Rock Bartley was never more than three steps away from her admiral during their stay on the alien world. She was shocked when War Speaker singled her out for personal introduction to the Lizard king. She was a bit embarrassed when she was presented as the "fierce female warrior—slayer of many Mekota—who first offered to exchange blades with me." He was wearing the Marine combat knife she had given him, and he drew it and ceremoniously presented it to his Leader for examination. She was wearing the ornate Akara blade he had given her, instead of the usual Marine-issue dress sword. Technically, she was out of uniform, but the admiral had suggested she wear it, noting that it might score a few points with the Lizards.

Charlie's point had been driven home—among the humans, female warriors were not to be trifled with, and Greenwood was the Heart of the Warriors before whom the Mekota would tremble in fear. With their leader's endorsement ringing in their ears, the Akara military people quickly got with the program. Sharing intelligence was no longer a problem.

In fact, Lorna was inundated with a flood of information—stellar topography of the frontier, Mekota deployments, Akara deployments, strengths, weaknesses, details of battles, assessments of Mekota tactics and capabilities. After a few days of that, she politely withdrew to her quarters on *Valkyrie*, telling the aliens she needed time to study the information. She returned two days later, armed with a few hundred questions that she fired at them in rapid succession. If they didn't have the answers, the Lizards scrambled to find them, and, after a dizzying day—dizzying for the Akara, at least—she retired once again to formulate a plan.

When she finally presented her plan, the Akara were horrified. She had invited the Akara leadership to *Valkyrie's* flag bridge for the presentation, knowing she would have to paint a picture for them.

"You mean to bring the plant-creatures *here...to our homeworld?*"

The simple question translated by Val didn't begin to convey the tail-twitching, hissing, talon-baring reaction she'd gotten. She was tempted to look over her shoulder to see if, perhaps, a legion of Mekota had suddenly materialized behind her. Instead, she directed Val to bring up the holographic display. "The Mekota are pressing you here, here, here, here, and here." She highlighted several star systems in the display. "They are pressing harder on these systems than anywhere else along the frontier. Why do you think that is?"

"They know where our homeworld is located," War Speaker replied. "This thrust is aimed at our heart, but that is why we *must* hold these systems."

"And how long will you be able to hold them?"

"Without your help, not long," the alien admitted.

"In fact, if it were not for their one great weakness, they would be here already, and your planet would be in ruins."

"Weakness?" The Lizards blinked at her.

"Logistics," she said. "You told me they push forward a little at a time, then pause and bring up their supply ships. They do not move forward again until they have garrisoned the system they have taken and set up a secure supply depot. They never launch what we might call a deep thrust, an attempt to penetrate far into your territory. Why is that?" She knew the answer, but she wanted them to say it.

"Their monstrous warships require frequent maintenance and re-supply. We believe the nutrients that keep them alive must be brought all the way from their homeworlds. Our scouts have seen the supply ships, huge things able to service three of their warships at a time. They never advance more than a few days' travel ahead of those ships."

"Yes," she said, "and that is why they must take these systems before they can advance on your homeworld. But they *will* take them, and you will have spent much of your strength for nothing, trying to defend them. The Mekota are slow-moving, but they are inexorable. They can replace their losses by drawing from anywhere in their sphere. But the only replacements *you* have are here in your own system, and they are gradually being diminished as you try to hold the enemy in five places at once. The other Clans cannot help you, as they have their own problems elsewhere along the frontier. Eventual-ly, one of these systems will fall, and that will free up Mekota forces to press home their attack on the next one and the next, until all of them have fallen. Then they will garrison those systems and bring up their supply lines. And then?"

"They will come *here*," War Speaker said, "and we will fight our final battle. But you are proposing that we retreat, that we *give* them those systems. What will that do other than hasten our destruction?"

"It will do several things. For one, it will preserve some of the strength that would otherwise be lost defending the indefensible. More importantly, it will make them think you have *no strength left* and will tempt them to break their own rules—to rush forward in haste instead of waiting, carefully preparing their supply lines, and replenishing their losses. And when they do rush forward, you will be waiting for them with a most unpleasant surprise."

"But…our system…we have seen how the Mekota operate. They will press forward to the inner system, absorbing whatever losses they must, to get within striking distance of the planet, of our eggs, our mates, and our young. They will rain down destruction on everything we fight to preserve, and it won't matter if we destroy every one of their ships, for by that time, there will be nothing left to defend."

"They won't get that far," she promised. "You'll meet them in the outer system. Oh, they'll press forward, until they are far enough from the hyperspace limit to make escape impossible. Then *we*—my people—will hit them from behind. We will have been waiting there, and they won't see us coming until it's too late.

"You need a decisive victory," she told them. "You need to catch a lot of their forces in one place and destroy them to turn the tide of this war. The only way to do that is to offer a target they cannot refuse and hit them with something they don't expect."

It was not an easy decision for the Lizards. Heart of the Copper Hills studied the plan and agreed with Lorna's logic, but if the plan failed, the consequences would be unthinkable. There was one thing that especially concerned him.

"We are told you are powerful, that you can crush the Mekota," he told Lorna and Charlie, "but we cannot rely on promises. Can you show us your strength, convince us you can destroy our enemies before they reach our world?"

Charlie looked at Lorna. "Firepower demonstration?"

"We can do that."

* * *

In any orbital system, there are points in space where the gravitational forces of orbiting bodies—a primary and its satellite—achieve balance. An object occupying one of those points will be in a stable orbit. Earth's astronomers refer to these as Lagrange points, named after mathematician Joseph Louis Lagrange, who first predicted their existence. Because of gravitational dynamics, rocks and other space debris tend to collect at the Lagrange points.

The star of the Copper Hills home system was like Sol, but older by half a billion years. Its planetary system was correspondingly older, with five rocky planets and one huge gas giant. Its Lagrange points were also dirtier because they'd had longer to accumulate the leftover debris from the system's formation. The L5 point of the homeworld, trailing behind the planet in its orbit, was home to several sizeable asteroids, the largest being the size of a Mekota dreadnought. Lorna selected this area as the firing range for her demonstration. Accompanied by several Akara observer ships, the Lunar squadron moved to a position approximately half a million kilometers from the target area.

With the forces at her disposal, Lorna could have turned the entire collection of asteroids into a dust cloud, but she decided to make her point with more finesse and less expenditure of ordnance. She assembled her group into a tight formation, briefed her people on the attack plan, and once the Akara were in place to observe, put the plan into action.

"Bravo Group, execute on my mark...three...two...one...mark!"

Two ships peeled out of the LFS formation, the light cruiser *Basilisk* and the destroyer *Starhound*. They drove straight for the targets at maximum acceleration, closing the range quickly. At 100,000 kilometers—still well out of a Mekota ship's beam range—they split up, slewing sharply in opposite directions as they launched missile broadsides, four missiles from the destroyer and eight from the light cruiser.

The missiles streaked for the targets with over a thousand gravities of acceleration. At 20,000 kilometers, they spread out and began to twist and turn erratically as their evasive action programs kicked in. By that time, they had already locked on to their selected targets. The two warships went wide around both sides of the target area, closing to 50,000 kilometers—still well out of Mekota weapon range—where they launched their second missile salvos. As they did, the first missiles arrived on target. The fire plan called for the first salvo to target the six largest asteroids, and each of them got two missiles. As the 20-megaton nuclear warheads detonated, those six targets vanished in the blinding glare of the explosions. When the fireballs faded, nothing was left but hot fragments in expanding balls of plasma.

The second wave of missiles were assigned to the next largest asteroids—twelve of them, targeted with one missile apiece. This time, the nuclear detonations were more widely scattered throughout the target formation, but the results were just as devastating.

As the fireballs faded, *Basilisk's* captain issued an order on the command frequency. "Bravo Two, this is Bravo Lead. Execute Red Dog…Execute."

The two warships turned sharply and poured on power, curving in on the asteroid field from opposite directions. At 10,000 kilometers, they opened fire with grasers. The results were not as spectacular as the missile hits, but the target area sparkled with brilliant points of light as the beam weapons found and vaporized any rocks deemed large enough to target. The two ships crossed above and below the target area, maintaining about 5,000 kilometers of separation, primarily to avoid collision with large rock fragments, and a few moments later, were once again out of Mekota weapon range.

Lorna looked at the screen on her flag bridge that held the image of Heart of the Copper Hills. "Have you seen enough, my lord?" Seconds later, after the brief transmission lag, he gave her the palm-inward hand gesture the humans had learned to recognize as an Akara nod of assent. "It is sufficient, Warrior Queen."

"Bravo Group, this is Flag. Disengage. Repeat, disengage. Return to formation," she ordered.

* * *

Heart of the Warriors—the Akara analog of fleet admiral and closest equivalent to Lorna in rank—was probably the oldest of the Lizards present in the large meeting chamber. His skin texture was not as smooth, his scales less iridescent, and his coloration more mottled than his younger fellows, which included Heart of the Copper Hills. In addition, the grizzled old war-Lizard was missing his left arm, which he had lost in some past battle with the Mekota. The other Akara treated him with deference second only to that of their clan leader.

"I am impressed, Warrior Queen," he said. "Especially since you chose to use just two ships—and not your most powerful ships—for this demonstration."

Lorna acknowledged his comment with the slight bow and hand gesture she had learned from studying the aliens. With their inability to speak or understand each other's language and the need to rely on computer translations, both sides were paying close attention to nonverbal signals.

"However," he continued, "I should point out that rocks do not shoot back." She noted that this comment was accompanied by the tongue-flashing equivalent of a smile, one bit of Lizard body language the humans were *not* inclined to imitate.

"True, Heart of the Warriors, but I'm sure you have also noted that, if these rocks had been Mekota ships, most of them would have been destroyed before they *could* shoot back—before our ships came within range of their weapons."

"Perhaps," he said, "but I might also point out that rocks cannot maneuver."

"Again, that is true. Because of that, you did not have the opportunity to see all that our missile weapons can do. They are intelligent weapons—self-guiding and able to maneuver as needed to engage a target. Within their operational envelope, they are faster and more maneuverable than any warship. Once they lock on to a target, evasive maneuvers are *not* an effective defense against them. The only way to stop them is to confuse their targeting systems, something the Mekota have no ability to do, or destroy them before they reach their targets. The Mekota can do that and have done it in our engagements with them, but with limited success. They lack anything in the way of an effective point-defense system. If they react quickly enough, they can destroy a few of the missiles. If we send missiles at them in large numbers, their chances of stopping them all are almost non-existent, and as you have seen, just *one* missile getting through their defenses is enough to destroy a ship or, at least, take it out of action.

"I will tell you the truth, my lords." She looked around, addressing her comments to the assembled aliens. "We are *not* invincible, and maneuvering is still one of the most important factors in such battles. If the Mekota scatter their forces widely, we must divide our forces to destroy them. If they force us to fire our missiles at extreme range, it is possible for a target ship to evade the missile long enough for the missile's drive to be exhausted. They learned quickly to shoot at the missiles coming at them. If the message they sent back to their homeworld provided any insight, they may have developed better point-defense tactics. *You* would not have noticed, since point defense is useless against beam weapons, and *we* won't discover it until we attack them with missiles again. Our ships have sophisticated defenses against missile attacks. Those defenses will be useless to us since the Mekota do not have missiles—unless they have developed such weapons since we last encountered them. I do not think it likely since they would probably have used those weapons against *you* if they had them.

"Each of our ships carries a limited number of missiles. If we use them all, and there are still enemies to be dealt with, we must close to energy range and attack them, which means we must come within *their* range. Our ships are tough, but they can be damaged or destroyed by Mekota weapons. Also, against *our* beam weapons, the Mekota ships are tough. We must chew them to pieces slowly, just as you do. We have the same advantage as you—our ships are faster and more maneuverable than theirs. Our beam weapons are *slightly* longer ranged and *slightly* more powerful. We will always do our best against them if we can hold the range open and attack them from afar, but in an action such as this, where we must prevent them from reaching your planet, that may not always be possible.

"War Speaker has visited our homeworld and has no doubt advised you that our fleet is much smaller than yours. If we commit to this action, there is a limit to how many ships we can provide. We must leave a sufficient force to defend our homeworld should the Mekota return. I brought twelve ships with me for this first visit to your world. For the action I have proposed, we could commit perhaps three times that number…less than a quarter the size of your fleet if you include the forces defending the outlying systems. If the Mekota attack in the numbers we expect, they may outnumber our combined forces by more than two to one. We have never met the Mekota in such numbers before.

"We believe we can defeat them and protect your world. In any case, the forces we commit will stand with you and fight with all their strength until we have defeated them or driven them off, or until we have nothing left with which to fight. I will be here to lead those forces, putting my life and the honor of my people at risk. But I realize you risk more than that—your world, your existence as a Clan of the People. So, it is you who must decide whether to do this or not. I have told you all that I can, the good as well as the bad, and if you choose not to do this, we can go back to discuss other strategies. But time is short, and the enemy is at the gates. I will await your answer."

Lorna deliberately gave them a conservative estimate of the forces the LFS could provide. Mick O'Hara had already agreed to commit half the Lunar Fleet to the effort, on the theory that, if the Akara fell, it wouldn't be long before the Mekota returned to the Sol System—if they weren't already planning to do so—Besides, the other nations of Earth, while reluctant to join the alliance with the Lizards, would stand with the LFS if their own planet were threatened. The American fleet would significantly strengthen the LFS forces that remained at home.

But she wanted to test the Akara—to see whether they accepted her assessment of the situation and whether they were willing to do what was necessary. In her view, the plan she offered was their best course of action, even if they had *no* help from the LFS. If they were willing to accept that, she planned to surprise them by providing more help than expected.

She thought she would have to wait, perhaps for days, while they discussed the matter. A silence had fallen over the Akara when she finished speaking.

But then Heart of the Warriors rose. "The Warrior Queen of the Humans has put *truth* in the air, and now she invites us to taste it." As if to demonstrate, he flicked his long, reptilian tongue and let it quiver in front of him. Then he drew it back and continued. "It has a bitter taste, but it is still the truth. There are two paths we can take. We can continue as we have, fighting the Mekota everywhere, being driven back until we finally fight them to the death here in our own system…and we will die here, and our Clan with us.

"Or we can risk all on a single, bold talon-slash that *may* cripple our enemies and send them fleeing back to whence they came. It is too much to hope we will inflict a fatal wound, but we might at least drive them back and have a chance to defeat them in the end. If we fail, we will die, and our Clan will die with us.

"All creatures die in the end, and even with no enemy to fight, I will probably die sooner than most of you. But I would rather die sooner, knowing I had given my Clan a chance to live, than remain alive longer and die knowing the Clan was dying as well. Is that not the lesson you seek to teach us, Warrior Queen?"

"Perhaps, my lord," Lorna said, "but I am reminded that a great Heart of our own warriors once said, 'I do not want warriors who will die for our Clan. I want warriors who will go out and make the *enemy* die for *his* Clan.' I would remind you that the intent of this plan is to make the *Mekota* die and to keep as many of our own as possible alive."

The clamor of approval from the Akara convinced Lorna that Patton's old axiom had translated well into their language. To her surprise, the old warrior-Lizard turned to her with a chop-licking "grin" and made the gesture the humans had learned to recognize as the Inferior Salute, half-drawing his blade and presenting the hilt to her as one of the Lizards would do to acknowledge a superior officer. Having been careful to learn the protocols for such things, she turned and presented the same salute to him, half-drawing her sword—the one Heart of the Copper Hills had presented to her— and offering him the hilt, thereby acknowledging him as an equal.

Still licking his chops, he turned to the other Akara once more. "There is great wisdom in that." But in a flash his "grin" vanished. "Death to the Mekota!" he shouted. His hand flew up, palm outward, and his talons shot out to their full extension.

In unison, the other Akara in the room jumped to their feet and repeated the epithet. At Lorna's side, Sergeant Bartley drew a sharp breath as she realized there were a *lot* of deadly, sharp talons in the room, but she relaxed as Heart of the Warriors slowly retracted his claws, and the others did the same and resumed their seats.

"Very well," the warrior-Lizard said. "We have all tasted the truth. Do we agree on what must be done?"

This time, only Heart of the Copper Hills responded. "I believe we do, old friend. So be it."

To Lorna's surprise, Heart of the Warriors turned to her again and extended his hand, with talons retracted, proving he had learned something about human gestures. Without hesitation, she accepted the handshake with a firm grip.

* * * * *

Chapter Twenty-Four

Alpha Akara System

The second fleet of the Lunar Free State—48 warships including three battlecruisers—waited quietly at the outer reaches of the system. The primary star was visible from Earth only with the aid of a telescope. It didn't have a name, only a number in various star catalogs, but to the LFS people, it was known as Alpha Akara, the home star of the Akara Clan of the Copper Hills.

The LFS home fleet, also with three battlecruisers—*Amazon, Athena,* and the newly-commissioned *Cassandra*—had remained at Luna under the command of Vice Admiral Sakura. The Americans, still reluctant to provide direct support to the Akara, agreed to put their substantial fleet at Sakura's disposal should defense of the Sol System be necessary.

Whether they went to Akara or attacked Earth, Lorna reflected, *the Mekota were going to get a surprise.* She sincerely hoped it would not be a pleasant one. *In any case,* she thought, *they're going to know they've been in a fight.*

It had taken Lorna three years from the time she'd first proposed her plan to Charlie Bender and Mick O'Hara to reach the point where she was that day, back where she most wanted to be, doing the thing she believed she did best.

From her command station on the flag bridge of LFS *Valkyrie,* Lorna Greenwood was conducting a commander's briefing. In a

425

moment of *déjà vu,* she thought back to another such briefing, over a decade before, on the original *Valkyrie.* Then, her command had consisted of nine ships—all that stood between the Lunar Free State and the Chinese assault on the Moon.

Now, the faces of her captains filled rows of windows spread over three screens in front of her, with two other flag officers in larger windows on two of those screens. Her deputy force commander, Rear Admiral Jeff Jones, commanded Bravo Group from his flag bridge aboard the battlecruiser *Nike.* The next in command, Rear Admiral Robin Torrey commanded Charlie Group from her flag bridge on *Nike's* sister ship, LFS *Isis.* Each of them had fifteen additional ships under their command, an assortment of heavy cruisers, light cruisers, and destroyers. Lorna, commanding Alpha Group as well as the overall fleet, had another fifteen of her own. It was, she reflected, a damned fine fleet and a far cry from the little force she'd taken into battle so many years ago.

"For now," she told the attentive officers, "we hold station here. Stay sharp. If the Akara are correct, we haven't got long to wait— five days at the outside. One group will run defense picket and recon each day, while another will run combat drills on station. Use computer sims if you want to practice anything fancy. The third group will stand down, and we'll rotate groups each day. For the group on picket and recon, I want full stealth in case our guests arrive early for the party. Any questions?"

None of the officers spoke up. They'd all been briefed on the main event and were just marking time until it started.

"Very well. Admiral Jones, you have picket and recon today. Admiral Torrey, your group can stand down. Commodore Ling—" her own flag captain, "—*Valkyrie's* group will go to battle stations at

0930. We will be running a group-level attack sim, so please come up to the flag bridge at 0900, and I'll give you the basic parameters. For this simulation, *I* will be running the opposing force, and *you* will assume command of Alpha Group. Thank you, ladies and gentlemen. That will be all."

* * *

"In this engagement, we do not expect to be conducting boarding actions," Major Jeremy McGuinness told the assembled Marines of Valkyrie Company. "That means your primary function will be damage control during the engagement. *However*, battle plans are not cast in stone, so it is always possible we *may* be ordered to board an enemy ship. Most of you have never been involved in close combat with the enemy. In fact, most of you have never *seen* a Turnip up close and personal. This briefing is intended to give you information that might save your lives, so listen up.

"You all know Sergeant Bartley of Second Platoon. What you may *not* know is that she's a badass Turnip-killer. She's boarded a Turnip warship, gone up against them, and taken them down. More importantly, she's still here to talk about it. So, if *you* still want to be here after this one, pay attention to what she has to say. Sergeant..."

Bartley stepped up with a twinge of nervousness. She might be a 'badass Turnip Killer,' but she didn't think of herself as an instructor and speaking in front of a group was not her idea of fun. She looked at the large photo of a Turnip on the bulkhead behind her and took a deep breath.

"All right, Marines, here's the deal," she began. "Turnips are big. Turnips are nasty. But Turnips are *not* invincible. You have the tools you need to make 'em into vegetable salad—*if* you use those tools properly.

"Let's talk about weapon selection. Forget about ball ammo, sabots, and armor-piercing. All they'll do is punch holes in 'em, and you can punch a *lot* of holes in a Turnip before it decides to die. In theory, you can kill one with a combat knife, but you'd better bring your lunch 'cause you're gonna be slicing and dicing for a long, long time.

"If you're packing a Rapper, you can chew 'em to pieces quickly, but a little finger-twitch on the trigger is *not* gonna do it. If you've got one of 'em standing in front of you, it's not the time to worry about conserving ammo.

"If you've got a Flamer, you're in luck, 'cause one sure way to take the fight out of a Turnip is to make it into a crispy critter. But the usual restrictions on Flamers still apply—you need to get 'em far enough away that you don't splash fire on yourselves or your buddies.

"Most of you will be carrying LCAWs with grenade tubes. For your LCAW, you want to lock and load with concussion HE rounds. Put one of those into a Turnip's middle, and you'll wind up with two halves of a Turnip—their body armor is *not* enough to stop that round from penetrating before it blows. But if you hit 'em low on the body, watch out, because the top half of the Turnip *might* still have some fight left. Your best bet is to put your round about two thirds of the way up the critter's trunk—right about here," She indicated the appropriate point on the photo. "That's a little higher than head-high for the average human. These suckers are *tall,* but a round that high up will take out whatever they use for a brain, and that'll be one less Turnip to worry about.

"If you're using grenades, make 'em concussion grenades, not frags. Again, these critters *do* wear body armor, and punching small holes in 'em doesn't do much good. But they don't handle massive trauma very well. If you knock 'em down, they have a hard time getting up again, which gives you time to get in and finish the job.

"If you have to take one of 'em hand to hand with a combat knife, your best bet is to get *inside* those long, snaky arms and stick 'em high, as high as you can reach. Those bumps near the top of the head are eyes. If you stick your knife in one of 'em, it'll probably spoil the Turnip's day. You only see two eyes in this picture, but they have a third one on the other side, so forget about sneaking up on 'em. They'll *always* see you coming. One more thing—they have three legs, and they can move in any direction without turning around. I can guarantee that kicking one of 'em in the crotch will produce no effect whatsoever."

That brought a chuckle from the Marines, and Bartley allowed herself a little smile. Then she got serious again.

"Let's talk about *their* weapons. They use hand grenades, and they can throw 'em pretty far, but not as far as you can launch one from a grenade tube. They also use concussion grenades—frags aren't effective against them, so I guess they never came up with the concept. Anyway, watch out, 'cause those concussions're pretty nasty.

"Their main weapon is a laser, and it's *definitely* nasty. They wear the thing like a belt, and it has three barrels, with one pointing out between each pair of arms. They use one arm to control each barrel, and can swing it up, down, sideways, or wherever to point it at a target. Don't know how they aim, since they shoot from the hip, but they're damned accurate. Having three barrels spaced around like that means they can fire in any direction, but they only seem to be able to fire one barrel at a time. Maybe the power packs can't handle more than one. We know the weapons take time to recharge. If a Turnip fires, you've got about three seconds before it can fire again.

"Each time they fire, the beam stays on for about two seconds. If you get hit, *stand still and wait for the cutoff.* I know it's a reflex action, and maybe you can't help it, but if you jerk away while the beam is still on, it will slice you open like a razor blade. Better to take one hole through the arm or leg than to wind up *without* an arm or leg. You might still be in trouble 'cause they like to swing their weapons while they fire to cut up their targets, but if you move you help them do it.

"You've been issued new body armor, and I've heard some half-assed comments about it being all shiny and sparkly and white and too easy for the Turnips to see. Fact is, they don't see the way we do. We think they are more sensitive to movement than to color, so if you stand still, they'll have a hard time seeing you even if you're wearing *pink* armor with purple polka-dots. The reason this stuff is shiny, sparkly, and white is simple—lasers are beams of light, people. They'll burn through anything dark with no problem, but those tiny sparkly beads will reflect and scatter the beam, making it less effective. The beam can probably still burn through, but the armor will give you some protection before it does. As for the old armor, well..." She bared her left arm and showed them the scar. "I was wearing that when they gave me this. I got lucky 'cause the beam just nicked me. Otherwise, I wouldn't have an arm at all."

* * *

When the Mekota arrived, they came in dismaying force.

"*Four hundred* dreadnoughts!" Jeff Jones shook his head. "Damn!"

"Closer to four-fifty," Lorna said. This time, her command conference involved five other people—her two rear admirals and the three flag captains of the attack groups. "And if the Akara are correct, there's another hundred and fifty ships behind them. If they follow their usual attack pattern, the first group will engage the Akara fleet and try to destroy it or drive it out of position. Their objective is to make a hole for the second group, which will head straight for the planet and bomb the hell out of it. *That's* the group we must knock out first. If we don't, the Akara will be very unhappy."

"Can't say I'd blame them," Jones said, "but where is the second group? It's been an hour since the first dropped out of hyper."

"According to the Akara, it shouldn't be more than another hour behind. It must be close to take advantage of the hole in the defense the first group is supposed to create. The Mekota departed from staging points in two different systems. The Akara didn't get a look at all of them, which is why their estimates of strength were a little off, and they can't give us a precise ETA for the second group."

"A *little* off?" Robin Torrey complained. "They told us three hundred ships. We're looking at nearly twice that number."

"I know, but it's the hand we've been dealt, so we've got to play it out. Missiles are our best advantage, and our supply is limited, so make every shot count. If the Turnips have anything in the way of point defense, we're eventually going to get down to graser range. I'd like as few of them left as possible when that happens. I'm sure the Akara aren't happy about the numbers either, but if we can thin the bastards out, our Lizard friends will be more effective in dealing with the remainder.

"We're going to be sitting here for almost another day. They dropped in way beyond the hyper limit to keep the Akara from seeing their hyper signatures, but they didn't count on our being here. We'll stay quiet and let them go by. On their present course, they won't get within five million kilometers of us.

"Once the second group is inside the limit, we'll light up and go after them, but it'll take eight hours to catch up. By the time they see us, our rate of closure should be such that they can't avoid engagement. They'll be inside the orbit of the gas giant, and the Akara fleet will already be engaging their forward group ...surprise, surprise. They won't have expected engagement until much closer in.

"They came in almost exactly on the predicted course, so we don't need to maneuver. The laws of physics are in our favor, and we should be able to put a hurting on them well before they get close to our friends' homeworld."

"Right," Torrey said without humor. "We've got them where we want them. Maybe we should tell them to go back and get reinforcements, just to make it fair."

* * *

The second Mekota force, 145 ships in all, arrived two hours behind the first. One LFS destroyer managed to get close enough to the enemy's line of approach to get some long-range visual imagery.

"What the hell is *that* thing?" Amy Ling asked.

The object was huge, even by Mekota standards. It was a flattened disk with a diameter five times that of the largest enemy dreadnought.

"Something we've never seen before," Lorna said, "but I'd guess it's the bombardment ship the Akara told us about—the planet-killer. That makes it target number one."

Ling glanced at her admiral. "Wolfpacks?"

"My thought exactly." Lorna's smile was grim. "If we're going to surprise them, let's make it count."

The Wolfpack system was the latest development in LFS missile technology. It consisted of a delivery vehicle—a large, powerful propulsion package—with a payload mounted on its forward end. The payload was made up of three Viper ship-killer missiles configured as slaves to the targeting system aboard the delivery vehicle. The assembled package was exceptionally large, and only heavy cruisers and battlecruisers could carry them externally in belts around the circumference of the hull, like huge bandoliers. Battlecruisers had two belts of twelve Wolfpacks each. Heavy cruisers mounted a single belt of eight amidships.

The concept was simple but elegant. As soon as an enemy was within the Wolfpack range envelope—within detection range but far beyond effective *targeting* range—the weapons would be launched. Ejection thrusters would shove them laterally outward to get them clear of the warship's gravity drive field. Then the delivery vehicles would bring up their gravity drives, which would propel them toward the target area with nearly 500 gravities of acceleration. When they built up a sufficiently high rate of closure, they shut down their drives, making them invisible to enemy defense systems. If the enemy maneuvered unexpectedly, the warship that launched the Wolfpacks could command them to fire up their drives again, make a course correction, and again shut down. The enemy *might* get a look at them when they did so, but the delivery vehicle had a much smaller drive signature than a warship. They were unlikely to be spotted until they got close.

Once a Wolfpack got within targeting range of the enemy, its internal targeting system would take control. If the enemy had not maneuvered, it would continue to wait, content to coast silently into the attack zone. If the enemy *had* maneuvered, it could make additional course corrections as needed, again shutting down as soon as possible to make detection difficult.

As it approached, the master targeting system would power up the three slaves and direct them to lock onto targets according to programmed parameters. In the initial lock-on, they used passive acquisition methods to minimize the possibility of detection.

After they locked on, the missiles would continue to ride the delivery vehicle until certain conditions were met. If onboard threat indicators told the master system it had been detected or if it reached a predetermined range where it could be detected by passive means, it would issue the firing order to the three missiles. If the enemy took extreme evasive action, scattering to the point where one or more of the missiles found the range to its target was *opening* rather than closing, that would also trigger the firing order. After being fired, the missiles would go hot and use active seeking systems to target the enemy.

As soon as the missiles fired, the delivery vehicle would begin its final task, launching tiny decoys, flares, and chaff clusters. It would also broadcast signals to jam and confuse enemy defense systems. Then it would bring up its own active seeker systems and head for a target. It wasn't as fast or maneuverable as the Vipers, but it carried an even larger warhead.

The enemy would suddenly find himself under missile attack without warning, at noticeably short range, perhaps even from within his own formation, while LFS warships were still far outside the normal engagement envelope. If the system worked as advertised, the enemy would not see the attack coming until it was too late to mount an effective defense.

The Wolfpacks had been thoroughly tested in the Sol System but had never been used in combat. Lorna and her people would be the first to find out if they were as good as the LFS engineers claimed they would be.

* * *

"Range down to one million kilometers, Admiral," Amy Ling said from her command station on *Valkyrie's* bridge.

"Very well," Lorna said from her flag bridge. "Time for turnover." She keyed her fleet command channel. "All ships, Flag. Prepare to execute Delta Two on my mark…three…two…one…mark!"

The maneuver had been pre-programmed by each ship's helmsman, and Lorna's countdown was an order to Val, the flagship's AI, to issue the execution signal to each ship's computer system. The LFS formation was spread out over several hundred thousand kilometers—more than a light-second. Val issued the signals to each ship individually at intervals precisely calculated to allow for the transmission lag. In perfect unison, forty-eight ships shut down their drives, flipped end for end, and went to 60 gravities of acceleration in the opposite direction.

The Mekota had not yet seen them coming and were still accelerating sunward at 40 gravities, but the LFS ships were closing fast.
Lorna's braking maneuver would slow the rate of closure to near
zero at 300,000 kilometers. At that point, the LFS ships would flip
again and match vectors with the Mekota. The battle would begin
with the LFS having the "weather gauge" on the enemy. With their
superior power curves, the Lunar warships would have control over
the range and direction of the engagement.

Normally, the Mekota would have been able to see the Lunar
ships at 500,000 kilometers or more, but Lorna was coming up directly behind them, where their gravity wakes hindered their detection gear. With luck, they wouldn't see her coming until—for some
of them, at least—it was too late.

The range continued to spool downward, quickly at first and then
more slowly as the braking maneuver took effect. The second turnover went as planned, and the LFS fleet accelerated again, still closing
but at a carefully controlled rate.

At 200,000 kilometers, Lorna touched her comm button. "Alpha
Group, Flag. Flush the Wolfpacks. Repeat, flush the Wolfpacks."

The weapons had a slight overtake advantage when they were
launched, and now they streaked ahead under full power. By the time
they shut down their drives, they had covered over half the distance
and were closing at almost 2,000 kilometers per second. The Mekota
were still accelerating at their ponderous 40-gravity maximum rate, so
the rate of closure would decrease with time, but they had less than
two minutes before mayhem would erupt in their midst.

That time was almost up when the aliens first realized they were
being chased.

"They're hitting us with active scans, Admiral," Amy Ling reported. "They know we're here."

The Mekota had just begun to react—twenty of their dreadnoughts suddenly cut power and dropped back to close with the LFS fleet—when Armageddon erupted in the middle of their formation. The bombardment ship, target of no less than six Wolfpacks—24 warheads in all—was engulfed in a cluster of nuclear fireballs. Moments later, it blew apart as its multiple fusion reactors went up in rapid succession.

Lorna's Alpha Group had fired all its Wolfpacks in the opening salvo, but she had ordered Bravo and Charlie groups to hold fire. She planned to conserve most of her "secret weapons" for use against the main Mekota force. If she could take *this* enemy force out quickly and completely, the main force wouldn't know what to expect. They were too far ahead to see the battle behind them. They would hear about it, of course—it was too much to hope that the rear force wouldn't get a message off. But she hoped those messages wouldn't tell them much, except that they should tremble in fear because a hellhound was on their trail. Fear of the unknown was an amazingly effective weapon.

Valkyrie and the four heavy cruisers in her group put 56 Wolfpacks into the heart of the enemy force. Even allowing for those that had been earmarked for the bombardment ship, that meant 200 warheads targeting the remaining 144 Mekota ships.

Not all of them got through. All had been programmed *not* to attack until after the first six launched their missiles against the bombardment ship, and six more had been programmed as backups for the first six. They were not allowed to seek other targets unless the bombardment ship was destroyed—which it was—in the first attack.

But the bombardment ship had been in the very center of the formation. Some of the leading Wolfpacks, programmed to attack on the far side of the enemy force, had already coasted into the midst of the Mekota before the first six launched, and some of them had been spotted by the aliens. Seven were picked off by Mekota lasers before they had a chance to launch, and 27 more Viper missiles were destroyed after launch but before reaching their targets. The Mekota fared even better against the bigger, slower delivery vehicles, killing 32 of them after they had launched their Vipers.

Despite efforts by the Wolfpack computers to stay in their assigned sectors, several Mekota ships found themselves targeted by multiple missiles, while others were not targeted at all. But when the last fireball faded, less than a third of the Mekota force remained—just 43 dreadnoughts, five of them heavily damaged by missiles that had *almost* reached them.

* * *

"**D**amn!" Amy Ling swore. "They *have* got point defense. Mr. Ashton, set missiles for Attack Plan Bravo. Admiral…" She glanced at Lorna's image on the screen in front of her.

"I heard, Amy. All ships from Flag," she ordered. "Upgrade missiles to Attack Plan Bravo."

LFS missiles, both the standard Broadswords and the heavier, longer-ranged Vipers, had four modes of attack programmed into them. Attack Plan Alpha presumed the enemy would have no point defense whatsoever. The missiles would go straight for their targets on a least-time course and without any ECM jammers, which were missiles without warheads designed to confuse the enemy's defense with decoys, false targets, and electronic countermeasures.

From Alpha level, each upgrade of the attack plan would program the missiles for more radical evasive maneuvers and would include more ECM birds in each salvo. Plan Bravo would typically include only one jammer for every eight warheads and would allow the missiles to turn and twist at random intervals but never stray far from their base course to the target. Under Plan Delta, the most extreme, nearly half the missiles would be jammers, and the incoming missiles would take radical evasive action, even shutting their drives down for periods of time to make it harder for the enemy to track them.

There was a cost, of course. The increased number of jammers decreased the number of actual warheads in each salvo. The evasive action also decreased the effective range of the missiles. Lunar Command *hoped* the Mekota hadn't learned much from their first encounters with humans in the Sol System, but it appeared they had. Their ships were equipped with, at least, a rudimentary point-defense system. They might not do as well against conventional missiles in an all-out attack at shorter ranges, but they had taken a significant bite out of the Wolfpacks.

Lorna hadn't brought a lot of jammers with her, as she had elected to use her magazine capacity for as many warhead birds as possible. She would run out of jammers quickly if she had to go to Attack Plan Charlie or Delta, but the warhead missiles could still be launched with high-level evasion programming. At this point, she wasn't sure how effective the jammers were since no one knew what kind of targeting systems the Mekota were using for point defense.

Well, she thought as the range fell below 100,000 kilometers, *I guess we're about to find out how good they are.*

"All ships from Flag. Execute fleet turn to starboard and present broadsides on my mark," she ordered. "Weapons are free. Stand by to engage with missiles when targets are acquired. Three...two...one...mark!"

* * *

The Mekota point-defense was good—especially considering that the aliens had not had a chance to test it in combat—but not good enough. Only six of the enemy ships survived Lorna's first broadside—78 Viper missiles fired by the battlecruisers and cruisers from all three groups. Not wanting to expend any more ordnance than necessary, she ordered her six light cruisers to close the range and finish the survivors with the shorter-ranged Broadsword missiles.

None of the Mekota got close enough to fire a single shot at an LFS warship, but as the last missiles closed on it, one Mekota ship tried to launch two couriers—one headed for the main Mekota formation to sunward and one headed for the hyper limit. The tiny messenger vessels were faster than a Mekota warship, capable of nearly 80 gravities of acceleration, but they were no match for Lorna's force. With their recently upgraded drive systems, LFS battlecruisers could pull 140 gees, and the lighter units were even faster. Lorna's destroyers ran both messengers down before they got far and destroyed them with graser fire.

Messenger drones were Lorna's primary security concern. She wanted no word of the battle to get back to the Mekota homeworld, and not just for psychological reasons. If the Mekota found out the

LFS was aiding the Akara, they might decide to attack Earth in force. The Mekota had dropped two such drones in the outer system, apparently to wait for orders and to carry messages back to their high command, but Lorna's force had seen them detach and drop back from the alien formation, marked their position, and destroyed them on the way to the battle. Now, the aliens would probably launch more of them. In the heat of battle, the small vessels might not be noticed and might escape.

Reluctantly, Lorna detached three of her new *Raptor*-class destroyers, one from each battle group, and ordered them to watch the back door and stop any such drones from escaping the system. The *Raptors* were designed for defense picket and reconnaissance missions. They sacrificed two broadside grasers and two missile tubes in favor of a more powerful drive and far better search-and-detection gear than their *Star*-class cousins. That made them the best choice to track and engage the tiny couriers.

* * *

War Speaker had a new title again—Heart of the Second Battle Group—but he had gotten it by attrition rather than promotion. There had been three Akara commanders in Second Group senior to him, and all of them were now dead or otherwise out of action. Heart of the Warriors still directed the action from his command ship with the First Group, but losses had been suffered there as well.

The outnumbered Akara ships had aimed deadly thrusts at the flanks of the Mekota formation and had destroyed nearly a hundred of the massive enemy dreadnoughts, but they had lost over sixty of their own in return. They now had less than a hundred ships left, while the Mekota numbered well over three times that many. Heart of the Second Group tasted bitter victory as yet another Mekota dreadnought blew up—bitter because he had lost two of his own ships to accomplish it.

The Mekota were changing their tactics. When the two Akara groups hit them from opposite sides, they had turned outward to meet the attacks and had pushed hard to drive the Akara away from their line of approach. Now, they were falling back toward their original course, regrouping. Heart thought he knew the reason, or at least he *hoped* he knew. The plant-creatures had tried to push the defenders outward to clear the path for their bombardment group. Now, they were consolidating again, perhaps because they no longer *had* a bombardment group and would have to attack the planet themselves.

No word had come from the humans, but none was expected. Even if they destroyed the rear group, Warrior Queen had no way of getting word to her allies without taking a chance the enemy would intercept the message and gain useful intelligence about the force behind them. The Akara commanders had agreed to simply fight on as if they were the only force that faced the enemy, until…

"My lord, the wolf is at the door!" Speaker of the Group reported.

Heart had no idea what a wolf might be, but the code phrase was the one he had been waiting to hear. "Group to disengage," he ordered. "All ships to head for the homeworld at best speed. We must get in front of them now, for others come to chew upon their flanks. Pass the word to First Group, in case they did not receive the message."

The Akara had just begun to disengage when the first Wolfpacks arrived at the rear of the Mekota formation. This time, there was no programmed delay, and the weapons went into attack mode as soon as targets fell within their envelope. The rearmost of the enemy dreadnoughts had no warning and little chance to escape. Fifty-two of them vanished in blinding fireballs in a matter of seconds. Those further in had better luck and managed to stop nearly two-thirds of the incoming warheads. Despite that, another 34 Mekota ships did not survive. That was the end of Bravo Group's Wolfpacks, but another salvo from Charlie Group was right behind it. The Mekota were fast learners, and now, their full attention was focused on their rear ranks. They did much better against the final wave of Wolfpacks but still lost another 25 ships. By the time the fireballs faded, they outnumbered the combined LFS and Akara forces by only about a hundred ships—a far cry from the three-to-one superiority of before.

By now, Lorna's fleet was visible to the Mekota and Akara, charging the enemy's rear at full power. They would reach Viper range for the cruisers and battlecruisers within ten minutes and Broadsword range for all LFS ships ten minutes after that. There was no longer any need for stealth, so Lorna sent her second coded message to the Akara.

"My lord, Warrior Queen says it is time to close the gates—"

"And make the plant-things *die for their Clan!*" Heart of the Warriors issued orders to his two battle groups. The Akara ships had rushed ahead, using their superior acceleration to get in front of the Mekota. Now they curved inward, aiming a combined thrust from both groups straight at the middle of the enemy formation.

As the Akara combined their forces, the LFS ships split into three groups, angling to go around the Mekota and rake them with missile fire from three directions. But as the first missile salvos streaked toward them, the Mekota did what Lorna had feared they might do: They scattered. Almost in unison, their formations broke apart and headed out in all directions. Whoever was in charge had obviously given an every-ship-for-itself order, for there was no pattern to their dispersal. From the LFS viewpoint, the timing couldn't have been worse.

Lorna's forces had fired a triple salvo, with each ship turning broadside to the enemy, firing all its tubes on one side, then rolling over and firing all the tubes on the other side. This was followed by a quick turn directly toward the enemy and a third, somewhat smaller volley as each ship emptied its forward chaser tubes. The idea was to give the enemy too many missiles for their point defense to handle. Meanwhile, the LFS ships would continue to close the range, reload their missile tubes, and fire again from a shorter distance.

The opening salvos were fired when the enemy was barely within range of the Broadswords. The missiles built up a high closure rate and were almost to the target area when the Mekota dispersed. To keep their target locks, the missiles had to make radical course changes, and many Broadswords didn't have enough drive capacity left to catch the fleeing dreadnoughts. The targets made it out of their range envelope, and the missiles burned out without ever getting close enough to trigger their warheads.

The larger, longer-ranged Viper missiles fared better, but those made up only about twenty percent of the salvo. Destroyers didn't carry them, and Viper tubes made up less than a third of a heavy or light cruiser's launch capacity. Only the battlecruisers could throw as many Vipers as Broadswords, but the enemy's sudden dispersal made the Vipers' task more difficult, forcing them to maneuver and giving the Mekota point defense more time to engage them. Worse, the failure of the Broadswords to reach the target left that point defense with fewer incoming missiles to deal with.

Not all the Mekota were successful in evasion or defense. The initial missile engagement destroyed seventeen ships and damaged eight more. But the LFS had spent over 400 of their precious missiles to achieve that result. With the missiles they'd expended wiping out the Mekota trailing force, some of the destroyers were down to only two full reloads for their tubes. Even cruisers and battlecruisers had no more than four reloads left. They would now have to adopt new tactics, which made the remaining missiles even more important.

Lorna's original plan had been dubbed "the Fist and the Talons" by the Akara. It had called for the Lizard warships to slam directly into the front of the enemy formation while the LFS forces enveloped them from all sides. Now, the Akara fist had nothing to smash, and Lorna's talons might as well have been closing on a handful of water. If the two allies maintained their tight attack formations, the enemy would simply squirt out in all directions. The only option was to break and go after the Mekota one ship at a time.

It was a possibility that both Lizards and humans had recognized and planned for, but it wasn't a desirable option. It would take a long time to run down all the enemy ships, and during that time, at least some of them would get too close to the Akara homeworld. The Mekota didn't have missiles, but they had bombs. If they got within half a million kilometers of the homeworld, they could launch those bombs. The unpowered weapons would be exceedingly difficult to detect and destroy.

There was also the problem of numbers. Lacking missile capability, the Akara warships could not go one-on-one with a Mekota dreadnought. Over the course of the war, they had developed effective tactics against the huge but sluggish enemy ships, but those tactics called for a coordinated attack by at least four Akara ships. They would need to split their attack groups into four-ship divisions, with each division going after a single enemy ship. Even if they destroyed all their initial targets, they would take losses and have to regroup, with fewer divisions to attack the next group. Worse, the enemy would scatter more widely with each passing minute, making it harder to find and intercept targets as the battle wore on. By Lorna's pessimistic estimate, the Akara could account for no more than thirty to forty of the attackers before the first ones got within range of the planet. That left over 140 enemy warships for the LFS to deal with.

Lorna's ships, even the destroyers, *could* go one-on-one with the Mekota, at least until they ran out of missiles. After that, they would have to form up in hunter groups and go after the remaining enemy ships the way the Akara did. A battlecruiser might be able to go *mano e mano* against a dreadnought at energy-beam range, but it wouldn't be pretty. None of her lighter ships dared to do so except as a last resort.

For the moment, Lorna still had missiles, and her ships were already scattering in pursuit of individual targets assigned by the battlecruiser AIs. The battle would spread over a huge area of space, perhaps many light-minutes. While her ships were still in real-time communication range, she called a quick command briefing. Once again, her screens were filled with the images of her captains.

"When you catch up with your target," she told them, "stay with it until you hit it, then go find another one as quickly as possible. If you hit one and only cripple it, break off and find another. If we get down to energy weapons, I'd rather be mopping up cripples than dealing with undamaged Mekota ships, so let's hit as many as possible while we still have missiles left.

"Destroyers, you'll most likely be the first to run out of missiles. When you do, *break off*. Do *not* attempt to take one of them alone with nothing but grasers. Find a few buddies who are also out of missiles, then get back in there and gang-bang them. You've all studied the Akara tactics, and we know they *work*. That's how the Lizards have managed to survive this long.

"If we get down to grasers, destroyers and cruisers should form up in groups of three or four if possible. If you can't find partners or targets, sing out for Val, Iris, or Nadia—they'll be keeping track of who's where, who has missiles left, and so on. Once we run out of missiles, only battlecruisers should go after one of those things alone, and even battlecruisers should operate with support if possible.

"We've broken this mess into three sectors, one for each battle group. Stay in your own sector and look to your own group command for guidance. We're going to be too spread out for effective single-point coordination. Remember, people, we've got to stop *every one* of the bastards. If even one of them gets within bombing range of the planet, a few million of our Lizard friends are going to die, and we will have failed in our mission. Any questions?"

There were none.

"Then good hunting, all of you." She closed the conference, and the faces blinked out on the screens, replaced by her tactical and status displays once again.

* * *

"**B**ravo Group, this is *Basilisk*. We are bingo for missiles, looking for partners and targets. Squawking IFF for position. Copy?"

The light cruiser was nearly four light-seconds from *Nike,* and Commander Ed Kellerman waited patiently for the delayed reply.

"*Basilisk,* Bravo Group," replied the soft contralto voice of Nadia, *Nike's* AI. "Your position and status are noted. Nearest target is marked on your plot. I have destroyer *Starhound,* also bingo missiles, at three oh seven plus four, your position, vectored to same target, also squawking IFF. Link up directly on channel two four and proceed—you are pack leader. No other wolves available at this time."

"Roger that," Kellerman said. "*Basilisk* out."

Damn! Just two of us, he thought. *Basilisk* had managed to kill one Mekota ship and severely damage another before her missile magazines ran dry, but the action had taken her far out in front of the group in the direction of the Akara homeworld. Except for the lone destroyer, nobody else was close enough to form a group with him.

"I have *Starhound* on twenty-four," his comm officer advised.

Kellerman opened the indicated channel. "*Starhound, Basilisk.* You ready for the dance, Willie?"

"Roger that. Let's do it," said Lieutenant Commander William Wilson, *Starhound's* captain. "Ah…stand by one, *Basilisk.*" A moment later, "*Basilisk, Starhound.* I have an Akara cruiser at two one five minus two, my position, sixty thousand klicks, squawking 'need assist.' Maybe we've got another partner after all."

A set of standard codes had been arranged for independent communication between LFS and Akara ships. While they still couldn't carry on a detailed conversation without the assistance of an AI, they could at least identify each other and exchange critical tactical information. The "need assist" code meant the Akara was combat-effective but was also looking for partners.

* * *

Heart of the Second Battle Group had accepted his fate and made his peace with the Goddess. Leading a four ship attack wing in pursuit of the scattering enemy, he had given his best—had destroyed two of the enemy dreadnoughts—but had lost two of his wingmates in the course of it.

His own ship had also suffered. His weapons systems were down, and his drive was damaged to the point where he could not stay ahead of the fresh enemy ship that was pursuing him. Even so, he was still doing his part, presenting the Mekota with a tempting target as he led it *away* from the homeworld. He had sent his surviving wingmate to seek another group to join rather than be destroyed in a futile attempt to take the Mekota ship alone.

Hopefully, he would delay this enemy long enough for others to engage and destroy it, but the delay would not last much longer. Even now, the ill-spawned plant-things were closing, and he was almost within range of their weapons. When that happened, he would reverse course and charge at them, hoping to drive his crippled ship straight into the oncoming behemoth. He had explained this to his surviving crew, and all of them had accepted it without question, though most of them knew they would be unlikely to close the distance before the enemy weapons wiped them out of existence.

The enemy was close enough for long-range visual imagery now. He could see the bloated globe of the dreadnought as it bore down on him. Once again, he checked the range. *Soon, very soon.* He knew he would never see the death shot. Lasers traveled at the speed of light, so if you saw the flash of the enemy's weapons, it could only mean they had missed you. Under such circumstances, with his ship unable to maneuver effectively, that was most unlikely.

But suddenly, he *did* see flashes, very *bright* flashes, a whole cluster of them erupting across the face of the enemy ship. Fascinated, he watched as the Mekota began to rotate and veer to the side, and yet *another* cluster of flashes erupted on the side facing him.

Heart turned his attention to his primary tactical display, where he was most pleased to note three friendly icons that had not been there a moment before. His wingmate had returned, with a pair of most unlikely—but most welcome—partners.

* * *

"**G**ood shooting, Guns," Kellerman said. "Now, get ready to do it again."

"Already locked in, sir," his tactical officer said. "The Akara is firing now. *Starhound* is up next. Just waiting our turn."

It was a tactic they'd all been required to study, one the Akara had used successfully against the Turnips many times in the past. Admiral Greenwood had called it peeling the apple.

When a Mekota dreadnought was attacked and hit hard on one side, it would invariably rotate in one direction or the other. In fact, it had no choice but to do so. Dreadnaughts had thick armor, sufficient to withstand two or perhaps three heavy volleys of energy fire. But after that, beam weapons would begin to penetrate deep into the ship and do serious damage. Mekota weapons and sensor arrays, however, were mounted externally on the hull and were less well protected. A heavy barrage would most likely tear them up, leaving the ship blind and defenseless on the side that was hit. Rotation was the only way to minimize further damage and possible penetration of the ship's armor. It was also necessary to bring undamaged weapons and targeting systems to bear on the attacker. If drive components were damaged in the attack, the ship would also need to rotate before it could maneuver away from the attacking force.

The trick was to keep up a steady concentrated fire, so each fresh section of the ship was hit as it rotated into view. A single ship could not carry out such an attack, because heavy beam weapons took time to recharge. The ponderous Mekota dreadnoughts were slow to rotate but not *that* slow, and a lone attacker would find himself taking fire before his weapons could recycle. But a coordinated attack, with two or more ships alternating fire in an orderly sequence, had a good chance of success. If they could keep it up with each one firing in turn, with accuracy, they could peel the apple and render the monster helpless.

The hardest part was to initiate the attack, since at least one ship would have to close within beam range and rake the Mekota without being hit first. In this case, however, the Akara cruiser had led *Basilisk* and *Starhound* back to where his crippled wingleader was drawing the enemy *toward* them. The three ships had cut their drives and waited to spring the trap, and it had worked perfectly. Less than two minutes after the first grasers were fired, the Mekota ship was a tumbling hulk, unable to maneuver or return fire. Thirty seconds after that it blew apart as Akara lasers found one of its power plants.

Heart of the Second Squadron took it in stride. "Well, my loyal Clansmen, it would seem it is not yet time for us to die. Now, if you could just restore our drive and weapons, perhaps we might even kill a few more Mekota before we go to see the Goddess."

It was a task they undertook with great enthusiasm.

* * *

LFS *Valkyrie* had done more than her share in the battle. She had killed five Mekota ships with missiles before running her magazines dry, then killed two more in one-on-one engagements with energy weapons. In the first of those engagements, thanks to deft ship handling and precision fire control, she had successfully peeled the apple by alternating fire among her port and starboard broadsides, her chase armament, and her top and bottom graser turrets. The enemy had scored only one hit, taking out one of her two top turrets, but the robotic turret was unmanned, and she'd suffered no crew casualties.

The second engagement hadn't gone nearly as well. The enemy scored on the LFS battlecruiser no less than five times, taking out both bottom turrets and half her starboard grasers with hits that wiped out two of her fire-control nodes. Worse, a hit in the aft engineering spaces had damaged her number three fusion plant. The fail-safes had done their job, and the reactor had shut down, but with additional damage to power feeds and drive nodes, she was down to just seventy gravities of acceleration. The loss of one fusion reactor also degraded the recycle times for her remaining grasers. There had been a human cost as well, with 24 of her crew dead and seven more critically injured.

The Mekota had not lived long enough to celebrate their gunnery, as *Valkyrie* had rolled over and slammed them with her port broadside. The 75-centimeter grasers had gone through the dreadnought's already-shattered armor and found one of its fusion plants, and the Mekota reactor had *not* shut down safely. All that remained was a cloud of expanding plasma and glowing hot debris.

The widely scattered battle had been raging for over eight hours, moving ever-closer to the Akara homeworld. In less than two hours, leading Mekota elements would be within bombardment range, and there were a lot of enemy ships still in action.

Which was why Amy Ling was proposing to go one on one with yet another undamaged Mekota dreadnought.

"Your ship, your call, Amy," Lorna Greenwood said.

"Frankly, Admiral, I don't *want* to take him on alone. We're far from a hundred percent effective, but there's nobody else available, and this bad boy is getting too close to his target."

"I understand." Lorna's status displays told her Ling's comment about *Valkyrie's* condition was an understatement, but she was right about the availability of assistance. With the battle spread over a huge area of space, it was hard enough to assemble cruisers and destroyers into attack groups. Battlecruisers were on their own.

Nor was *Valkyrie* the only ship with battle damage. *Nike* was in worse shape, with two of her three reactors down, most of her grasers out of action, and her long-range communications knocked out. She had accounted for another five Mekota ships, but now, with over a hundred dead among her crew, she was effectively out of it, and Jeff Jones was coordinating Bravo Group's actions through LFS *Stardancer.* The destroyer had also taken heavy damage but still had long-range comm capability and was staying close to *Nike* to relay signals to the rest of the group.

According to Lorna's status displays, one heavy cruiser, two light cruisers, and four destroyers were gone, presumed lost with all hands. Three other ships were out of action with battle damage and heavy casualties, and several others had lesser damage. The Akara only had 38 combat-effective ships remaining, but they were still in there, slugging it out. In a few cases, they'd formed up with LFS warships in mixed attack groups, since they were also having trouble finding partners.

The allies had wrought terrible carnage on the attackers. Few, if any, Mekota warships would survive the battle. But if even *one* got close enough to bomb the planet...

"Do what you have to do, Amy," Lorna said. "I'll worry about the rest of the fleet."

* * *

The Mekota First Leader was no longer on the bridge of her ship. She was on a lower deck in a compartment humans might have called a boat bay. Having released her ships to proceed independently, there was no need for her to remain in command, and nothing she could do would mitigate the disaster in progress. She told her subleader she needed to prepare a message for the homeworlds, and she left the bridge and went to the lower deck instead.

The deck shuddered under her, sending sharp vibrations through her feeding tendrils into her root nerves. *Another hit by the accursed reptiles and their vermin allies.* No less than four enemy ships were closing for the kill—a kill that was almost certain since her ship no longer had power to maneuver or weapons with which to fight.

Her battle sphere had been First of the Twelves, what humans would have called the flagship. It had been positioned to the rear of center of the Thrust Force. All had gone according to plan for most of the inward journey but then word had come from the Termination Force to the rear. They were being attacked by an unknown enemy that had come up from behind. They were being hit by strange and deadly missile weapons. A final message had come, with just one word... *Humans!* Then silence.

First Leader had dismissed it as the panicked reaction of a subordinate commander. Rogue humans were the demons most feared by inexperienced subleaders, but the Mekota had encountered them only once before, in the humans' own system. *Those* humans hadn't had the secret of Otherspace, so the Guardians had elected to leave them alone and isolated, to be dealt with after more pressing issues had been addressed. Since then, no sign of them had been found anywhere, and there was no reason to expect them here, so far from their own world. Still, what *had* happened to the Termination Force?

Then the reptiles had attacked, sooner and in greater force than expected, giving First Leader other matters to deal with. She had not been surprised when a second enemy force appeared behind her— she had expected it ever since communication from the Termination Force had ceased—but to her shock, the new attackers *were* humans! She had seen the Guardians' records of the abortive expedition to the human world, and there was no mistaking the distinctive ship types.

Her forces were much more numerous. If she scattered them, the reptiles and humans had no chance of stopping all of them. She gave the order to scatter just as the humans unleased another barrage of their deadly missile weapons. The flagship barely escaped destruction, and others of her force were not so fortunate, but, for the most part, her fleet escaped with little damage, and the enemy forces began to scatter in pursuit.

At first, she was puzzled. The reptile-things formed up into their usual little attack groups, further enhancing the Mekota numerical advantage. But the humans had gone after her fleet ship for ship. She thought it most foolish of them, until she saw one of the *smaller* human ships unleash a volley of missiles that wiped out one of her battle spheres in a blinding flash from *outside* the sphere's weapons range.

Other battle spheres fared better, and she was thankful for the new defensive lasers. They hadn't expected to encounter *this* enemy here, but the humans had shown that missile weapons were possible. The Mekota might encounter another race that used them. To remain invincible, they'd had to prepare for such things. The homeworld was working on Mekota missile weapons, but those had not yet been deployed.

In the early part of the battle, First Leader had been lucky. Her ship had been ignored by the humans, bypassed in their haste to engage the leading elements of her fleet. This had not displeased her, for she was content to let others take the damage and wear the enemy down. She expected hers would be one of the ships that—after the humans and reptiles were defeated—would bomb the reptile planet and return in triumph to the homeworld. She expected appropriate rewards, since she had been the one who'd pressed for a rapid strike against the reptiles when their nearby system defenses collapsed. The annihilation of a major reptile nest would bring high praise from the Guardians no matter how many ships she lost in the process. Perhaps she might even attain Guardian rank, might even be allowed to flower and procreate. But now...

The enemy ships moved on, out of detection range. Her own ships remained in her holographic plot, thanks to the beacons they carried that allowed her to track them as tiny yellow icons making their way inexorably toward the reptiles' nest. But as the battle wore on, those icons disappeared in alarming numbers. Some ships might have had their beacons disabled by battle damage, but more likely, given the violent effectiveness of the human weapons, those ships had been destroyed. With a shock, she realized that less than five twelves of ships remained. Then four new icons, *red* icons, appeared on the plot as enemy ships came within range of her sensors, and she realized they were coming for *her.*

Her systems identified them as one human—not one of their largest—and three reptile cruisers of substantial size. They spread out as they approached. They were almost within weapons range when suddenly the human ship launched one of those abominable missile weapons!

* * *

Raoul Sanchez, commanding the light cruiser *Wraith*, had only one missile left—a Broadsword that had failed to launch earlier but had now been put back online by his weapons techs. A lone missile had little chance of getting past the Mekota point defense, but Sanchez had a plan. He *hoped* he'd managed to convey the plan to his partners—three Akara ships he'd linked up with when Iris couldn't find any LFS ships in the area. He'd relayed the details to the AI and asked her to explain it to the Akara, but the battlecruiser was almost twenty light-seconds away, too far to coordinate the timing. He had to hope the Lizards picked up their cues and did what they were supposed to do.

* * *

458 | JOHN E. SIERS

rantically, Mekota gunners brought their defense lasers into action and tried to target the incoming missile, but the thing twisted and turned fiendishly and periodically disappeared from their plot as its drive shut down then restarted again. And it was *fast*. It had gotten all too close to them when they finally managed to hit it, producing a monstrous fireball and an EMP spike that played hell with their sensors. They were just beginning to recover, nervously scanning for more of the demon-weapons, when their battle sphere was rocked by a barrage of laser fire from an Akara cruiser that had run in on their opposite flank while they were distracted.

They hesitated. To rotate the ship to face this new threat would force them to take their already-primed defenses away from the human ship. But hesitation was nearly fatal, as the *second* Akara cruiser hammered them with fire from the same direction as the first. Now, they began to rotate. The Akara were too close, their fire too effective to be ignored, but, as the massive dreadnought started to turn toward that threat, the *human* ship attacked again. Not with missiles this time, but with a barrage of beam weaponry that was all too powerful for such a small ship. Busy with the missile, they hadn't even noticed the enemy had crept into beam weapon range.

From then on it was hopeless. No matter which way they turned, they were taking heavy fire from two sides, as the third Akara joined the human ship and added its lasers to the melee. Within moments, their power systems were failing and their weapons offline. They were spared the searing flash of a nuclear fireball as their reactors shut down; but with nothing remaining but emergency power, they were helpless, and the enemy ships bored in without mercy, hitting them again and again. At that point, First Leader left the bridge.

After reaching the boat bay, she went straight to the messenger ship that was preparing to carry the last word of the fleet's ignominious defeat back to the homeworld. She had ordered it to hold until she gave the launch order, and now she planned to deliver that order in person.

The tiny courier only had room and life-support for its crew of three. Without hesitation, she seized the nearest crew member—one of the sexless carriers who normally performed such missions—dragged it from the ship, and hurled it to the deck, making certain to cause sufficient injury so that the drone would no longer trouble her. She inserted herself into its place in the cabin, plugged her three legs into the nutrient wells that would sustain her for the journey, and ordered the other two crewmembers to seal the ship and prepare to launch.

"Do not use the drive," she ordered. "When we are ejected from the ship, let us drift. Make the enemy think we are just another piece of wreckage." The accursed reptiles and their hell-spawned ally were blasting away great chunks of the battle sphere's armor and hull structure, providing plenty of cover for her tiny ship to slip out unnoticed. She secured herself into place and braced herself as the outer hatch opened, and the launch mechanism catapulted the messenger ship into the void.

The ploy worked. Spewing debris with every hit, the maimed battle sphere soon shrank to a tiny dot in the distance, taking its attackers with it. First Leader began to plan. She would order the messenger's remaining crew to take her out of the system on a devious course, slowly and carefully, with minimum energy emission.

Once they were far enough out-system, they would jump into Otherspace and make their way to the nearest occupied system. She examined the interior of the tiny cabin. It was a most uncomfortable space in which to spend that much time, but it was better than being dead.

The ship was designed to be crewed by carriers, who were smaller than a mature female and had lower metabolic requirements. She would need to kill another of the crew to ensure adequate life support and nutrients for herself. She would allow the third one to survive, to serve her needs until they reached safety. Then it would have to be killed as well. It wouldn't do to have another first-hand report of the debacle, a report that might conflict with her own. She would have to purge some data from the ship's systems—the data it was *supposed* to bring back. If she was selective, she could make it appear as if the human vermin had a much larger force. She still could not believe they had done this with so few ships!

Other messengers might survive as well but would likely provide only a microscopic view of part of the engagement—nothing she couldn't work into her plan. A few of her ships might even succeed in bombing the reptiles' home planet, but she doubted they would fully destroy the Akara nesting place. She would detain any other survivors on the frontier while she alone went back to the homeworld to report to the Guardians and convince them she was not to blame for the defeat. With luck, she might even claim some small success. There was a chance she might survive the Guardians' wrath.

* * *

"**F**usion one and three are offline. Fusion two is forty percent. Forward impeller segments three, four, and seven are out. Ma'am, we've barely got maneuvering power."

"Grasers are down, and it looks like he's rotating for another shot. I think he's only got one battery left, ma'am, but he's gonna use it, and we can't do much about it."

"Then hit him with point defense, Mr. Ashton," Amy Ling ordered. "Anything you've got. I don't care if you throw rocks at him. We are *not* going to curl up and die."

Valkyrie had savaged the Mekota dreadnought and had been savaged in return. Neither ship could be called combat-effective, but neither was out of action yet. Both had severely limited maneuvering capability, and the LFS battlecruiser's graser batteries were out of action. Worse, nearly a hundred of her crew were dead or dying. The two combatants hung in space, separated by only twenty kilometers.

Unfortunately, one of the Mekota ship's lasers was still in service. In desperation, *Valkyrie's* tactical officer opened fire with countermissiles. The tiny birds carried no warheads; they were simply projectiles designed to knock out an incoming missile with sheer kinetic energy. But their outrageous acceleration gave them a *lot* of kinetic energy, and the battlecruiser threw over a hundred of them in that first salvo. They were meant to home in on a small, fast-moving targets hundreds of kilometers away. At twenty kilometers, they could hardly miss the massive enemy ship.

Ashton had done his best to narrow their targeting to the part of the enemy ship where the surviving laser battery was located. One of them struck the exposed snout of the huge Mekota laser, shattering the monocrystal rod just as the weapon started to fire. The resulting explosion ended the aliens' last chance to hit *Valkyrie* again, but the Mekota were not finished yet.

"Ma'am! They've just grabbed us with a gravity beam. They're trying to drag us together!" *Valkyrie's* helmsman couldn't believe it. "I don't have the power to break loose, ma'am. Best I can do is slow 'em down."

Ling keyed her channel to auxiliary control, far aft in the battle-cruiser's hull. "Mr. Swenson."

"Yes, ma'am," the exec responded promptly.

"How's it going back there, specifically Fusion Three?"

"Working on it, ma'am. Engineering says they've got to replace a lot of power runs to the containment coils. At least an hour."

"Roger that. Keep me advised."

Fusion One was a wreck—a dockyard job, according to the engineers—but without another reactor online, *Valkyrie* couldn't break free of the alien's grip. Even with Fusion Three online, they might not be able to do it. They might just end up dragging the massive Mekota ship along with them. *What the hell is the bastard playing at?*

"Val, are the docking buffers operational?"

"Yes, ma'am, that system is fully functional."

"About the only thing that is," Ling growled. "Helmsman, power up the docking buffers and stand by."

The helmsman blinked at her, then realized what she had in mind. "Yes, ma'am!" He started bringing up the system.

Ling's first thought was that the Mekota intended to smash *Valkyrie* against their hull. But with her docking buffers operational—small but powerful counter-grav units that were intended specifically to prevent such a collision—that wasn't going to happen. Once they got within a hundred meters, it would take a lot more than a tractor beam to overcome the buffers.

The range continued to close. Now at less than five kilometers, the Mekota ship was getting exceptionally large on the main bridge display. Lieutenant Commander Ashton continued to rake the enemy ship with point-defense lasers, but the small beam weapons, powerful enough to knock down a missile, had little effect on the dreadnought's armored hull.

Then the lasers went offline, another victim of *Valkyrie's* damaged power systems. Moments later, Ashton reported the last of the countermissiles were gone. He had peppered the alien with the tiny projectiles, and a few of them had found chinks in the Mekota armor, punching small holes through the hull and no doubt wreaking molten-metal havoc inside. But the alien ship was so big, it was like throwing darts at an elephant. The countermissiles had gotten less effective as the range closed and they had less time to build up velocity on their way to the target.

"What the hell is *that*?" *Valkyrie's* communications officer exclaimed, calling the bridge crew's attention to the main screen. Swarms of small, white, cylindrical objects poured out of several openings in the alien ship's side, now less than a kilometer away.

"Val, magnify main screen," Ling ordered.

In close-up view, the cylinders showed three flexible tubes protruding from the bottom, and three more about midway up the sides. They also appeared to have various types of equipment attached all around the midsection. With a shock, Amy Ling realized what they were. *Vacuum suits! Mekota vacuum suits…and probably battle-armored.*

She keyed the all-hands channel and issued an order she had never expected to give in her entire career. "Attention all Marines, say again, *all Marines*, this is the captain. Equip with weapons and stand by to repel boarders. Repeat. Equip with weapons and stand by to repel boarders."

* * *

The scene on *Valkyrie's* flag bridge was surprisingly calm, but there were a few hints that the situation was far from normal.

"Your sidearm, ma'am." Commander Weathers handed Lorna the holstered weapon. "For once, I think I'm going to envy you that antique cannon of yours."

"I'm not sure a .45 will stop a Turnip, Bill," she replied with a grim smile as she checked the old semi-auto pistol and slipped it back into the holster, "but if they get in here, I'm sure as hell gonna try to *hurt* a few of them."

The entry chime for the main hatch sounded, and Chief Petty Officer Sandy Parks checked the monitor screen, then unlocked the hatch, admitting two armored Marines with slung LCAWs and a carry-bag of equipment.

The leading Marine saluted Lorna as he came through the hatch. "Corporal Barnes and Private Simpson reporting, ma'am, flag bridge security detail."

"Carry on, Corporal. Glad to have you with us." Lorna returned the salute.

"Uh, ma'am," the corporal hesitated, "Sergeant Bartley's compliments, ma'am. She said to tell you she wished she could be here, but Major McGuinness has another use for her talents at the moment."

"I'm sure he has," Lorna said, "and I'm sure the two of you can handle it. Besides, if the Turnips get this far, we're probably screwed. But we can make them pay for whatever they get."

"Yes, ma'am." The Marine nodded grimly, locking a magazine into his LCAW. "We can do that."

Lorna turned back to her status displays and regarded them with frustration. Like the Mekota First Leader, she realized the battle was out of her hands. But unlike her alien counterpart, no thought of her own safety entered her mind. Instead, she wracked her brain for anything she could contribute to the mission. Her tactical displays were better than those of the Mekota—she could see her own ships *and* most of the enemy's as well as the ships of her Lizard allies. But the battle was scattered, and her ship captains were doing their best without her intervention. Still, *someone* had to be in command, and it didn't look like she would be able to fill that role much longer. She'd been lucky so far—*Valkyrie*'s communications systems remained fully functional—but she couldn't count on them staying that way. "Val, what's the communication lag to *Isis*?"

"LFS *Isis* is forty-two light-seconds from our position, Admiral," the AI replied.

Too far for anything resembling a conversation, but at least I should be able to get an acknowledgement.

LFS *Isis* was the only undamaged battlecruiser in Lorna's fleet—*relatively* undamaged, at least. She'd taken a few minor hits, but after running her missile magazines dry—and accounting for four Mekota ships in the process—she'd managed to link up with the light cruiser *Werewolf*, and the two of them had killed three more of the enemy in rapid succession. According to Lorna's displays, they were about to engage a fourth one.

It appears that battlecruisers can take on a Mekota ship alone, Lorna reflected, *but pairing them with just one other ship makes a big difference. Need to remember that next time...if there is a next time.*

"Val, record for transmission to LFS *Isis*, tagged personal to Charlie Group commander, Admiral Torrey," she ordered.

"Ready to record, Admiral."

"Charlie Group Command, this is Flag. *Valkyrie* is severely damaged and still engaged with the enemy. We may soon be condition Omega. Bravo Group Prime is out of action, with communications impaired. I am passing fleet command to you. Effective immediately, you have the flag. Please acknowledge and confirm. Robin," she continued, "I need you to finish the job. Don't let the bastards wear you down. Good hunting. Message ends. Send it, Val."

"Message sent," the AI said.

"Record for transmission to all ships. *Valkyrie* out of action. Fleet command passed to Admiral Torrey aboard *Isis*. You've done your best, people, but I need you to keep doing it. Don't let up until the last of the enemy are finished. Good hunting. Greenwood out. Send it, Val."

"Message sent to all ships, Admiral."

"Translate and send it to the Akara as well. They need to know Robin's now in command."

"Translated and sent, Admiral."

* * *

"Warrior Queen has fallen?" Heart of the Akara Warriors was shocked. This did not bode well with so many of the Mekota yet to be dealt with so close to the homeworld.

"Not yet fallen, my lord," his communications officer said. "But her ship is badly damaged and still engaged in single combat with one of the enemy. She has passed command to the Heart of her Third Group."

"Another female. It appears human females *do* know how to fight."

"They are strong, my lord," Talons of the Fleet said. "Warrior Queen's ship destroyed seven of the enemy and is still engaged with the eighth. The one who now commands has also destroyed seven and is engaging her eighth as we speak. In total, the humans have destroyed more than a hundred since our fleets linked up and have assisted our own groups in destroying many more. The remaining Mekota no longer have sufficient force to destroy our homeworld, but the humans are still killing them, as are we."

"You are telling me we have victory in our grasp," the old war-Lizard grumbled, "but we have yet to tally the cost."

"Yes, my lord," Talons replied.

* * *

"All ships, this is Charlie Group Command." Robin Torrey had acknowledged Lorna's message and was about to issue her first orders as fleet commander. "Per Admiral Greenwood's orders, I am assuming temporary command of the fleet. All ships still combat-effective and not currently engaged, rally to *Isis* at one one four mark seven. Acknowledge and advise status.

"We've thinned the bastards out, but I want to make sure we're *between* any stragglers and the Akara planet. Let's concentrate our strength and build a wall in front of them, one they'll have to go through before they can get in bombing range. We may not know where all of them are right now, but we know where they're trying to go, so let's get there first. Flag out."

* * *

On *Valkyrie's* flag bridge, Lorna Greenwood heard the message. *Good thinking. Robin's got it together, and she's taking charge.* She relaxed a bit, knowing her surviving fleet was in good hands.

* * *

"We've got about a hundred Turnips in boat bay three. How the hell did they get in there?" Lieutenant Mathis demanded.

"Hull's breached just aft of frame 212. Laser hit," Major McGuinness said. "According to Val, they're trying to seal the breach behind them. Looks like they want to pressurize the compartment."

"They're in pressure suits. Why would they want to do that, sir?"

"Makes it easier to advance. If they have to cycle through the airlocks, it'll slow them down, and it's too easy for us to trap them in small groups. Of course, we can put a stop to that in a hurry. I'm thinking we'll just blow the boat bay doors off. Bet they can't seal up a hole *that* size."

"Uh, sir?" Sergeant Bartley was in the group of non-coms around the two Marine officers, waiting for orders.

"What is it, Bartley?"

"What are the chances the Turnips can stop us from blowing the doors?"

McGuinness turned to the engineer who had been assigned to assist the Marines.

The young ensign shrugged. "Poor to zero, I'd say. The charges are built into the door frame, and there must be a hundred control runs in the area. Unless they know exactly what they're looking for, they won't be able to find them, let alone disable them."

"In that case, sir," Bartley suggested, "I think we should let 'em get the compartment sealed up and pressurized and *then* blow the doors off. I'm not an engineer, but the term 'explosive decompression' does have a certain ring to it."

"You have an evil mind, Sergeant." McGuinness grinned at her. "I expect you'll go far in this world." He turned to the engineer. "Any reason we can't do what the sergeant suggests, Ensign?"

"No, sir." The young officer was grinning as well. "We'll probably lose any unsecured equipment in the bay, but that'll just give the Turnips a few more flying objects to dodge."

"Great!" He turned back to Bartley. "I wish I could let you stay here to see the results, Sarge, but I need you to take your squad aft. Val says she *thinks* more Turnips are coming in through the wreckage of number four turret, but she has lost video coverage in that area. I need you to check it out, report, and respond as needed. Understood?"

"Yes, sir." Bartley tossed him a salute and turned to her waiting troops. "Second squad, you're with me." She started off at a trot down the passageway.

* * *

By ones and twos, the surviving Mekota ships approached. Many of them, on first detecting the remnants of the allied fleet arrayed in front of them, tried frantically to reverse course, but for most of them, it was too late. They had built up too much velocity, and by the time they saw the defenders, they could no longer avoid engagement. A few charged forward, trying to bull their way through the defensive shield. These were met by swarms of human and Akara ships—ships with crews that had been through the fire and gotten plenty of practice in conducting coordinated attacks. With their forces consolidated again, the allies had no problem forming attack groups, and each incoming attacker found itself engaged by as many as seven or eight defenders at once. None of the attackers made it through the defensive lines.

Those who tried to flee survived a little longer but met even more certain destruction in the end. Their attempts to decelerate made it easy for the defenders to get in front of them, go into stealth mode, and simply wait for them to slide into the trap.

"I cannot believe how *stupidly* the bastards are fighting." Robin Torrey shook her head. "If they had made *any* attempt to regroup, they could have made our job much more difficult."

On the screen in front of her, the Akara she thought of as the Lizard admiral made a gesture of agreement. He replied in his own language, which Iris translated. "They have won victory by brute force for so long, they have never needed to learn the arts of strategy and tactics. I am content to leave them in ignorance so let us make sure that none return to their kind to teach the lesson."

"Two of them tried," Torrey said, "but they encountered the destroyers Admiral Greenwood stationed out-system. It was unfortunate for them since those destroyers still had full missile magazines."

Greenwood's original intent had been to guard against Mekota messenger ships escaping with word of the battle, but the Iron Maiden also made sure they were equipped to deal with any enemy warships that came their way.

"Have you any word of the Warrior Queen?"

"No, your Lizardship," Torrey replied. She wasn't sure of the proper form of address for the Akara leader, but she was certain Iris would translate the makeshift honorific into proper Lizard-speak. *On the other hand*, she mused, *AIs do have a sense of humor. They always translated Lizard references to Admiral Greenwood as Warrior Queen rather than fleet admiral.*

"We lost all contact with *Valkyrie* a short while ago. When last we heard, the Mekota were trying to board her, and her Marines were resisting them."

"*Board* her?" The Akara cocked his head in surprise. "You mean they actually sent individual warriors to try to gain entry to her ship in open space? I have never heard of the plant-creatures doing such a thing. I cannot imagine how such an attack could be carried out. We have put people aboard their ships in the past, but only *after* they surrendered. To do this while an enemy is still resisting..."

Torrey shrugged. "Actually, we've done it to *them* on a couple of occasions. It's one of the reasons our ships carry Marines, and they are trained for such an action. Of course, you have to knock out the enemy's drive and heavy weapons systems first."

"But why would you do that? Under those conditions, why not just stand off and destroy the enemy ship?"

"We wanted to gain intelligence about their technology. In this case, we know *Valkyrie's* drive and main weapon batteries are down, but it is possible the Mekota's drive and weapons are out as well. It may have been a desperation move. If so, one can hope it is going badly for them. Our Marines are trained for such an action, and they know how to *oppose* one as well. *Valkyrie's* IFF beacon is still transmitting, so we know where she is. With your permission, I would like to send a couple of ships to assist her now that our primary mission is well in hand."

"Of course." The Lizard admiral made a gesture of assent. "We can spare the ships. As you have said, the plant-creatures are fighting stupidly. We must remain vigilant, but it appears victory is ours."

* * *

Bartley and her squad entered the huge reactor room known as Fusion Three through the forward hatch on the starboard side, just as several Mekota forced their way in through the *aft* starboard hatch. A half-dozen engineering techs dove for cover as lasers hissed down the length of the compartment and were answered by a volley of screaming HE rounds from the Marines' LCAWs. The engagement lasted less than ten seconds. When it was over, one Marine was down, and three Mekota lay in scattered pieces at the aft end of the compartment. One of the tripeds managed to backtrack out of the compartment, pulling the hatch closed behind it, but the alien had not taken the time to secure the hatch, and it swung open again, giving Bartley a clear view of the retreating Mekota. She raised her LCAW, took careful aim, and blew the alien in half at nearly fifty meters.

"That's how it's done, people," she told her Marines. "Aim carefully and take 'em down. Spraying doesn't help, 'cause the bastards are too stupid to take cover."

She remembered an instructor in basic combat training who had told her that most rounds fired in battle weren't aimed at anything but were expended just to keep the enemy down and unable to return fire. The Marines were taught *not* to do that but to aim carefully and fire for effect. *Blow a few of 'em away*, the instructor had said, *and the rest of them will keep their heads down anyway.*

It wasn't that the Mekota were too stupid, she reflected. It was just that they were too big and clumsy to take cover. They didn't seem to be able to lie down—if you knocked one down, it had a lot of trouble getting back up. The best they could do was a sort of squat which reduced their height from three meters to two, a serious disadvantage in close combat. *And one I'm not complaining about,* she decided.

"Rockwell! Dawes! Secure that hatch." She pointed to the opening through which she had just shot the fleeing Mekota. "Taylor! Marks! Cover the portside. Make sure this compartment is secure. Benson, how're you doing?" She turned to the wounded Marine, who was being worked on by one of his squadmates.

His face was tense with pain, and his breathing was labored, but he looked up at her and attempted a smile. "I'm okay, Sarge. I think you were right about that new armor." The laser hit had scored a deep gouge across his armored chest plate before finally penetrating somewhere in his lower right rib cage. Without the armor, it would probably have sliced him nearly in half.

Bartley keyed into the command channel and reported the engagement. "We've got one down. We need a medic, and we could use a backup squad to keep Fusion Three secure while we press on. Copy that?"

"Understood, Sergeant," Val replied. The AI still had control of the ship's internal communications, which made coordination a whole lot easier for the Marines. "Major McGuinness has already dispatched another squad—ETA is five minutes. He suggests you hold for their arrival before pressing further."

Bartley smirked. Like all AIs, Val was invariably cool, collected, and very polite, even under extreme conditions. If she said the Major had suggested something, Bartley understood that to be an order. She turned to the engineering lieutenant, who was approaching her while the rest of his crew cautiously emerged from their hiding places.

"Your people okay, sir?" she asked.

"Yes, thank you, Sergeant. Your arrival was timely." He turned back to his crew. "All right, you apes! The Marines are here to protect your sorry asses, so get back to work. I told the captain we'd have this plant online in ten minutes!" Actually, he had told the XO it would be *thirty* minutes, but he wasn't about to share that with them.

"You have any people working aft of this compartment, Lieutenant?"

"Yes. I've got two techs in Impeller Five—next compartment aft, starboard side, upper deck. They just checked in, and they haven't seen any Turnips, but…"

"Riley, Jones." Bartley pointed at the stairway to the catwalk above. "Get up there to the upper deck. Next compartment aft—should be two techs working back there. Secure the compartment and keep 'em covered. Sing out if the Turnips show up."

"Aye, aye, Sarge." The two Marines hustled off.

"There's also people further aft in the engineering shops, and a crew of three working on Number Two turret, topside. Number Four is a write-off, so we don't have anyone down there."

Bartley flipped her visor down and called up the ship's deck plan. She knew what she would find—Marines had to be familiar with the layout of a ship for their damage-control responsibilities—but she wanted to confirm it. The reactor room was near the centerline of the ship, wrapped in armored bulkheads. It was surrounded on both sides, above, and below by machinery and equipment spaces, including a pair of primary broadside graser batteries on each side, port and starboard. Except for narrow access tubes too small for Mekota to negotiate, those compartments were accessible only from Fusion Three. The enemy would have to come through there to get forward.

Aft of the reactor room, the impeller rooms quartered the ship's hull on two decks, port and starboard. Those rooms were mostly packed with machinery, with only a narrow passage down the center. If she split up her squad, she could hold those rooms.

Aft of that, the ship divided into three decks with a maze of compartments, including the engineering shops on the middle deck and the machinery room for Turret Four on the lower deck, where the Mekota may have gained entry.

"Val, have you got contact with anyone aft of frame two six two?"

"Negative, Sergeant," the AI said. "I have no communication and no video coverage in that part of the ship."

Gonna be one nasty Turnip hunt back there, Bartley reflected.

"So, how are we doing, Sarge?" the engineer asked.

"Well…I'm doing just fine, Lieutenant," she said. "And it looks like your people are fine, too. We should be able to keep this place

Turnip-free. Aft of the impeller rooms...don't know yet. Forward of here...that's somebody else's problem, and it's not my mission."

"I guess it's not mine, either," he conceded and turned back to his crew working on the reactor.

* * *

"Well," Ensign Martin said, "the bay's under pressure."

"So, the Turnips got it figured out, sir?" Corporal Lee asked.

"I don't think so. I think Val gave them a little help."

"That is correct, Ensign." The AI's voice came through their headsets. "Knowing your plan, I brought the pressure up as soon as they sealed the hull breach. They have been under pressure for about two minutes."

"Val, can you put overpressure in the bay for a little extra effect?"

"Yes, Ensign. I can pressurize the bay to one-point-five atmospheres. It will take about thirty seconds. Do you wish me to do that?"

"Yes, please," Martin said.

"Now, sir, that's downright *nasty*." Lee's grin was wicked.

The Marine corporal had been detailed to stay with the engineer and assist as needed, which meant making sure Martin didn't have Turnip trouble. Here in the bay control center, an armorplast-windowed gallery that overlooked the docking bay, there wasn't much danger of that. But when they cautiously peered over the top of the console, they could see hundreds of aliens in the bay below.

The gallery was dark, so there was little danger of the aliens noticing them.

"Pressure at one point five atmospheres," Val said.

"Right." Martin took a deep breath. "Here goes…" He opened a black and yellow striped panel on the bulkhead. Inside, he lifted two red safety covers and flipped the switches under them.

"Warning! Bay door jettison armed! Warning! Bay door jettison armed!"

Martin glanced nervously at the aliens below. Apparently, the warning had sounded in the bay as well as the gallery because most of them had tensed up and stopped moving around.

"We know that, Val. You could have skipped the warning." Martin gritted his teeth.

"Sorry, Ensign." This time her voice sounded only in his headset.

"It's not an option. Certain warning messages are pre-recorded, and I don't control them. It's a safety issue, and I can't override it. That's why I couldn't trigger the doors myself—it requires human intervention for safety reasons. When you trigger the doors, there will be additional warnings and a fifteen-second delay before the door charges fire."

"Great," Martin muttered. "Let's hope they don't understand English. Better lock your helmet down, Corporal. These windows are *supposed* to withstand decompression, but we've taken a lot of damage, and I wouldn't bet my life on it."

The Marine hastily locked his helmet visor in place, and Martin did the same. He reached into the panel, grasped two red levers, and pulled them down. In the bay below, a series of bright red strobes along the overhead began to flash, while a loud warning horn started blaring. "Warning! Warning! Bay decompression in fifteen seconds!

All unprotected personnel evacuate *immediately*! Bay decompression now in ten seconds…nine…eight…seven…"

The aliens below had frozen in place. A few of them grasped their weapon belts nervously. They knew something bad was going to happen, but they didn't know what.

"Say goodbye, you bastards," Lee muttered as Val's countdown reached "three… two…one…"

The system worked as it was supposed to, and the two docking doors—each large enough to admit two Marine assault landers side by side—blew out into space. The docking bay was huge, but, with openings that size, all the air inside shot out in less than three seconds, creating a brief hurricane force blast that carried every loose object in the bay with it. The Mekota warriors, some already dead or injured by collisions with flying equipment, were spit out of the ship at velocities on the order of fifty meters per second. A moment later, any that survived the ejection died as they crashed into the hull of their own ship 100 meters away.

The windows of the gallery held, and the two men watched the whole thing happen.

"Hot damn!" Lee exclaimed. "Ensign, I think you just killed more Turnips than any Marine unit has ever done in combat."

* * *

"Two of the Mekota are now in the portside access passage to the flag bridge," Val reported.

Lorna and her staff tensed, and the two Marines gave their weapons a final check. They could see the advancing aliens on the monitor that covered the passageway in question.

Suddenly, mayhem erupted in the narrow corridor, and something spattered against the lens of the camera, obscuring the view.

"Correction," Val said. "There are two *dead* Mekota in the portside access passage." Some of the obscuring fluid dripped off the lens, giving them a blurry view of the three Marines advancing up the passage. Lorna smiled as her staff gave a ragged cheer.

* * *

"Val, internal security status?" Amy Ling asked. "All secure forward of frame two six two, Captain," the AI said. "There is still activity aft of that point, and Major McGuinness is sending additional Marines. I am blind in that area, so I cannot give a more detailed report; however, we control everything forward of Fusion Three and the aft impeller rooms."

On the bridge, Ling breathed a sigh of relief. The ship was still hers, and her Marines were kicking ass. The Mekota had tried to send another wave of boarders, but engineering had managed to get point defense six and eight back online. The fast-tracking, rapid-fire lasers had turned the space between the two ships into a killing zone. None of the would-be invaders reached *Valkyrie*, and after a while, they stopped coming.

Still at a stalemate, though, Ling thought. *Until something changes, neither side has won this battle.*

* * *

"Yes, sir, that's *Valkyrie*, but she's locked up tight against the Turnip ship. There can't be more than a hundred meters between them."

Commander Sanchez studied the imagery. LFS *Wraith* and the two destroyers were 20,000 kilometers from the stricken flagship, but they needed to get closer before they could assist. *Maybe we're too late. Maybe they've captured her and killed everyone aboard. We can give them some serious payback, but I don't dare open fire until I know the situation.*

* * *

"I think that's the last of 'em, sir," Bartley reported to Major McGuinness. "We're back in Fusion Three now, and First Platoon is checking every compartment and equipment closet aft of here, just to make sure we got 'em all. Looks like about thirty Turnips got in the back door, and they're all dead now. I lost two Marines in the process, plus two wounded."

"Roger that, Bartley. Sorry about your casualties, but you did a good job. Take a break where you are. Watch the engineers work for a while."

"Aye, sir."

Seated on the deck with her back against the bulkhead, Bartley watched as the engineering officer stepped up to a large console at the far end of the compartment.

"Okay, boys and girls, time for the smoke test," Lieutenant Murtaugh said. It was an old engineering joke: *How do you test a piece of equipment? Answer: Turn it on, and if nothing starts smoking, it's good.*

He turned to the console and keyed in the commands that would initiate Fusion Three's start-up sequence. Anxiously, he watched the readouts as the reactor went through its self-test, then started to come alive. Reaction mass, mostly ionized deuterium, filled the containment chamber, laser initiators fired, and a miniature star was born inside. Power generators kicked in to harness the energy. Murtaugh watched the displays come up to full power, but he held it there for another thirty seconds just to make sure. Then he began feeding the output to the ship's power grid.

He opened the channel to damage control central. "Fusion Three is online."

* * *

"Ma'am, Fusion Three's back up. Starting to get response from some of the sub-systems," Amy Ling's systems tech reported.

At the tactical station, Lieutenant Commander Ashton stared at his console in disbelief, as three lights came on that had been dark for some time. For the moment, they were yellow, but his display showed a word that brought him great excitement: CHARGING.

"Captain, I've got *grasers* coming online! Numbers eight, ten, and twelve are charging now."

"I suggest you pick your targets carefully, Mr. Ashton," Ling replied calmly. "At this range, I'd prefer that you *not* hit their fusion reactors."

* * *

"Oh, *shit!*"

Raoul Sanchez didn't notice who on *Wraith's* bridge had uttered the expletive and, at the moment, he didn't care. He was captivated by the high-resolution image on the screen in front of him.

Grasers are tight, coherent beams of energy, but their effect diminishes with distance. At 10,000 kilometers, *Valkyrie's* main graser batteries might not have penetrated the Mekota dreadnought's heavy armor. But at 100 *meters*, that armor was worse than nonexistent—worse because the heavy metal it was made of converted instantly to a jet of star-hot metallic plasma that stabbed straight into the bowels of the alien ship.

On the side of the Mekota dreadnought facing *Valkyrie*, the full effect wasn't apparent. The 75-centimeter beams produced neat, round, glowing holes in the alien hull. But inside that hull, the fires of Hell erupted. Decks, bulkheads, atmosphere, and anything else that got in the way of the beams added fuel to the plasma storm. Compartments blew apart, equipment vaporized, and Mekota crewmembers simply ceased to exist. On five of the ship's thirty-six decks, not a single alien survived, as the destruction spread upward, downward, and outward from the points of impact. The deeper the beams penetrated, the worse it got until, on the side of the huge ship facing *away* from the LFS flagship (the side that Raoul Sanchez was seeing), a huge section of the alien hull blew outward in a massive explosion of white-hot fragments. Then slowly, almost gracefully, the rest of the Mekota ship began to break apart.

On *Valkyrie's* bridge, Amy Ling turned to her tactical officer. "I believe you can cease fire, Mr. Ashton," she said in a perfectly matter-of-fact tone as the bridge crew broke out in wild cheering. Noting the gravity tractor holding her ship no longer existed, she said, "Helm, take us out of this junkyard."

* * *

In the streets of the capital city, there was wild jubilation. It was part of a victory celebration that involved almost the entire population of the planet that the humans now called CHP, for Copper Hills Prime. Inside the executive palace known as the Halls of the Heart, the mood was joyful but somewhat more subdued.

"Truthfully, Warrior Queen," Heart of the Warriors confided, "I expected this battle to be our last. Victory has taken us by surprise, and now we must consider what to do with it. Much as I would like to go outside and join the revelry, duty bids me stay here and plan how best to press our advantage. Since you were the architect of that victory, I welcome your advice."

"I agree we must press the advantage," Lorna said, "and I wish we had the strength to launch a thrust all the way to the Mekota homeworld. We probably won't get a better chance for a long time, but our victory has been costly. We don't want to make the same mistake our enemy made—to overextend ourselves.

"Having said that," she continued, "there are a number of things we ought to do. The first thing—one that can be done without using any resources—should be to spread the word along the Akara frontier, telling every clan what we have done and encouraging them to hit the Mekota *now*, as hard as they can. If your estimates of the enemy's fleet strength are accurate, they must have pulled forces from all along the line to mount the attack on us. That will leave them weakened in other places, and now, they can't reinforce those places quickly."

"Word will spread, even without encouragement," Heart of the Copper Hills replied, "but you are right. We need to dispatch couriers to all the clans to get them moving. Besides, I look forward to hearing apologies from those Hearts who told me I was wrong to ally myself with humans." He favored the assembled group with a royal Akara tongue-flashing grin.

"Some have been defending so long, I wonder if they even re-member how to mount an offensive," Heart of the Warriors grum-bled. "But as you say, Warrior Queen, it costs us nothing to twist their tails and maybe some of them will surprise us."

"As for us," Lorna said, "we cannot mount a major offensive un-til we've had time to repair and rebuild our fleets. In fact, my lords, I must advise you that I will be leaving you shortly. I have many ships that are in sore need of the Lunar dockyards. I have enough undam-aged—or at least combat-effective—ships to form a battlecruiser division around LFS *Isis*. I intend to leave that group with you under Admiral Torrey." She nodded to Torrey, who was seated on her right. "We have also brought in our missile colliers from the outer system, so *Isis* and her group will have full loads of missiles again. The colliers will remain here and can rearm the group several times over if necessary.

"There are actions you can take that will make the most of the forces available. I suggest you dispatch raiding forces to the five sys-tems the Mekota recently took from you—not to retake those sys-tems, but simply to destroy the Mekota support infrastructure. If you move quickly, you may be able to destroy the service vessels they've brought up before they have a chance to pull back again. Destroying them may do more to cripple the Mekota than any other action we might take."

"Agreed." Heart of the Warriors made a gesture of assent. "Much as I'd like to let our crews celebrate victory, we need to get some of them back into action immediately. At least, this mission should be easier for them than the last.

"Heart of the Second Group," he turned to the Lizard Lorna still thought of as Captain, "you have served the Clan well since the day you first encountered these humans who have become our Clanbrothers. Now, I have another mission for you. You will plan these attacks on the five systems and lead them yourself. You may requisition whatever forces you need, but I will need a plan from you by tomorrow, with your mission to depart no later than three days hence."

"Yes, my lord."

"Admiral Torrey," the old one-armed warrior continued, "I would be pleased if you would spare a few ships to accompany these raiding missions to protect our precious tails and help us suppress any Mekota warships we might happen to meet."

"I would be honored to do so, my lord," Torrey said.

* * * * *

Chapter Twenty-Five

The Mekota Homeworld

"Explain why you should continue to exist, Fifth of Yellow," the First Guardian said, "and do not think to misdirect us. At the moment, I am inclined to give you a swift and merciful end, but if you are not truthful, the fleshworms await."

The Guardian's use of her title reminded First Leader that, while she might have been a supreme commander of forces on the Akara frontier, in this chamber, she was of lowly rank, too low to even be present had she not been summoned. At the mention of fleshworms, all color drained from her crest. The tiny creatures, discovered on a planet in the outer reaches of the Sphere, would feed on almost anything organic and seemed to have a taste for Mekota flesh. A few of them would burrow into the victim's body, unnoticed at first, but they would reproduce rapidly. By the time symptoms of infestation appeared, it would be too late. It would take twelves of days for an infected Mekota to die, having been literally eaten alive from within; but long before that, the unfortunate victim would be begging for death.

Execution by fleshworms was a punishment reserved for those whom the Guardians wished to make a horrible example.

"First Guardian," she began, "I did not return to beg for my life. I would have died in battle most willingly, but the battle was already lost, and I had no means to continue to fight. The only duty that remained was to return and report to the Guardians. My ship's systems were damaged. I could not even transfer records of the battle to the courier. There was no one else who had seen the fullness of it, so I brought the information myself. I have given my knowledge to you, and you may now execute me unless there is additional information I can provide."

It was a lie, of course. She *was* begging for her life while trying not to appear to do so. She had deliberately left many details out of her first report. As long as the Guardians had questions, she would survive to provide answers, answers she hoped would convince them to spare her in the end.

She was right. They had many questions, and she gave them her prepared answers. No other witnesses survived to contradict her. Those she'd allowed to live could only provide details to support her version of the battle. In the telling of that version, the human fleet grew to many times its actual size, and the enemy's ships and weapons became even more formidable. By the time she finished, the horrified Guardians were convinced no Mekota fleet of any size could have prevailed against them.

There were uncomfortable moments, however.

"Did it occur to you," Second of the Yellow asked, "that, perhaps, the humans trapped you so easily because you used *the same plan* you have used in every planetary assault since you took command on the frontier?"

"It was a proven plan, Guardian, one that has worked well in many battles. You yourself used the same plan against—"

"I used it *once!*" the Guardian snarled. "And it succeeded. Since then, other fleet leaders have followed it blindly instead of using their brains to come up with a plan of their own. Our enemies may be inferior, but they are not *stupid*. You were dealing with *humans*, the most devious and cunning vermin in the galaxy. Did you think they would not learn your tactics when you use them repeatedly?"

"Forgive me, Guardian, but I had no way of knowing I would be dealing with humans. This was a mission against the Akara—"

"The reptiles are just as bad! They have hampered your efforts, despite our superior numbers and technology. Now, with the aid of the humans, they were able to crush you. Even without the humans, they might have stopped you once again."

"No, Guardian, they would *not* have done so!" She decided the time had come to be a bit defiant. She sensed that First Guardian was becoming weary of the Yellow's attempts to blame the failure entirely on her. "The reptiles fought hard and were tougher than we thought they would be, but without the humans, they would have fallen."

"Enough!" First Guardian commanded. "As of this moment, the war with the Akara is ended. The true threat to us comes from the humans, and we must deal with it. Withdraw our forces from the Akara frontier and leave only enough to defend against a reptile invasion of the Sphere. Without humans to assist, the reptiles do not have the strength to conduct such an invasion. We must make sure the humans cannot provide that assistance.

"This one battle cost more than two twelve-parts of our forces. With what we leave to defend the Akara side of the Sphere, we will have but half our force available, and some must be held in reserve to defend the homeworlds. What remains will still be a much larger force than was just defeated and will be sent against the human home system. We must remove this threat from within the Sphere!"

"First Guardian!" The Second of the Yellow sounded shocked. "This is a frightening gamble. If we lose that battle…"

"I am aware of the consequences, just as I am aware of the consequences if we do *not* crush the humans." Her crest was a ripple of color, the Mekota equivalent of a sigh. "We thought to simply leave them alone and hope they would take no further action. They did not even have Otherspace technology, but now they are loose among the stars. If we do not stop them now, they will come for us—*here*, to the homeworld. No doubt, their reptile allies have already told them where to find us."

"But leaving the Akara unchecked…" the Second of the Yellow persisted. "Surely that is unwise. The reptiles have launched offensives against several worlds, have destroyed parts of our fleet support structure, and are attacking all along the frontier."

"I have seen the reports. This is not a coordinated offensive. They are harassing us, but I am convinced if we pull back, they will pause. We *must* pull back to positions we can defend, not try to defend positions we cannot hold. I understand your concern. We will pull back and hold for a time, and if they do not press us, we will gather our forces and attack the humans. We can come back and deal with the reptiles once their allies have been removed.

"The attack on the humans is a gamble, one that must succeed, or we are lost. For that reason, Second of the Yellow, you will lead that attack yourself. You are a skillful warrior-leader, and you have complained about the tactics used in this battle. Now, we give you the opportunity to demonstrate how it *should* have been done.

She turned to the lowly Fifth of Yellow who, for a few moments, had been grateful *not* to be the center of attention. "As for you, I have decided to be merciful. You will join the attack force as a lowly

Triforce leader, and I'm sure Second of the Yellow will find a suitable place for you at the forefront of the battle, where you will once again have the chance to prove yourself against these humans. This time, you will not return, unless it is to report victory. Otherwise, you *will* be given to the fleshworms."

* * *

TerraNova City, Luna

"**C**ome now, lass, do you nae think you're bein' just a wee bit modest?"

Mick O'Hara's affected Irish accent brought a smile to Lorna's lips, but it was a fleeting smile.

"Admiral, I—"

"Oh, come on, Lorna, it's me, Mick. You can skip the formalities. There's nobody here but us old-timers, and besides, *you* had this job before I did."

"All right, then, *Mick*...and Charlie." She aimed a nod at Bender. "But I lost seven ships and a lot of good people. Over half the fleet took heavy damage. The yard dogs are still shaking their heads over *Valkyrie's* condition, and *Nike's* not much better. Sure, we won the battle, but it was costly.

"The Copper Hills Akara are even in worse shape," she continued. "They lost over half their fleet outright and half of those left are out of commission for repairs."

"I don't have a lot of military experience," O'Hara admitted, "but you went against an enemy that outnumbered you ten to one, and you *annihilated* them. Wiped 'em out. You can complain about losses and battle damage, but on their side, there's nobody left to complain."

"I *do* have military experience," Bender said, "and I agree with Mick. The Akara may have taken losses, but from what their diplomats are telling us, they can rebuild their fleet three times over just using the wreckage of Turnip warships you've left scattered all over their system. Besides, you've done more than win a battle. You've cemented a solid alliance with an alien race. They tell me there are little villages on Copper Hills Prime where ordinary Lizard citizens are hanging pictures of you on their walls. I hear they're building a huge statue of you in the public square in front of the Halls of the Heart."

"It's *not* a statue of *me*," Lorna insisted, reddening with embarrassment. "It's a monument to our combined forces. I've seen the plans, and it should be impressive. It depicts humans and Akara together, advancing to meet a common enemy. But you're right—at the moment, we can do no wrong as far as the Copper Hills Clan are concerned. Unfortunately, we may need that alliance in the future."

"You really think the Mekota will come for us?" Mick seemed doubtful.

"I don't know, but we have to assume some of them survived and returned to their bases. I don't *think* any of their big warships got away, but the battle was spread out over a huge area of space, and we destroyed many of their courier ships. We probably didn't catch them all. That means the Mekota must know who maimed them so badly. If the Akara are even close to being right about Mekota fleet strength, they can still put together a force much larger than the one that attacked Copper Hills Prime, and the logical place to send it would be here. They know where we live, and, right now, they probably see us as more of a threat than the Akara."

* * *

Outer Reaches of the Sol System

Lorna was right, and, eventually, the Mekota came. But the delay while the Mekota waited to see if the Akara would press forward proved to be their undoing. Not only did it give the humans time to repair and strengthen their fleets, it gave the Akara time to rebuild their own forces as well. And the Lizards made good on their promise to support their human allies.

The Mekota came with a much larger force—over a thousand ships—and their tactics were better than those used against the Akara. They'd also made improvements in their point-defense systems, and a few of their ships were equipped with primitive missiles. But in the end, none of those factors had much effect on the outcome.

They entered the Sol System from three directions, on the theory that at least one of their thrusts ought to penetrate far enough into the inner system to attack Earth itself. But the tactic gave the humans the advantage of interior lines. They could shift their forces from one front to another, while the Mekota could not do the same without significant delay. More importantly, the human forces were operating at home this time. They were able to dispatch missile colliers from Earth and Luna, allowing their warships to disengage briefly, rearm with the one weapon that was most effective against their enemy, and rejoin the battle with full magazines.

As for the Mekota missiles, they had never been tested in battle against enemy ships that mounted an effective point defense. Not one human ship fell prey to them and, unlike their enemies, the Mekota could not replenish their missile supply once they'd engaged.

Lorna was aware of the difficulties involved in coordinating a multi-national fleet, so she did her best to eliminate the need. Once the Mekota triple thrust tactic was apparent, she led the LFS fleet against what appeared to be the strongest Mekota force. The Americans and Japanese were given the responsibility of handling one of the other enemy formations, while British and Australian forces took on the third. The Brits and Aussies made up the lightest of the human fleets, but they decimated the incoming aliens and harassed the survivors until reinforcements arrived in the form of the Akara, who fell on the Mekota from the rear just as the LFS forces had done in the battle for Copper Hills Prime.

If the Mekota had been able to achieve surprise, they might have had a chance of success, and they might have come close enough to inflict damage on Earth and Luna. But the Akara, scouting their frontier and sending probes into the Mekota sphere, had not failed to notice the drawdown of enemy forces there. They'd correctly deduced that the Mekota were preparing an offensive, and when their deep scouts reported a fleet being assembled on the side of the sphere where Sol was located, they sent their own fleet, as many warships as they could spare, to assist their human allies. They were already in place in the outer system when the attackers arrived, and they watched silently as the Mekota forces lumbered by without seeing them. When they attacked, the Mekota recognized them and tried to engage them in the usual manner, only to discover—to their dismay—that the Lizard warships now had missiles as well!

It had been Lorna's suggestion. Charlie Bender hadn't been comfortable with it, but she had managed to overcome his objections.

"The Akara can't duplicate our missile technology," she'd told him. "They lack ultra-miniature electronics. We could give them our best missiles tomorrow, and they wouldn't be able to figure out how they work, let alone replicate them. But that technology is built into the missiles themselves. You don't need that degree of miniaturization for a basic launch system.

"We have thousands of Broadsword Mark IIs in our stockpiles, strictly for reserves since they're technically obsolete. But they can still be launched from any standard Broadsword rail or tube system. Suppose we come up with a basic launcher, something that could be mounted externally on an Akara ship—a non-reloadable box launcher, for example, or a belt system like we use for the Wolfpacks. Since the Mark IIs don't have the slave-guidance or command mode capabilities of the Mark IV, the control system can be simple—two lights and two switches. You switch the missile on, you get a ready light. You aim your ship at the enemy, close the range until the target lock light comes on, and hit the second switch to launch. I'm sure the engineers can come up with something that simple. The only sensitive technology we'd be giving them is the missile itself, and they don't have the ability to figure it out or duplicate it."

"True," Mick O'Hara said, his 'engineering brain' suddenly coming online, "but if they don't have the ship's targeting and control capabilities, they'd have to get close enough for the missile's seeker head to lock on to the target."

"Right," Lorna said, "they'd have to get within about twenty thousand kilometers, at which point the missile's kill probability would be about ninety-nine percent. But the main laser batteries of a Mekota dreadnought only have an effective range of about twelve thousand kilometers. Our Lizard friends can still attack them without coming under fire."

She had proposed the idea immediately after the battle of Copper Hills Prime, and it hadn't taken long to convince them. O'Hara dispatched a shipload of the obsolete missiles and a gaggle of Lunar engineers to the Akara. By the time they arrived, the engineers had already worked out a design for the launchers and control systems. While the Lizards were nowhere near the LFS in micro-electronics, their engineers were competent with their own technology. It took them only a month to come up with a prototype launcher and mount it on a ship for testing. Within three months, they had equipped a significant number of ships with the new system. By the time the Mekota decided to move, nearly the entire Akara fleet was missile-armed.

The new Akara weaponry was not as sophisticated as that of the LFS or the other Earth nations, nor could they carry anywhere near the missile load of a human warship, but it was more than a match for any defense the Mekota could mount. To Lorna's delight—and that of her alien allies—the Akara were able to inflict crushing damage on the Mekota with minimal losses of their own.

When the tattered remains of the Mekota fleet finally turned to flee, the allies made only a token effort to stop them. There was no longer any need for operational secrecy, and both humans and Akara agreed the few dozen battered dreadnoughts that survived would only convince the enemy not to return.

As for Fifth of the Yellow, the fleshworms were denied their meal after all. At the vanguard of the Mekota main thrust, her Triforce had encountered the LFS Third Battle Group, led by the new-ly-built battlecruiser *Sorceress*. The encounter lasted less than a minute, but the drifting wreckage of the Triforce and the scattered remains of its Mekota crews would eventually have to be marked with a beacon as a hazard to navigation.

The crushing defeat caused a radical change in Mekota leadership. First Guardian was assassinated, her place taken by Second of the Red, unchallenged by the Yellow, whose leadership had been decimated in the battle. The remains of the Mekota fleet were summoned home for fear of an invasion of their own worlds. In a short time, the Mekota Sphere of influence contracted to less than half its former size. Earth was now thirty light-years *outside* the Sphere, as were the worlds of the Akara frontier.

Six months later, an LFS battle squadron, probing in the direction of the Sphere, encountered a lone Mekota ship—a commerce vessel of the Blue—and forced it to surrender without a shot. To the surprise of the Mekota crew, the ship was released and sent on its way with a message:

Neither the humans of Earth nor the Akara wish to continue a war with the Mekota. If you make no further attacks, we will not retaliate. We will consider commerce with the Mekota if you keep your warships in your own space. To reply to this message, send one ship—alone and unarmed—to Earth or to the Akara world of the Copper Hills. We await your answer.

Several months passed before a small Mekota ship appeared in the Sol System, crewed only by carrier drones and carrying a return message. The message described the now-smaller boundaries of the Mekota Sphere and advised them that the Mekota wished no further contact with the humans or their reptile allies. The Mekota would remain within their territory, and the humans and Akara were warned to stay out of it. The Mekota, the message said, had no desire for commerce with "inferior races."

After conferring with the Akara, Mick O'Hara sent the Mekota ship home with a simple reply: We agree. Stay within your boundaries and we will take no further action. We will not enter your territory unless you violate this agreement.

This would be marked by historians as the beginning of the so-called Pax Galactica—a period of relative peace in Earth's corner of the galaxy. There would be other conflicts as the LFS ventured outward to explore and conduct trade, but it would be more than a century before either humans or Akara found themselves in a war for survival.

* * * * *

Epilogue

The Akara Homeworld

"**O**migosh, Mom! That's *you!*"

Lorna winced. She had hoped that detail would escape Carla's notice. "No, it's not, honey. That's the Valkyrie. They took the image from the ship's hull artwork."

"It may be the Valkyrie," the teenager replied skeptically, "but she's got *your* face. Look, she's even got that little scar on her left cheek, the one you're so self-conscious about." Carla began walking back and forth, taking in details of the sculpture. The massive work of art was nearly fifty meters wide and over twenty meters high. "Besides, the Valkyrie on the ship has bigger boobs. These look more like yours."

"Her boobs are *covered*," Lorna protested, "and so are mine…at least they have been whenever these people have seen me. I'm sure you're mistaken."

"Hers are *barely* covered." Carla giggled. "And I've seen yours. You can't fool me. C'mon, Mom, it's *you*, isn't it?"

Lorna sighed as her daughter continued to examine the sculpture from all angles.

"Aha, here's more proof. The one on the right is supposed to be Isis, the Egyptian goddess. I suppose you're going to say that comes from ship artwork, too, but *this* one has Aunt Robin's face, and *her* flagship was LFS *Isis* in the big battle. Hmmm…not sure about the one on the left, though."

"Nike?" Lorna smiled. "Well, that one's tough since Nike's female, but they did manage to make her look a *little* like Jeff Jones, and they definitely gave her a more masculine, African-ancestry look. The original Nike—and the one in LFS *Nike's* hull artwork—is a *Greek* goddess if you recall."

"I knew it!" Carla crowed. "These *are* supposed to be the real heroes—the Valkyrie is you!"

The monument was impressive. It dominated the courtyard in front of the Halls of the Heart, and Lorna was forced to admit the Lizard sculptors had done an amazing job of capturing the human faces and figures—enough so that she'd been *very* embarrassed the first time she'd seen it many years ago.

The statuary depicted a horde of Lizard warriors, clad in ancient armor and armed with blades, battle-axes, and lances, charging fiercely into battle. At the front and center of the charge was a Lizard who towered over the other warriors, brandishing a sword that looked suspiciously like an oversized LFS Marine combat knife and wearing an ancient headdress that marked him as a clan war-leader. He was flanked on either side by the equally towering figures of Nike and Isis, the former armed with a drawn bow, the latter with a long spear.

But in the center of the sculpture, towering over *everything*, were two more figures. On the right, mounted on a snarling dragon-like creature of Akara mythology, was an ancient Lizard warrior with only one arm, holding a huge battle-axe. On the left—the position of honor, for the left-handed Akara—rode the Valkyrie on her winged horse, with her longsword raised above her head.

"Okay," Lorna admitted. "You win. But just so you get this in the proper perspective, the Akara riding the dragon is the old Heart of the Warriors, the one you met at the fancy dinner at the embassy."

"Right, with one arm, I see that."

"And the one here in front, between Nike and Isis, is the new Heart of the Warriors. You met him as well. He was the Akara second-in-command in that battle."

"Awesome!" Carla said. "My mom, the Babe on the Horse."

"I am soooo going to have words with Auntie Roni about that." Lorna grimaced. "I wish she had never told you that story."

"Aw, c'mon, Mom. Just because the Marines think you're Superwoman...I think it's great."

"Look, honey." Lorna sighed. "I just happened to be in the right place at the right moment in history. Yes, I think I'm rather good at what I do, but the rest of it was just...fate, or destiny, or whatever you want to call it. Other than that, I'm still your mom, I still put my boots on one at a time, and I still wear a bra to keep my not-so-spectacular boobs from sagging. And by the way, young lady, don't think I haven't noticed that *you* aren't wearing one." She tried to put a stern expression on her face.

"Mom!" Carla rolled her eyes. "It's too hot here, and besides, I'm only fifteen. And the Lizards don't pay attention anyway."

"The Lizards may not, but you distracted that young ensign at the embassy this morning to the point where he almost walked into a wall. You may only be fifteen, but you've already got a well-developed figure. Obviously, you take after your *other* mother in that department."

"I wish I'd known Momma Carla," the girl said wistfully. "From what you've told me, she was a really special person."

"Yes, she was," Lorna said quietly, "and you're her daughter as much as you are mine. I can see her in you, and that makes me incredibly happy."

She walked over to a long stone bench in front of the great monument and sat down. Carla continued to prowl around the statuary for a while, taking in all its details and capturing images of it from all angles with her data pad.

Finally, she came and sat beside Lorna. "I guess this explains a lot of things. The Lizards have treated me like a minor goddess ever since we got here. They kept calling me *segrana,* a word I didn't recognize, so I uplinked to Val, and she told me it means 'from the egg of the queen.' It's their word for 'princess.'"

"You've certainly talked to a lot of them. At least you know the Gadget really works."

"Well, I knew that already. But it's different, using it myself—and not just with Val or Mike."

Lorna looked at her daughter with pride. Perhaps the girl would never be a fleet officer, but Lorna was certain she was destined for greatness. The Gadget was just one example. At fifteen, Carla had already completed her high school studies and been accepted for an advanced program in science at Luna University, where she would pursue her passion for astrophysics. This trip was a graduation present for her. Even as a little girl, she'd been fascinated by the Lizards and had peppered her mother with questions about them and their world. That fascination had led to her most recent accomplishment.

Two years ago, she'd taken top honors in the LFS Youth Science Competition, with a study on heavy element formation in supergiant stars, a study that impressed even Luna's top astrophysicists. For this year's competition, though, she'd decided to do something different, something totally outside her favorite field of study.

She'd once asked Mike why humans couldn't speak Akara. The AI explained that it was mostly a matter of pitch. The human palate could shape the sounds of the Akara language, but human vocal cords couldn't reach the broad range of high-frequency sounds that were as vital to the language as the words themselves.

"You mean, if my voice were a couple of octaves higher-pitched, I could do it?" she had asked.

"No, more like five octaves, and you'd have to cover a four-octave range as well," Mike explained. "Akara speech pushes beyond the limit of human hearing. The part of it that humans *can* hear sounds like high-pitched bird calls. And to an Akara, our speech is a low-pitched rumbling, much of it below the lower limits of *their* hearing. They can sense low-frequency vibration with their tongues, but they can't make sense of it."

"But suppose you used a frequency converter to raise the pitch and maybe some kind of expander to stretch out the range. Couldn't you learn to form words that could be electronically converted into something the Akara could understand?"

Thus was born the idea for the Gadget. The actual construction was simple, at least for a teenager who regularly designed her own molycirc chips just for fun. But to use it, she had to learn how to speak Akara—or at least, the human-pitched version she dubbed Low Akara. With Mike as a tutor, she'd become reasonably fluent in a matter of weeks. She'd also had to make the Gadget work both ways, using a downward frequency conversion and audio compression to convert Lizard speech into Low Akara. She'd done that part first so she could hear what Low Akara would sound like. Mike, the only person available to her who spoke and understood real Akara speech, had willingly served as her test subject.

When she'd presented her project at the Competition, the judges had been skeptical. Despite Mike's assurances, they'd asked a member of the Akara trade delegation to come to the exhibition hall and verify that the device worked. The Lizard had been astonished and delighted, and after a few minutes of conversation, had told them that, while her accent was strange, her words were perfectly understandable—as, apparently, were his words to her.

Still, one of the judges, a commander in the Lunar Corps of Engineers, had been unconvinced. "Obviously, it works," she'd told Carla. "And it's a novel concept, but it really hasn't much practical application. It requires a person to learn a language—this Low Akara, as you call it—to use it. Why bother with that when an AI can interpret for you without a strange accent and with nearly instantaneous translation?"

At that point, another judge, an executive of Terra Corporation, had intervened. "I don't think you understand, Commander. This is revolutionary! We've dealt with the Akara for well over a decade, but we've never been able to speak with them unless an AI is available to translate.

"We've puzzled out each other's *written* languages to some degree, and we've developed a limited sign language, but the sign language requires a learning curve on both sides since it's not a native language for either of us. We can pass notes to each other—a very cumbersome method of communication—but again, one side has to be able to read the other's language.

"For all these years, the LFS fleet contingent stationed at Copper Hills Prime has *always* included a battlecruiser for the sole purpose of having an AI available so we could *talk* to the Akara, and that's no help to researchers, traders, and diplomatic people on other Akara worlds, or even those on Copper Hills Prime who don't have access to fleet communication channels. What I see here is a device that solves all those problems and probably costs less than a tenth of a Gold Lunar to manufacture. With this device, a human who has learned to speak this Low Akara language can speak to *any* Akara, *anywhere.* Many of my commercial people have to learn other languages to deal with suppliers, clients, and so forth. I don't see that as an obstacle at all. And if I understand it correctly, this device will work even with those Akara clans who don't speak the common Akara language. It'll just be a different Low language for the user to learn."

"Yes, sir," Carla had replied, "as long as the person you want to communicate with is an Akara. The frequency conversion is specifically set up for their audio range."

At that point, the Akara had joined in, asking Carla if—assuming the Lizards could learn to speak a high-pitched variant of a common human language—a comparable device could be made to convert *that* into regular *human* speech.

"I don't see why not," she'd told him. "If I can learn to speak Low Akara, there's no reason why an Akara shouldn't be able to speak High English. And I don't think you'd even need a new device. This one should be able to handle both applications. It's not doing a translation. It's just processing sounds and converting them to a different frequency range.

"Here, try this," she told him in Low Akara. "Repeat these words, just as you hear them—the quick brown fox jumps over the lazy dog." She said it in English. Normally, she used an earbud for the low-frequency output, but this time, she switched it to the unit's small speaker so all of them could hear.

The Akara shrugged. The words, or rather, the high-frequency version that he'd heard from the Gadget, meant nothing to him, but he dutifully repeated them as best he could. "Tsee queek brun fokes choomps ovar tsee lahzy tog," came out of the Gadget's speaker.

"See!" Carla crowed as the judges' jaws dropped. "If you can get that close on the first try without even knowing the language, you've just proved it. An Akara *can* speak English...er, *High* English, that is."

In the end, they'd given her the top prize. More importantly, the Terra Corporation people had come to see her before the presentation. Lunar law was extremely strict about intellectual property rights, and Carla had more business sense than many citizens twice her age. With guidance from Lorna and other well-placed LFS 'family members,' including CEO 'Uncle Mick' O'Hara, she'd agreed to sell them the design specifications and the rights to manufacture the Gadget, but she hadn't sold them cheaply, and she'd insisted on royalties per unit as well. In addition, they'd paid a handsome retainer for her services as a consultant on future improvements to the device.

Carla had worked with Mike to develop a teaching program that would help humans learn the Low Akara language, and another to teach High English to the Akara. Again, Terra Corporation had paid her handsomely for the rights to those programs, including royalties. The first 10,000-unit production run of the Gadget—now officially dubbed the AHSI, for Akara-Human Speech Interface—was sold out within days, with nearly half of the run being purchased by the Akara Copper Hills Trade Consortium. The Lizards also paid in advance for another 5,000 units to be delivered from the next production run.

At fifteen, Carla was on her way to becoming a very wealthy young woman. "At least," she told her mother, "I won't have to worry about research grants when I get my degrees."

Now, Lorna looked at her precocious daughter with a pride that almost brought tears to her eyes. *I'm sure she got her brains from Carla as well as her hair and figure, but she does have my eyes, and she's going to be tall, like me.*

"So, Egg of the Queen, what do you think of Copper Hills Prime so far?" she asked, with a smile.

"I like it here. I could live here. I've been off Luna a few times, but it's still kind of weird, standing under an open sky like this with no dome and no pressure suit. This planet is a lot warmer than I'm used to, but it's a beautiful place, and the Lizards are nice people. Are you really thinking about coming here when you retire?"

"Well, maybe not permanently, but Heart of the Copper Hills insisted on giving me a nice piece of land up in the mountains. It'll be a great place for a vacation home where we can spend a few months at a time. You'll see. I'm going to charter a flyer to take us up there in a couple of days."

"That'll be great. I really want to see it. But you know, Mom, the best part of being here is being with you. I know how busy you are with the fleet, and you spend time with me at home. But it's nice to have you all to myself for a while."

"Thank you, honey." Lorna felt her eyes starting to mist up. "I wish we'd been able to do this more often over the years."

"It's okay, Mom, I understand. You've been out there, making the galaxy safe for me and everybody else. You're a real heroine, and everybody respects you for it, especially me.

"Besides," she added with an impish grin, "being the Egg of the Queen is okay, but I'd *really* rather be known as the Valkyrie's daughter."

# # # # #

About John E. Siers

John E. Siers is a Viet Nam–era Air Force veteran who spent several decades working as a software developer, designing analytical systems for corporate clients.

An avid reader of science fiction since grade school, John started writing in the late 1970s, mostly for his own enjoyment. He wrote for more than 20 years and produced three complete novels before ever showing his work to anyone.

Escaping from the overcrowded northeast, John moved to Tennessee in 1997. Encouraged by friends, he finally published his first novel, The Moon and Beyond, in late 2012, followed by Someday the Stars in 2013. The latter won the 2014 Darrell Award for Best SF Novel by a Midsouth Author.

John's Lunar Free State series had grown to four novels—with no thought of doing anything outside his own comfort zone—when he encountered William Alan Webb at MidSouthCon in 2019. Bill led John astray, tempting him with visions of other universes, whispering names like Four Horsemen, Last Brigade, and finally, Hit World.

John succumbed to the temptation, and The Ferryman and The Dragons of Styx are the results. He has since entered a rehab program and produced a fifth novel in his own universe.

John lives with his wife, son, dog, and two cats in west Tennessee. In his spare time (what there is of it) he runs his own firearm repair and service business under the trade name of Gunsmith Jack. Readers can follow him on Amazon, Facebook, or his own website at www.lunarfreestate.com.

* * * * *

Meet the author and other CKP authors on the Factory Floor:

https://www.facebook.com/groups/461794864654198

* * * * *

Did you like this book?
Please write a review!

* * * * *

The following is an

Excerpt from Book One of Abner Fortis, ISMC:

Cherry Drop

_____

P.A. Piatt

Available from Theogony Books

eBook and Paperback

Excerpt from "Cherry Drop:"

"Here they come!"

A low, throbbing buzz rose from the trees and the undergrowth shook. Thousands of bugs exploded out of the jungle, and Fortis' breath caught in his throat. The insects tumbled over each other in a rolling, skittering mass that engulfed everything in its path. The Space Marines didn't need an order to open fire. Rifles cracked and the grenade launcher thumped over and over as they tried to stem the tide of bugs. Grenades tore holes in the ranks of the bugs and well-aimed rifle fire dropped many more. Still, the bugs advanced.

Hawkins' voice boomed in Fortis' ear. "LT, fall back behind the fighting position, clear the way for the heavy weapons."

Fortis looked over his shoulder and saw the fighting holes bristling with Marines who couldn't fire for fear of hitting their own comrades. He thumped Thorsen on the shoulder.

"Fall back!" he ordered. "Take up positions behind the fighting holes."

Thorsen stopped firing and moved among the other Marines, relaying Fortis' order. One by one, the Marines stopped firing and made for the rear. As the gunfire slacked off, the bugs closed ranks and continued forward.

After the last Marine had fallen back, Fortis motioned to Thorsen.

"Let's go!"

Thorsen turned and let out a blood-chilling scream. A bug had approached unnoticed and buried its stinger deep in Thorsen's calf. The stricken Marine fell to the ground and began to convulse as the neurotoxin entered his bloodstream.

"Holy shit!" Fortis drew his kukri, ran over, and chopped at the insect stinger. The injured bug made a high-pitched shrieking noise, which Fortis cut short with another stroke of his knife.

Viscous, black goo oozed from the hole in Thorsen's armor and his convulsions ceased.

"Get the hell out of there!"

Hawkins was shouting in his ear, and Abner looked up. The line of bugs was ten meters away. For a split second he almost turned and ran, but the urge vanished as quickly as it appeared. He grabbed Thorsen under the arms and dragged the injured Marine along with him, pursued by the inexorable tide of gaping pincers and dripping stingers.

Fortis pulled Thorsen as fast as he could, straining with all his might against the substantial Pada-Pada gravity. Thorsen convulsed and slipped from Abner's grip and the young officer fell backward. When he sat up, he saw the bugs were almost on them.

* * * * *

Get "Cherry Drop" now at:
https://www.amazon.com/dp/B09B14VBK2

Find out more about P.A. Piatt at:
https://chriskennedypublishing.com

* * * * *

The following is an
Excerpt from Book One of Murphy's Lawless:

Shakes

_____

Mike Massa

Available from Beyond Terra Press

eBook and Paperback

Excerpt from "Shakes:"

"My name is Volo of the House Zobulakos," the SpinDog announced haughtily. Harry watched as his slender ally found his feet and made a show of brushing imaginary dust from his shoulder where the lance had rested.

Volo was defiant even in the face of drawn weapons; Harry had to give him points for style.

"I am here representing the esteemed friend to all Sarmatchani, my father, Arko Primus Heraklis Zobulakos. This is a mission of great importance. What honorless prole names my brother a liar and interferes with the will of the Primus? Tell me, that I might inform your chief of this insolence."

Harry tensed as two of the newcomers surged forward in angry reaction to the word "honorless," but the tall man interposed his lance, barring their way.

"Father!" the shorter one objected, throwing back her hood, revealing a sharp featured young woman. She'd drawn her blade and balefully eyed the SpinDog. "Let me teach this arrogant weakling about honor!"

"Nay, Stella," the broad-shouldered man said grimly. "Even my daughter must cleave to the law. This is a clan matter. And as to the stripling's question...

"I, hight Yannis al-Caoimhip ex-huscarlo, Patrisero of the Herdbane, First among the Sarmatchani," he went on, fixing his eyes first on Volo and then each of the Terrans. "I name Stabilo of the Sky People a liar, a cheat, and a coward. I call his people to account. Blood or treasure. At dawn tomorrow either will suffice."

517

Harry didn't say a word but heard a deep sigh from Rodriguez. These were the allies he'd been sent to find, all right. Just like every other joint operation with indigs, it was SNAFU.

Murphy's Law was in still in effect.

* * * * *

Get "Shakes" now at: https://www.amazon.com/dp/B0861F23KH

Find out more about Myrphy's Lawless and Beyond Terra Press at: https://chriskennedypublishing.com/imprints-authors/beyond-terra-press/

* * * * *

Made in the USA
Coppell, TX
29 November 2021

66719298R00285